Youth Without Youth

Mircea E L I A D E

Youth Without Youth and Other Novellas

Edited and with an Introduction
by Matei Calinescu

Translated by Mac Linscott Ricketts

FOREST BOOKS

London 1989

Copyright © 1988 by the Ohio State University Press.
All rights reserved.

Printed in the U.S.A.

Published by Forest Books
20 Forest View, Chingford, London E4 7AY
First published in the United States of America 1988
by the Ohio State University Press
First published in the United Kingdom 1989

Jacket design © Janet Hart

British Library Cataloguing in Publication Data

Eliade, Mircea, *1907-1986*
    Youth without youth and other novellas
    I. Title
    859'.3'32 [F]

ISBN 0-948259-74-4

Contents

Biographical Note on Mircea Eliade

Born in Bucharest, Romania, on March 9, 1907, Mircea Eliade received his Master of Arts degree from the University of Bucharest with a thesis on the philosophy of the Renaissance (1928). He then studied Indian philosophy (mainly with Surendranath Dasgupta) at the University of Calcutta between 1928 and 1931. Back in Romania, he obtained his Ph.D. with a dissertation on Yoga (1933) and taught philosophy and the history of religions at the University of Bucharest until 1938. Between 1940 and 1945 he served as Romania's cultural attaché, first in London, then in Lisbon. An émigré after World War II, he lived in Paris between 1945 and 1956, lecturing at the Sorbonne as well as at several other European universities, and participating in many conferences, including the yearly Ascona meetings of the Eranos group, whose *spiritus rector* was C. G. Jung. It was during those years that Eliade established himself as one of the foremost contemporary scholars of religion and myth. From 1956 to 1983 he taught the history of religions at the University of Chicago, where a chair named for him was established after his retirement. He died in Chicago on April 22, 1986.

The two major directions of Eliade's work—literature and scholarship—were clearly visible from the beginning of his career. Even though, during the 1930s and even later, Eliade was better known to the Romanian public as a writer, his great originality as a thinker and scholar could already be discerned in his impressively erudite *Yoga. Essai sur les origines de la mystique indienne* (1936), in his study *Alchimie asiatică* (1935; Asiatic alchemy), in his essay in English, *Metallurgy, Magic and Alchemy* (1938), and in his profound little book about the archetypes of *coincidentia oppositorum*, particularly the myths of androgyny, entitled *Mitul reintegrării* (1942; The myth of reintegration).

As a novelist, Eliade was definitely a "modernist," with his literary reputation enhanced by a youthful note of nonconformism and aggressive authenticity. The unifying element of his early fiction is a strong, immediately recognizable autobiographical bent. Some of his most characteristic works of this period were actually outgrowths of his journal, conceived (as he would later reveal) as a "storehouse" of reflections, intimate experiences, recollections, intellectual discoveries, observations, reveries, and even imaginative experiments. From the existential-sexual obsessions straightforwardly presented in *Isabel şi apele diavolului* (1930; Isabel and the devil's waters) to the thinly disguised love story between a young European and an Indian teenage girl, poetically recounted in *Maitreyi* (1933; Maitreyi), to the unconcealed use of his Indian diary in *Şantier* (1935; Work in progress), Eliade's early novels are clearly derived from the personal experiences of a young intellectual torn between his Western urge for "modernity" and his fascination with the Eastern negation of time. Even his fiction on Romanian themes, as exemplified particularly in *Întoarcerea din rai* (1934; Return from paradise), was built in large part on episodes from his personal life (see, for instance, Pavel Anicet's simultaneous love for two women in the novel, and the corresponding biographical episode, as recounted many years later in the chapter "Man Without Destiny" in *Autobiography*, volume 1). The presence of autobiographical material continued to be felt even when Eliade attempted, as in *Huliganii* (1935; The hooligans), to draw a more objective portrait of the "collective self" of his generation of metaphysical "hooligans" (reincarnations of the nineteenth-century "nihilists" as adherents of a new cult of death), intent on demolishing their society and culture in the name of a feverishly expected revolutionary apocalypse.

The most forward-looking of Eliade's early works was, curiously, the one that was received least favorably by the critics of the time, *Lumina ce se stinge* (1934; The light that fails), a novel with an important "fantastic" or "epiphanic" dimension but difficult to read because of its use of an experimental (Joycean) stream-of-consciousness technique. Increasingly from the mid-1930s on, he undertook broader explorations of the realm of the fantastic and of the ways in which the supernatural both hides and reveals itself in everyday "reality," for example in the powerful tale of terror, *Domnişoara Christina* (1936; Miss Christina); in *Şarpele* (1937; The snake)—a short novel that starts realistically only to end mythically, on a paradisal island, with a vision of sexuality as a cosmological force and a direct manifestation of the sacred; and, most explicitly, in the two tales of the occult included in *Secretul Doctorului Honigberger* (1940; *Two Tales of the Occult*, 1972; reprinted as *Two Strange Tales*, 1986).

The major part of Eliade's intellectual efforts in his postwar years as an exile went into scholarship. This is not the place to try to assess or even to superficially characterize the significance of his contribution to religious phenomenology and the history of the sacred. It will suffice to just mention some of the works in which his dialectic of the sacred and the profane, his theory of hierophany, his understanding of mythical time and space, and his notion of the "camouflages" of myth in modern, historical, and desacralized societies are forcefully articulated and fascinatingly illustrated by myriad examples drawn from the most diverse religious traditions. The scope of Eliade's scholarship, far beyond the religions of the Book (Judaism, Christianity, and Islam) and classical Greco-Roman paganism, includes the archaic religions of Asia, the Americas, and Australia, as illustrated in such studies as *Le mythe de l'éternel retour* (1949; *The Myth of the Eternal Return*, 1954); *Traité d'histoire des religions* (1949; *Patterns in Comparative Religion*, 1958); *Le chamanisme* (1951; *Shamanism*, 1964); *Yoga. Immortalité et liberté* (1952; *Yoga: Immortality and Freedom*, 1964); and, the crowning synthesis of his later years, the three massive volumes of *A History of Religious Ideas* (1976–83).

With the exception of the symbolic novel of initiatory quest, *Forêt interdite* (1955; *The Forbidden Forest*, 1978) — written, like all Eliade's literary works, in Romanian but first published in French translation; eventually published in Romanian in Paris as *Noaptea de Sânziene* in 1971 — Eliade's fictional production in the postwar years consisted mainly of stories of the fantastic, in which the finest narrative and poetic qualities of his prose were most effectively realized. Some of these novellas are already available in English: one of the best pieces in *Nuvele* (1963; novellas), "La ţigănci" ("With the Gypsy Girls") was collected with "Les Trois Grâces" (1976) in *Tales of the Sacred and the Supernatural* (1981), and *Pe Strada Mântuleasa* (1968) was published as *The Old Man and the Bureaucrats* (1979). To this list are now added the three outstanding pieces included in this volume. The over twenty works of short fiction written by Eliade in the postwar years stand, in many ways, in stark contrast to his early novels: they display a freer, richer, and more generous fantasy; their deep archetypal themes are more universal and at the same time more authentically personal; and they contain, unlike the rather loosely structured and often overwritten early works, numerous examples of a refined, suggestive, complex, and powerful narrative craft. Between *Isabel şi apele diavolului* and the postwar novellas, Eliade has gone all the way from a certain modernist obsession with self and existential immediacy to the serene joys of storytelling.

While Eliade's novellas retained only rudiments of autobiography, and then treated them as points of departure for unpredictable fantastic (symbolic) developments, the autobiographical strain of his work continued in openly personal writings, such as *Fragments d'un journal, 1945–1969* (1973; the latter part of this volume was translated as *No Souvenirs, Journal 1957–1969*, 1977), *Fragments d'un journal II, 1970–1978* (1981; Fragments of a diary II), or in the two volumes of straight autobiographical narrative, *Autobiography*, volume 1 (1981) and its sequel, *Autobiography*, volume 2, scheduled to appear in 1988.

Selected Critical Bibliography

This short and highly selective bibliography refers exclusively to critical works dealing primarily, or at least in good part, with Mircea Eliade's literary work and aesthetic ideas. Indispensable to any serious study of Eliade is *Mircea Eliade: An Annotated Bibliography* by Douglas Allen and Dennis Doeing (1980). The cutoff year for Allen/ Doeing is 1978 and, unfortunately, there is no comparable bibliographical tool for the particularly rich last decade of Eliade publications and studies.

Alexandrescu, Sorin. "Studiu introductiv." In *La ţigănci şi alte povestiri*, Mircea Eliade, v–xlx. Bucharest: Editura pentru literatură, 1969.

Allen, Douglas, and Dennis Doeing. *Mircea Eliade: An Annotated Bibliography.* New York: Garland, 1980.

Apostolos-Cappadona, D. "To Create a New Universe: Mircea Eliade on Modern Art," *Cross Currents,* 33, 4 (1982–83): 408–19.

———. "Introduction: Mircea Eliade: The Scholar as Artist, Critic, and Poet." In *Symbolism, the Sacred, and the Arts,* by Mircea Eliade, ed. by D. Apostolos-Cappadona, xi–xxi. New York: Crossroad, 1986.

Calinescu, M. "Imagination and Meaning: Aesthetic Attitudes and Ideas in Mircea Eliade's Thought." *The Journal of Religion* 57, no. 1 (January 1977): 1–15. Reprinted in *American Critics at Work,* ed. by V. A. Kramer, 368–96. Troy, New York: Whitston, 1984.

———. "Between History and Paradise: Initiation Trials." *The Journal of Religion* 59, no. 2 (April 1979): 218–23.

———. " 'The Function of the Unreal': Reflections on Mircea Eliade's Short Fiction." *Southeastern Europe,* 7, pt. 1 (1980): 62–73. Reprinted in *Imagination and Meaning: The Scholarly and Literary Worlds of Mircea Eliade,* ed. by N. J. Girardot and M. L. Ricketts, 138–61. New York: Seabury, 1982.

Culianu, Ioan P. *Mircea Eliade.* Assisi: Cittadela Editrice, 1978.

Dorian, Marguerite. Review of *Bei den Zigeunerinnen* (Frankfurt a.M.: Suhrkamp, 1980). In *World Literature Today* 55 (1981): 299–300.

———. Review of *Memoire I, 1907–1937: Les promesses de l'equinoxe* (Paris: Gallimard, 1980). In *World Literature Today* 55 (1981): 300.

———. Review of *A l'ombre d'une fleur de lys* (Paris: Gallimard, 1985). In *World Literature Today* 60 (1986): 94–95.

Duerr, Hans Peter, ed. *Die Mitte der Welt: Aufsätze zu Mircea Eliade.* Frankfurt/ Main: Suhrkamp, 1984. (Essays by M. Calinescu, I. Culianu, A. Marino, M. L. Ricketts, Claude-Henri Rocquet, E. Simion.)

Girardot, N. J., and M. L. Ricketts, eds. *Imagination and Meaning: The Scholarly and Literary Worlds of Mircea Eliade.* New York: Seabury Press, 1982. (Essays by S. Cain, M. Calinescu, A. Marino, M. L. Ricketts, E. Simion.)

Handoca, Mircea. *Mircea Eliade — Contribuţii biobibliografice.* Bucharest: Socieatea literară "Relief românesc," 1980.

Kitagawa, J., and C. Long. *Myths and Symbols: Studies in Honor of Mircea Eliade.* Chicago: University of Chicago Press, 1969. (Essays by E. M. Cioran, V. Horia, V. Ierunca, M. Popescu, G. Spaltmann, G. Uscatescu.)

Marino, Adrian. *Hermeneutica lui Mircea Eliade.* Cluj-Napoca: Editura Dacia, 1980. Translated into French as *L'herméneutique de Mircea Eliade.* Paris: Gallimard, 1981.

Mincu, Marin, and Roberto Scagno, eds. *Mircea Eliade e l'Italia.* Milan: Jaca Book, 1987. (Essays by Sorin Alexandrescu, Adrian Marino, Ion Negoiţescu, Andrei Pleşu, Mihai Zamfir.)

Mircea Eliade et les horizons de la culture. Aix-en-Provence: Publications Université de Provence, 1985. (Transactions of an international colloquium at Aix-en-Provence, France, 3–5 May 1984.)

Nemoianu, Virgil. "Wrestling with Time: Some Tendencies in Nabokov's and Eliade's Later Works." *Southeastern Europe* 7, pt. 1 (1980): 74–90.

———. "Naming the Secret: Fantastic and Political Dimensions of Charles Williams' and Eliade's Fiction." *Bulletin of the American-Romanian Academy of Arts and Sciences* 4 (1983): 50–59.

Simion, Eugen. "Mircea Eliade." In *Scriitori români de azi II,* 319–36. Bucharest: Cartea românească, 1976.

———. "Postfata: Nivelele textului mitic." In *In curte la Dionis,* by Mircea Eliade, 619–60. Bucharest: Cartea Romaneasca, 1981.

Spariosu, Mihai. "Orientalist Fictions in Eliade's *Maitreyi.*" In *Fiction and Drama in Eastern and Southeastern Europe* (Proceedings of the 1978 UCLA Conference), ed. by H. Birnbaum and T. Eekman. Columbus, Ohio: Slavic Publications, 1980, 349–360.

Strauss, Walter A. Review of *The Old Man and the Bureaucrats* (Notre Dame: University of Notre Dame Press, 1979). In *Western Humanities Review* 35 (1981): 276–280.

Tacou, Constantin, ed. *Mircea Eliade.* Cahiers de l'Herne, no. 33. Paris: Editions de l'Herne, 1978. (Essays by Ion Balu, Jean Biès, M. Calinescu, Richard Comstock, W. A. Coates, Sergiu Al. George, Simone Vierne.)

Introduction

The Fantastic and Its Interpretation in Mircea Eliade's Later Novellas

Matei Calinescu

The main characteristic of modern fantastic literature — the suggestion of an unresolved conflict between our natural world and a threatening world of the supernatural — suffers an interesting modification in Mircea Eliade's novellas. Traditionally, the literary fantastic achieves its most typical effects through the manipulation of our sense of the coherence of the universe. The supernatural (the incomprehensible, the insane, the demonically meaningless) suddenly irrupts in the flow of our ordinary civilized life and challenges our ideas of causality and order. Our natural response to this challenge is to cling stubbornly to our sense of everyday reality and seek reassurance in its logic. The everyday may have been invaded and occupied by the supernatural, but this cannot last. The everyday remains, in other words, our principal frame of meaning-making, and the intrusion of the terrifying forces from the *other* world can bend this frame but will never be able to break it. It is only insofar as the everyday continues to be a reliable and renewable source of meaning that it can be effectively played off against the obscure and malevolent world of the supernatural and that we, as readers, can derive an aesthetic pleasure from the horror associated with the fantastic. With Eliade this relation is reversed: the transcendent or the supernatural is no longer a threat to the coherence of the world; on the contrary, it holds the only real promise of such coherence; and it is the everyday that, on closer consideration, turns out to be incomprehensible, cruel, and ultimately meaningless. Only when we recognize the secret but powerful pull of the *other* world of "miracle," the sacred, and the mythical, can we go beyond the inherent meaninglessness of quotidian life and perhaps be given a chance of access to true meaning. This mere chance, however remote, is infinitely more precious than anything "reality" in the accepted sense might offer.

For Eliade this *other* world does not exist objectively — materially, physically — "out there," waiting to be discovered: rather, it is an invention or a creation, but one that paradoxically, entirely mysteriously, carries ontological weight. I am aware that other students of Eliade might take issue with what I have just said. But this is not the place to go into a complex philosophical argument about the sense in which myth exists for Eliade. In support of my opinion that Eliade views the *other* world as the result of a process of invention, or re-invention, I would like to quote just one text in which Eliade illuminates, perhaps more directly than elsewhere in his work as a thinker, his conception of myth and creativity, personal and impersonal:

> Every exile is a Ulysses traveling toward Ithaca. Every real existence reproduces the *Odyssey*. The path toward Ithaca, toward the center. I had known all that for a long time. What I have just discovered is that the chance to become a new Ulysses is given to *any* exile *whatsoever* (precisely because he has been condemned by the gods, that is, by the 'powers' which decide historical, earthly destinies). But to realize this, the exile must be capable of penetrating the hidden meaning of his wanderings, and of understanding them as a long series of initiation trials (willed by the gods) and as so many obstacles on the path which brings them back to the hearth (the center). That means: seeing signs, hidden meanings, symbols, in the sufferings,

the depressions, the dry periods in everyday life. Seeing them and reading them even *if they aren't there;* if
one sees them, one can build a structure and read a
message in the formless flow of things and the monoto-
nous flux of historical facts.[1]

The possibility of understanding oneself in terms of
mythical models is at the basis of Eliade's ontology of the
imaginary, which is so enchantingly dramatized, or, better,
"novelized," in his short fiction, and particularly in the novellas
of his later years. That is why Eliade's fantastic not only refers
to myth (myth being a paradigmatic act of creation) but aspires
to function like myth, that is, to create new worlds, meanings,
and realities. If we are allowed to paraphrase Eliade as theorist
in order to describe the universe of Eliade as a writer, we may
say that his literary use of the supernatural is meant to disclose
"various and sometimes dramatic irruptions of the sacred into
the world"; to bear witness to "an irruption of creative energy
in the world"; and, significantly, to show that what happens
in the imagination can add to *being* or, as Eliade puts it, "bring
about a surplus of ontological substance."[2]

Eliade is of course aware of the historical predicament
of mythical imagination in the modern world. He seems to
agree with C. G. Jung that modern rationalism, while unable
to completely eradicate myth from the human psyche, has
managed to push it out of the sphere of consciousness. Con-
fined to the unconscious, myth continues to be active, however.
For Jung, dreams, fantasies, or other such phenomena often
carry mythical messages from the unconscious, to be deciphered in light of traditional symbolisms. In his capacity as
a psychologist and psychiatrist, Jung believes that these messages can offer the therapist extremely precious indications as
to the cure of certain mental disturbances, particularly of a
neurotic character. Eliade will naturally be less interested in
the purely psychological implications of the repression of the
sacred. He will turn his attention instead to the various cultural
consequences of the expulsion of mythical imagination from

the activities controlled by consciousness. Using a biblical metaphor, Eliade once proposed that the occultation and marginalization of the experience of the sacred in the modern world might be described as a "Second Fall." After the Fall, he argued, man lost paradise, that is, the possibility of direct communication with God, but preserved the ability to *see* the traces of the divine in nature as well as in his own conscience. But, Eliade wrote, "After the 'Second Fall' (corresponding to the Death of God announced by Nietzsche) modern man has lost the possibility of experiencing the sacred on the level of consciousness, although he still continues to be guided and nourished by it in his unconscious."[3]

Eliade's vast scholarly work contains numerous examples and detailed analyses of the modern repression of myth or de-sacralization of the world. To give an idea of how he approaches this subject, it is enough to mention one example, namely, his notion of the "camouflage" of the sacred in modern art, which offers an excellent insight into his larger model of the dialectic of the sacred and the profane as it functions in the specific conditions of our modern times. (In his fantastic prose, Eliade uses this model with highly original effects.) "The West," Eliade writes, "can no longer create a 'religious art.' . . . In other words, the artists do not accept any more to exalt mere 'idols'; they are no longer interested in religious imagery or in traditional religious symbolism. This doesn't mean, however, that the sacred has entirely disappeared from modern art. But the sacred has become *unrecognizable;* it has camouflaged itself in forms, intentions, and significances that appear to be 'profane.' The sacred is no longer *in full view.* . . . It can no longer be recognized *immediately* and *easily.*" And he adds: "Modern man has 'forgotten' religion, but the sacred has hidden itself in his *unconscious.*"[4]

Unrecognizability, camouflage, and forgetfulness (as well as their opposites, recognition, revelation, and spiritual recollection or anamnesis) are the keys for penetrating and orienting oneself in the tumultuous narrative world of Eliade's novellas. These terms name some of the major recurrent and even obsessive themes of Eliade's thought, of which his stories are wonderfully unexpected and illuminating variations. There is perhaps only one larger, indeed over-arching, theme in the work of the later Eliade, a theme whose presence heightens the sense of tension and secret unity conveyed by all the others: interpretation. In their different ways, all three stories discussed here thematize "interpretation" and illustrate an original type of the fantastic, in which the clashes between reality and unreality become a focus of interpretation, of what might be defined as an imaginative or creative hermeneutics.

In this light let us first examine "The Cape," written in 1975, one of Eliade's best later stories. According to the author's own testimony, "The Cape" originated from a highly unusual, if not plainly surreal image. In the summer of 1975, feeling one of his periodic urges to write fiction, Eliade had a "vision," which he described in his personal diary: "The scene is today's Bucharest: a rather ordinary man, wearing a threadbare and shabbily patched cape, stops the passersby in the streets, asking them, 'Could you please tell me what year we are in?' "[5] Letting himself be almost completely absorbed by his work on the novella, Eliade managed to finish it in only ten days (19–28 July 1975). The few entries for this brief period do not add much of interest to the "story of the story." There is one little exception, namely, the information that the author decided to call the piece "The Cape" on July 26, that is, when the writing of the story was nearing its end, thus underscoring the importance of the initial generative image. We will see why this is so.

The title — "The Cape" is a translation of the original Romanian "Pelerina," which could have been rendered equally well as "The Cloak" — has the advantage of being symbolically appropriate for the hermeneutic drama unfolding in the story. The symbolism of the cape or the cloak highlights the esoteric associations produced by clothing imagery (covering, protecting, hiding, shrouding in secrecy), and such associations intensify the sense of mystery derived from a tale of ciphered messages and apocryphal communications.[6] Naturally, everything in "The Cape" revolves around the question of meaning, of how true meaning can be extracted from among so many falsifications, camouflages, and deceptions. From the very beginning the reader is assaulted by questions such as: Why does the otherwise unremarkable former political prisoner Zevedei insist on wearing his shabby, suspicious-looking cape, with its "two symmetrical and provocative patches sewn on the shoulders as if . . . to hide the traces of epaulettes"? Is he simply a fool or is he trying, at great personal risk, to convey a special, coded message to an unknown party? Or is he involved in a diversionary maneuver, trying to decoy the secret police to protect another, possibly international, operation? Is there any link between this cape and the illicit alterations performed by unknown people on the old uniforms on display at the Military Museum? And is there any connection between the cape and the altered uniforms, on the one hand, and the circulation of a parallel, "apocryphal" edition of the Romanian Communist Party newspaper, *Scînteia*, on the other? Who could be responsible for the falsified edition of *Scînteia*, antedated by exactly three years (1966 instead of 1969), with one word changed in the logo (which now reads "Dreamers of all countries unite!"), and containing numerous cryptic typos and letter transpositions? And how is one to account for the flabbergasting coincidences — first pointed out to the secret police by the young chemist Pantelimon, the principal suspect in the investigation — between the patterns of typographical errors in the apocryphal newspapers and the lunar calendar of the year 1966? The reader is presented with a rapidly growing number of unusual, unexplainable, and increasingly surreal (mysterious and at the same time often preposterous) events. What holds them together is precisely the feeling that they are not devoid of meaning, although this meaning is not easily grasped. That is why the search for meaning in the story is paralleled by a search for meaning in the mind of the reader.

Here I would like to open a brief parenthesis: the reader's search for meaning might well go beyond the text of the story, beyond, that is, the primarily *intra*textual aspect of the reading, to look for hints and leads in other texts that are alluded to or evoked, if not directly invoked, by the story. This latter way of searching for elements of the meaning of a literary work in other works is subsumed, in the technical jargon of poetics, under the label of "*inter*textuality." Intertextually I find it almost impossible to read Eliade's "The Cape" without thinking of Gogol's *The Overcoat*. In a certain sense, I would argue, Eliade's story could be seen as a rewriting of Gogol's masterpiece in a new mode, a rewriting that implies a drastic revision of the traditional, social or realist, reading of *The Overcoat*. Here I can only describe this new reading in the broadest of outlines. In the interpretation I have in mind, an interpretation made possible by comparing *The Overcoat* with "The Cape," the story of the pathetic little copyist who is robbed of his new overcoat the very first night he wears it carries an oblique, secret religious significance. In Gogol's work, the little man, represented by the ineffably grotesque Akaky Akakievich, is doomed to be the victim of contempt and suspicion in a world of laughable, but at the same time demonic, banality. The overcoat, which Akaky Akakievich has obtained with such excruciating efforts and sacrifices, is at once his vision of grace and the principle of his demise. At the police station where the shy clerk tries to report the theft of his almost mystically cherished overcoat, the commissioner considers him with rudeness and, more significantly, *suspicion:* "Instead of attending to the main point, he began asking Akaky Akakievich questions: why had he been coming home so late? wasn't he going, or hadn't he been, to some bawdy house?" Later on, when Akaky Akakievich appeals for help to the Person of Consequence, his request seems so out of place, so derisory, so utterly insignificant, that the Person of Consequence can only feel offended and, in the perverse *logic of suspicion,* accuse the harmless clerk of subversive feelings: "What?what?what? . . . Where did you pick up such ideas? What insubordination is spreading among young men against their superiors and their chiefs?" (I have quoted from the standard English translation of Constance Garnett.) Akaky Akakievich is crushed and literally killed by the enormity, by the cruel absurdity of it all. In Eliade's free-wheeling rewriting of *The Overcoat*, the symbolic ambivalence that surrounds Gogol's overcoat is preserved not only in the centrally important image of the cape, which eventually becomes a metaphor for the text itself, but also in the recurrent references to the old uniforms in the Military Museum. Also reminiscent of Gogol is Eliade's sensitivity to the complex links between the fantastic and suspicion. Finally, the line that separates delirium from banality in the two stories can be equally fluid. What differs in Eliade, to the point that the presence of Gogol may become almost "unrecognizable," is the ascendancy of sheer narrative invention over character creation — unlike Gogol's, Eliade's characters are unmemorable as fictional individuals.

Returning now to the *intra*textual discussion of "The Cape," let me point out that, like other later novellas by Eliade, it describes two opposite ways of approaching the problem of meaning *(suspicion* versus *trust)* through two sets of contrasting characters. First, there are the secret service investigators, from the low-ranking Petrescu Doi to the top-ranking Pantazi, who are intent on discovering *the reason* behind the whole apparent charade, that is, the motivation and goals of the organizers of what seems to be a perfidious Plot. We encounter these character types in many of Eliade's novellas, starting with "The Old Man and the Bureaucrats" (1968) and including such later pieces as "Les Trois Grâces" (1976) and "Nineteen Roses" (1978). They represent, in the larger drama of interpretation, some of the more extreme and occasionally grotesque practical consequences of what Paul Ricoeur has called the "hermeneutics of suspicion." Simply put, such a hermeneutics of doubt (whose most influential modern masters, according to Ricoeur, are Nietzsche, Freud, and, more significant for our present discussion, Marx) would consist of a philosophical refusal to take the languages and actions of man at face value. Real human motives, from the point of view of suspicion, are always masked by lies (lies in which the liar himself often believes or half-believes) and to uncover them one must become an expert de-mystifier, demythologizer, debunker, breaker of codes, and solver of riddles. Eliade's commentary, which is incorporated in the way he portrays his main fictional investigators, would be that oversuspicion can lead to forms of credulity by far more absurd than even the most childish naiveté.

Conceived from the point of view of suspicion, interpretation appears as an activity of *detection,* an activity that involves *hypothetical thinking* in order to reconstruct real situations from *clues.* The complicating factor in the plot of "The Cape" is that such clues are not only identified and gathered but indeed continuously fabricated by the secret police investigators themselves. Their suspicious gaze makes any image, symbol, gesture, statement, or action, no matter how innocuous, into a potential clue to be fitted with other clues in an effort to solve a menacing and frustrating puzzle. The deeper trouble, however, is that many of the pieces of this puzzle have been falsified and that the falsifiers themselves can no longer tell the difference between the legitimate pieces and the countless fakes. A fine narrative artist, Eliade has exploited with remarkable effects the rich possibilities offered by such a situation. "The Cape" is a particularly intriguing example of the type of novella—at once a "metaphysical" detective thriller, a humorous mystery, a slightly nightmarish fantasy, a modern-day fairy tale, and an extended parodic/poetic allegory—bearing Eliade's unmistakable fantastic signature.

The possibilities of the second, confident-imaginative attitude toward meaning is represented in "The Cape," abundantly but indirectly, by the naive, youthful dreamer, Pantelimon. Through this character—one of his numerous variations on the prototype of the "holy fool"—Eliade discloses the deep interconnections between imagination and meaning, even though Pantelimon's is largely the story of a failure to recognize the truly mythical and sacred. Other heroes of Eliade's prose, such as Dominic Matei in "Youth Without Youth" or the stage director Ieronim, his two pupils, Serdaru and Niculina, and the novelist Pandele in "Nineteen Roses," directly illustrate the imaginative-mythical alternative to paranoid suspicion. By and large, this alternative is premised on what I would call a hermeneutics of trust—a trust first and foremost in the principle of the imagination, in the richness of images and symbols, and in their ultimate soteriological function or power to save us. To be sure, the fantastic tension in Eliade's novellas comes from the suggested conflict between two worlds, as pointed out earlier; but these two worlds themselves appear as the product of two kinds of interpretation—demythologizing and reductionist, on the one hand; (re)mythologizing and creative, on the other. To be able to interpret life in the latter fashion one must definitely be a dreamer and a muser and a passionate explorer of images. Eliade's figure of the dreamer is not unlike Gaston Bachelard's *rêveur*, whose philosophical portrait appears in his *Poétique de la rêverie* and in other essays in the phenomenology of the imaginary. Interestingly, Eliade not only knew and admired Bachelard, but, in speaking of his own urge to write fiction, appropriated one of the key notions of the Bachelardian theory of the imagination, namely, *la fonction d'irréel*, "the function of the unreal." Here is a significant diary entry, dated 20 June 1963: "I'm working on the short story. I tell myself that what I am doing is absurd: losing these last few weeks of freedom writing a story and without even knowing how it will end. But I feel I must write for my moral health. How right G. Bachelard was when he spoke about 'the function of the unreal,' which, if it is not satisfied, leads to neurosis and sterility."[7] This same "function of the unreal" is, in the novellas, a constitutive element of the broader vision articulated by the writer, a vision in which, to paraphrase Bachelard, fiction provides us "with hypotheses of life that enlarge our life" and places us in a relationship of trust in regard to the world. And Bachelard adds, underscoring the key concept of *trust:* "Through the imagination, and thanks to the subtleties of the function of the unreal, we return to the world of trust, to the world of trusting being, to the very world of reverie."[8] As we see, insofar as the hermeneutics of trust is itself an extension of the imagination, it is not a direct, dialectical, or polemical negation of suspicion, but rather a turning away from it and a return, by way of interpretive musement, to a lost world of confident enchantment and to a forgotten paradise. Particularly in Eliade's view, imagination wouldn't be itself if it didn't have, however secret, a genuine paradisal vocation.

If we choose to read "The Cape" as an allegory of interpretation (and let me make it clear that this is only one among many other possible readings), we may ask ourselves: does this story attempt to make a larger statement about interpretation? To answer this question we need to consider more closely the ending and the retroactive light it may throw on the earlier parts. There are two characters in the last scene, the shrewd high secret service official, Pantazi, and the young stargazer Pantelimon, whose loony hypotheses—based on certain odd declarations of Zevedei concerning rockets and trips to the moon—have against all odds helped the police in deciphering the worrisome coded messages. We understand from Pantazi, again unexpectedly, that the laborious cryptanalysis has resulted in a plainly embarrassing situation: the mysterious "conspiratorial" communications have turned out to be, ironically and perversely, nothing but a collection of tired Christian platitudes. However, by a semantic reversal typical of Eliade's art of fantastic story-telling, the most insipid clichés may well point the way to the genuinely mythical. Such is the case with the deciphered message, "Blessed be the poor in spirit," which suddenly reminds Pantelimon of his former fiancée, who had repeated this phrase to him to the point of humiliation and annoyance. At this juncture, the reader is reminded that Pantelimon had separated from his fiancée (for motives that remain obscure) three years earlier, in the late spring of 1966, which is to say, *precisely* at the time inscribed on the antedated apocryphal issues of *Scînteia*. A close review by the reader of what he has learned about Pantelimon's life will highlight the intriguing and somehow unsettling chronological parallelisms and symbolic contrasts between the stages of the political investigation, in which the principal suspect is none other than Pantelimon, and Pantelimon's personal story. Curiously, the efforts of the secret police to solve what seems to be an over-complicated conspiracy have a metaphorical and ironic correspondence with Pantelimon's own efforts to elucidate a personal mystery and to recover the memory of a lost love. The young man's fault, which he seeks to understand, has consisted of a failure of the imagination, of an inability to read the "signs" of the sacred. That is why Pantelimon could not *recognize* in his fiancée, Sanda Irineu, the embodiment of the mythical figure of feminine spirituality or *Anima,* or, to resort to a literary analogy, a new incarnation of Dante's Beatrice. On this largely implicit plane, the story's profound message is one of love — personal love at the core of the cosmic love that moves the sun and the other stars. Regarding the latter, one may note the twofold astronomical reference in "The Cape" to the lunar calendar as well as to the solar calendar. Insofar as the solar cycle is concerned, the action of the story is placed at a time of the year of paramount importance in the mythology of love. It is the summer solstice,[9] June 22–23, when in Bucharest the fragrance of linden flowers is at its most intoxicating. In this regard, "The Cape" could be seen as an exotic and indeed improbable rewriting of that summer-solstice classic, Shakespeare's *A Midsummer Night's Dream.*

The reader gets a better insight into the hermeneutical drama of "The Cape" when focusing on the story's central allegory of investigation/reading. I would summarize Eliade's paradoxical final statement about interpretation in the following way: interpretation is fundamentally a quest, and ultimately a quest of the quest itself; when the quest ends, for whatever reason and irrespective of the result, interpretive activity loses its raison d'être and meaning itself disappears. The words addressed by Pantazi to Pantelimon in the closing scene seem to bear this out: "There have been many poor in spirit in this great world of ours. But the most famous one remains Parsifal. For he was the only one who asked the question, 'Where is the chalice of the Holy Grail?'. . . 'Hurrah for our Goddamn Grail!' " he continued in a tired, far-off voice. "Hurrah for the Goddamn Grail which we have been fated to seek! To seek — and to find!" It should be clear that Pantazi's "we" refers to himself and to his suspecting colleagues, whose search has been successful, not to Pantelimon. Pantelimon, who had been under investigation throughout the story, is finally free to search, like a new Prince Charming, for his mythical bride and for the *Anima* or feminine part of his own psyche. "The Cape," in conclusion, invites us to reread it as a fairy tale.

"Youth Without Youth" (in Romanian "Tinereţe fără de tinereţe," written in 1976) alludes by its very title to one of the best-known Romanian *basme* or folktales, "Tinereţe fără batrî-neţe şi viaţă fără de moarte" (Youth Without Old Age and Life Without Death). The folktale is based, like Eliade's novella, on the ancient motif of the search for eternal life or for paradise. This motif is woven into a plot halfway between a romantic Chamisso-like tale (we recall that Chamisso's Peter Schlemihl loses his shadow while Eliade's Dominic Matei loses the external attributes of old age to become, literally, a youth without youth) and a modern-day piece of science fiction. The thriller stuff is not missing, but it no longer derives, as in "The Cape," from a narrative model of detection. It now comes from a more dynamic pattern of flight and pursuit. Like "The Cape," "Youth Without Youth" contains elements of a secret story of lost love. In his first youth, to indulge his passion for books, Dominic Matei separates from his enigmatic wife, Laura, who believes that his real "genius" is for life, not culture. But now, in contrast to "The Cape," the theme of lost love never becomes the symbolic keystone of the whole narrative edifice.

The reason is that the failure of Dominic's Petrarchan love for Laura is part of a larger and deeper spiritual failure. Given his huge ambitions for humanistic learning and erudition, Dominic Matei's intellectual endowment, particularly his *memory*, has always been pitifully mediocre. All he has achieved of his youthful aspiration to heroic scholarship has been to become a modest Latin and Italian teacher in a provincial Romanian lycée. Retired, and increasingly aware of a rapid loss of memory, the seventy-year-old teacher decides to commit suicide. Although irreligious, he curiously sets the date for his demise on Easter night, 1938. We remember that at the beginning of Goethe's *Faust*, the hero, aware of the failure of both science and magic to give meaning to life, attempts to kill himself precisely on Easter night. Faust decides not to drink the poison at the very last moment, when he hears the bells announcing the Resurrection and suddenly feels that life, symbolized by the Earth, is stronger than his wish to die. The allusion to Faust in "Youth Without Youth," backed by a number of quotations or direct references to Goethe, is hard to miss. In this light, it is possible to see Dominic Matei—a petty provincial scholarly crank on the brink of senility—as a mock-heroic or parodic variation on the motif of Faust's second youth. But the parody remains subdued, a free-wheeling indirect commentary of allusions that eventually dissolve into an intricate symbolic reverie. Thus, in spite of structural similarities, the second youth granted to Dominic is of an entirely different quality from the one gained by Faust as part of his bargain with Mephistopheles.

The mysterious force that stops Dominic from taking his life and leads to his miraculous rejuvenation does not come from the Earth, but from the Heaven: it is a hierophany of electricity, manifested in the form of a tremendous lightning bolt. At this point I think that a brief outline of the story might help us to isolate the key symbolic moments. Struck by lightning in a freakish spring thunderstorm in Bucharest, an old man, who later turns out to be the retired teacher Dominic Matei, is rushed to the nearest hospital, where he is expected soon to die. To the amazement of the doctors, however, the almost completely charred body of the man undergoes a rapid process of regeneration, defying all the laws of biology. In a few weeks, Dominic Matei has become unrecognizable. His skin is soft, elastic, and tight, his muscles are strong, he has grown a new set of perfect teeth, and his general appearance at seventy is of a healthy and energetic young man. Even more incredible is his mental condition. Not only is his amnesia gone but he finds himself endowed with a supernatural memory, a memory that has retained more than he ever learned or knew, more than any individual, even a genius, could possibly learn or know in a lifetime. So, Dominic Matei discovers that he is fluent in ancient oriental languages that he never studied. His case naturally produces great excitement in the medical world. A French specialist, Dr. Bernard, comes to Bucharest to see him. The Nazi Dr. Rudolf, who believes that electric shocks of great voltage could produce a mutation of the human species, would like to observe him in his laboratory in Germany. Availing himself of his high connections within the Nazi Party, Rudolf gets the Gestapo to try to kidnap the old/young Dominic Matei. This may be meant to illustrate the dangerous ambivalence of the sacred, which can so easily be put to monstrous uses. To protect him, the Romanian secret police alter his physical appearance and get him out of the country under a false name. (This is the second time Dominic becomes unrecognizable, a way by which Eliade stresses the sacred or mythical quality of the character's experience.) Thus camouflaged, the hero settles in Geneva. He lives on, a young man who doesn't show any signs of aging until close to his one-hundredth anniversary. His fantastic biography records many extraordinary events, encounters, journeys, and epiphanies.

The ending, as in the case of "The Cape," reshapes the meaning of the whole story. A few weeks before turning one hundred and one, around Christmas, 1968, Dominic Matei decides to visit his home town of Piatra Neamţ. (Note this intriguing symmetry: Dominic's rebirth, after his symbolic death by lightning, happens on Easter night, and his real death coincides with the nativity of Christ.) So the young-looking Dominic arrives at a hotel in Piatra Neamţ and checks in. The receptionist is surprised that this man, a foreigner according to his passport, speaks such good Romanian. The visitor gets his room assignment and then goes out for a short walk to the café where he used to meet his friends three decades earlier. His friends are there and they immediately recognize him (to them he looks like his forgetful seventy-year-old self), a suggestion that the scene occurs in fact thirty years earlier, in December of 1938. Strangely, though, the decrepit Dominic knows "about Hiroshima and the hydrogen bomb, and Neil Armstrong, the astronaut who landed on the moon last summer, in July." (This would suggest that the scene takes place in a fantastic time in which Dominic Matei can, in December 1968, speak of a future event, namely, Armstrong's walk on the moon of July 1969, as having occurred "last summer.") To his friends these glimpses of the future are of course nothing but ravings of advanced senility. The next day (we have again moved thirty years forward, to December of 1968), we learn that the young man who had gone out for a short walk has never returned to his hotel. We also learn that the frozen body of an extremely old man has been found in the snow, in front of the house that had once belonged to Dominic Matei. The reader is informed that the old man's body was dressed "in an elegant suit and an expensive fur-lined overcoat. But the overcoat and the other clothing were much too large for him, leaving no room for doubt that they were not his. Moreover, in the pocket of the jacket a billfold was found containing foreign currency and a Swiss passport bearing the name Martin Audricourt, born in Honduras, 18 November 1939." (By now, the reader has little trouble identifying a new instance of disguise and unrecognizability, but how it should be interpreted is not immediately clear.)

The ending of "Youth Without Youth" raises two interesting hermeneutic issues. The first one, centering around the notion of identity, is summarized by the question: *Who* died? The second one, in which the focus is on time and temporality, might be rendered by the question: *When* did this death occur? To start with the first question, it is clear that the body found in the snow is old Dominic's. But a related matter — the question of what happened to the young hero of the story, the rejuvenated Dominic — is not so easy to answer, or to dismiss. Within the fantastic logic of Eliade's prose, to explain the presence of an elegant and athletic young man's garments on a frail body shrunk by old age and found frozen in a street at the end of a story, there is no way of avoiding a larger symbolic scenario. It turns out that a good starting point for building such a scenario is, once again, the symbolism of clothing. If in "The Cape" we called upon the analogies between clothing and *hiding* (covering, masking, shrouding, making secret or inaccessible), what we need to stress now is a different set of affinities between clothing and *habitus* (condition, character, disposition). Interestingly, *habitus* is the etymon of the old word "habit," meaning precisely clothing — but clothing as *indicative* of condition (social, professional), of character, and of mental disposition as in the case of mourning. In this latter sense, the symbolism of garments suggests the exact opposite of hiding — showing, indicating, expressing, declaring, displaying. This remarkable ambiguity has naturally attracted Eliade, whose view of the sacred has always been that it hides itself in the very act of revealing itself and, conversely, that it reveals itself in the very act of hiding itself. The "elegant suit" and the "expensive fur-lined overcoat" in the above passage serve, I would argue, as *indications* that the rejuvenated Dominic indeed existed, that he successfully escaped death and now is restored to his truly paradisal condition. His abandoned clothes suggest to us that he finally enjoys the paradisal nudity of a sacred body. The one who dies is the "historical" Dominic. The Dominic who embodies the dream or the imagination of eternal youth actually cannot die, because he exists within a different, recurrent structure of mythical time where death in our sense of an ineluctable, absolute end is inconceivable.

This brings me to the second hermeneutical problem, namely, that of the *when* of the death. Did it occur in 1938 or in 1968? And, if in 1938, did it occur at Easter or at Christmas? And what about the thirty years of "historical" life of the "post-historical" young Dominic? Were these years a hallucination (with strange anticipatory elements) of the thunderstruck Dominic or, perhaps, of the old teacher dying in Piatra Neamţ, in 1938? Another interesting question would be: Do these years have anything in common with the paradoxical time found in some of Jorge Luis Borges's best stories? I am thinking, for instance, of "The Secret Miracle," in which Jaromir Hladik, a Jew in German-occupied Prague during World War II, prays to God to postpone his execution by one year so that he might finish his tragedy in verse, *The Enemies*; Hladik's wish is granted, even as the firing squad takes aim at him, and one entire year passes between the command to fire and its execution. That particular quality of time, in which a second can take a year to pass, and one year just one second, would not be out of place in Eliade's fantastic universe. In spite of the differences between the two writers (Borges being cerebral, bookish, and extraordinarily laconic, in contrast to Eliade's more expansive, romantic, unsparing imagination), they seem to arrive at similar paradoxes of time. This is all the more remarkable if we consider how distant their points of departure are: Borges starts from the purely logical aporias involved in our conceptualization of time, and Eliade from an intuition of both rupture and interpenetration of sacred and profane time. So the story — or stories — of Dominic Matei actually unfolds in two distinct temporal frames, one historical and irreversible, the other mythical and recurrent. The interpretive complications to which the text gives rise, such as the ones surrounding the death of Dominic, have their origin in the unexpected collisions, superpositions, and divergences between the two frames, or, to use one of Eliade's favorite expressions, in the way they incorporate the principle of *coincidentia oppositorum* or the union of opposites.

If in "Youth Without Youth" interpretation was less a concern of the characters than the reader — and I am referring here not to an external or "real" reader but to the "implied reader," whose figure is defined by the text — in "Nineteen Roses," as in "The Cape," and perhaps with even more urgency, the problem of interpretation confronts the main characters themselves. In "The Cape," as we saw, interpretation was for the most part seen from the angle of what I called "the hermeneutics of suspicion"; in "Nineteen Roses," more attention is devoted to the opposite practice of interpretation or "the hermeneutics of trust." The question of interpretation here is closely linked to the broad question of memory — memory as a way, beyond personality, to mythical truth. In "Nineteen Roses," Eliade comes closest to presenting in vivid narrative terms a coherent program and a methodology for reading the signs, messages, and symbolic images that carry with them a sense of transcendence, and can thus help us to enlarge our life. The program can be described in one word—anamnesis. Anamnesis, literally recollection or remembering (we recall that Plato used it to denote the soul's *reminiscence* of the world of Ideas), is defined by one of the characters as "a mode of giving meaning to the events of one's life." As for the methods by which anamnesis can be achieved, Eliade focuses in "Nineteen Roses" on theatre, performance, and acting, that is, on ways of orchestrating and interpreting *roles*.

The story is about Pandele's anamnesis or recovery of his forgotten Orphic self through the discovery of the spiritual meaning of dramatic performance or *spectacle*. Specifically, Pandele embarks on a quest for one crucial moment in his life that had been completely obscured by amnesia, a moment in which personal time intersected with mythical time, a moment in which he had experienced true love. Like "The Cape," "Nineteen Roses" is a story of nostalgia for lost love. But whereas Pantelimon's nostalgia is largely unself-conscious until the very end, Pandele's is a constant inspiration through all phases of his anamnesis. The spiritual adventure begins one summer evening, when Anghel D. Pandele, an aging literary celebrity in Bucharest, receives the unannounced visit of two unknown young actors, Serdaru and his fiancée, Niculina (on the basis of clues deftly scattered throughout the text one can calculate the exact day of the visit, August 23,* 1966). Serdaru claims that he is Pandele's unknown natural son and (even more strangely) asks him to give his paternal consent and blessing to his marriage with Niculina. Of course Pandele is startled, but his search for himself and his essential past (including the

---

*We note that August 23 is the national holiday of Communist Romania, which celebrates the country's "liberation from the domination of Fascism." Historically, it commemorates the events that took place on August 23, 1944, when a successful palace revolution staged by King Michael led to the arrest of the dictator, Ion Antonescu, an ally of Nazi Germany. This made it possible for Romania, in part occupied by the Red Army, to sign an armistice with the Allies and to declare war on Germany. The official position of the Romanian Communist Party is that Romania's changing of sides during World War II was caused by a Communist-inspired popular insurrection.

forgotten encounter with Serdaru's mother) has already begun. The significance of Pandele's search is skillfully suggested by successive, increasingly far-reaching mythical hints and associations. Consider the first extended mythical allusion found in the story. Serdaru tries to explain how he arrived at the conviction that Pandele was his father. He recalls that, some eight months before, he had been rehearsing, together with his fiancée, in an anti-religious propaganda play, *The Star Is Rising*, to be performed at Christmas. This play was the last-minute replacement for a mythological *Orpheus in the Underworld*, which the Communist authorities had forbidden. We soon realize that Serdaru's story has a hidden meaning, a meaning whose presence can be better ascertained when it becomes clear that the events it recounts are the mysterious echoes of certain earlier events. Serdaru goes on to remind Pandele that some thirty years earlier, more precisely in December of 1938, Pandele's own play, *Orpheus and Eurydice*, which was being rehearsed in the town of Sibiu, had been forbidden by the authorities of the royal dictatorship of King Carol II and replaced with a conventional folkloric-religious performance, coincidentally bearing the same title as the later atheistic play, *The Star Is Rising*.[10] Serdaru's actress-mother had been cast as Eurydice in Pandele's old play. The construction of the episode reveals one of Eliade's favorite techniques, a technique, I would say, of ambiguities and ironic doubles, mirror images and reflections, and echoes and reverberations, which attempts to translate the dialectic of mythical unrecognizability into concrete, situational symmetries and oppositions.

As the story unfolds, Pandele's anamnesis proceeds along the lines of a classical initiation scenario, with the hero's symbolic death (his disappearance from the everyday world where he was a highly regarded novelist) and his mysterious rebirth under a new, unrecognizable identity. In remembering and re-imagining his love for the woman who had been Eurydice in his play, Pandele eventually reassumes his mythical role as Orpheus, which he had abandoned for the sake of a socially successful literary career in postwar Communist Romania. If he is indeed "saved" from amnesia, from the ineluc-table forgetting brought about by "history," this is due primarily to the soteriological virtues of theater and performance. Acting, impersonating, role-playing, enacting, and re-enacting are ac-tivities that can mediate between the world of the ordinary and that of the mythical; understood spiritually, they are effec-tive techniques of liberation from the tyrannical meaningless-ness of the profane. Serdaru and Niculina represent the hidden sacrality of spectacle. Niculina, an intriguing embodiment of the Jungian *Anima,* is actually in immediate contact with the sacred as she changes identities, and even ages, with the ease and grace with which she changes the theatrical costumes she always carries with her in a valise. Here we note, after "The Cape" and the final part of "Youth Without Youth," which we discussed at some length earlier, another twist in the use of the symbolism of clothing in Eliade's work: changing costumes is a way of changing mythical identities. Significantly, it is through Serdaru and Niculina that Pandele is introduced to Ieronim Thanase, the enigmatic theatrical genius and theorist of performance, whose ideas inspire and guide Pandele's anam-nesis. Fitting this broad context of theatricality and drama, Pandele's own fundamental experience, his love for Eurydice, long-repressed in his unconscious, had been essentially *theatri-cal.* This love was rendered possible by his Orpheus play, the only one he wrote in an otherwise rich literary career; likewise, the recovery of this mythical love, after thirty years of amnesia, could be possible only through a rediscovery of theater, through what amounts to a veritable psychoanalysis of spectacle.

Opposed to the world of "spectacle" is the world of history, more precisely, "the terror of history." Its main represen-tative in the story is Colonel Albini, the secret police inves-tigator, whose inquiries are premised on the notion that what-ever looks unusual or strange or extraordinary in the world poses an imminent danger to the ideas of hierarchical order and institutional stability, which to him are the only guarantees against chaos and anarchy. Albini, whom we encounter either under his name (for instance in "Les Trois Grâces") or under different (dis)guises in many of Eliade's novellas, is a convinced practitioner of the "hermeneutics of suspicion." But, ironically, in fighting for a de-mythologization of the world, Albini unwittingly embraces a no less fantastical world view than the one he combats.

Here I would like to point to an interesting characteristic of Eliade's work. With few exceptions, both his scholarly and his fictional worlds are largely devoid of portrayals of radical evil. In the later novellas one can speak of a quasi-absence of the demonic or, to put it differently, of the final absorption of the demonic into the sacred in keeping with the principle of *coincidentia oppositorum*.[11] Going back now to Albini, a representative of suspicion and repression and one of the characters in Eliade's later fiction who might have become a credible focus of evil, it is curious to see how benevolently he is treated. The tolerant serenity with which an abhorrent personage like Albini is portrayed puzzled me to the point that, after having read the manuscript of the story in 1979, I expressed my bewilderment in a letter to the author. "Of course," Eliade answered, "Albini is impossible in socialist Romania, but he may be accepted in a story in which a sled with four people penetrates a forest that was destroyed twenty-five years earlier." In other words, in drawing Albini, he sought not a "realistic" but a fantastic credibility. Eliade concluded: "Albini is a sort of 'Grand Inquisitor.'" But, unlike Dostoevsky's character, Eliade's Albini is a Grand Inquisitor who ends up playing into the hands of what he most fanatically opposes—Myth. Speaking of *The Old Man and the Bureaucrats*, the first novella, finished in 1968, in which he presented the conflict between the logic of myth and the counterlogic of power and suspicion, Eliade noted:

> *The Old Man and the Bureaucrats* relates the tale of the intrusion of the bizarre personal memories of an old man on the official bureaucratic world. In this story the style becomes a counterpoint to the narrative which depicts the encounter of two different, antagonistic, and *yet finally identical mythological worlds* [the italics

are mine, M.C.]. In an attempt to explain himself to the city police, the old man, Fărâmă, becomes involved in writing out a long, rambling, and hopelessly labyrinthine history of his earlier experiences and memories as headmaster of the primary school in Strada Mântuleasa—an account that seems to the officials to be more legend and folklore than history. In the frustrating process of interrogation the two worlds gradually impinge and merge, and the bureaucratic world begins to function fantastically.[12]

Even though its action starts on a day (August 23) charged with political significance in Romanian history, "Nineteen Roses" is in no way intended as a piece of political literature. That is perhaps why the date of August 23 is deliberately hidden in the text, which can be read and reread as a delightful and captivating fantasy, without any specific historical reference. But once the reader puts together the hints contained in the text ("We've been dreaming of this meeting for 243 days," says Niculina at the end of the first scene, and the reader gathers that her counting starts a couple of days before Christmas Eve, that is on December 22 or the exact day of the winter solstice), the question arises: how should one interpret the oblique, indirect, but also quite precise allusion to August 23? Here I can only sketch an answer to this question: "Nineteen Roses" can also be read as a meditation of the self-exiled Eliade on the situation of the (Romanian) artist, symbolized by Pandele, but also by Ieronim Thanase, in the face of the "terror of history" (August 23 is the beginning or, metaphorically put, the "seed" of the whole post–World War II history of Romania as a Soviet-Bloc country, including the traumatic experience of forced Russification and rampant Stalinism). The artist, Eliade seems to suggest, can find the road to freedom, and even to "absolute freedom" (the modifier "absolute" is emphasized at key moments in the novella), even from the midst of "history": this road, full of pitfalls, difficulties, and paradoxes, leads ultimately to the mythical, to a sort of imaginative-mythical universalism, in which the most diverse traditions reveal their profound unity. In "Nineteen Roses," this unity is suggested by the structural role given to the Orpheus/Christ analogy.

Aside from the two extreme hermeneutical positions represented by Pandele and Albini, we find a third one in "Nineteen Roses," and one that is quite important if we think that it is embodied in the narrator of the story. The narrator, Eusebiu Damian, Pandele's devoted secretary, far from being a mere narrative convention, is an essential character. The way he tells the story may be a misinterpretation of the events, but it is a misinterpretation from which we glimpse their true significance. In an allegorical reading of "Nineteen Roses," the complex relationship between Pandele and Damian may stand for the paradoxical contacts, mutual reflections, and stark contrasts between the sacred and the profane. We might say that insofar as one is touched by the sacred, one ceases to have a voice of one's own. If one goes on speaking, one does so only through the voice of the profane. Thus, the story of the successful anamnesis of Pandele cannot be told by Pandele himself. It needs someone like Damian. A close and honest witness, Damian, I would say, represents the profane in its good-natured, generous, candid mediocrity. Unable to concentrate his attention when it is most needed, absent-minded and forgetful in spiritually important moments, Damian remains a good storyteller. The main reason why he is ultimately reliable is that he doesn't hide his failings. So, when relating his visit to the summer camp where Pandele, in the first phase of his disappearance, was the guest of Ieronim and his troupe, Damian confesses that he could not really understand what was happening around him. At a symbolic-mythical spectacle directed by Ieronim at the camp, Damian was fascinated by what he saw, yet could not help falling asleep and missing the very moment of the epiphany. The next day, when he hoped to learn what the performance really meant, he simply could not keep his mind from wandering even as Serdaru was getting close to the essential point. Along similar lines, later, when typing the manuscript of Pandele's new mystical play (entitled, in the logic of the union of opposites, *In the Beginning Was the End*, and written according to the teachings of Ieronim), his memory was again unable to retain anything specific. Fascinatingly, it is from the narrator's recognized failures to understand that the reader receives some of the most helpful interpretive cues.

Finally, I would like to stress the difference between a modern mode of the fantastic, which I call the *fantastic of presentation,* and the "home-made" variety used by Eliade in his later stories, the *fantastic of interpretation.* In the first case, the reader is presented with often highly ambiguous events, with the irruption of profoundly disturbing alien forces in the midst of a recognizably ordinary world. Of course, interpretation is involved at almost every step in the reader's attempt to deal with such ambiguities. But the sense of a hallucinatory presence, enigmatic and grotesque — as in Kafka's *The Metamorphosis* — seems to stimulate interpretation only to frustrate it. This may be an indirect expression of hermeneutical malaise. Eliade's later novellas engage the reader in an ultimately optimistic hermeneutic adventure. The fantastic of interpretation attempts to free the reader's imagination, to revive his sense of wonder, and to make him discover the credible within the incredible, or the converse. Furthermore, Eliade's fantastic of interpretation persuades the reader to look at images, symbols, metaphors, stories, dreams, or inventions as possible bearers of epiphanies or remembrances. By means of these devices the imagination breaks out of the amnesia in which modernity has trapped it to recall and revive lost worlds of meaning. The larger message of Eliade's fantastic prose is, in brief, that interpretation remains our best hope for an anamnesis of mythical truth.

Notes on the Introduction

1   See *No Souvenirs, Journal 1957–1969* (New York: Harper & Row, 1977), entry of 1 January 1960, p. 84.

2   See *The Sacred and the Profane* (New York: Harcourt, Brace & World/Harvest, 1959), p. 97.

3   *Briser le toit de la maison* (Paris: Gallimard, 1986), p. 27. The quotation is from the essay "La permanence du sacré dans l'art contemporain," originally published in 1964.

4   Ibid., p. 26.

5   *Fragments d'un journal II* (Paris: Gallimard, 1981), p. 243.

6   The etymology of the Romanian word "pelerina," coming from the French "pèlerine," originally the garment worn by a "pèlerin" or pilgrim, might also be interesting to consider. Could we read the title of the story also as an allusion to a "pilgrim cape"? Such a cape, as we know, was meant not to hide but, on the contrary, to disclose the purpose of the pilgrim's voyage to a sacred place. What makes this reading improbable or marginal is the detail that the cape in our story might have been part of a military uniform, although it is impossible to confirm this with any historical precision. But as an item of military uniform, the cape would have again been meant to disclose an allegiance, a rank, etc., and to make the wearer *recognizable*. The symbolic coincidence of hiding (as conveyed by the cape or cloak) and disclosing (the pilgrim cape or the item of military uniform) would fit Eliade's general view of the ambiguous relation between the sacred and the profane. But it remains an open question whether the associations produced by the religious etymology of "pelerina" or those deriving from its surmised military origin, play as important a structural role in the story as the symbolism of concealment, disguise, secretiveness, and dissimulation.

7   *No Souvenirs: Journal 1957–1969* (New York: Harper & Row, 1977), p. 190. For a look at how "the unreal" functions in Eliade's prose (with special emphasis on the novellas "With the Gypsy Girls" and *The Old Man and the Bureaucrats*), see my essay " 'The Function of the Unreal': Reflections on Mircea Eliade's Short Fiction," in *Imagination and Meaning*, ed. by N. Girardot and M. L. Ricketts (New York: Seabury, 1982), pp. 138–61.

8   *Poetique de la rêverie* (Paris: Presses Universitaires de France, 1960), p. 12.

9   The use of solstitial symbolism, if not always immediately visible, is important for understanding Eliade's novellas, both individually and in terms of common recurrent patterns. For a discussion of solstitial mythology in Eliade's major novel, whose Romanian title, *Noaptea de Sânziene* or Midsummer Night, was translated as *The Forbidden Forest* (Notre Dame, Indiana: Notre Dame University Press, 1979), see my review article, "Between

History and Paradise: Initiation Trials," *The Journal of Religion* 59, no. 2 (April 1979): particularly 218–19.

    10   This is another instance of Eliade's recurrent solstitial thematic — in this particular case the Orphic symbolism of death, associated with the end of the year, in combination with the symbolism of birth, as in the obscure, initially *unrecognizable* nativity of the Messiah, associated with the beginning of a new year. Beyond that, we note the quasi-obsesssive return of the year 1938, one of the most troubled in Eliade's life, as well as in the pre-World War II history of Romania. Since I am not interested here in the biographical-historical significance of certain features of Eliade's novelistic world, such as its chronological and geographical patterns, nor, more broadly, in an "esoteric" reading of his postwar fiction, I limit myself to mentioning these possible interpretive perspectives. It is only on the basis of a very careful and thorough biographical-historical exegesis that the questions raised by a possible "esoteric" reading of Eliade's fantastic prose could be intelligently entertained. The limited space available to this introductory essay clearly excludes the possibility of such an attempt. The perspective adopted in the present study has been an entirely "exoteric" one, namely, the perspective of a literary hermeneutics which looks at texts as complex and, as we saw, multi-layered literary-symbolic constructs, to be interpreted (both *intra-* and *inter*textually) in terms of the notion of an *explicit literary system.* Those interested in a biographical approach to Eliade's prose could start by reading his *Autobiography* and, in regard to the importance of the period 1937–38, specifically chapters 15 and 16 of volume 2 (Chicago: University of Chicago Press, forthcoming).

    11   A clear presence of the demonic, along the lines of the classical fantastic, can be found in only one of Eliade's prewar pieces, the fantastic novel *Domnişoara Christina* (Miss Christina), published in Bucharest in 1936.

    12   "Foreword — Literature and Fantasy," in *Tales of the Sacred and the Supernatural* (Philadelphia: Westminster, 1981), pp. 11–12.

The Cape

The Cape

1

He recognized him from a distance. He was wearing the same cape as before: short, old-fashioned, with two symmetrical and provocative patches sewn on the shoulders as if he wished to hide the traces of epaulettes. (But Pantelimon knew now that capes with epaulettes had not been a part of any uniform of the Romanian army; "At least not in our century," Ulieru had assured him. They would have been worn at another time, perhaps in the feudal era. "And if it could be proved that the patches really do hide traces of epaulettes," Ulieru had added after a pause, "I mean, if one could prove it by modern, scientific means, then it would be a serious matter!" He stopped speaking and looked at him hard. "How long have you known him?" "I? I don't know him. I have no idea who he is or what's his name. I spoke to you about his cape because the two patches caught my eye. I said, they seem to be sewn on the shoulders exactly like a pair of epaulettes." "Rather suspicious," Ulieru interrupted. "And if it could be proved positively by scientific methods, it might even be very serious. I think you understand why." Pantelimon shrugged, perplexed. "No," he said, "I don't understand." "Because in that case, the cape was *certainly* stolen. Stolen from the Military Museum . . . And yet," he added thoughtfully, "you say you don't know him." "I've seen him

3

only two or three times coming out of the Mătăsari Grocery Store. He was going out as I was heading toward entrance B. I was going to buy some salami and sausages.")

This time he slackened his step in order to be able to get a better look at the cape. He had not been mistaken: the patches were sewn exactly where epaulettes would have been, and they were of the same size. Perhaps Pantelimon's eyes or his smile encouraged him, because he stopped abruptly, a step in front of him.

"Please, if you don't mind, could you tell me what year this is?"

"The nineteenth of May," Pantelimon replied.

"No, you misunderstood me. The nineteenth of May, this I know. But the *year*—what year is it?"

Pantelimon drew up slightly against the wall to allow a woman leading a child by the hand to pass.

"1969!" he said. "May nineteenth, 1969."

"I thought so myself!" exclaimed the other man. "I can even say I was sure of it: 1969. And yet, there are people who believe differently. To be more precise, there are people who claim this is 1966! They even showed me newspapers. I read them with utmost attentiveness: I had to admit that they were papers from March, April, and May of 1966."

"I don't understand," said Pantelimon, with a puzzled smile.

"Please believe me," continued the other, tossing back the cape with a surprisingly youthful gesture. "I'm a serious-minded man; I have, as they say, my head on my shoulders. But in the face of the evidence, of the newspapers, I mean, I had to give in."

"What kind of newspapers?" asked Pantelimon.

"Our most popular daily, *Scînteia*.* I read it every day. This morning's *Scînteia* I read from the first to the last line."

"And so?" Pantelimon interrupted him irritably, realizing that several passersby had stopped to listen to them. "I

Scînteia (The Spark) is the official newspaper of the Romanian Communist Party.

4

read it too, from front to back."

"Yes, but the newspaper of which I speak assured me that this is May, 1966!"

"Perhaps it was an old number," suggested a young man with a kepi drawn down on his forehead, right to the eyebrows.

"Yes, but you see . . . ," he started to explain, and again he shook his cape as though he wished to throw it off his shoulders and onto his back entirely.

"What's the matter?" someone standing beside the wall asked, without removing the cigarette from his mouth. He took a few steps toward Pantelimon.

"The comrade maintains this is 1966."

"I beg your pardon, Comrade; *I* don't maintain this. I only permitted myself to ask what year this is. More precisely, I wanted to persuade myself that I am not wrong in affirming that this is 1969, although . . ."

"Although what?" He had taken the cigarette from between his teeth and his voice sounded different now, almost severe.

"Although, as I said, the newspaper which I read this morning, *Scînteia,* I mean, indicated precisely: 19 May 1966. And this wasn't the first time. Three days ago and twice last week, and before — the whole month of April — all the copies of *Scînteia* I received and read indicated, without exception, the year 1966!"

"It has happened," declared someone. "I have a friend at Slatina, and he showed me himself; I saw it with my own eyes. . . . Issues of *Scînteia* . . . All dated 1966."

"That was in the provinces," someone interrupted. "Slatina is a beautiful city, but it's in the provinces."

Several people began laughing. Pantelimon felt a touch on his arm and turned his head. The old man smiled meaningfully.

"You ought to hurry to Slatina too," he said. "Perhaps you'll find yourself back in the year 1966 again. And . . ."

But he met the other man's gaze, he saw how hungrily

5

he drew on his cigarette, and he stopped speaking, smiling sheepishly.

"Take it easy!" he whistled between his teeth, crushing his cigarette under his foot. "You're listening to a lot of foolishness. . . . Instead of minding your own business."

2

A half hour later, when he emerged from the grocery, he found him leaning with his back against the wall, waiting for him.

"Pantelimon," he asked, "how long have you known Zevedei?"

Pantelimon swallowed hard and shifted the bag of groceries to the other hand.

"I don't know him. I didn't even know his name was Zevedei. I've seen him two or three times and I was struck by the patches on his cape: they look as though they were sewed on in place of epaulettes. But, as our Director, Comrade Ulieru, says, the Romanian army has never had capes with epaulettes. That's why he's under suspicion. . . . Perhaps, in the Feudal era . . ."

"Never mind the Feudal era," the other man interrupted. "Why do you say he's under suspicion?"

"Because, as Comrade Ulieru says, if it could be proved positively, by scientific means — I mean, if one could prove the patches were sewn in place of epaulettes, then the cape must *surely* be stolen from the Military Museum."

"That's another kettle of fish," said the other, taking out a pack of cigarettes. "Forget the Military Museum. How long have you known Zevedei?"

Pantelimon passed the bag back into his left hand. But he quickly changed his mind, and, taking it in his right hand again, he retreated a step backward toward the wall.

"I told you. I met him a half hour ago. I was going into the grocery for some salami and sausages, and he stopped me and asked, 'Please, if you don't mind, can you tell me what year this is?' And I answered . . ." Pantelimon lifted his head suddenly and smiled. "I didn't understand him. I thought he was asking about the day, and I answered, the nineteenth of May. But he interrupted me: 'No,' he said, 'I know this is May 19. But the year — what year is it?' "

" 'What year is it?' " the other repeated, smiling. "And you didn't suspect anything?"

Pantelimon drew closer to the wall.

"I thought perhaps he was a little out of his mind, or that . . ."

"What do you mean by that? That something was wrong with him? That he was mixed up in some suspicious business and that, ultimately, everything stemmed from that?"

"Something like that, yes; or perhaps that . . . actually . . . you know what I mean."

The other man smiled again, then lit a cigarette absently.

"But why in *1966*?" he asked suddenly, squinting at him severely. "Did it not seem suspicious to you that Zevedei specified *1966* and not some other year, for instance 1956 or 1960?"

"No," admitted Pantelimon timidly. "But now that you mention it, it *does* seem suspicious. Because after all, why 1966?"

The other man broke into a laugh. "You take me for more of a fool than I am, Comrade."

Pantelimon paled and tried in vain to smile. "I?" he began. "Why do you say that I think that? I . . ."

But he stopped abruptly, seeing the young man with the cap pulled down on his forehead coming toward them in great haste, almost as if fleeing from someone.

"He left the house," he whispered, panting. "He left five minutes ago."

"From Number 13?"

"No, from Number 13½."

"Then he's tricked you again. I told you that at Number 13½. . . . But anyway, for the time being it doesn't matter." Then, turning to Pantelimon, he asked suddenly, "How do you come to know about the Military Museum?"

7

"I? I don't know anything about it."

"Comrade Pantelimon," the other man said firmly through his teeth, "I'm a good man for my sort, but . . ."

Pantelimon's shoulders sagged, and he flattened himself against the wall.

"Our administrative director, Comrade Ulieru, pointed it out to me and said that if one could prove positively, by modern, scientific means, that in place of the patches . . ."

"All right, all right, this you already told me. But why the Military Museum?"

"Comrade Ulieru said it was serious, because it was a museum piece. In other words, it was a piece stolen from the Military Museum."

The other man took out a cigarette and interrupted him, shaking his hand several times very close to Pantelimon's cheek.

"And if you understood this, why didn't you understand the connection with 1966? — Because Zevedei spoke to you about 1966, not 1960 or 1956!"

He looked straight at him again with his eyes almost closed, then whistled through his teeth.

"You take me for more of a fool than I am, Comrade!"

"I, Comrade?" exclaimed Pantelimon, holding his free hand close against his heart.

"Take it easy!" Then, turning abruptly to the youth in the military cap: "What was it with the man from Slatina? Does anyone know him?"

"He's from the same section as Făinaru. He referred to the matter of September."

"Then he's suspect."

"That's what Făinaru said. Therefore . . ."

"All right, I understand!" he interrupted, looking him deep in the eyes threateningly.

3

As he did each day, a few minutes before the lunch hour, he

set off in the direction of Ulieru's office. But in front of the elevator he met the typist.

"Don't waste your time going up — he hasn't come in today. . . . Business affairs," she added, smiling. "May 20, May 21, and so on."

It seemed to Pantelimon that the secretary had tried to wink her left eye at him, and he blushed in confusion.

"I understand," he said, and started toward the door. But after a few steps he turned back and asked her, lowering his voice, "Is it something special? I mean, the twentieth or twenty-first of May — have they any special significance?"

The typist looked at him again in surprise, and this time Pantelimon was certain: the young woman really did wink her left eye at him, with meaning.

"It depends on the city," she said. "In certain provincial cities May 20 is more important than May 21."

"Provincial cities," Pantelimon repeated dreamily. "How odd! I don't know why, but just last evening I was thinking about provincial cities — about Slatina, for instance."

As if she had not heard him, the young woman smiled and, giving a nod of her head, she turned her back.

On the following day, Pantelimon decided to eat lunch in the laboratory. He had taken a package of sausages out of the bag and was about to open a bottle of beer when Ulieru appeared in the doorway.

"You've returned!" Pantelimon greeted him happily. "We'll go to the canteen then."

But because Ulieru made no reply and stood staring as though preoccupied, he opened the beer bottle, filled a glass, and offered it to him.

"How did you find out that I was at Slatina?" asked Ulieru after carefully taking several swallows.

"You were at Slatina? May God strike me dead if I knew it!"

"Then why did you tell the typist that your favorite city is Slatina? Why Slatina of all places, just where I was? Because we're friends and I trust you, I can tell you I was sent there on an inspection trip."

Pantelimon emptied his glass and sat down on a chair.

"To start with, I never said that Slatina is my favorite city. All I said was that, on the evening before, I was thinking — I don't rightly know why — I was thinking about provincial cities, for instance Slatina."

"But why *Slatina*?" Ulieru interrupted, trying to catch his eye.

Pantelimon shrugged in confusion.

"Because, if you'll give me time to say it, because, the day before yesterday as I was heading into the grocery, I ran into that individual with the cape again, you know who I mean. The chap about whom you said that if one could prove positively . . ."

Ulieru walked on tiptoe to the door, opened it quickly, looking to the right and to the left, and then returned and sat down again.

"I thought he was a little touched in the head," continued Pantelimon.

"Did you speak with him?"

"Just a few words. I didn't have time to say much, because . . . Oh, it's a long story."

"But did he say something to you about Slatina?"

"Not he. A whole group of people gathered there on the sidewalk, and someone, I don't rightly remember who, said that at Slatina too *Scînteia* had appeared with the date, let's say, of May 19, 1966, instead of May 19, 1969, as it should be. You see how it was."

As he listened, Ulieru wiped his handkerchief across his brow from time to time. Then, ashamed, he hid it in his pocket and began rubbing his hands together.

"It could be a very serious matter," he said at last. "You've gotten me — I realize, unintentionally — you've gotten us both into a predicament, and God only knows who'll get us out of it."

"But why is it so serious?" asked Pantelimon, troubled.

"Because that very suspicious individual, that fellow

with the cape, brought up the matter of newspapers from 1966."

"But what happened in 1966?"

Ulieru stood up suddenly and opened the door again, looking to the far end of the hallway. "Good, good!" he cried, waving his hand. Then he stepped close to the chair 'where Pantelimon was sitting and continued in a whisper.

"Let's speak more softly. Petrescu Doi has returned to check on the equipment."

He paused and took a deep breath.

"What happened in 1966? Many things happened. In any case, it was better in 1966 than now, in 1969. Then too, you understand, if people read the newspaper for May 1966, when we are, in fact in May 1969 . . . At any rate, it's a subversive thing. It's against the State."

He stopped a moment, turned his head toward the door, made a sign to Pantelimon, and continued in a louder voice.

"It's against our Socialist system. You encounter saboteurs in any undertaking. There's nothing remarkable about that. The class enemy does not renounce the privileges which, by right, the party and the people . . ."

The door opened and on the threshold appeared Ioanichie Petrescu. He entered, holding out an open cigarette case temptingly.

"I know, I know, you don't smoke, but I put you to the test anyway." Then turning to Ulieru, he asked, "How's the inquiry developing, Comrade Engineer?"

"It wasn't an inquiry," Ulieru replied, trying to sound casual, almost bored. "I was on a supervisory mission. Everything's developing in accord with the Plan."

Ioanichie Petrescu looked at him, smiling ironically.

"And yet, we haven't delivered twenty percent of our orders."

"They will be delivered, they will be delivered, in full accord with the Plan . . . But I'm hungry," he added, suddenly getting to his feet. "And since salami and sausages don't agree with me very well, I'm going to the canteen."

11

"Today they have bean soup," Petrescu informed him, still smiling.

He allowed an interval to pass, playing absently with his cigarette case; then, without looking at him, he addressed Pantelimon.

"I didn't know you knew Năstase."

Pantelimon had just finished unwrapping the package of salami.

"I don't believe I do know him. Who is Năstase?"

"You had quite a conversation with him the day before yesterday in front of the Mătăsari Grocery. You must know that he's a very capable agent. And a man of integrity. You can have perfect confidence in him. But," he added, trying to catch his eye, "because we're by ourselves I can tell you that you rather disappointed him."

"I?" exclaimed Pantelimon, bringing his hand to his chest.

"You. You were reticent, as though you were afraid of him. You told him nothing about your connection with Zevedei, how long you've known him, etc."

Pantelimon swallowed hard, and, seizing Ulieru's glass, he gulped down the rest of the beer.

"If you're thirsty," continued Petrescu, "come to the laboratory with me, to my place. I always have a bottle of cold beer."

"No, thank you, I'm not thirsty. But because you raise the matter of Comrade Năstase and the fellow with the cape . . ."

"This is his mania — Zevedei's," Petrescu broke in, "to wear the cape of his uncle, the Colonel."

"Comrade Ulieru suspects he stole it from the Military Museum."

"No, he didn't steal it. His uncle, the Colonel, was in the Austro-Hungarian army. He died a very old man, almost a hundred, at the end of the last war. But Zevedei is a curious man: he wishes to distinguish himself from the people, and so he resorts to any distinctive sign."

Taking courage, Pantelimon began to place the slices of sausage on a plastic plate. "Actually, he wants to declare himself openly to be a class enemy."

"Something like that," said Petrescu, opening his cigarette case. "It's his right."

"His right?" said Pantelimon in surprise. "In a socialist society like ours?"

"So he believes. And he has taken the consequences. You know he spent fifteen years in prison — fifteen years, till he was pardoned."

Pantelimon had taken a big bite out of a slice of bologna and was laboring now to chew it as quickly as possible. Petrescu watched him, amused.

". . . And since he was pardoned," he continued after a pause, "he can't be arrested again for wearing his uncle's cape. . . . But, you see, he won't take it easy. Năstase's right. There are people who, no matter what happens to them in life, won't take things easy."

Gradually, Pantelimon's face lighted up. "He asked what year it is," he said.

"Exactly. And that's why you disappointed Năstase, trying to pretend . . ."

"I what?" exclaimed Pantelimon with some difficulty, because his mouth was full.

Petrescu laughed heartily and then selected a cigarette from the case.

"A foreign one, with a filter, for big days . . . Yes, you," he said calmly in a neutral tone of voice. "You tried to play the role of the naive young man with his head in a fog, when we all know you and appreciate you as a brilliant element, trustworthy, with a future."

"I don't understand," said Pantelimon. "May God strike me dead if I understand what you're referring to."

"You respond as if you didn't know Zevedei. . . ."

"But I don't know him."

"Let me finish, please," Petrescu interrupted, raising his arm in the air. "As if you didn't know him, while, on the other hand, you pretend you don't understand the connection with *1966*."

"Now I understand," Pantelimon declared with an air of triumph. "Very probably, 1966 was the year he was pardoned."

Ioanichie Petrescu looked at him for several moments in silence, smoking absently.

"I admit you're a great master; you know how to hide your game. . . . It's your right," he added, finding his smile again. "But in case you don't know, I'll tell you: Zevedei was pardoned, like all the others, in 1964. Everyone knows that."

4

As usual, when the neighbors were listening to the evening news, Pantelimon propped his elbows on the desk, stuck his fingers in his ears, and stubbornly continued his reading. Every time he came across a foreign name, he syllabized it several times aloud. The famous English physiologist, John A. Davenport . . . Da-ven-port. Da-ven- . . .

But then he heard the well-known signal — the five knocks on the door, with a short pause after the third — and he hurried to open it.

"You ought to get married, like all the rising young men," said Ulieru. "You'll have a television, you'll listen to the evening newscast. . . ." He lowered his voice suddenly and added, "Come on, let's get a beer."

After they had crossed the boulevard, Ulieru asked, "What did Petrescu Doi say to you after I left?"

He listened closely, turning his head around from time to time to make sure they were alone. After a while he stopped walking and took several long, deep breaths.

"In other words, he knows something. He knows two things at least: first, that Slatina has been in a great commotion ever since the explosion at the ink factory. And second, he knows the result of the inquiry."

He fell silent suddenly, lifting his head as if by chance to look at an open window on the third floor. Pantelimon followed his gaze; then the two of them started off again abruptly, walking faster than before.

"That is — ?" he ventured to ask at length.

"He knows that in the course of the inquiry we discovered the origin of the ink with which, two or three weeks ago, the issues of *Scînteia* falsely dated February and March 1966 were printed."

"In other words," exclaimed Pantelimon, "Zevedei was right!"

"Speak more softly," Ulieru interrupted him. "Your man was right because apocryphal editions do exist: I've seen them myself. I saw them at Slatina."

"And — ?" asked Pantelimon excitedly.

"I don't understand, but, of course, I don't know the main thing. All I know is what I've been told: that there's a vast and very cleverly organized plot at the bottom of it." He paused and exclaimed, ". . . A great misfortune!"

He stepped to the curb and spat furiously several times.

"Great misfortune! Both for me, since I was sent to Slatina, and for you, because you were interested in a cape with patches in place of epaulettes, and so fell into the hands of Năstase. No matter what we do from here on, we're suspect, both of us. You saw Petrescu Doi? Did he ever visit you like that before, out of a clear sky, at lunchtime?"

"I don't think so."

"That was because he saw me when I opened the door."

Pantelimon walked with his eyes cast on the pavement, absent, preoccupied. "But I don't understand what sort of plot it could be," he murmured after a long silence.

"Nor do I. Those who bought both editions — the real issues of 1969 and the apocryphal editions from 1966 — say that the texts are *almost* identical. Just a few modifications, apparently of little significance, and many typographical errors, more than usual."

"So?"

"They say it's a plot. Meanwhile, an effort is being made to discover who is receiving such antedated copies. They arrive in the morning mail, together with copies of the current edition. But of course, people have gotten wind of what we're doing and hide them, perhaps even destroy them." He paused again, then added, "Although, on the other hand, I've heard that in some provincial cities they're sold on the black market."

Very carefully they both felt the bench to see if it was dry, before sitting down in silence.

"It's strange, as strange as it can be," Pantelimon said softly, mostly to himself. He hesitated a moment, then continued in a firm voice. "I mean, it's a strange kind of plot. . . . To reproduce whole numbers of *Scînteia*, taking care to antedate them by three years, that is, to give away the fact that they're apocryphal!"

"I said the same thing. But if the organizers of the plot wanted to transmit messages throughout the country, they couldn't find a surer way than to send them through the very organ of the Party."

Pantelimon nodded his head. "Yes, but now that they've been discovered, they won't have another chance. The copies will be inspected one by one before being sent out."

"You can't inspect tens of thousands of copies every night. It would paralyze the circulation of the paper. . . . Besides, the apocryphal copies appear irregularly, sometimes two or three days in a row, then none at all for a whole week!"

He fell silent, rubbing his hands together nervously. Then, staring at the curb, he spoke softly. "You ought to get married, have a family, buy a television. You're young. Don't end up like me."

He sighed deeply, wearily, and turned toward Pantelimon. "What I told you just now I didn't find out at Slatina. Năstase told me these things this evening. He came to my place and told me. In order to gain my confidence, he claimed. And of course he questioned me, asked me everything under the sun, asked especially about you—how long I've known you, and so on. And as he was leaving he told me something

16

else. He told me he'll expect you tomorrow, in his office, about lunchtime." "Don't worry," he added, "if he should detain you beyond the lunch hour, he'll arrange himself for you to be excused."

5

It had been raining again all morning, and as soon as he reached the street, Pantelimon glanced at the sky uneasily. He turned up the collar of his raincoat, pulled his beret down to his ears, and set off at a fast pace. But in a few minutes the rain intensified and he had to open his umbrella. He pretended not to notice the smiles of passersby, turning their heads to look at him almost running, huddled up under the half of an umbrella, but he knew he was blushing. A few houses away from Number 4 he decided suddenly to close the umbrella.

"You're soaked to the skin, Comrade!" exclaimed Năstase when he saw him. "Don't catch cold. Perhaps it would be a good idea to take an aspirin. If you don't have any handy, I'll give you one."

"No, thank you, I don't believe that will be necessary. I don't catch cold so easily."

Leaning on the back of an armchair, Năstase regarded him ironically and yet amiably, almost sympathetically.

"I've heard nothing but good concerning you," he began abruptly. "In particular, your director, Comrade Ulieru, has praised you to the heavens. He says you're on the road toward making a great discovery. I don't know what the substance is you're working with, in any event. . . ."

Pantelimon smiled in embarrassment. "Yes, it has to do with one of the primary materials. . . . But, you see, it's a rather delicate matter. In a sense, it's a State secret. . . ."

"I know, and for that reason I won't insist. . . . Don't you smoke?" he asked him, taking a package of cigarettes from his pocket.

"No, thank you. I've never smoked."

17

"You do well. . . . Do you know why I summoned you?" he asked, looking him in the eye.

"Comrade Ulieru told me last evening."

"What did he tell you?"

"He told me to present myself at your office at the lunch hour. And if you should detain me . . ."

"He didn't tell you everything. Besides, I didn't expect him to. . . . So, let us come to the point."

He inhaled the smoke hungrily, then continued without removing the cigarette from his mouth.

"The essential point for us is *not* the story you heard from Zevedei. The essential thing *for us* is the connection that you mentioned three days ago, the connection between the explosion at the ink factory in Slatina, the clandestine printery where the false issues of *Scînteia* were printed and especially — I emphasize *especially* — the incident at the Military Museum, *precisely* in 1966, the incident that led to the trial of the assistant director. You know the details, I needn't remind you of them. . . . But," he added, taking the cigarette from his mouth and leaning over the desk a little, gazing directly into Pantelimon's eyes, "you know something more. . . ." He paused again briefly, then continued: "You know, for instance, the formula for the dyes by means of which the colors of several uniforms of the nineteenth century were altered. The assistant director of the museum said 'modified,' but in fact they were altered, because they were changed radically from their original colors. Now, it was proven at the inquiry that the substances used could have been obtained in 1966 from only two places: the ink factory at Slatina or the laboratory where you were working in 1966."

He extinguished his cigarette, crushing it for a long time in the ashtray.

"That is why I summoned you," he began again at length. "From our brief conversation of four days ago, I realized that you also noticed the connection. Since then, I've found out several other things. . . . So now that you know what interests us — begin wherever you wish."

18

Pantelimon realized all at once that he was smiling, and he began to twist and turn in his chair, embarrassed.

"If I tell you the truth," he began abruptly in a firm voice, "you'll think I'm either a fool or a madman—and I'll lose my job, I'll be demoted. But I'll tell you everything, because you've driven me to the wall. The truth is that three years ago, in 1966, I was working on the same project I told you about, the one having to do with raw materials. I know absolutely nothing about the chemistry of inks. And as for the change of colors of certain uniforms in the Military Museum, I heard about that for the first time today, from you. So far as the explosion at Slatina is concerned, I know only what Comrade Ulieru told me last evening."

"You didn't understand me rightly," Năstase interrupted him almost severely. "I did not say that you were involved, directly, in the preparation of the inks. I only reminded you that you were working in a laboratory where the inks could have been manufactured. Not only did you work there, but among your colleagues in the laboratory was a certain young and very beautiful woman, who . . ."

Pantelimon blushed. "It was my mistake," he said. "We weren't right for each other and we parted."

"No, I'm not referring to that. I'm just reminding you that the young female chemist lived on strada Luceafărul,* Number 13—while Number 13½ was Zevedei's residence."

Pantelimon swallowed several times with an effort, as if trying in vain to recover his voice.

"It is difficult to believe you never met Zevedei."

"And yet, that's the truth!" Pantelimon exploded. "I never met him!"

"Let's accept that also," Năstase continued calmly. "But it's inconceivable that you never learned anything about what was being done and said in the other divisions—for instance, in the ink laboratories."

"I told you, I know nothing about the chemistry of inks."

*That is, Luceafărul Street.

"And yet your coworker, domnişoara* Sanda Irineu, worked in the inks division."

Pantelimon shrugged his shoulders in embarrassment. "When we were alone," he said, "we never discussed problems of chemistry."

"But what about when you were in a group? At the canteen, for instance, or on the outing you went on with twelve other colleagues, men and women, in the Neamţ Mountains, in the summer of 1966?"

"That was the last time we were together," Pantelimon declared solemnly, lifting his head. "After we returned to Bucharest there was nothing more between us."

"And nothing that was said and discussed then struck you? You remember none of it now? For instance, about Dr. Magheru, who was afterwards transferred to Slatina? Your fellow workers say you were friends."

"We were not friends. Besides, if you want to know the truth, it was on account of him that I broke up with Alexandra."

Năstase continued to look at him, slowly nodding his head.

"And yet you have not severed completely your relationship with Comrade Irineu. You write to her from time to time."

"Picture postcards," smiled Pantelimon, "because she has a collection of them."

"The past year you even sent her a book."

"It was a pamphlet in the German language. I knew it would interest her, I wanted to do her a favor."

"But it never reached her," Năstase continued, "because in the meantime, Comrade Irineu changed her address again. She was sent on a mission to Sweden, and remained there."

Pantelimon turned pale, ran his hand through his hair, and began to wipe away the drops of rainwater, as if he were

*Domnişoara is "Miss," that is, the title prefixed to the name of an unmarried woman or girl.

20

feeling them for the first time.

"Didn't you know she remained in Sweden?"

"No," Pantelimon replied absently. Then he looked at his wet hand and let it fall awkwardly into his lap.

"If your hair stays wet, you'll catch cold for sure," said Năstase, getting to his feet. "Let me give you an aspirin."

Pantelimon swallowed it obediently and emptied the glass of water in one swallow. "Thank you," he said, setting the glass on a corner of the desk.

"But, you know, the climate of Sweden did not agree with her, and she went away — far away. . . . It seems she settled in Uganda."

6

After listening to the conversation recorded on the tape recorder, Ghibercea turned his head and asked, "Why did you tell him she's settled in Uganda?"

"Just to see how he'd react."

"He couldn't have reacted better. . . . Either he knows nothing, in which case by his speech he's a fool; or else he conceals his game so well that, again by his speech, he seems to be half crazy."

He stopped speaking and, lifting his head, fixed his gaze on the ceiling. "Time passes, clandestine issues continue to appear — at irregular intervals, it's true — and we're exactly where we started from three months ago when we discovered the first apocryphal issue."

Năstase shifted his position on the chair — then, seeing that the silence was prolonged, he ventured to speak.

"If I may say so, Comrade Colonel, we have learned a few things."

"For example?"

"For example, the connection between Slatina and the Military Museum."

"If only we could be sure a connection does exist."

"Or, that the modifications introduced into the text, and especially the typographical errors, constitute a code by which messages are transmitted."

Ghibercea turned the swivel chair slowly toward the window, still intent on examining the ceiling.

"Modifications introduced into the text," he repeated slowly. "The most important is also the most mysterious: 'Dreamers of all nations, unite!' Or, as you say, *especially* the typographical errors: 'providence' instead of 'provenance,' 'confusion' instead of 'diffusion,' and others of the same sort. The majority with a letter missing or two letters extra."

"In conformity with a code," Năstase suggested timidly.

"But after three months, Special Services still hasn't deciphered the code."

Năstase shifted his position in the chair again. "We know, at least, that messages of some particular subversive group are being transmitted; very probably acts of sabotage are being arranged, or more probably, a plot of some sort."

Ghibercea swung the chair around decisively toward Năstase and stared at him from under his eyebrows.

"You know very well, Comrade, that if class enemies exist and if criminal acts of sabotage are being committed, no changes have been noticed in the past three months. Everything has gone along as if the apocryphal editions had not circulated. It is, certainly, a clandestine act against the State. But the results have not been seen."

"Perhaps they haven't yet passed from talk to action," suggested Năstase.

"This is a possibility. . . . The only argument in favor of the hypothesis of an organized action is Zevedei."

"I'd say so too."

"But not in the sense you think," continued Ghibercea. "An error was made in the beginning, when you gave Zevedei to understand that we had learned a great deal about him, and thus that he was being followed day and night. It's a good thing you didn't arrest him! As much as he deserved it! . . . But, at any rate, Zevedei's behavior cannot be explained except by assuming there exists a secret organization in which, directly or indirectly, he participates. Otherwise, he would have to be considered mad, and a madman he *certainly* is not!"

"And yet . . . ," Năstase began timidly.

"Those who don't know him well would agree with you," Ghibercea interrupted. "Because what could be the sense in accosting people in front of the Mătăsari Grocery, which he knows is under your surveillance — accosting them and asking them what year it is, thereby bringing up the matter of the apocryphal newspapers? And what could be the sense in his cape with the two patches sewn in place of epaulettes? No one who ever met him or heard him talking about the newspapers dated 1966 could ever forget him. That man behaves as if he wanted to draw attention to himself and in such a way that *one could not forget him.* Especially when someone like you — in the interest of the Services of course — sends couriers to strada Luceafărul, Number 13, and repeats the address in a loud voice."

Năstase changed his position again, preparing to make a defense of himself.

"I know, you had to do it, but it was a mistake. . . . But, to return to the objective Zevedei's pursuing. There's only one explanation: the man has lost contact with his agent or his superior. He knows he's here somewhere in the Capital, and he keeps sending him signals. Probably today or tomorrow all Bucharest will find out about him. And Zevedei hopes one night to run into the man who's waiting for him."

"Both dwellings are under surveillance, twenty-four hours a day," Năstase declared. "Both Number 13 and Number 13½. We have men watching at numbers 10, 12, and 14. Everyone who has visited Zevedei or his neighbor, Ioan Roata, has been followed and, when necessary, interrogated. But at night, no one comes looking for him. And Zevedei himself never leaves the premises after ten P.M."

"I know, I know," Ghibercea interrupted him. "But sooner or later, in the daytime or at night, he'll contact the man who's waiting for him. Otherwise . . ."

23

"And so, it's a matter of a plot," said Năstase, in order to break the silence.

"In a sense, yes. But if it's a plot, and Zevedei has lost his contact man and keeps looking for him all the time, how does it happen that today, May 26, we've discovered examples of antedated papers in fourteen cities already, to say nothing of Bucharest. How does it happen?"

He fell silent and began to drum on the desk with his fingers. Then he pressed the button to the left of the telephone, and when the door opened, he said without turning his head, "Bring me the latest file with the results of the Special Services' investigations."

He waited silently, continuing to move his fingers in a curious rhythm, first as if he were fingering the keyboard of a harpsichord, then as if beating on a drum.

"This last file seems just as worthless as the one of the week before," he sighed, after leafing through the first pages. "They've recorded all the typographical errors, they've made tables and statistics, they've consulted two eminent mathematicians and even a computer specialist—and so far, nothing. We know nothing!"

He raised his eyes from the file and, smiling wearily, looked at Năstase.

"But why should we beat around the bush, Comrade Năstase? You know what I'm referring to," he added after a pause, lowering his voice. "We understood, it was understood higher up, and then still higher. This was understood long ago. There does not exist anywhere in the country, and there could not exist, a printery capable of furnishing these apocryphal editions. Therefore we can console ourselves with this hypothesis: that the apocryphal copies are possibly being printed at one of the embassies in the Capital. An embassy of a friendly country . . . Or one not so friendly," he added, trying to smile. "But that's only an hypothesis."

"And yet," ventured Năstase, "the ink is manufactured at Slatina."

"If only we could be sure of that!" exclaimed Ghibercea.

24

"Let's assume, however, that it is the same ink. Where is the printing press, and how is the circulation managed? And for what purpose, what object? *Cui prodest?* — if you perchance studied Latin in school and you still remember. *Cui prodest?* 'Dreamers of all lands . . . ' Where do they come from? And who are they?"

7

Every day, a few minutes before lunchtime, Pantelimon would start out resolutely for Ulieru's office. But the nearer he got to the office, the more slowly he walked. At the elevator door, he would lean against the wall and open his newspaper. But he could not read it, no matter how hard he tried. Every few moments he would lift his eyes and look at the clock on the wall. Then, folding up the paper, he would set off slowly for the canteen. He would be among the last to arrive and would eat in a rush, without appetite, staring at his plate. If anyone happened to speak to him, he would jump, startled, and blink, doing his best to smile. He ended the lunch hour always by looking at umbrellas in the nearest shop window.

"So it's true what they say," he heard Ulieru's familiar voice behind him. "You really do want to buy an umbrella!"

After shaking his hand vigorously, Ulieru looked at him closely, frowning.

"What's the matter with you? You seem to be from another world."

"The insomnia attacks have come back," Pantelimon replied, somewhat embarrassed. "Comrade Năstase was right: I caught cold last week. The rain soaked me, and although he gave me an aspirin, my hair was wet, especially at the back of my neck, and I caught cold. So, I wanted to buy myself a good umbrella. Maybe one of those over there," he added, pointing.

"If you haven't anything else to do, come with me. . . . I haven't seen you for a week," he continued, lowering his voice. "But in that week I've found out more about you than I did in two years."

Pantelimon turned suddenly and gave him a puzzled look.

"And I'm sure you've found out just as much about me." Ulieru continued, smiling. "Because, although we haven't been meeting, we've communicated with each other through an intermediary. Năstase repeated to me everything he discussed with you, and sometimes he played the tape recorder and asked me to comment on certain passages. I have no doubt the same thing has happened with you."

"The same thing," whispered Pantelimon, lowering his eyes. "Exactly the same thing."

"Don't let your conscience bother you," Ulieru consoled him. "That's the way the times are." He turned his head and then stopped, sighing deeply. "But that's not the reason I was looking for you. Your interpretations interested me."

"What interpretations?" Pantelimon asked in fright.

"All you said about Zevedei. He's fascinating. And so," he added, lowering his voice considerably, "you know him well. When did you meet him?"

"I don't know him at all. I've met him only once, the time when he stopped me and asked what year it was. . . . But Comrade Năstase has a whole collection of conversations recorded on tape, and I've listened to them — some, even two or three times."

He stopped walking and turned to look at Ulieru. This time a great smile illuminated his whole face. "That Zevedei," he continued with an unexpected fervor in his voice, "is more than just an interesting man. He's unique! Probably that's why I go to sleep so late. There is no night I don't think about him and try to figure out what he means when he declares, 'I practiced politics for fifteen years . . .' "

" '. . . and I was a prisoner for another fifteen years,' " continued Ulieru, " 'and I want to understand . . .' "

" 'I want to understand the meaning of those thirty years,' " Pantelimon continued. " 'Because the two periods constitute a totality.' "

"I believe he said, 'The two phases,' " Ulieru interrupted. "But it amounts to the same thing."

" 'And that's why the problem of time interests me,' " Pantelimon continued to quote. "The problem of time," he repeated pensively.

He stopped speaking and sought Ulieru's eyes. "But this couldn't have any connection with the newspapers antedated 1966."

"And yet, Năstase suspects him," Ulieru remarked absently. "Come on, we'd better keep walking."

"Of course, antedated newspapers betray a certain preoccupation with the 'problem of time.' But all that Zevedei said before that, if he was sincere, and I believe he was—perhaps he's insane, but he's sincere—all he said before indicated something else. . . . I don't know if you listened to the whole conversation recorded that day or not."

"I listened to a good share of it, but I don't know if it was the whole conversation. You refer, very likely, to what Zevedei said about von Braun."

"Exactly!" exclaimed Pantelimon. "I listened to that passage three times and I know it almost by heart. What enchanted me most of all was his sincerity when he emphasized that he is now quite indifferent to politics."

"He said something else, even before that," Ulieru interrupted. "He said, 'The mystery of the antedated newspapers is a pseudo-mystery. It's simply a technological feat.' "

"I believe he said that later, *after* he insisted he was quite indifferent now to politics. But that's not important. After he spoke about the 'problem of time,' he added, 'You ought to encourage me, because people like me, captivated by the problem of time, do not have, and cannot have, any political power.' "

" 'Remember von Braun's reply,' " Ulieru continued, quoting from memory, " 'Von Braun's reply when Hitler asked him to hurry with perfecting the rockets, to ensure victory.' "

Pantelimon stopped and took hold of his companion's arm.

" 'He said, "I'm not interested in how to win the war more quickly; what interests me is how to arrive sooner on the moon!" And so it happened: the Germans lost the war, but, thanks to von Braun, the Americans reached the moon!' "

"Come on, let's go," Ulieru urged, after turning around once to search the street.

"And yet," Pantelimon said, at length, "the example of von Braun could be taken in two ways. Perhaps Zevedei meant to say, the problem of time doesn't interest me, and von Braun illustrates admirably the triumph of those who look *far ahead*, across the years, beyond time. On the other hand, one could reply: but the triumph of von Braun is purely technological, and as such finds expression through political power."

"In that case —?" Ulieru interrupted.

"In that case, by citing the example of von Braun, Zevedei was thinking of something else. . . . But what? . . . That's why I can't sleep," he added after a pause. "I toss and turn on my bed and I keep wondering, what was he thinking about?"

"Maybe he wasn't thinking about anything," Ulieru suggested.

"Then that would be even more interesting, because, in that case, without meaning to, without realizing it, he betrayed himself!"

Pantelimon stopped suddenly and seized his companion's arm. "Shall I tell him, or will you?" he asked in a whisper. "Because it could be the first step in deciphering the code."

"You tell him, because you're young and you need the stripes. But tell me too. I'll repeat it to him and perhaps he'll be convinced I'm not hiding anything."

Before continuing, they both looked all around them.

"Von Braun, the moon, lunation," Pantelimon began. "The messages might be transmitted by means of a code based on the phases of the moon. The typographical errors and the other modifications made from the original editions might make sense if we take account of indications on the lunar calendar."

"I don't understand," whispered Ulieru.

"And yet, actually, it's rather simple. You open the newspaper, you read the information for that day: full moon, first quarter, third quarter, etc., and you look for the typographical errors. Let's say, today is the full moon. You count twelve words—or twelve letters—after the first typo, then you go to the next error, to the third, and so on. You copy those words, or perhaps only the initial letters, and you arrive at the message."

"Could this be so?" whispered Ulieru, greatly excited.

"I don't know, because I've never seen a copy of the apocryphal editions. But it could be verified. . . ."

"Let's go!" said Ulieru.

He walked thoughtfully, now and then turning his head toward Pantelimon, looking at him with curiosity, admiration, and at the same time fear.

"I congratulate you," he whispered after a while. "And it makes me happy that you've confided in me. You know, I felt bad when I heard you talking about your former sweetheart, domnişoara Irineu. I didn't realize. We've known each other for almost two years, and you never told me anything about her."

8

"I kept thinking this morning on the airplane," Pantazi began, after shaking hands with the others, "I thought, what does this remind me of? And just now, as I was entering, it came to me: it's like that story of the village that killed all its old men. They killed them all, leaving not one alive. And when things got in a muddle . . . you know the rest."

"They made a lot of errors," said Ghibercea, smiling awkwardly.

Pantazi glanced at him curtly, nodded his head, and sat down in the armchair.

"The Party never makes errors," he continued, removing the toothpick from his mouth and placing it on the rim of his coffee cup. "Only the circumstances are changed. . . . And what a delight," he added, casting his eyes around the table, "what a delight to see you haven't forgotten my manias: Turkish coffee without cream."

A shy smile flickered for a few moments on their faces. Then all six men turned their gaze toward Ghibercea. With an almost imperceptible tremor of his hand, Pantazi picked up the cup and sipped slowly, with fascination.

"Exactly as in the good old days . . . But the fable of the village without old men," he added, turning toward Ghibercea, "set me thinking. The fact that you've brought me here by special plane means that things have gotten into quite a bad muddle. And because, in the good old days, it was said that I had the magic dogbane."*

As if a signal had been given, all six broke into a short, timid laugh, watching Ghibercea's expression.

"You think that all I have to do is to pull the dogbane out of my pocket, touch the lock, and by magic all the bolts will be broken."

He picked up the cup, drained it, and then addressed a question to Ghibercea. "What's it all about?"

Ghibercea held out a file folder.

"I imagine you already know what it's about."

Pantazi opened the file and took out a copy of *Scînteia*. He skimmed it in a single glance, then replaced it in the folder carefully.

"It's from June 6, 1966," he said.

"It appeared and was distributed three days ago," Ghibercea informed him. "Haven't you heard about the apocryphal issues of *Scînteia*?"

Pantazi took the toothpick, broke it into pieces, and began chewing a piece of it slowly, concentrating.

"For two years I've been checking the identity and examining the files of the workers at the factories, as you know. I haven't had much time for anything else. Of course, like every-

*In Romanian folklore *iarba fiarelor* (dogbane) is a magic plant which has the power to open any lock and break metal bolts, fetters, etc. Here it is used figuratively for "breaking the code."

body else, I've heard a lot. But I don't know anything precise," he added, beginning to deposit meticulously and unhurriedly the fragments of the toothpick on the edge of his saucer.

Ghibercea spoke to a half-bald youth wearing dark glasses, who was seated at the end of the table. "You begin, Dumitrescu."

Pantazi listened to him, at the same time leafing through the file. After a few minutes he lifted his hand to stop him.

"These newspapers, apocryphal as you call them, were either printed on the presses of *Scînteia* or else procured from one of the embassies in the Capital."

"We think so too," smiled Ghibercea. "And because we're certain they weren't printed on our presses, we wonder why they were introduced and distributed by an embassy. Keep listening."

Pantazi drew another toothpick from his pocket, and with his head bowed, eyes half closed, he listened to the results of the investigations undertaken by the Special Services: the analyses of the paper and ink, the statistics on the typographical errors, the attempts to decipher the code by which messages are transmitted.

"But how do we know that messages are being sent?" asked Pantazi.

"Otherwise, what point is there in all these considerable efforts to print and distribute thousands of apocryphal copies throughout the country?" asked Ghibercea. "Because, as you will see, there are other elements too. Listen further."

Pantazi leaned his elbows on the desk and listened, sucking discreetly on the end of his toothpick.

"What's this about Zevedei's cape?" he asked suddenly. "I used to know that man in the old days."

At a signal from Ghibercea, Năstase opened the dossier in front of him and quoted several sentences; at the same time there appeared on the screen a slide of Zevedei leaving the Mătăsari Grocery, beaming and tossing the cape over his shoulders.

"His sort has little to be cheerful about," added Năstase. "But that day he had found some ham."

Immobilized on the screen, Zevedei continued to smile, holding his little package in his left hand, and preparing with his right to arrange his cape.

"The cape belonged to an uncle of his, Colonel Bruno Flondor, of the Austro-Hungarian Army," Năstase explained. "But now I think it will be useful for you to listen to one of his first conversations," he continued, reaching for the tape recorder.

"I practiced politics for fifteen years," he heard Zevedei's voice saying, "and I was a prisoner for another fifteen years. That is why I *must* understand the problem of time . . ."

A few minutes later Pantazi asked to have the passage about von Braun repeated. A second cup of coffee was brought, and he began to sip it slowly, listening to Năstase reading from the memorandum on Pantelimon.

"A socially healthy origin. Son of workers in Valea Jiului. Outstanding student, though lacking in political spirit. Even before taking his doctorate, he accepted a rather bold project at Section C. After six months of research, the results proved so unexpected that the project was passed with priority to Section A. He was promoted to head of the laboratory with the rank of assistant professor. For reasons unknown, he broke his engagement with Comrade Sanda Irineu, a coworker in the laboratory. He became suspect in November of 1967 and has been under surveillance ever since. He has no friends. The only person he talks with at the canteen and sometimes meets is Comrade Ulieru from the accounting office."

"What does he look like?" asked Pantazi.

He saw him on the screen: first, in front of the Mătăsari Grocery, then in the laboratory, frowning at the contents of a retort, then walking along the street with Ulieru; in the last view, he was taking the arm of a young woman, as though he would have liked to embrace her.

"She is Comrade Sanda Irineu," Năstase explained. "She studied for four years at the Faculty of Chemistry in Moscow. She specialized in aniline dyes and inks. In November

1967, she was sent to a conference at Stockholm, and she never returned. She's presently in Uganda. She collects picture post-cards from all over the world."

Năstase then summarized his conversations with Uli-eru and Pantelimon, leafing through the file and frequently reading whole sentences, or, at Pantazi's request, switching on the tape recorder and allowing it to speak. After a quarter of an hour, listening for the second time to Pantelimon's explana-tions relative to the possibility of a code based on phases of the moon, he turned to Ghibercea.

"Well—?" he asked. "Have you tried it?"

Ghibercea smiled with unconcealed satisfaction and shrugged.

"Special Services began calculations that very night, June 2–3, on the basis of the apocryphal edition of the previous morning. Nothing resulted. Then they investigated all the ear-lier issues. Nothing . . . Pantelimon's hypothesis is rather in-genious, but the code, assuming there is a code, has not yet been deciphered."

Pantazi remained pensive and no one dared disturb the silence.

"Before proceeding any further," he began at length, "I must make a confession: you have brought me here for nothing. I cannot help you, for the simple reason that this problem transcends the territorial limits. I'm of no use in prob-lems of an international nature. You ought to consult the ser-vices of certain friendly nations."

"We did that long ago," said Ghibercea. "We had to, in fact, because they found out about the matter, probably a few hours after we did. They followed the same course as we: the explosion at the ink factory, the case against the assistant director of the Military Museum, the surveillance of the print-ery, and the distribution of the paper. We ran into them every-where. And very likely they utilized computers . . . without any positive results."

"And yet," Pantazi began, chewing calmly on the re-mainder of his toothpick, "the affair *can only be* international.

We're a small country and our internal enemies have long since been annihilated or reduced to impotence. It is impossible to imagine that, under our very noses, there could have been organized in the last three or four months a subversive activity of such proportions and possessed of technical means that would be the envy of many nations."

Ghibercea looked around triumphantly as he listened to this statement. "We've arrived at the same conclusions," he said. "But the question continually keeps arising: why? for what purpose? If the apocryphal editions carry subversive messages, why hasn't something more happened, something *different* from what occurred last winter? Whatever the subversive action may be, the means used are too complex and too costly."

The man sitting next to Ghibercea raised his hand.

"If you will permit me, Comrade Colonel, I'd like to put a question to Comrade Pantazi. When you said that the problem is international, what were you thinking about?"

Before replying, Pantazi gave him a long look, as if he were seeing him for the first time. "I was thinking that maybe it was the authors of the operation themselves who suggested to us the idea of a subversive operation and a plot."

"I don't quite understand . . ."

"Nor do I," added Ghibercea. "Why would they go to all that trouble?"

Pantazi took hold of the saucer and drew it slowly to him.

"Thanks," he said. "Only here can one drink the best coffee *without cream*. I don't understand how you do it." He brought the cup to his lips and sipped carefully. "And, as usual, it's piping hot. Excellent! . . . But to get back to what I said a little while ago. I said, it could be that a message exists, but that it doesn't refer to a subversive activity in *our country*. It could be that the message is addressed to other groups in other lands, and in order to make it more certain to arrive at its destination, they send it through counterfeited editions of our newspaper."

"That's hard to believe," Ghibercea interrupted, smiling. "Too complicated."

"I said, *it could be.* Simply an hypothesis. But one could devise others also."

"Such as — ?" asked Ghibercea.

"I'll tell you later, after I've learned more details. In the meantime, I'd like to know if such apocryphal copies have been sent across the border. More precisely, if they've turned up in the collections of central libraries or in the offices of Communist newspapers in Europe or anywhere else in the world that *Scînteia* is sent. Do you think it would be possible to get precise information on this within a reasonable length of time?"

"It's possible," replied Ghibercea. "But if they were sent, it's hard to believe they were kept in the collections. Seeing they were dated 1966, the recipients would have supposed that there had been a mistake or an oversight on the part of the sender, and they'd have thrown them away."

"Nevertheless, it's worth a try. If it had been observed that an error or oversight was repeated, the administration of the newspaper would have been notified. Do you know about any complaint of that sort?"

"Yes," spoke up the man next to Pantazi, the one who had brought him the coffee. "There have been at least two complaints: one from the Central Library in Mexico City, and the other from the offices of the Italian newspaper *Unita.*"

"What sort of complaints?" asked Ghibercea.

"Both the same: that we had sent them, at intervals, old numbers, and thus their collection was not complete. But it never occurred to me that there might be some connection with the apocryphal issues," he added, blushing.

"When were the complaints made?"

"The one from Mexico in March, the one from Italy a few weeks later. *Unita* even sent us a list of the issues missing from their collection. Obviously, it's a matter of . . ."

"Then it's quite simple," Ghibercea interrupted him, at the same time pressing one of the red buttons beside the telephone.

9

The session resumed at 2:15. In front of each man was a thermos with orange juice and, in a glass, espresso coffee with ice. Only at Pantazi's place there was Turkish coffee and a carafe of cold water. They listened absently to the report of an inspector concerning the cities where apocryphal exemplars had been collected, what kind of people had received them, and what they had stated at their interrogations. The great majority of them were workers or heads of organizations. Very few intellectuals, and almost all members of the Party. At first, they threw away the apocryphal copies, especially since some of them received the current edition the same morning. But lately they had heard about them, and they brought them to headquarters or sold them to connoisseurs.

"What kind of connoisseurs?" asked Pantazi.

"People of all sorts, collectors of curiosities. They've been questioned, too. They don't appear suspicious. Apparently they're trustworthy; but, of course, they talk here and there, and intentionally or unintentionally they publicize the matter. . . . It's known in all the provincial cities now."

"That's how I myself found out about it," said Pantazi, meticulously breaking a toothpick. "Some are amused, others are happy. They say: Look, it's possible to commit acts of sabotage and get away with it; the Security can't find a trace of the perpetrators."

"This is the most serious part of the whole business," Ghibercea broke in. "The publicity. It's hard to know how many are aware of the modifications in the texts and the typographical errors. Many people haven't noticed even the main modification: 'Dreamers of all lands, unite!' But they're fascinated by the success of the operation."

"Perhaps this is part of the program," said Pantazi. "But if it were just this and nothing more! . . . I'm listening," he added, seeing that the silence was prolonged.

"I believe I've covered the essentials," concluded the inspector, after leafing through the file one more time.

Pantazi automatically stuck his fingers in the upper pocket of his coat, but he found nothing. In a matter of moments, Ghibercea held out to him a cellophane tube full of toothpicks. Looking around, he caught the other four in the same gesture.

"Thank you," said Pantazi. "I'm glad to see you haven't forgotten my tics and manias. . . . But I should like to return for a moment to our principal suspects: Pantelimon, Zevedei, and domnişoara Irineu. If it's a case of some planned action, and therefore of an organization, I understand the role of domnişoara Irineu, but I don't quite understand that of the other two—or three, if we count Ulieru."

"So far as Zevedei's concerned," intervened Ghibercea, "there may however be a clue." And he expounded his hypothesis: Zevedei's behavior can be explained only by presupposing he has lost his contact. Pantazi listened intently, sucking on his toothpick from time to time.

"Very interesting, your hypothesis. But I wonder if perhaps they have drawn us off our course from the beginning, decoying us with false tracks: Zevedei's cape, the explosion at the ink factory, the irregularities at the Military Museum, and perhaps additional ones of which we're unaware."

"But still," Năstase interjected, "a connection *does* exist between them, because Sanda Irineu, when she was engaged to Pantelimon, lived right beside Zevedei, and Dr. Magheru, on whose account Pantelimon broke his engagement, was moved to the ink factory in Slatina."

"True," agreed Pantazi, "But it could be that this connection, which seems rather suspicious, has been used as a decoy to cause us to mobilize all our energy around a fictitious internal plot, thus camouflaging the source and international character of the operation. If that is so, then they've succeeded, because we've lost three months."

Ghibercea paled slightly and frowned.

"But what could we have done?"

"I'm not reproaching you," Pantazi continued. "Certainly, you questioned Zevedei quite efficiently, you communicated his declarations to Pantelimon—I refer in particular to the passage about von Braun—and thus you identified the structure of the code."

Ghibercea looked around the table smiling wryly. "You're joking, Comrade," he said, still smiling. "I pointed out to you this morning that the Special Services have labored day and night, taking as a basis the phases of the moon in 1966 and the present year, with absolutely no success. They've been unable to form a single word, let alone a message."

Pantazi began to drink thoughtfully from the fresh coffee one of the men had brought him.

"Of course, it's simply an hypothesis. But because we know now that apocryphal editions were sent across the borders—to Mexico, Italy, and certainly to other places—that, therefore, it is a matter of an international action, we must not calculate on the basis of the phases of the moon *here*, in Romania. We must take account of the lunar calendar in other countries, even a great many countries. I believe the Special Services will be able to start this very evening, utilizing the computer. The Observatory will be able to put at their disposal tables of great precision, indicating the phases of the moon for the whole surface of the earth. We ought to begin first with our neighbors; then France, Italy, Mexico, Sweden . . . But don't forget Uganda," he added after a short pause.

10

When he saw him approaching, the young man folded up his newspaper, looked for something in his briefcase, then got up from the bench lazily, as though he could not bear the thought of leaving the shade of the linden. He set off slowly, with sluggish steps, in the opposite direction, glancing back frequently at the bench. Only after he saw him sitting down did he walk faster; in a few moments he had disappeared.

"I'm very glad that, at last, I have the occasion to meet you," said Pantazi, "and especially here, under the lindens.

It's been three years since I came here," he added, taking a toothpick from his pocket and beginning to roll it around between his fingers. "I want to congratulate you and ask you a question: When did you decipher the code? How many days before you informed Năstase of your discovery?"

Pantelimon turned suddenly with his whole body, and looked at him with surprise. "But I didn't decipher it! They made all possible calculations, Comrade Năstase told me, but without success."

Pantazi studied him for a few moments in silence, meanwhile beginning to break the toothpick meticulously.

"Don't get upset watching me suck on toothpicks, break them in pieces, and masticate them. This habit — a detestable one, I admit — is the price I pay even now, five years later, for giving up smoking. . . . As I was saying," he continued in a more serious tone, "I'm curious to know how many days elapsed between the moment when you made the connection — von Braun–lunation–phases of the moon, — and the moment when you informed Năstase of your hypothesis?"

"Not more than four days. Of course the day before, I had spoken with Comrade Ulieru — the day when we met by chance in front of the umbrella department."

Pantazi did not attempt to conceal his satisfaction. "In other words, three days. You kept the secret to yourself for three days. Why?"

"I didn't dare divulge it to anyone. It seemed to me — the principle, I mean — seemed to be *obvious*, and at the same time absurd, inapplicable — as it turned out to be, in fact."

"And why to Ulieru?"

"Because we are — how shall I say? — not friends, but — well, he's the only man I trust completely, the only person I talk with."

"And so," Pantazi interrupted, "if your friend Ulieru had revealed it to someone else that very day, that other person would have had an advantage of twenty-four hours."

Pantelimon shrugged his shoulders in embarrassment.

"But never mind about that," Pantazi continued. "The

remarkable thing to me is the fact that you succeeded in unlocking the code, thanks to Zevedei's cape! Because, isn't it true? Didn't you admit from the very first interrogation that you were impressed by the patches sewn in the place of the epaulettes?"

Pantelimon began to squirm a little on the bench.

"If it hadn't been for the patches, Zevedei wouldn't have stopped you in front of the Mătăsari Grocery to ask you what year it was, and today you'd be going about your business peacefully in your laboratory. You wouldn't have become the number one object of several secret services, to such an extent that they've watched you day and night. Because," he added smiling, "I believe you've understood it too: the fact that you were removed to the provinces hastily, then interned in a sanatorium under the pretext that you were in danger of a pulmonary congestion; and the fact that today you were returned to Bucharest in the ambulance of the Ministry for an alleged consultation, and then invited to stroll in the park accompanied by an intern; and finally invited to sit on this bench. . . . I believe you've understood this was all for your own good."

"I haven't understood anything! I only imagined that I became suspect afterwards."

"You were suspect even before," Pantazi interrupted him. "But this time it was a different matter. We had to watch you. Men can disappear more easily than you imagine. They disappear today, and tomorrow they turn up on who knows what continent. That's the way times are. Other people found out about your discovery, and they found out twenty-four hours before we did."

"But they made calculations. . . ." Pantelimon tried to excuse himself again.

"Let's get back to this. I spoke to you about Zevedei's cape, without which . . . I know Zevedei, and I knew about the cape, too, but I didn't know he wore it patched that way, summer and winter. I know Zevedei well. It was I who sent him to prison. I learned he was getting ready to run off to the mountains to join a group of rather well armed saboteurs. And because I knew that the group had been surrounded, I felt sorry for Zevedei. I had known him as a youth, and before that I had been well acquainted with his uncle, Colonel Bruno Flondor. So I had to arrest him that very night and implicate him in a fictitious plot. I hoped that he would get no more than five years, but at the trial he talked too much, intentionally or unintentionally, and he was sentenced to twenty-five years. I was sorry, but at least he had escaped with his life. The others in the mountains were caught and executed a few days later."

He paused a moment and looked Pantelimon directly in the eyes.

"If you should meet him, don't say anything about this to him. It's an old story, and he knows nothing of it. . . . But the cape!" he exclaimed, lifting a hand in the air as if he wished to display the toothpick he had just taken from his pocket. "I read and reread all the stenographic reports just to find out why he decided to wear that cape!"

"With two patches sewn on in the place of the epaulettes," Pantelimon specified.

"The epaulettes were ripped off on the night he was arrested. I had given instructions to search for foreign currency; if any had been found, he would have been implicated in another case and given the minimum sentence of three years. But Zevedei was a man of integrity: he wanted to fight in the mountains. In his house they didn't find so much as a single Swiss franc."

He paused a moment, then smiled and began again. "It is probable, though, that the whole city found out about the thoroughness of the search and the ripping of the epaulettes, because, since then, we have found hardly any jewels or foreign coins hidden in the linings of coats. And one of the blackest pages of our Service is precisely this: we didn't think about the collection of national costumes, and above all the collection of uniforms, in the Military Museum. The organization was able to work, undisturbed, for at least ten years. They had reliable men working at the museum, and very skillful liaison agents. Under different pretexts — moths, dust, checking the records, etc. — certain pieces were removed from the glass cases and taken to a special room. The rest you can imagine. . . . It was thus that many managed to save their jewels and foreign currency — and, yes, some of them even their gold coins. Of course the operation cost dearly: almost half the value of the objects thus hidden. But some uniforms had been ripped open and sewed up so many times that after several years they began to be badly tattered. At that point the assistant director of the museum had an unfortunate idea: he decided to restore them; inferior dyes were used, though, and the uniforms came out looking worse than before. The assistant director then suggested they change the colors. . . . And so he was caught, and the scandal erupted."

"It's like an adventure novel!" said Pantelimon.

Pantazi looked at him curiously, as if trying to hide his disappointment.

"And yet I still don't understand *why* Zevedei decided to wear *only* that cape, and to wear it summer and winter. As well as I know him, I'm sure there *must* be a reason. But what? At any rate, we ought to be grateful. Thanks to the cape, you met Zevedei, you found out about the apocryphal issues, about von Braun and lunation, and you suggested a hypothesis, the only one worth being considered. Except that you didn't relate it in its entirety. The last part you kept to yourself."

"I don't understand what you mean," Pantelimon whispered, quite intimidated.

For a few moments Pantazi examined him again, smiling.

"It's hard for me to believe you stopped half-way. I'd have expected you to suggest that Năstase proceed with the deciphering of the messages by taking account of the phases of the moon outside our territory — taking account, for instance, of the lunar calendar in France, or Russia, or Mexico. Or Uganda."

Pantelimon paled and lifted his head suddenly.

"But that's utterly absurd!" he exclaimed. "If clandestine editions appear in Romania with their messages coded, the messages can only be in the Romanian language and addressed to Romanians."

"It does seem absurd," Pantazi agreed, seeking a new toothpick. "And yet, *it's so*: by taking account of the lunar calendars from the whole surface of the earth, the computers have deciphered up to the present time over a hundred messages, composed in fifteen languages, including Romanian."

"Impossible! Absurd!" Pantelimon repeated. "What kind of messages?"

"Rather placid and insipid ones. Quotations from Gandhi and the Gospels, from the Charter of the United Nations, from Marcus Aurelius, Confucius, and many other sources of the same sort. But especially from the Gospels. In fifteen languages so far, but the entire collection has not yet been exhausted."

Pantelimon listened in amazement, staring at him with eyes dilated, as though straining to see him better.

"But *why*?" he whispered at last. "What could be the sense of a polyglot edition, coded and printed here, containing messages indecipherable in Romania?"

"In a sense," Pantazi resumed, still smiling, "it's pacifist propaganda on a global scale, effected by international means."

"But it's absurd, absurd! Propaganda using methods so complicated that only computers can decipher the messages!"

"I don't exactly understand it myself," Pantazi admitted. "But don't forget that only *we* here in Romania had to resort to computers. The reader in France or Sweden or Mexico deciphered it by himself. He looked at the date on which the paper was printed, he sought the position of the moon on that day in his country; then, in accord with the system that you discovered, he began to decipher it. Of course, if he sees that the first group of letters doesn't make sense, he abandons the effort. He knows, because he was informed beforehand, that the edition for that day doesn't contain any messages addressed to his country."

"It's so extraordinarily complicated!" Pantelimon repeated. "And it seems downright absurd, when you consider that the paper is printed in the Romanian language."

"There *is* an explanation, nonetheless." He paused, then added, "I'm telling you because you've proved to me that you can keep a secret, at least for three days. But yours was, indeed, a very precious secret. What I shall tell you now are only hypotheses, and they don't involve our country directly. But if you can, it would be better if you kept them to yourself."

"I give you my word of honor," whispered Pantelimon, placing his hand over his heart.

"We are a small country," said Pantazi, with a trace of sadness in his voice, "and we, like many other countries, constitute a more or less closed society. This is our historic situation, and we must take account of it. . . . Among our neighbors, certain structural changes have been attempted — what Occidentals call 'liberalization.' You know the results. But it is difficult to imagine that this tendency toward liberalization can be radically annihilated. On the other hand, it is hard to imagine that certain superpowers would not try to take advantage of such a tendency."

He stopped speaking, removed the fragments of the toothpick from his mouth, and placed them, very carefully, one beside the other, on the edge of the bench.

"What I'm telling you now, I repeat, is simply a hypothesis. And I'm telling you because you understood the lesson of von Braun: only those who see far ahead will triumph. You're young, and you will see many things. To be specific, what sense can there be, as you say, in an apocryphal edition of *Scînteia* whose coded messages cannot be deciphered in Romania and are only rarely composed in Romanian? Only one explanation is possible: certain services of a superpower are trying an experiment, and, for reasons I don't understand, they're trying it in our country. But in order to avoid a possibly erroneous interpretation, and especially to avoid diplomatic complications, the messages are written in a code impossible to be deciphered in our country. Moreover, the content of

44

these messages is politically without significance; that is, at least for the time being, it is simply pacifistic propaganda."

"It seems incredible!" exclaimed Pantelimon. "To go to all that expense of money and energy, just to transmit in coded form texts from the Gospels and Gandhi!"

"If my hypothesis is correct, the experiment has an extraordinary importance. Later, it might have rather serious consequences. I shall return to this aspect of the problem in a minute. Meanwhile, let us analyze the purpose of the experiment. The organizers are trying to verify to what extent they can transmit — to the whole world — certain slogans or information, or, later on, precise instructions of a political or military nature. To what extent — that is, to what limits — they can make use of a code that is, on the one hand so simple that it can be learned by heart, yet on the other hand recodifies itself automatically and infinitely in the case of its discovery by an adversary. Because, you know as well as I do, on an invariable base — the phases of the moon — you can change the cipher an infinite number of times: in our case, one counts the words — or letters — to the right or the left of the typographical errors; but they can modify the order in which one must count, and they can constitute new systems on the basis of letters or groups of letters — ad infinitum. Only one thing matters: the existence of an invariable and easily accessible structure, that is, one present at any longitude or latitude. As you so well guessed, the only structure of this sort is the lunar calendar."

"But . . . ," intervened Pantelimon.

"I know," Pantazi interrupted him. "It is, as you say, extremely complicated: printing apocryphal editions, introducing them by legal or illegal means into different countries, instructing the readers beforehand in the system of recoding deciphered codes, and so on. It is extraordinarily complicated, but it is a system that can never be abolished. As long as a lunar calendar exists, and as long as there are superpowers with unlimited technical means at their disposal, the diffusion of any category of messages on a worldwide scale cannot be interrupted. For the present," he added smiling, "they're making pacifist propaganda. Zevedei, for instance, has no idea about the code, but he's convinced that it is a matter of religious messages announcing Universal Peace. Because, while endeavoring to understand, as he says, the fundamental unity of two antagonistic phases of his life — fifteen years of political activity and fifteen years of meditation in prison — he has arrived at the conclusion that only a universal reconciliation, that is, World Peace, can save mankind from catastrophe. Ever since he set eyes on copies antedated by three years he has been convinced that a powerful spiritual offensive has been launched in several parts of the world. But because he cannot read the messages, he asks now and then — as he did with you — what year it is, hoping one day to meet someone who knows the code and can relate to him the messages. . . . If you meet him," he added with a wistful smile, "tell him that he was right: the majority of the messages are taken from the Gospels, above all from the Beatitudes."

"The Beatitudes?" asked Pantelimon. "What are they?"

"Haven't you ever heard of the Beatitudes proclaimed by Jesus? 'Blessed are those who hunger, for they shall be satisfied. Blessed are those who mourn, for they shall be comforted. . . . Blessed are the lovers of peace. . . .' "

"Oh, yes," exclaimed Pantelimon, blushing. "I know. I've heard them. But I didn't know they were called the Beatitudes."

"There are eight Beatitudes," added Pantazi, placing the last fragment of the toothpick on the edge of the bench with trembling fingers. "If I were to make an effort, I believe I could recall all eight."

He was quiet, with eyes closed, as though trying to remember and count them.

"You said that there were messages transmitted in the Romanian language also," Pantelimon asked at length, venturing to break the silence.

"Only one, actually, but it was sent several times: 'Blessed are the poor in spirit, for theirs will be the Kingdom of Heaven.' "

Pantelimon blanched and wiped his hand across his forehead several times.

" 'The poor in spirit,' " he repeated in a whisper. "If I'm not being indiscreet . . ."

"Not at all. This message, the only one in the Romanian language, can be deciphered only by taking account of the lunar calendar of Uganda!"

"It was her favorite expression," Pantelimon murmured dreamily. "She would repeat it to me over and over. At the time, I found it humiliating, and I didn't understand why she would say it to me. Why to me, of all people?"

With a quick motion, Pantazi flicked the remains of the toothpick away, then ground them under his foot, mingling them with the gravel, trying to hide them.

"You will understand, perhaps, later," he said. "There have been many poor in spirit in this great world of ours. But the most famous one remains—Parsifal. For he was the only one who asked, 'Where is the chalice of the Holy Grail?' . . . Hurrah for our Goddamn Grail!" he continued in a tired, far-off voice. "Hurrah for the Goddamn Grail for which we have been fated to seek! To seek—and to find!"

He stood up, shook Pantelimon's hand, and set off slowly, tilting his head slightly upward, as if he had just become aware of the fragrance of the linden blossoms.

1975

Youth Without Youth

for Sybille

Youth Without Youth

1

Only when he heard the bell of the Metropolia Church did he remember that it was the night of Easter. And suddenly the rain seemed unnatural — the rain which had greeted him as he had emerged from the railway station and which threatened to become torrential. He made his way forward hastily with the umbrella brought down to his shoulders, his eyes downcast, trying to avoid the rivulets. Without realizing it, he began to run, holding the umbrella close to his chest, like a shield. But after some twenty meters he saw the traffic signal turn red, and he had to stop. He waited nervously, standing on tiptoe, hopping from one foot to the other continually, looking in consternation at the little pond that covered a good part of the boulevard directly in front of him. The red orb went out, and in the next moment he was shaken, blinded by an explosion of white incandescent light. He felt as though he had been sucked up by a fiery cyclone that had exploded at some mysterious moment on top of his head. A close strike of lightning, he said to himself, blinking with difficulty to unseal his eyelids. He did not understand why he was clutching the handle of his umbrella so hard. The rain lashed at him wildly from all sides at once, and yet he felt nothing. Then he heard the bell at the Metropolia again, and all the other bells, and very close

51

by still another, striking in a solitary, desperate way. I've had a fright, he said to himself, and he began to shiver. It's because of the water, he realized a few moments later, becoming aware of the fact that he was lying in the puddle near the curb. I've taken a chill. . . .

"I saw the lightning strike him," he heard the breathless voice of a frightened man saying. "I don't know if he's still alive or not. I was looking over there, where he was standing under the traffic signal, and I saw him light up from head to toe — umbrella, hat, coat, all at once! If it hadn't been for the rain, he would have been burnt to a crisp. I don't know if he's still alive or not."

"And even if he's still alive, what can we do with him?" The voice seemed to come from far away and it sounded to him tired, bitter.

"Who knows what sins he's committed, that God would strike him on the very night of Easter, right behind a church!" Then, after a pause, he added, "Let's see what the intern says about it."

It seemed strange to him that he felt nothing, that he did not, in fact, feel his body at all. He knew from the conversation of those around him that he had been moved. But how had he been transported? In their arms? On a stretcher? On a cart of some sort? . . .

"I don't believe he has a chance," he heard another voice saying later, also far away. "Not a single centimeter of his skin is untouched. I don't understand how he stays alive. Normally, he would have . . ."

Of course, everybody knows that. If you have lost more than fifty percent of your skin, you die of asphyxia. But he realized quickly that it was ridiculous and humiliating to reply mentally to the people bustling around him. He would have liked not to have had to hear them, just as, with his eyes shut tight, he did not see them. And at the same moment he found himself far away, happy, as he had been *then*.

"And then, what else happened," she asked him in

jest, smiling. "What other tragedy?"

"I didn't say it was a tragedy, but in a sense it was that: to conceive a passion for science, to have but one desire — to dedicate your life to science."

"To which science are you referring?" she interrupted him. "To mathematics or to the Chinese language?"

"To both — and to all the others I've discovered and fallen in love with, insofar as I've learned about them."

She put her hand on his arm to keep him from getting angry at being interrupted again. "Mathematics I understand, because if you didn't have a vocation for it, it would be useless to persevere. But *Chinese*?"

He didn't know why he burst into laughter. Probably he was amused by the way she had said, "But *Chinese*?"

"I thought I'd told you. Two years ago in the fall when I was in Paris I went to a lecture by Chavannes. I saw him after class in his office; he asked me how long I'd been studying Chinese and how many other Oriental languages I knew. No need to repeat the whole conversation. I understood just one thing: that if I didn't master in a few years — in a *few years* — Chinese, Sanskrit, Tibetan, and Japanese, I would never become a great orientalist."

"All right, but you must have told him that you wanted to study *only* the Chinese language."

"That's what I said, but I didn't persuade him. Because even in that case I'd still have to learn Japanese and a lot of South Asian languages and dialects. . . . But this wasn't the important thing; it was something else. When I told him I'd been studying Chinese for five months, he stepped to a blackboard and wrote some twenty characters. He asked me to pronounce them one by one, and then to translate the passage. I pronounced them as I had been taught, and I translated some, but not all, of them. He smiled amiably. 'That's not bad,' he said, 'But if after five months . . . How many hours a day?' 'At least six hours,' I replied.

'Then the Chinese language is not for you. Probably you don't have the necessary visual memory. . . . My dear sir,' he added with a smile that was ambiguous, affectionate, and ironic at the same time, 'My dear sir, in order to master Chinese you must have the memory of a Mandarin, a *photographic memory.* If you don't have it, you will be obliged to make an effort three or four times as great. I don't believe it's worth it.' 'So, basically it's a matter of memory.' 'Of a photographic memory,' he repeated gravely, emphasizing the words."

He heard the door opening and closing several times and other noises, including strange voices.

"Let's see what the Professor says. If you ask me, I'd say that frankly . . ."

The same thing, over and over again! But he liked the voice; it was, no doubt, that of a young doctor, clever and enthusiastic about his profession, generous.

". . . His skin was burned one hundred percent, and yet he's survived twelve hours, and so far as we can tell, he's not in pain. . . . Have you given him any shots?"

"One, this morning. I thought he groaned. But maybe he was just moaning in his sleep."

"Do you know anything about him? Was anything found beside him?"

"Just the handle of the umbrella. The rest was inciner-ated. Curious — the handle, of all things, a wooden han-dle. . . . The clothes were turned to ashes. What the rain didn't wash away was saved in the ambulance."

He knew it would have had to be that way, and yet hearing the intern say it lifted his spirits. So, the two envelopes in his pocket had been incinerated, too. . . .

Without intending to, because he had not been care-ful to close the door completely behind him, he had overheard: "The Old Man's getting quite decrepit! He told us the same thing three or four times."

It was true. He had been impressed by the news he had read in *La Fiera Letteraria*, that Papini was almost blind and no surgeon dared to operate on him. For a ravenous and indefatigable reader like Papini, this was an unparalleled tragedy. That is why he kept talking about it all the time. But perhaps Vaian was right: I *am* beginning to get decrepit.

Then he heard the voice again. "And what other tragedy befell you? You gave up the Chinese language. What else?"

"As a matter of fact, I didn't give it up; I continued to learn ten or fifteen characters per day, but this was mostly for my pleasure and because it helped me to understand the translations of the texts I read. Actually, I was a dilettante."

"So much the better," Laura interrupted him, placing her hand on his arm again. "There have to be a few intelligent men with enough imagination to enjoy the discoveries made by your great scholars. It's a good thing you dropped Chinese. . . . But what are the other tragedies you referred to?"

He looked at her a long time. She was far from being the best-looking female student he had known, but she was *different.* He did not understand what attracted him, why he sought her continually, going through the lecture halls where he had not walked for three or four years, since he had taken his Degree. He knew he would always find her at Titu Maiorescu's class. There he had met her an hour ago, and, as usual, when he escorted her to her home, they had stopped to sit on a bench beside a lake in Cişmigiu.

"What are the other tragedies?" she repeated, maintaining her calm, smiling gaze.

"I told you that while I was still in the lycée, I was fond of mathematics and music, but I also liked history, archeology, and philosophy. I wanted to study them all; obviously, not as a specialist, but still rigorously, working directly from texts, because I have a horror of improvisation and hearsay learning."

She interrupted him, raising her arms in a boyish gesture.

"You're the most ambitious man I've ever met! The most ambitious and the most driven! Driven, especially!"

He knew the voices well, and had learned to distinguish them. There were three nurses by day and two at night.

"If he had any luck, he'd die now. Because they say that whoever dies during the Week of Light goes straight to Paradise."

She has a good soul; she pities me. She's better than the others because she's thinking about my salvation. . . . But what if she gets the idea of pulling the I.V. needle out of my vein? Probably I'd survive till morning when the intern comes. And if he doesn't notice it, the Professor will. The Professor is the only one who's desperate and humiliated over the fact that he doesn't understand; the only one who wants at all costs to keep me alive, to find out what happened. He had heard him one day — no use asking *when* — he had heard him talking after he had touched his eyelids with infinite care:

"The eye seems intact, but if he's blind or not, I don't know. I don't know *anything*, in fact. . . ."

He had heard this also: "I don't even know if he's conscious or not, if he hears or if he *understands* what he hears." It wasn't his fault. Several times before that he had recognized the voice and had understood it perfectly. "If you understand what I say," the Professor shouted, "squeeze my finger." But he could not feel his finger. He would have liked to squeeze it, but he didn't know how.

That time the Professor added, "If we can succeed in keeping him alive another five days . . ."

In five days, one of his assistants found out, the great specialist from Paris, Professor Gilbert Bernard, would come to Bucharest en route to Athens.

56

"Especially, ambitious!" Laura repeated. "You want to be what all those other people are: philologist, orientalist, archeologist, historian, and who knows what else. That is, you want to live a strange life, a different life, instead of being yourself, Dominic Matei, and cultivating your own genius exclusively."

"My genius?" he exclaimed with a pretended modesty in order to hide his delight. "That presupposes I *have* genius!"

"In a sense, certainly, you do have it. You don't resemble anyone I have ever met. You live life and understand it differently from us."

"But up to now, at age twenty-six, I haven't accomplished anything. I've just taken all the exams and passed with good marks. I haven't discovered anything, not even an original interpretation of Canto XI of *Purgatorio*, which I have translated and written a commentary on."

"Why would you have to discover something? Your genius ought to be to fulfill yourself in the life you live, not in original analyses, discoveries, and interpretations. Your model ought to be Socrates or Goethe; but imagine a Goethe *without a written opus!*"

"I don't exactly understand," he said.

"Do you understand everything?" asked the Professor.

"I don't understand you very well, especially when you speak fast."

He understood very well. The Professor's French was impeccable; without doubt he had taken his doctorate in Paris. He seemed to speak more precisely and elegantly than the great specialist. Bernard was, probably, of foreign origin. But he guessed from his slow, hesitating sentences that—as Vaian had said about their last director, whenever he had had to make a grave decision quickly—he did not dare to express himself.

"When did you become convinced he's conscious?"

"Only the day before yesterday," said the Professor. "I had tried several times before to get a response, but without result."

"And you're *sure* he squeezed your finger? You *felt* him squeeze it in response to your question? Couldn't it have been a reflex gesture, involuntary and therefore without significance?"

"I repeated the experiment several times. Try it yourself, if you wish, and you'll be convinced."

He sensed, as at so many times in the past few days, a finger introduced gently, with exaggerated precaution, beneath his own fingers drawn up in a fist. Then he heard the Professor's voice: "If you understand what I am saying, squeeze my finger!" He must have squeezed it with sufficient force, because Dr. Bernard withdrew it quickly, surprised. But a few moments later, after whispering, *"Traduisez, s'il vous plait,"* he introduced it again and said, pronouncing the words clearly and slowly: *"Celui qui vous parle est un médecin français. Accepteriez-vous qu'il vous pose quelques questions?"* Before the Professor had finished translating, he squeezed the finger as hard as before. This time the doctor did not withdraw it, but asked, *"Vous comprenez le français?"* He repeated the squeezing, but with less conviction. After hesitating a few moments, Dr. Bernard asked, *"Voulez-vous qu'on vous abandonne à votre sort?"* With great delight, he kept his whole hand inert, as if it were a plaster cast. *"Vous préférez qu'on s'occupe de vous?"* He squeezed hard. *"Voulez-vous qu'on donne du chloroforme?"* He immobilized his hand again, and kept it that way, without the slightest twitch, while listening to the final questions: *"Etes-vous Jésus-Christ? Voulez-vous jouer du piano? Ce matin, avez-vous bu du champagne?"*

That night, everyone stood with champagne glasses in hand, surrounding them and shouting at them with a sad, mediocre lack of modesty that surprised them both: "Don't drink any more champagne till you get to Venice, or you'll be sick!"

"I was afraid that they drank more champagne than they should have," said Laura, after the train had left the station.

Then he heard the Professor's voice: "Let's try one more time. Perhaps he didn't understand your questions properly. I'll question him in Romanian." And he continued, raising his voice. "We wish to find out your age. For every ten years squeeze my finger once."

He squeezed it, harder and harder, six times; then, without understanding why, he stopped.

"Sixty years?" marveled the Professor. "I'd have thought less."

"In this larval state," he heard the voice of Dr. Bernard saying, "it is hard to estimate. Ask him if he's tired, if we can continue."

They continued the dialogue for another half hour, learning by this means that he did not live in Bucharest, that he had only one relative, a distant one, whom he did not care to inform about the accident, that he would accept any test no matter how hazardous, to verify whether the optic nerve was damaged. Fortunately, they did not ask any more questions, because if they had he probably would not have listened to them. The blindness that threatened Papini had been the first sign. He had told himself, that week, that perhaps it was not a matter of the inevitable decrepitude of old age, that if he repeated the story of Papini (Papini, on whom no surgeon dared to operate), he did it because the tragedy of one of his favorite writers preoccupied him. But soon he realized he was trying to deceive himself. One year before that, Doctor Neculache had acknowledged that, for the time being, arteriosclerosis was incurable. The doctor had not told him that arteriosclerosis was threatening him, but he had added: "At a certain age, you can expect anything. I myself am losing my memory," he continued, smiling sadly. "From a certain time, I've been unable to memorize the verses of younger poets whom I discover and like."

"Nor can I," he had interrupted. "I once knew by heart the whole of *Paradiso*, and now . . . And as for the young writers, after I read them, I retain almost nothing."

And yet . . . Lately, as he lay there in bed with his eyes closed, he remembered many books he had read recently, and he mentally recited poems by Ungaretti, Ion Barbu, and Dan Botta — texts he hadn't realized he had ever memorized. As for *Paradiso*, for many days and nights he fell asleep reciting his favorite *terze rime*. He was seized suddenly by a strange fear, which he did not understand because it seemed to arise from the joy of the discovery he had made. Don't think anymore! he ordered himself. Think about something else! . . . And yet, for much of the time he did nothing else but recite poems and repeat books that he had read. I've been a blockhead! I was frightened for nothing! . . . Although, once when he had left the house he realized on reaching the street that he had forgotten where he wanted to go. . . . But perhaps it was just an accident. Perhaps I was tired . . . although I didn't have any reason to be tired.

"Actually, the great specialist didn't explain very much," he heard one of the interns saying.

"He did say that a few other cases are known. For instance, that Swiss pastor who was burned by lightning over almost his whole body and who nevertheless lived many years afterward. True, he was left mute — as our man is also, probably," he added, lowering his voice.

"Don't talk anymore; maybe he can hear you," whispered someone whose voice he could not identify.

"That's what I want — I want him to hear me. Let's see how he'll react. Perhaps he isn't mute after all."

Involuntarily, without realizing what he was doing, he slowly opened his mouth. At that moment he heard exceptionally loud noises in his ears, as if on both sides of him several freight cars loaded with scrap iron were tumbling down a rocky mountainside. But even though the echo of the explosions kept ringing in his ears, he continued to hold open his mouth. And suddenly he heard himself articulating, "No!" He repeated the word several times. Then after a short pause, he added, "Not mute!" He knew he had meant to say, "I'm not mute," but he had not succeeded in pronouncing the syllable "I'm." From the noises in the room and the sound of the door opening and closing quickly he understood that the two words had provoked a sensation. He held his mouth wide open, but he dared not move his tongue. When Doctor Gavrilă, his favorite, the one about whom he had been sure from the first that he had a medical vocation, approached the bed, he repeated the words again. Then he understood why he had so much difficulty pronouncing them: with each movement of the tongue he could feel his teeth rattling, as though they were ready to fall out.

"That was it," whispered Gavrilă. "The teeth. Even the molars," he added with a preoccupied air. "Call Dr. Filip on the telephone. Tell him to send someone immediately — ideally, he himself should come — and have him come prepared with everything necessary."

Then he heard him speaking at a distance.

"They're barely holding. If he were to swallow very hard, he'd be in danger of choking on a molar. Tell the Professor."

He felt pincers of some sort grasping a tooth in front and pulling it out without effort. He began to count: in a few minutes, with the same ease, Dr. Filip had extracted nine incisors and five molars.

"I don't exactly understand what's happened. The roots are healthy. It's as though they were being pushed out by wisdom teeth. But that's impossible. We'll have to take an X-ray."

The Professor stepped to the bed and put two fingers on the patient's right hand.

"Try to pronounce something, any word, any sound."

He tried moving his tongue without fear now, but he did not succeed in saying what he meant. Finally, resigned, he began to pronounce at random various short words: pin, cock, cow, man, pen, foam.

The third night after that, he had a dream he remembered completely. He had returned unexpectedly to Piatra Neamţ and was on his way to lycée. But the closer to school he came, the more pedestrians there were. He recognized around him on the sidewalk many of his former pupils, looking as they did when he and they had parted, ten, twenty, or twenty-five years before. He took one of them by the arm. "Where are you all going in this crowd, Teodorescu?" he asked. The boy gave him a long look, smiling quizzically; he did not recognize him. "We're not going to school. Today is the centenary of Professor Dominic Matei."

I don't like that dream very much, he repeated to himself several times. *I don't understand why, but I do not like it.*

He waited for the nurse to leave. Then, with high emotion and great caution, he began to half-open his eyelids. He had found himself one night looking at a luminous, bluish spot, without realizing he had opened his eyes and without understanding what he was seeing. He felt his heart racing fast, frightened—and quickly he closed his eyes. But the next night he awoke again, staring with eyes opened wide at the same luminous spot. Not knowing what to do, he began counting mentally. When he reached 72, he suddenly realized that the light was coming from the venetian blind at the other end of the room. He could hardly control the happiness he felt looking, unhurriedly, one wall at a time, at his room, the one to which he had been transferred on the eve of Dr. Bernard's visit. After that, whenever he was left alone, especially at night, he would open his eyes, move his head slightly, then his shoulders, and begin to investigate the forms and colors, shadows and half-lights, around him.

"Why haven't you showed *us* that you could open your eyes?" It was the voice of one of the interns. In the next moment he saw him, and he was almost as he had imagined him by the inflections of his voice: tall, dark, lean, with the beginning of a bald spot. So, the intern had suspected something and had kept watch for a long time, to catch him.

"I don't know w'y," he replied, pronouncing his words only partially. "Maybe I wan'ed to convin' myself firs' that I hadn' los' my sigh'."

The intern looked at him, smiling vacantly.

"You, sir, are a curious man. When the Professor asked you your age, you answered sixty."

"I'm older."

"That's hard to believe. You heard, no doubt, what the nurses said."

With the respectful gesture of a repentant schoolboy, he inclined his head. He had heard them: "How old did he say he was — sixty? That man's hiding his age. You saw him this morning, a little while ago, when I was bathing him. He's a young man, in the prime of life; he's less than forty."

"I don't want you to think I spied on you so I could report you to the Director. But I must inform the Professor. And he will decide. . . ."

Another time he would have been angry or afraid, but now he found himself reciting — at first mentally, then slowly moving his lips — one of his favorite poems, *La morte meditata*, by Ungaretti:

> *Sei la donna che passa*
> *Come una foglia*
> *E lasci agli alberi un fuoco d'autunno. . . .*

He remembered that when he had read that poem for the first time, they had been separated for a long while already: almost twenty-five years. And yet, reading it, he had thought of her. He did not know if it was the same love he had had at the beginning, if he loved her still as he had confessed on the morning of October 12, 1904, after they had left the courthouse and were headed for Cişmigiu. When they parted, kissing her hand he had added: "I wish you . . . Oh, you know what I mean. . . . But I'd like you to know something else, that I'll love you till I die." He was not sure he still loved her, but it was of her he thought when he read, *"Sei la donna che passa . . ."*

"So, you're persuaded that you're out of danger now."

Thus the Professor greeted him the next morning, approaching him with a smile. He was more impressive than he had imagined. Though not very tall, his manner of holding his head high and his body erect, as though he were on parade, gave him a somewhat intimidating martial air. If his hair had not been almost white, he would have seemed severe. Even when he smiled he remained grave, distant.

"Only now do you begin to become an 'interesting case,' " he added, seating himself on a chair facing the bed. "I believe you understand why. Up to now no one has found any plausible explanation, neither here nor abroad. The way the lightning struck you, you *had* to have been killed on the spot, or else to have died of asphyxiation in ten or fifteen minutes; at best you would have been left paralyzed, mute, or blind. The enigmas that confront us multiply with each passing day. I don't know to what reflex to attribute your inability to open your mouth for twenty-three days so that you had to be fed intravenously. Probably you succeeded in opening it when you had to eliminate your teeth, which your gums could no longer retain. We had planned to make a set of dentures to allow you to eat and above all to speak normally. But for the time being we can do nothing; the X-rays show that in a short time a whole new set of teeth will be ready to appear."

"Imposs'ble!" he exclaimed, dumbfounded, mutilating the word.

"So say all the doctors and dentists — that it is simply impossible. And yet the X-rays are quite clear. That is why, finally, I said that only now does your case become extremely interesting. No longer is it a case of a 'living dead man,' but of something else entirely. *What*, exactly, we still don't know."

I must be careful, I mustn't make a mistake and give myself away. Today, tomorrow they'll ask my name, address, occupation. Still, what have I to be afraid of? I haven't done anything. No one knows about the white envelope or the blue envelope. . . . And yet, without knowing why, he wanted at all costs to preserve his anonymity, the way it had been at first when they had shouted at him, "Do you hear me or not? If you understand what I'm saying, squeeze my finger." Fortunately, now, without any teeth, he spoke with difficulty. It would be easy to pretend, to mangle those few words he managed to pronounce. But what if they asked him to write? He looked at his right arm and right hand closely for the first time. The skin was smooth, fresh, and was beginning to acquire again its old coloring. He felt the arm slowly, cautiously, up to the elbow; then with two fingers he caressed his biceps. How odd! Perhaps the almost absolute immobility for nearly four weeks, and those nutritive fluids they injected directly into the veins . . . "He's a young man, in the prime of life!" the nurse had said. And a day before, he had heard a door being opened cautiously, then steps approaching his bed, and the intern whispering, "He's asleep, don't waken him." Then a strange voice, hoarse: "It can't be he. . . . Still, we'll have to see him without the beard. But the guy we were looking for is a student, not past twenty-two, and this man here looks older, close to forty."

Then he remembered again about the storm. "The curious thing about it," one of the interns had said, "was that it was raining only in that one place where he was walking, between the North Station and bulevardul Elisabeta. It was a sudden shower, like in the middle of summer, which lasted long enough to flood the boulevard, but a few hundred meters away — not a drop!" "That's true," someone had added. "I passed there on my way back from church, and the water on the boulevard still hadn't drained away." "Some say there was an attempt at a bombing, because supposedly a lot of dynamite was found, but the torrential rain caught them by surprise and they had to give it up." "That could be an invention of the Security, to justify their arresting students." Then they had all fallen silent.

I must be very careful, he repeated to himself. They might confuse me with one of the hidden Legionaries* the Siguranţa (Security) is looking for. And then I'll have to tell them who I am. They'll send me to Piatra to verify it. And

---

*Representatives of an extreme rightist, fascist-type movement, also known as the Iron Guard, against which a massive crackdown had been ordered by the Romanian government in the spring of 1938, the time when the action of *Youth Without Youth* starts.

then . . . But, as usual, he succeeded in uprooting the thought that annoyed him. He found himself reciting Canto XI from *Purgatorio;* then he tried to remember the passage from the *Aeneid: Agnosco veteris vestigia flammae* . . .

"The trouble with you, *Cucoane** Dominic, is that you never finish anything you start. You jump from one book to another, from one language to another, from one science to another. Perhaps that's why you two separated," he added with a sad smile.

He had not been angry then. Nicodim was someone he liked, a good Moldavian, honest and quiet.

"No, *Domnule*† Nicodim, the Japanese language manual had nothing to do with our separating."

"What's this about a manual of Japanese?" Nicodim asked, surprised.

"I thought that was what you were referring to, to the rumor that circulated in the square."

"Which was—?"

"It was said that when I came home with a Japanese language manual, Laura, seeing me open my notebook immediately and begin to study, said . . . well, in short, she's supposed to have said that I started too many things and didn't carry any of them to a finish; and on account of this we separated."

"No, I never heard that. What I heard from one person and another is that *Duduia*‡ Laura became rather tired of your gallant adventures; that, in particular, this past summer in Bucharest you went around all the time with a French girl, saying that you knew her from your Sorbonne days."

"No," he interrupted wearily, shaking his head slowly. "That was something else entirely. It's true that Laura was suspicious, because she had found out

*Respectful form of address to a man in Romanian *(archaic).*
†Form of polite address to a man in Romanian.
‡Respectful form of address to a woman.

about another, earlier affair, but she's an intelligent woman; she knows I don't *love* anyone but her; and that the others, well . . . But I must tell you also that we've remained very good friends."

But he had not told him anything else. He had not told anyone, not even Dadu Rareş, his best friend, who died of tuberculosis twelve years later. Although Dadu, perhaps, had been the only one who had guessed the truth. Maybe Laura had even confided something to him, because they were very congenial. . . .

"I'm listening to you," said the Professor with a slight irritation in his voice. "I'm listening to you and I don't understand. For several days now, no progress. It even seems to me that last week you could pronounce certain words that today . . . You must cooperate with us. Don't be afraid of reporters. The orders are strict: no one will interview you. Obviously, your case was too important not to have become known in the city. News stories and feature articles have appeared in different papers, the majority of them absurd, ridiculous. But to return to the point, you *must* cooperate. We have to know more about you: where you're from, who you are, what your profession is, and so on."

He nodded his head obediently and repeated several times, "Yes, yes." This was no joke. He had to be on the lookout. Luckily, the next morning, while running his tongue over his gums, he felt the point of the first canine. With an exaggerated innocence, he showed it to the nurses, then to the interns, pretending it was impossible to say anything else. But the teeth appeared rapidly, one after another. By week's end, all of them had emerged. Every morning a dentist came to examine him and took notes for the article he was preparing. For several days he suffered with gingivitis, and even if he had wished, he could not have spoken very well. Those were the most serene days, because he felt, likewise, an energy and a confidence that he had not known since the time of the Great War, when at Piatra Neamţ he had organized a "Movement of

Cultural Renaissance" (so the local newspaper dubbed it), un-
equaled anywhere else in Moldavia. Even Nicolae Iorga had
spoken of it with praise in a lecture he gave at the lycée.
Professor Iorga had spent part of an afternoon at his house,
and he had not hidden his surprise on discovering those many
thousands of volumes of Orientalia, classical philology, ancient
history, and archeology. "Why do you not write, colleague?"
he had asked him several times. "I have been working, Domnule
Professor. I have labored for some ten years to finish a work."
Then Davidoglu had interrupted him with his inevitable joke:
"But ask him, Domnule Professor, what kind of work! *De omni
re scribili!*" It was an old joke of theirs, which they repeated
every time they saw him coming to the office with a bundle
of new books freshly arrived from Paris, Leipzig, or Oxford.
"When do you plan to stop, Cucoane Dominic?" they would
ask him. "How can I stop, when I haven't even reached the
halfway point yet?" As a matter of fact he knew, in those days
before the War, that by spending what little funds he had left
on expensive books and study trips, he was obliged to remain
a teacher there, in the lycée, and that consequently a good
part of his time would be wasted with preparing lessons. For
a long time Latin and Italian had ceased to interest him; he
would have liked, if it had been possible, to give himself over
to the history of civilization or to philosophy. "The way you
want to do everything, ten lives wouldn't be enough." Once
he had replied, almost with conviction: "I'm sure of one thing,
at least: that for philosophy you do not need ten lives." "*Habe
nun ach! Philosophie . . . durchaus studiert!*" the professor of
German cited solemnly. "You know the rest," he added.

From the indiscretions of the assistants, he understood
why the Professor was so on edge: Bernard was pressing him
all the time for more ample and more precise information.
"*En somme, qui est ce Monsieur?*" he asked in a letter. (But
that was not certain, someone had observed. Dr. Gavrilă had
said it, but he had not seen the letter.) Of course, Bernard
had found out long before that the unknown person whom
he had examined at the beginning of April had not lost his

sight and that he had begun to speak. He was more curious now than ever. Not only the stages of the physical restoration but also as many details as possible about the patient's mental capacities interested him. The fact that the patient understood French led him to believe that he was a man of some education. He wanted to find out what he had retained and what he had lost. He suggested a series of tests: vocabulary, syntax, word associations.

"But when will you finish it, Domnule?"

"I still have to write the first part; the other parts — Antiquity, the Middle Ages, and the Modern Era — are almost completely written. But the first part — you understand, the origin of language, of society, of the family, of all the other institutions — this calls for years and years of research. And with our provincial libraries . . . I used to buy as many books as I could find, but now, with straitened means . . ."

As a matter of fact, the more time passed the more clearly he understood that he would never be able to finish his one and only book, his life's work. He awoke one morning with the taste of ashes in his mouth. He was approaching age sixty, and he had finished nothing of all that he had begun. Meanwhile, his "disciples," as some of his very young colleagues, overwhelmed with admiration, liked to call themselves, who had gathered at least one evening each week in the library to hear him speak about the enormous problems he had to resolve — his disciples had scattered with the passing of the years, moving to other cities. There was no one left even to entrust with the manuscripts and the materials he had collected.

When he heard that at the cafe they called him the Old Man or Papa Dominic, he realized that the prestige he had acquired during the War years, when Nicolae Iorga had praised him at the beginning of the lecture and had sent him now and then from Iaşi a student to request books from him — that prestige had begun to pale. Little by little he realized that in the faculty office or at the Cafe Select he was no longer the center of attention, that he no longer "shined" as formerly. Recently, since he overheard Vaian saying, "The Old Man's really getting decrepit!" he had hardly dared speak about the new books he had read, about articles in *NRF, Criterion,* or *La Fiera Letteraria.* And then there had followed, one after the other, what he called in his secret language, "crises of consciousness."

"But what are you doing here, Domnu' Matei?"

"I'm taking a walk. A migraine hit me again, and I went out for a walk."

"But like this, in your pajamas, on Christmas Eve? Don't catch cold!"

The next day the whole city found out about it. Probably they were waiting for him at the cafe, to cross-examine him — but that day he didn't go, nor the next.

"At the first opportunity!" he exclaimed one afternoon in front of the Cafe Select, laughing. "At the first opportunity!"

"What will you do at the first opportunity?" Vaian queried him.

Indeed, what would he do? He frowned, trying to remember. At last he shrugged and set off for home. Not until he had put his hand on the door knob did he remember: At the first opportunity he would open the blue envelope. But not here, where everyone knows me. Far away, in another city. In Bucharest, perhaps.

One morning he asked the nurse for a piece of paper, a pencil, and an envelope. He wrote a few lines, sealed the envelope, and addressed it to the Professor. Then he began to wait, sensing the rate of his heartbeat accelerating.

When before had he experienced a similar emotion? Perhaps on the morning when he had learned that Romania had declared a general mobilization. Or earlier, twelve years earlier, when, as he entered the parlor, he realized that Laura was waiting for him and that she wished to speak with him. It had seemed to him then that her eyes were moist.

"I have to talk to you," she began, forcing a smile. "It's very important for both of us, and I can't hide it any longer. . . . It has to be brought out into the open. I felt this a long while ago, but for some time now it has obsessed me. I sense that you aren't *mine* any longer. Please, don't interrupt. It's not what you think . . . . I sense that you are not mine, that you aren't *here* with me, that you live in another world. I'm not thinking of your research, which, in spite of what you believe, *does* interest me. But I feel you're living in an alien world, one I cannot enter with you. Both for my sake and for yours, I believe it would be wiser for us to separate. We're still young, we both love life. . . . You'll see later. . . ."

"Very well," said the Professor, after he had folded the paper carefully and inserted it into his appointment book. "I shall return later."

An hour later he returned. Locking the door in order not to be disturbed, he sat down on the chair facing the bed.

"I'm here to listen to you. It's not necessary that you make a very great effort. The words you can't pronounce you can write," he added, handing him a pad of paper.

"You will understand why I must resort to this stratagem," he began, obviously tense. "I wish to avoid publicity. The truth is this: my name is Dominic Matei. On January 8 I reached the age of seventy. I was instructor in Latin and Italian at Lycée Alexandru Ion Cuza in Piatra Neamţ, where I now reside. I live on strada Episcopiei at No. 18. It is my house and it contains a library of nearly 8,000 volumes, which I have willed to the lycée."

"Extraordinary!" exclaimed the Professor, after taking a deep breath. He looked at the patient again, somewhat frightened it seemed.

"I believe it will not be hard for you to verify my story. But, I implore you, be very, very discreet! The whole city knows me. If you wish additional proof, I can draw you a plan of the house, I can tell you what books are on the desk and any other detail you ask me for. But, at least for the time being, it isn't necessary for anyone to know what's happened to me. As you yourself said, it's a rather sensational thing that I've escaped safe and sound. If it were to be learned that I've been hospitalized, I'd have no peace. I'm telling you all this because agents from Security who have been here already will never believe I'm past seventy. Therefore, they won't believe I am who I am, and I'll be interrogated — and anything can happen if you are interrogated! . . . I pray you, if you consider that my case deserves to be studied — I mean, that it deserves to be studied over a period of time here at the hospital — please find me a fictitious identity. Of course, it will be temporary, and if, later on, you become dissatisfied with my conduct, you may reveal the truth at any time."

"That's no problem," the Professor interrupted. "For the time being, the one thing that matters is for you to have a regular situation. This, I hope, will not be too hard to obtain. But what age can we give you? When we shave off your beard, you'll look like a man of thirty or thirty-one. Shall we say thirty-two?"

He asked the street and number of the house again, and noted them in his date book.

"The house, of course, is closed?" he began again after an interval.

"Yes and no. An old woman, Veta, my housekeeper for my whole life, lives in two little rooms attached to the kitchen. She keeps the keys for the other rooms."

"Probably there is an album of photographs some-where, more precisely with pictures of you when you were young."

"All of them are in the upper drawer of the desk; there are three albums. The key to the drawer is under the cigar box on top of the desk. . . . But if the person you send says anything to Veta, the whole city will find out."

"There's no danger if he proceeds with caution."

He returned the date book to his pocket pensively and was silent a few moments, keeping his eyes on Dominic all the while.

"I admit, your case excites me," he said, getting up. "I don't understand it, and neither does anyone else at the hospital. Probably you do exercises when you're alone at night."

He shrugged his shoulders, embarrassed.

"I felt my legs were 'asleep,' so I got out of bed and here, on the rug . . ."

"Didn't anything surprise you?"

"Yes, indeed. I felt of myself all over. I sensed my muscles were as they were years ago, strong, robust. I didn't expect that. After so many weeks of almost absolute immobility, it would have to be, how to say it? a sort of . . ."

"Yes, it would have to be that," the Professor interrupted. He started toward the door, but stopped, turned, and sought his eyes. "You didn't give me any address for here, in Bucharest."

He felt himself blushing, but with an effort he managed to smile. "I have no address, because I'd scarcely arrived. I came by train from Piatra Neamţ. It was almost midnight when I arrived, the night of Easter."

The Professor stared at him in disbelief.

"But you must have been going somewhere. And on the sidewalk, next to you, there was no valise found."

"I didn't have a valise. I brought nothing with me except a blue envelope. I had come with the intention of committing suicide. It seemed to me I was a condemned man: arteriosclerosis. I was losing my memory."

"You came here to commit suicide?" the Professor echoed.

"Yes. I saw no other solution. The only solution was the blue envelope. I had been keeping there, for a long time, a few milligrams of strychnine."

2

He knew he was dreaming, and he kept wiping his hand across his freshly shaved cheek, but he did not succeed in fully waking up. Only after the car had reached the end of the boulevard did he recognize the neighborhood; he recognized it mainly by the fragrance of the lindens in flower. We're headed toward Şosea, he realized. He had not passed through here for several years and, moved, he gazed at the old houses, which reminded him of his student years. Then they entered an avenue lined with tall trees; the following moment a gate opened and the car, moving slowly over the gravel drive, came to a halt in front of stairs of bluish stone. "Why don't you get out?" he heard an unfamiliar voice asking. Looking around in surprise, he saw no one. It appeared that up above, at the head of the stairs, a door had opened. So, he was expected. I ought to get out, he said to himself.

Waking up, the bright light from outside blinded him, and he looked in surprise at the clock. It was not yet 6:00. Probably they forgot to draw the blinds. Presently he heard the door open.

"I've brought you your clothes," said the nurse, smiling as she approached the bed, her arms laden.

She was Anetta, still rather young, the most daring of the nurses. (A few days earlier she had said, "When you're released, maybe you'll take me to the cinema some evening!") She helped him dress, although he would not have needed any help. He guessed from her look of disappointment that the jacket didn't fit very well ("Too tight in the shoulders," she said) and the tie, blue with little gray triangles, did not go well with the striped shirt. Soon the intern in residence entered. He began to examine him carefully, frowning.

"It looks from a distance as though those are not your clothes. You could become suspect. We'll have to find you something else. Dr. Gavrilă said that he has some outfits of the best quality, left by an uncle of his."

"He inherited them after the uncle died," Anetta specified. "And it isn't good to wear clothes from other families' dead. From your own dead, it's different. You wear them in memory, as a souvenir."

"It doesn't matter," he said, smiling. "Anyway, there isn't time today. Perhaps on another occasion, when I pass this way again."

"Yes," the intern agreed, "but with that jacket you'll attract attention and risk being followed."

"If he hunches down in the back seat of the car, maybe he won't be noticed."

Two hours later he went downstairs and out into the courtyard, accompanied by Dr. Chirilă, the one he liked the least, because, after Chirilă had caught him opening his eyes that night, he had had the impression that the doctor was spying on him all the time. Setting eyes on the car, he stopped abruptly.

"I've seen that car before!" he whispered. "I saw it last night, in my dream. Some would say it's a bad sign, that we might have an accident."

"I am not superstitious," Dr. Chirilă proclaimed, speaking slowly and sententiously as he opened the car door. "In any event, they're waiting for us."

When the auto started for the boulevard, he felt a strange peace, broken now and then by almost violent upsurges of happiness.

"Open the window," he added. "Now we're approaching Şosea." And later: "Look at that beautiful building with the tall trees, and that neat drive with gravel, and the stairs of bluish stone."

The intern kept looking at him curiously, frowning silently. The car stopped in front of the steps.

"Why don't you get out?" he heard a voice saying.

"We're waiting for the orderly to come, to take charge," the driver replied.

Soon hurried footsteps were heard on the gravel, and from behind the car there appeared a bespectacled man, with a face pinched by age and hair close-cropped, military style.

Chirilă opened the door.

"He is the person about whom you were informed. You are not to treat him like just another patient. From now on, you're responsible for him."

"I understand," he said. "Don't worry. I'll keep on the lookout."

"What he does inside or in the garden doesn't concern you. Your job is to guard the gate."

He liked the room: it was spacious, with windows opening on the park and, as the Professor had assured him, it had a wooden table and, on the walls, shelves for books. He stepped to the open window and breathed deeply. It seemed the fragrance of wild roses was reaching him from somewhere. Yet, he could not, somehow, feel happy. He smiled, caressing his left cheek with his hand, but it seemed to him that all that had happened for some time past did not concern him *really*, that it had to do with something else, with *someone* else.

"Try to describe, as precisely and with as many details as possible, what you mean when you say, 'Someone else,' " the Professor interrupted him once. "In what sense do you feel *alien* to yourself? Are you not yet 'installed' in your new situation? This is very important. Note down all that passes through your mind. If you aren't in the mood to write or if you have too much to say, use the recorder, indicating always the day, hour, and place, and specifying whether you are dictating while lying in bed or walking about your room."

During the last several days at the hospital he had filled almost a whole notebook. He wrote all kinds of things: books that he remembered (and he enjoyed indicating the edition, year of publication, and year when he had read it for the first time, in order to verify his miraculous recovery of memory), poems in all the languages he had learned, algebraic exercises, a few dreams that seemed significant. But some recent discoveries he did not confess. He sensed an incomprehensible resistance, about which he had spoken once with the Professor. "It's very important for us to learn the significance of this resistance," the Professor had said. "Try at least to make some allusion, so we will know if what you don't *want* to say (*cannot say!* he interjected mentally) refers to certain events from the past, or if it is a matter of something else having to do with your new condition—about which, I repeat, we still know very little."

He turned away from the window and, after pacing the room several times—walking as he used to do, in his youth, with his hands clasped behind his back—he stretched out on the bed. He lay there with his eyes open, staring at the ceiling.

"I've brought you your family album," the Professor said to him one morning. "The one with your pictures from lycée, the university, Italy. . . . Aren't you curious to see it?"

"To tell you the truth, no."

"But why?"

"I don't know why myself. I'm beginning to feel detached from my past. It's as though I weren't the same person."

"That's strange," said the Professor. "We ought to discover the reasons."

At last, resigned, he decided to leaf through it. The Professor was sitting beside the bed, in a chair, watching him closely, incapable of concealing his curiosity.

"What are you thinking about?" he asked him abruptly after a few minutes. "What sort of memories? What sort of associations?"

He hesitated, rubbing his cheek with his left hand. ("I know that gesture has become a habit of mine, a tic," he had admitted several times.)

"I remember perfectly the year and location where they were taken, every one of them. I can even say I remember the *day;* it's as though I can hear the voices of those around me and the words they spoke, and I seem to sense in my nostrils the smell peculiar to that place and that day. . . . See here, for instance, where I'm with Laura, at Tivoli. When I set eyes on that snapshot, I sensed the heat of that morning and the fragrance of the oleander flowers. But I sensed also a strong odor of hot crude oil, and I recalled that some twenty meters from the spot where we were photographed there were two pails of crude oil."

"It's a kind of hypermnesia with lateral effects," said the Professor.

"It's awful," he continued. "It's too much, and it's so useless!"

"It seems useless because we don't know yet what to do with it, with that fantastic recovery of memory. . . . In any event," he added, smiling, "I have good news for you. In a few days you will receive from your library at Piatra Neamț the books you noted on your first list, that is, all the grammars and dictionaries you said you'd need. Bernard is enthusiastic. He told me we couldn't find a more suitable test. He was interested especially in the fact that you began to study Chinese in your youth, then you neglected it for ten or twelve years, then you took it up again before and during the war years, and finally, quite suddenly, you gave it up completely. We have to deal, therefore, with several strata of the memory. If you will take pains to analyze yourself and make careful notes, we shall see which of the strata will be revived first."

For some time they looked at each other, as if each were waiting for the other to begin.

"And what do people at Piatra Neamț believe about my disappearance?" he asked suddenly. "I'm not too curious, but I'd be interested to know about what my chances are now."

"What kind of chances?"

He smiled, embarrassed. As soon as he had uttered the expression it had seemed vulgar and inappropriate.

"My chances for continuing the life I recently began, without the risk of reintegrating it into my previous biography."

"For the time being, I can't tell you anything precise. Your friends in Piatra believe you are in a hospital in Moldavia, suffering from amnesia. Someone remembered that he saw you at the station on the Saturday before Easter, but he doesn't know what train you took; the man was in a hurry to get home."

"I have an idea who it was that saw me at the station," he whispered.

"In order to be able to collect the books you listed, the police staged a search. They pretended that, having learned of your disappearance, one of the wanted Legionaries might have hidden in your library."

He remained pensive for a while, as though reluctant to continue.

"But of course the more time passes, the more difficult it will get. Soon it will be learned at Piatra Neamţ what all Bucharest knows: that someone, an older man of unknown origin, was struck by lightning and after ten weeks appeared perfectly healthy and young again. Let us hope the rest will not be found out."

Two weeks later, upon coming downstairs to the garden, he met face to face with a young woman of strange beauty — a beauty that, for reasons hard to grasp, she tried to attenuate by means of a deliberate vulgarity, applying makeup in an exaggerated and clumsy manner. The way she smiled at him then, provocatively and yet chastely, the girl reminded him of one of his most recent dreams. He inclined his head slightly and spoke.

"Haven't we met somewhere before?"

The young woman began to laugh. (Too bad, he said to himself, she laughs in the same vulgar way she paints her face.)

"You're as discreet as you can be!" she said. (And it seemed she spoke as if on stage.) "Of course we've met before; several times, in fact."

"Where? When?"

The young woman wrinkled her brow in a slight frown and sought his eyes again.

"Most recently, last night, in Room Number 6. Your room is next door, Number 4," she added, walking away.

The Professor came that same evening, to return the notebook and to read the latest notations. He listened, perplexed, confused, without smiling, avoiding his gaze.

"I believe you know what it's all about, and that you understand — how to say it? — the scientific intent of the experiment. No analysis is complete without the index of the sexual capacity. You remember the question Bernard asked you the last time. . . ."

He wanted to laugh, but succeeded only in nodding his head and smiling.

"Do I remember! I fell through the floor with shame! Naked, spread out on the table, in front of all those foreign doctors and scholars!"

"I warned you in advance that there would be a sort of international consultation. They all came on account of you. They couldn't believe the reports I published in *La Presse médicale.*"

"I wasn't expecting such a question. Especially since I was still in the hospital and therefore didn't have any way to confirm or rule out the sexual possibilities."

The Professor smiled, giving a shrug.

"We found out something, of course, from the nurse."

"From the nurse?"

"We thought the initiative was yours. In any other circumstances, the patient and the nurse involved would have been penalized. But in your case, we not only shut our eyes, we valued the information. In the last analysis, the context doesn't matter. All that matters is the information. . . . But in the case of the young lady in Room 6," he resumed after a pause, "we have to do with something else. It's better I tell you now, lest complications arise later. That woman has been imposed on us by Security."

"By Security?" he repeated with some fear. "But why?"

"I don't claim to understand very much of it, but I *know* that Security is very interested in your case. Probably they aren't convinced that I've been telling the whole truth and actually, of course, they're right. At any rate, Security does not believe in your metamorphosis. They're convinced that the story circulating in the city about the lightning on Easter night, your unconsciousness, and your recovery of your

80

health and youth is an invention of the Legionaries. They believe that in fact this legend was fabricated to camouflage the identity of an important Legionary leader and pave the way for his flight across the border."

He listened, surprised and yet serene.

"Then, my situation is graver than I had imagined," he said. "But since, for the time being, there is no other solution . . ."

"A solution will be found, in time," the Professor interrupted. "I must add, so that you may be better informed, that you are, and have been from the beginning, under the supervision of Security. That is why an outfit was procured for you in which you would not dare go out on the street because you would be arrested immediately. Neither would you dare to circulate in the city in that 'cassock,' the uniform of the clinic, which is, in fact, rather elegant. And, as you have understood from the first, if you want to walk, you can't go outside the gate. . . . This is what we know. But who can tell how many other members of the clinic staff are informers for Security?"

He began laughing and rubbed his left hand over his cheek several times.

"Actually, perhaps it's better this way. I feel safe from surprise."

The Professor sat looking at him for a long time, as though hesitating to say more. Then suddenly he decided to continue.

"Let us return, now, to a more important problem. Are you *sure* that, in your memory, all your sexual experiences have passed as erotic dreams?"

He was pensive for some moments.

"I'm not so sure any more. Up to this evening, I was convinced they were only dreams."

"I ask, because in your notebook which I read, you recorded all kinds of dreams, but without any *manifestly* erotic elements."

"Perhaps I should have noted the others too, but I didn't think they were significant. . . . In any event," he continued after a short pause, "if I've confused real experiences with erotic dreams, things are more complicated than I had imagined."

With a childish, almost ridiculous gesture he put his hand to his temple as if he wanted to show he was concentrating.

"I'm listening," said the Professor at length. "In what sense could they be more complicated than they seem to be?"

He raised his head suddenly and smiled a puzzled smile.

"I don't know whether or not you understood certain allusions in the notebook, but for some time I've had the impression — how to say it? — I've had the impression that I was learning during the time I'm asleep; more precisely, I dream that I'm studying. For instance, I open a grammar in my dream, I read over and memorize several pages, or I leaf through a book. . . ."

"Very interesting!" said the Professor. "But I don't believe you've recorded all these things with precision and clarity in your notebook."

"I don't exactly know how to describe them. They were a series of dreams, in a sense didactic, and they seemed to be continuations of readings done during the day. I even thought I was dreaming grammatical rules, vocabulary, and etymologies, because I used to have a passion for such things. . . . But now I wonder if in a more or less somnambulic way I get up during the night and continue my work."

The Professor continued to stare at him closely, frowning slightly — a sign, as he had observed long ago, that he was tempted by several questions at the same time.

"In any event," he said, "you don't seem tired, you don't have the expression of an intellectual who spends a good part of the night reading. . . . But if it were true, why hasn't anyone noticed a light, a lamp burning late in your room?"

He rose from the armchair and extended his hand.

"What seems paradoxical to me is the fact that this hesitation, more precisely this confusion between oneiric experiences and the waking state, has developed in parallel with your hypermnesia. . . . What you said to me then about the smell of oleanders and crude oil that you sensed while looking at a picture taken almost forty years ago . . ."

"But now I'm not sure about that any more!" he exclaimed. "I'm not sure about anything now!"

After the Professor had gone, he found himself thinking: *It was a good thing that you said, I'm not sure about anything anymore. In that way, you're always covered. You can answer anytime, I dreamed it! Or when it's convenient you can say the opposite. But watch out! Don't ever tell the WHOLE truth!*

He turned his head and looked around in surprise. A few moments later he whispered as if he were addressing someone present, yet invisible: "But even if I wanted to tell, *I couldn't!* I don't understand why," he added, lowering his voice even more, "but certain things are impossible for me to say."

That night he wrestled a long while with insomnia. (It was his first insomnia since he had left Piatra Neamţ, and that fact annoyed him. He had suffered from insomnia almost all his life, and recently he believed he was cured of it.) As usual, he thought about the mystery of his recovered memory. In fact, he realized, it was not just a matter of a recovery, because his memory now was more extensive and more precise than it had ever been. "The memory of a Mandarin," as Chavannes had said every Sinologue needed. He had begun to believe he had even more than that: a hypermnesia. Even before the grammars and dictionary had been brought him from Piatra, he found himself one day reciting Chinese texts, at the same time visualizing the characters and translating as fast as he recited. Several days later he verified the ideograms, pronunciation, and translation by using Giles's anthology and dictionary. He had not made a single mistake! He wrote several lines in a notebook, with a slight feeling of regret: Bernard would be disappointed. It was impossible to specify which stratum of the memory had appeared first. He found himself suddenly in possession of the Chinese language, as he had never known it before. Now he could open any text, and reading it understand it as easily as he could a text in Latin or Old Italian.

It was a very warm night and he had left open the window facing the park. Thinking he heard footsteps, he got out of bed and without turning on the light crept to the window. Outside he saw the orderly and he realized the man had seen him too.

"Don't you ever sleep?" he asked, speaking as softly as possible in order not to wake the others.

The orderly shrugged, then moved off toward the park, becoming lost in the darkness. If I ask him about it tomorrow, he said to himself, probably, he'll tell me I was dreaming. And yet I'm *certain* this time that I'm not dreaming. He went back to bed and said to himself, as he used to do when he was suffering from insomnia: In three minutes I'll be asleep! *You must go to sleep, he heard himself thinking, because in sleep you learn best of all. Didactic dreams, as the Professor said this evening. You must have another series of didactic dreams, not related to Chinese, but to something else, something more important!*

He liked to listen to himself think, but this time he sensed a mysterious uneasiness, and he whispered to himself threateningly: If you don't go to sleep by the count of twenty, I'll go down and take a walk in the park! But he got no further than the number seven.

Several days later the Professor asked him, without lifting his eyes from the second book of notes: "Do you remember that one night you climbed out the window and walked to the back of the garden where the beds of roses are located?"

He sensed himself blushing, and he felt intimidated. "No. I *do* remember that I couldn't go to sleep, and at a certain moment I said to myself, 'If you don't go to sleep by the count of twenty, I'll go down and take a walk in the park!' After that I remember nothing. Probably I fell asleep immediately."

The Professor smiled at him enigmatically. "In any event, you didn't fall asleep immediately. . . . Because you spent a period of time in the vicinity of the roses."

"Then I'm a sleepwalker!" he exclaimed. "For the first time in my life I've had an attack of somnambulism!"

84

The Professor got up suddenly, strode to the window, and stood staring straight ahead for some time. Then he returned to the armchair and reseated himself.

"That's what I thought, too. But things are not so simple. When the orderly gave the alarm, two staff members — probably Security agents — ran to search the street, not knowing the orderly had discovered you already. They saw a car with its headlights turned off waiting in the street, right in front of the rose bed where you were found. Of course, the auto disappeared before they could get the license number."

He put his hand to his forehead and removed it again, nervously. "If I didn't know you, . . ." he began.

"I know, it seems incredible," interrupted the Professor. "Nevertheless, there are three witnesses, simple men but trustworthy and experienced."

"And what did they do with me? Did they take me back to my room?"

"No, there was no one but the orderly in the garden. He says that as soon as you caught sight of him, you went back to the house. You climbed into your room through the window, the way you had left. . . . Sleepwalking or not, it doesn't matter. The serious thing is that Security no longer doubts an escape is being planned for you. The fact that you were caught in the very place where, on the street, a car was waiting, proves, in their opinion, that you knew what was going on and were in agreement with it. I had to intercede for you in high places to prevent your being arrested."

"Thank you," he said with some embarrassment, wiping his forehead.

"Meanwhile, they've doubled their guard. The street is patrolled continually all night; a sergeant in street clothes will look after things during working hours right outside your window — as he is doing now," he added, lowering his voice, "while at night the orderly will sleep on a folding cot in the corridor outside your door."

He stood up again and began pacing the floor, absently passing the notebook from one hand to the other. Suddenly he halted in front of him and looked him deeply in the eyes.

"But how do you explain this series of coincidences: for the first time you have insomnia, followed, as you admit, by the first attack of somnambulism you ever had in your life; at the time of the attack you head straight for the rose bed, *exactly* in the place where, across the wall, a car is waiting with its lights out. A car that," he added after a few moments, "disappeared immediately after the alarm was given. How do you explain all that?"

He shrugged his shoulders, discouraged. "I don't understand it at all. Until last week it was hard for me to admit that I'd confused some dreams with the waking state; I had to be convinced by certain evidence. But this time . . . an attack of somnambulism, the car waiting for me . . ."

The Professor opened his almost-full briefcase and slipped the notebook carefully between the magazines and pamphlets.

"To repeat an expression you used a little while ago, if I didn't know you from your family picture albums, if I hadn't seen photographs of you from thirty to sixty-some years, I'd be ready to accept the hypothesis of Security: that you are who Security thinks you are. . . ."

Why are you so agitated? he heard himself thinking once the light was out. *Everything is unfolding normally. It had to happen like this, for you to be confused with others, to have people think you can't distinguish dream from reality, and other confusions of the same sort. You couldn't have found a better camouflage. Ultimately, you will be convinced that there is no danger, that you are being taken care of.*

He broke off abruptly; then, after a short pause, he whispered, "Who is taking care of me?" He waited several moments. Then he found himself asking in an unfamiliar voice, *Do you think that all you've gone through is due to chance? It's not a question of what I believe or what I don't believe,* he interrupted himself crossly. *Who is it that is watching over me?* Again he waited for some time, with fear. Then he heard: *You'll find out later. That doesn't matter now. Besides, you've guessed some of it, but you don't dare admit it. Otherwise, why don't you ever say anything to the Professor about CERTAIN THOUGHTS, and why don't you mention them in your notebook? If you didn't know SOMEONE ELSE existed, why don't you refer to all that you've discovered in the past two weeks? But, to return to my question . . . ,* he tried to interrupt his thought. He waited a while, and when it seemed that he was beginning to distinguish the response, he fell asleep.

It is better we talk in dreams, he heard. *While you are sleeping, you understand more quickly and more profoundly. You told the Professor that in sleep you continue the studies of the daytime. As a matter of fact, you were convinced long ago that this is not always true. You haven't learned anything, either while sleeping or while waking. Little by little you discovered you had mastered Chinese, just as you discovered later you had mastered other languages that interested you. You no longer dare to believe that you are remembering NOW what you learned in youth and forgot. Think about the Albanian grammar!*

The memory of this struck him so forcefully that he awakened from sleep and turned on the light. He could not believe it then, and he could scarcely believe it now, a week after the discovery. He knew he had never studied the Albanian language. True, he had purchased G. Meyer's *Grammar* some twenty years ago, but he had never read further than the preface. Nor had he consulted it since that time. And yet when he unwrapped one of the packages brought from Piatra and set eyes on it, he opened it at random toward the end of the book and began to read. With a thrill and a fright, he realized he understood everything he was reading. He looked up the translation of the paragraph and he was convinced: not a mistake! He got out of bed and stepped to the bookshelves. At all costs he must verify it again, now. Just then he heard an unfamiliar voice coming from outside the open window.

"But aren't you sleeping?"

He returned to bed, shut his eyes with fury, and repeated in a whisper, "I must not think! I mustn't think of anything!"

I said that to you on the first night at the hospital, he heard.

He thought he was beginning to understand what had happened. The enormous concentration of electricity that, by exploding directly above him, had shot through him, had regenerated his entire organism and amplified fabulously all his mental faculties. But this electrical discharge had made possible likewise the appearance of a new personality, a sort of "double," a "person" whom he heard speaking to him especially during his sleep, with whom he sometimes had friendly discourse and sometimes disagreed. It was probable that this new personality had been built up gradually, during the time of his convalescence, from the deepest strata of his unconscious. Every time he repeated this explanation, he heard himself thinking, *Quite correct! The formula of the "double" is correct and useful. But don't be in a hurry to inform the Professor!*

He wondered, amused and vexed at the same time, why he kept repeating to himself such invitations to precaution when he had decided long ago not to touch this problem (in fact, it had not even been necessary for him to make a decision: he knew that he *could not* do otherwise). In conversations the Professor returned continually to hypermnesia and his progressive detachment from the past.

"We could bring you the manuscripts and portfolios with notes," he had proposed recently. "With the possibilities you have at your disposal now, you could finish the work in a few months."

He raised his arms high in a gesture of protest. "No, no!" he exclaimed, almost in panic. "It doesn't interest me any more!"

The Professor looked at him, surprised and somewhat disappointed. "But it's your life's work!"

"I would have to rewrite it from the first to the last page, and I don't believe it's worth it. It will have to remain what it was: an *opus imperfectum*. But there's something I'd like to ask you," he continued as if he wanted to change the subject as quickly as possible, "although I'm afraid I may seem indiscreet. What's been happening to me in the past week? What have the orderly and all the others reported?"

The Professor stood up and walked to the window without answering. He returned to the chair after a few moments, pensive.

"They know how to make themselves invisible when they need to, but they are all on duty," he said. "They haven't reported anything sensational: just that you turned on the light several times at night, then switched it off again quickly a few minutes later. . . . At least, so I have been informed. But I suspect they haven't told me everything," he added, lowering his voice. "I suspect they've found out something rather important, or they are on the road to discovering something. . . ."

"With regard to me?" he asked, successfully controlling his excitement.

The Professor hesitated a few moments, then rose suddenly and went to the window again. "I don't know," he answered at length. "It could be that it's not *only* with regard to you."

On the third of August he came to see him unexpectedly.

"I don't know if we ought to be happy or not. You've become famous in the United States. An illustrated magazine has even published an 'interview,' obviously apocryphal: 'How I Was Struck by Lightning.' The article created a sensation and has been reprinted and translated everywhere. From the Press Office I have been informed that three correspondents from large American dailies arrived last evening and wish without fail to talk with you. I told them that for the time being the doctors are against any visits. But how long will we be able to hide? It is likely that at this very hour the reporters have already begun their questioning. The interns and nurses will tell them all they know, and so will many others higher up. And they'll find informers here also," he added, lowering his voice. "With regard to the photographers, I have no illusions: you've been photographed certainly many times, walking in

the park, standing at the window, perhaps even lying in bed.
. . . But I see that this news doesn't impress you very much,"
he added after regarding him carefully. "You say nothing."

"I'm waiting for the sequel."

The Professor stepped closer, still looking him deeply
in the eyes. "How do you know there is a 'sequel?' " he asked.

"I guessed it from your nervousness. I've never seen
you so nervous."

The Professor shrugged and smiled bitterly. "You
haven't seen me so, maybe, but I'm a rather nervous individual. . . . But to return to your case. A lot of complications
have arisen, especially during the two weeks I was away."

"On account of me?" he asked.

"Not on your account, nor mine. You've stayed in your
room almost the whole time (I know, because I telephoned
nearly every day). As for me, in the two weeks I spent at
Predeal, I did not discuss your case except with a few colleagues,
of whose discretion I have no doubt. But something else has
happened," he went on, rising from the chair. "First, the young
lady from Room 6, the agent Security imposed on us, disappeared some ten days ago. Security suspected long ago that
she was a double agent, but they did *not* suspect she was in
the service of the Gestapo!"

"Very strange," he whispered. "But how was it learned
so fast?"

"Because the network with which she was connected
was discovered and three agents were arrested, the men who
were waiting for you on several different nights in the car with
its lights turned off. Security guessed rightly: you were to be
abducted and passed across the border into Germany. They
were wrong, however, about identities: it was not a matter of
a Legionary leader, but *you.*"

"But why?" he asked, smiling.

The Professor stepped to the window but quickly returned, looking at him closely, as though he expected him to
say something more.

"Because you are the way you are, after all that has

happened to you. I never entertained any illusions," he continued, beginning to pace slowly back and forth between the
door and the chair. "I knew that one day it would be found
out. That is why I also informed *La Presse médicale* in a few
lines. I wanted what was learned to be learned directly from
the source. Obviously, I didn't tell everything; I was content
to report the stages of physical and intellectual re-establishment
just by an allusion, and that rather obscure, to regeneration
and rejuvenation. Nothing about the hypermnesia. But everything was found out: about your phenomenal memory and the
fact that you've recovered all the languages you studied in your
youth. Therefore, you have become the most valuable human
specimen existing today on the face of the earth. All the medical
schools in the world would like, at least temporarily, to have
you at their disposal."

"A sort of guinea pig?" he asked, smiling.

"In certain cases, yes: a guinea pig. Having access to
the information transmitted by the woman from Room 6, it is
easy to understand why the Gestapo wants, at all costs, to
abduct you."

He stood pensive for some moments, then suddenly
his face brightened in a big smile.

"Your companion of a night, or several . . ."

"I'm afraid it was several," he admitted, blushing.

"Your companion was more intelligent than Security
considered her. She was not content to test your sexual potential
and, taking advantage of your parasomnambulic condition, she
quizzed you, trying to decipher your identity. She proceeded
scientifically: she recorded on a minuscule recording device all
your conversations including, in fact, your long monologues,
and she transmitted them to Security. But she noticed something
else, too: for example, that you recited poems in a great many
languages, and when she asked you questions in German and
then in Russian, you replied without difficulty in the languages
of the questions. Then, after you received the books, she made a
list of all the grammars and dictionaries you had consulted.
Wisely, she preserved all this information for her bosses in

Germany. It is probable that after listening to the recordings someone high up in the Gestapo decided to kidnap you."

"I understand," he said, rubbing his forehead.

The Professor stopped in front of the open window, gazing out on the park.

"Of course," he added at length, "the guard has been increased tenfold. Probably you weren't aware of it, but for several days many of the neighboring rooms have been occupied by agents. At night, you can imagine how the street is patrolled. And yet, in spite of all this, soon you will have to be evacuated from here."

"Too bad!" he said. "I'm used to it—and I like it here."

"I have been advised to begin your camouflaging already. For the time being, you are to let your moustache grow as thick and bushy as possible. I've been told that they will try to modify your face. I imagine they'll also dye your hair and change your hair style, so that you will no longer resemble the photographs that have certainly been taken in recent weeks. They've assured me that they can add ten to fifteen years. When you leave the clinic, you'll look like a man in his forties."

He stopped speaking and sat down in the chair wearily.

"Fortunately," he added later, "those attacks of para-somnambulism, or whatever they were, have not recurred. At least, so I've been told."

The day promised to be torrid. He took off his cassock and put on the thinnest pajamas he could find in the wardrobe. Then he stretched out on the bed. *Of course,* he heard himself thinking, *you know very well it wasn't somnambulism. You've behaved as you ought, in order to create the necessary confusion. But from now on we won't need such devices.*

"The double," he whispered, smiling. "He always answers the questions I'm ready to ask him. Like a true guardian angel." *And that's a correct and useful formula.* Are there others? *Many. Some of them are anachronistic or out of use, others are rather current, especially in places where Christian theology and practice have known how to preserve the immemorial mythological traditions.* For example? he asked, amused. *For example, along with angels and guardian angels, there are Powers, Archangels, Seraphim, and Cherubim. Intermediary beings par excellence.* Intermediary between consciousness and unconsciousness? *Of course. But also between Nature and man, between man and the divine, reason and Eros, feminine and masculine, darkness and light, matter and spirit.*

He came to, laughing, and sat bolt upright. For several moments he looked around, then whispered, pronouncing the words slowly: "So, I've come back again to my old passion, philosophy. Will I ever succeed in demonstrating logically the reality of the exterior world? Idealistic metaphysics still seems to me today to be the only perfectly coherent construct." *We've gotten off our subject,* he heard the voice say. *The problem was not the reality of the exterior world, but the objective reality of the "double" or the guardian angel — pick any term that suits you. Isn't that true?* Very true. I can't believe in the *objective* reality of the "person" with whom I'm conversing; I consider him my "double." *In a sense, that's what he is. But that doesn't mean he does not exist in an objective way, independently of the consciousness whose projection he appears to be.* I'd like to be convinced, but . . . *I know, in metaphysical controversies empirical proofs have no value. But wouldn't you enjoy receiving, right now, in a moment or two, a few fresh roses picked from the garden?* Roses! he exclaimed with feeling and some trepidation. I've always liked roses. *Where would you like me to put them? Not in the glass, at any rate. . . .* No, he replied. Not in the glass. But a rose in my right hand, as I'm holding it now, open, and another on my knee. And a third, let's say. . . .

At that moment he suddenly found himself holding between his fingers a beautiful rose the color of fresh blood, and on his knee, in an unstable balance, another was rocking. *And the third?* he heard himself thinking. *Where do you want me to put the third rose?*

"Things are more serious than we anticipated," he heard the voice of the Professor saying. It seemed he was hearing it through a thick pillow, or else that it was coming from very far away. And yet he was right there in front of him, in the easy chair, with the briefcase on his lap.

"More serious than we anticipated?" he echoed absently.

The Professor stood up, went to him, and put a hand on his forehead. "Don't you feel well?" he asked. "Did you have a bad night, perhaps?"

"No, no. But just now, when you entered the room, it seemed . . . Actually . . ."

"I must speak to you of something urgent and very important," the Professor continued. "Have you come to your senses? Do you think you can listen?"

He wiped his hand slowly across his forehead and, with an effort, managed to smile. "I'm even very curious to listen to you."

The Professor sat down in the chair again. "I said that the situation is more serious than we suspected, because now we know the Gestapo will try anything — *anything*," he repeated, emphasizing the word, "in order to get their hands on you. You will understand why immediately. Among the intimates of Goebbels there is an enigmatic and ambiguous personage, a certain Dr. Rudolf, who for the past several years has been elaborating a theory that on first view is fantastic, but incorporates certain scientific elements also. He believes that electrocution by a current of at least a million volts could produce a radical mutation of the human species. Not only would the person submitted to such an electrical discharge not be killed, but he would be completely regenerated. . . . As things have happened in your case," he added. "Fortunately or unfortunately this hypothesis can't be verified experimentally. Rudolf recognizes that he cannot specify the intensity of the electrical current necessary for the mutation; he maintains only that it must exceed a million volts, perhaps even two million. . . . You understand now the interest your case presents."

"I understand," he repeated absently.

"All the information they have had about you — and they have had plenty — confirms the hypothesis. Some members of Goebbels's entourage are enthusiastic. They have made appeals through diplomatic channels, in the name of science, for the good of humanity, etc. Several universities and scientific institutes have invited us for a series of lectures — me, you, Dr. Gavrilă, and anyone else I want to bring; in a word, they want us to lend you to them for a period of time. And because we are reluctant, the Gestapo has been given a free hand. . . ."

He stopped, as though he had suddenly lost his breath. For the first time he seemed tired, aged.

"We had to hand over to them copies of the reports made in the first weeks at the hospital. It's a customary thing to do, and we couldn't refuse. Of course, I haven't informed them of everything. As far as the most recent materials are concerned — among others photostats of your notebook and copies of the recordings — all these were shipped to Paris. Bernard and his coworkers are studying them now, and later they will be deposited at one of the laboratories of the Rockefeller Foundation. . . . But I see you aren't listening anymore," he added, getting to his feet. "You're tired. You'll learn the rest later."

"The rest" seemed interminable. And sometimes it seemed of no interest to him, and at other times it seemed he was hearing things he had learned already, although he could not specify when or under what circumstances. He was amused in particular by the investigations made in connection with the lightning of Easter night. How had it happened that the cloudburst did not extend beyond a certain perimeter, and that only one bolt of lightning had struck — and in a rather unusual way, because the faithful who were waiting in the narthex of the church had seen the lightning as an endless incandescent spear? In any event, along with the specialists sent by Dr. Rudolf, who gathered all sorts of information about the form and intensity of the light in the flash, there came also a famous dilettante, the author of several studies on the Etruscans. In less than a week he had succeeded in reconstructing the perimeter covered by the rainfall, and he was now interpreting the symbolism of the space where the bolt had struck.

"But these inquiries and investigations have only an anecdotal value," the Professor continued. "The only serious thing is Dr. Rudolf's decision to begin experiments in electrocution, once he has completed his file by having a few conversations with you."

"But what else could I tell him?" he asked.

"That, no one knows. Perhaps the additional information will be obtained through certain laboratory experiments, by producing, for instance, a series of artificial lightning flashes and hoping you will recognize by the intensity of the light the one that struck you. Perhaps he wants to find out straight from your mouth what you felt at that moment, and why you had the sensation of being sucked up by a fiery cyclone that had burst directly over your head. I don't know. It is suspected, however, that the electrocution experiments will be made on political prisoners. And *that* crime must, at all costs, be avoided."

He had let his moustache grow as he had been told, thick and bushy.

"The modification of your face will take place later," he was told on the evening of September 25.

The Professor could scarcely contain himself. "Chamberlain and Daladier are in Munich," he said as he entered the room. "Anything could happen now, any day. . . . Those who are concerned with you have changed their plan," he began after a pause, taking his usual place in the chair. "You will be evacuated at night, in great secrecy, but in such a way that the others find out, or more precisely, so that they see the car in which you will be transported. Then, twenty or twenty-five kilometers away . . ."

"I believe I've guessed the rest," he interrupted, smiling. "Twenty or twenty-five kilometers from Bucharest an accident will be staged."

"Exactly. There will even be several witnesses. The

press will speak about a routine accident in which three men perished by incineration. But the various wire services will learn that the victims were you and the two agents who were accompanying you, en route to an unknown destination. They will be given to understand that the agents wanted to hide you away in a very safe place. . . ."

"That's the way it will happen," the Professor resumed after a pause. "I don't know where you'll be hidden. But there they will make the modifications of which I spoke. In a month at most, with a regular passport, you will be transported to Geneva—how, I don't know; I wasn't informed. Bernard proposed Geneva. He believes that at the present moment Paris is not the safest place. He will come to see you as soon as possible. I'll come also," he added. "At least, I hope to."

3

He never saw the Professor again. At the end of October the older man died. Dominic had been afraid that would happen ever since the day when the Professor had burst into his room saying, "Things are more serious than we expected!" He had had a vision then of the doctor putting his hand to his heart and collapsing, moaning; then he had heard a scream, doors slamming, footsteps rapidly departing on the stairs. Only when the Professor had approached him and asked, "Don't you feel well? Did you have a bad night?" did he return to his senses. But from then on, the vision had kept haunting him. When Dr. Bernard told him, "I have a piece of sad news to give you," he was ready to reply, "I know, the Professor has died."

Dr. Bernard came to see him at least once a month. They would spend almost the whole day together. Sometimes, after listening to him answer certain questions, he would bring the recorder closer and ask him to repeat the answers. Fortunately the questions had to do with memory, the modification of behavior (relations with people, animals, events as compared with his previous way of behaving), his adaptation of his personality to a paradoxical situation (did he believe he could still love someone in the same way he did when he was that age before?), questions to which he could respond without fear. Each time he came, Bernard brought him a sum of money (from a fund put at his disposal by the Rockefeller Foundation, he explained). He had assisted him also in getting a job at the university, entrusting to him the task of coordinating materials for a history of medical psychology.

After the occupation of France, there was a long interval during which he received no news, although, until December 1942, he continued to receive a check each month directly from the Rockefeller Foundation. At the beginning of 1943 a letter arrived from Dr. Bernard, posted in Portugal. It informed him that he would soon write "a long letter, because there is much to tell." But he had received nothing more. Only after the liberation of France, through one of his assistants, did he find out that Dr. Bernard had been killed in an airplane accident in Morocco in February of 1943.

He went each day to the library and asked for many books and collections of old periodicals. He leafed through them attentively, took notes, wrote bibliographical cards; but all this work constituted a camouflage. Once he had read the first few lines he *knew* what would follow. Without understanding the process of anamnesis (as he was accustomed to call it), he discovered that with any text he had before him, if he wanted to find out the content, he immediately *knew* it. Some time after he had begun work at the library he experienced a long, dramatic dream, which he remembered only fragmentarily, however, because he had interrupted it by waking up several times. There was one detail in particular he remembered: in the aftermath of his electrocution, his mental activity anticipated somewhat the condition men will attain some tens of thousands of years hence. The principal characteristic of the new humanity will be the structure of its psycho-mental life: all that has ever been thought or done by men, expressed orally or in writing, will be recoverable through a certain exercise of concentration. In fact, education then will consist in the learning of this method under the direction of instructors.

In short, I'm a "mutant," he said to himself on awakening. I anticipate the post-historic existence of man. Like in a science-fiction novel, he added, smiling with amusement. He made such ironic reflections primarily for the "Powers" that were watching over him. *In a certain sense, what you say is true,* he heard himself thinking. *But in distinction to characters in science-fiction novels, you have retained the freedom to accept or reject this new condition. At the moment you wish, for one reason or another, to return to the other condition, you are free to do it.*

He breathed deeply. "Therefore, I'm free!" he exclaimed after looking around carefully. "I'm free, and yet . . ." But he did not dare continue the thought.

Already in 1939 he had decided to describe his recent experiences in a special notebook. He had begun by commenting on this fact (which, he thought, would confirm the "humanity of post-historic man"): spontaneous knowledge, which in a sense was automatic, did not destroy his interest in research or the joy of discovery. He chose an example easily verified: the pleasure with which a lover of poetry reads a poem he knows almost by heart. He can recite it, yet sometimes he prefers to read it. This is because the new reading gives him the opportunity to discover beauty and meanings that he had not suspected heretofore. It was the same with all that science he received ready-made, all the languages and literatures he had discovered he knew: they had not diminished the joy of learning and investigating.

Reread after several years, some of the sentences fascinated him: "You learn well or with pleasure only that which you know already." "Do not compare me with a computer. Like me, if the computer is correctly 'fed,' it can recite the *Odyssey* or the *Aeneid*, but I recite them *differently* each time." Or, "The blessings that any cultural creation (*n.b.: cultural creation*, not only artistic) can afford are unlimited."

He always remembered with a thrill the mysterious epiphany of the two roses. But from time to time it pleased him to contest the validity of the philosophical argument. There ensued then long dialogues that delighted him. He even promised himself to write them down, primarily for their literary value (which it seemed to him they possessed). The last time, however, the dialogue had ended rather quickly, even abruptly. Basically, he repeated to himself that winter evening in 1944, such parapsychological phenomena can be the effect of forces we do not know, but which can be controlled by the unconscious. *That's very true,* he heard himself thinking. *Every action is effected by a force more or less unknown. But after so many experiences, you ought to revise your philosophical principles. You suspect what I'm referring to.* "Yes, I believe so," he acknowledged, smiling.

Several times during the last years of the War he had discovered that his reserves at the bank were exhausted. Each time he would wait for the solution of the crisis, curious and at the same time impatient. The first time he had received a money order for 1,000 francs from a person of whom he had never heard. His letter of thanks was returned with the indication: "Unknown at this address." Another time he had met by chance one of his colleagues in a restaurant at the train station. On learning that he was going to spend a week at Monte Carlo, he asked him to enter the Casino three days hence at seven P.M. (at *exactly* seven, he insisted) and, at the first table in the first roulette salon, to put 100 francs on a certain number. He requested him to keep the matter secret, and he repeated the request after the young man had returned in great excitement bringing him 3,600 francs.

The last time in particular delighted him. (It was this of which he thought first when he heard, *You suspect what I'm referring to.*) He was passing the three windows of a stamp dealer's shop as he did every time he returned from the library. This time, without understanding why, he stopped and began to look, at random, at the stamps displayed there. Philately had never interested him, and he wondered why he could not pull himself away from one of the windows, apparently the least attractive one. When he set eyes on an old and modest-appearing album, he realized that he *had* to buy it. It cost five francs. At home, he began to thumb through it, attentive, curious, although he did not know what he was seeking. Undoubtedly, it had been a beginner's album, perhaps that of a lycée pupil. Even an amateur like himself realized that the stamps were recent and commonplace. All of a sudden, he took a razor blade and began cutting open the cardboard bindings. He removed several cellophane envelopes, full of old stamps. It was easy to guess what had happened: someone, persecuted by the regime, had succeeded by this device in removing a large number of rare stamps from Germany.

He returned the next day and asked the proprietor of the shop if he remembered who had sold him the album. He did not know: he had bought it in a lot of old albums at an auction several years previously. When he showed him the stamps he had removed from the binders, the dealer paled.

"Such rarities have not been seen for a long time, neither here in Switzerland nor in other countries!" If he were to sell them now, he could obtain at least 100,000 francs. But if he were to wait a while, at any international auction he could obtain as much as 200,000.

"But since I bought them from you for nothing I consider it only fair that I divide the money half and half with you. Right now I need a few thousand francs. The rest of my share, according to how you sell the stamps, you may deposit to my account at the bank."

How such events would have thrilled Leibniz! he said to himself, smiling. To feel yourself obliged to revise your philosophical principles because, because in a mysterious way . . .

Beginning in 1942 he understood that the official version of the accident no longer was accepted either by the Gestapo or by other secret services — which, for various reasons, were interested in his case. Very probably, indiscretions had been made in Bucharest, corroborated later by certain particulars obtained at Paris from the circle of Dr. Bernard's assistants. But if it had been discovered that he was living at Geneva, it was not known what he looked like, and his name was not

101

known. To his surprise, he discovered one evening, when leaving a cafe, that he was being followed. He succeeded in losing the pursuer, and he spent the next week in a village near Lucerne. Soon after he returned to Geneva, the incident was repeated: this time two men dressed in trench coats were waiting for him in front of the library. One of the librarians came down just then; he asked to be allowed to accompany him. After a while, when the librarian could no longer doubt that they were indeed being followed, they caught a taxi. A brother-in-law of the librarian was a functionary of the Bureau of Aliens. From him he learned later that he had been mistaken for a secret agent, and a telephone number was given him that he could call in case of need. It amused him that although the Gestapo and probably other Services were looking for him, the immediate risks were due to a confusion with an ordinary informer or secret agent.

From the first year on, on the advice of Dr. Bernard, he had kept his books of personal notes in a safety deposit box in the bank. Then he gave up using notebooks; he wrote instead on a pad that he carried with him at all times. Certain pages containing too intimate confessions he deposited at the bank as soon as he had written them.

The same evening he had taken refuge near Lucerne, he had decided to complete his autobiographical notes:

> I am not a clairvoyant or an occultist, nor do I belong to any secret society. One of the documents in my safety deposit box summarizes my life which began in the spring of 1938. My first experiences were described and analyzed in the reports of Professors Roman Stănciulescu and Gilbert Bernard and sent by the latter, later, to a laboratory of the Rockefeller Foundation. But they concern only the external aspects of the mutation process set in motion in April 1938. I mention them nevertheless because they validate in a highly scientific way some of the things contained in the other documents deposited at the bank.

I do not doubt that the eventual investigator, beginning to read through the aforementioned documents,
will ask himself the same question that I have asked
many times in the past seven years: Why *me*? Why has
this mutation happened to me, of all people? From
the short autobiography that will be found in Portfolio
A it will be seen clearly that even before being
threatened by total amnesia, I had not succeeded in
doing any major thing. I was attracted, in my youth,
to many sciences and disciplines, but, except for an
enormous reading, I accomplished nothing. So then,
why me? I don't know. Perhaps because I had no family.
Perhaps I was chosen because as a young man, I wanted
to possess a universal education, and then, at the very
moment when I was on the verge of losing my memory
completely, I was gifted with a universal erudition such
as will become accessible to man only many thousands
of years from now.

I have written this note because if, contrary to all
expectations, I were to disappear now, I want it to be
known that I had no merit and no responsibility in
the process of mutation that I have described as fully
as possible in the notebooks grouped in Portfolio A.

The next day he continued:

For reasons explained in Portfolio B, I was brought to
Switzerland and camouflaged in October 1938. That
up to today, January 20, 1943, I have not been identified
(and eventually captured) might seem incomprehensible. The reader will wonder how I could have passed
unobserved for so many years, although I constituted
an exceptional case: I was a "mutant" and had access
to means of knowledge still inaccessible to mankind.
This question I asked myself also, several times, between 1938 and 1939. But I quickly realized that I did
not risk betraying myself—and therefore being iden-

tified — for the simple reason that in the presence of others I behaved like an average intellectual. In 1938–39 I was afraid I would give myself away conversing with professors and colleagues of mine at the university: I *knew* more than any of them and I *understood* things they never suspected existed. But to my surprise and great relief, I discovered that in the presence of others, *I couldn't make myself appear as I was,* just as an adult, having a conversation with a child, knows that he cannot communicate — and therefore he does not try to communicate — anything but facts and information accessible to the mental capacities of the child. This continuous camouflage of the immense possibilities that have been put at my disposal has not forced me to lead a "double life"; not in the presence of children, nor parents, nor pedagogues have I lived a "double life."

In a sense, my experience has an exemplary value. If someone were to tell me that there exist among us saints or authentic magicians, or Bodhisattvas, or any other kind of person endowed with miraculous powers, I should believe him. By virtue of their very mode of existence such men could not be recognized by the profane.

Beginning with the morning of November 1, 1947 he decided to cease writing notes in French, but to use instead an artificial language that he had constructed with passion, almost as a man possessed, over the past few months. What fascinated him about it especially was the extraordinary flexibility of the grammar and the infinite possibilities of the vocabulary (he succeeded in introducing into the system of purely etymological proliferation a corrective borrowed from the theory of aggregates). Now he could describe situations that were paradoxical, apparently contradictory, impossible to express in existing languages. The way this linguistic system was constructed, it could be deciphered only by means of a perfected computer; therefore, he estimated, not before 1980. This certainly permitted him to reveal facts that until then he had not dared to confess in writing.

As usual, after a morning devoted to work, he went for a stroll along the shore of the lake. Upon returning he stopped at the Cafe Albert. As soon as he saw him, the waiter brought coffee and a bottle of mineral water. The waiter also brought him the newspapers, but he did not have time to look at them. A tall, distinguished looking man (seemingly emerged from a portrait by Whistler, he thought to himself) stopped in front of him and asked permission to sit at his table. The man was still rather youthful, although the old-fashioned style of his jacket added six or seven years to his appearance.

"It is curious that we should meet on just this day," he said, "a day so important for you. I am Comte de Saint-Germain. At least so I'm told," he added with a wry smile. "But is it not curious that we meet today, the day following the discovery of the Essene manuscripts from the Dead Sea? Surely you have heard . . ."

"Just what the papers have written."

The man looked at him for a moment, then raised his hand. "The same, and without sugar," he ordered.

"All meetings of this sort," he began after the waiter had brought the coffee, "all meetings between incredible people like us have an air of artificiality about them. The consequence of bad literature, pseudo-occultist books," he added. "But we must resign ourselves: nothing can be done about folklore of mediocre quality. The legends that enchant certain contemporaries of ours are in detestably bad taste. I recall a conversation I had with Matila Ghyka in London in the summer of 1940. It was soon after the fall of France. That admirable savant, writer, and philosopher (in parenthesis let me say I value highly not only *Le nombre d'or,* as does everyone, but also his early novel, *La pluie d'étoiles*) — that incomparable Matila Ghyka told me that the Second World War, which at that time had scarcely begun, was in reality an occult conflict between two secret societies, the Templars and the Teutonic Knights. If a man of intelligence and learning could believe that, it is not surprising that occult traditions are treated with contempt. . . . But I see you aren't saying anything," he added, smiling.

"I'm listening. It's interesting."

"Anyway, there is no need for you to say very much. I shall ask you only, at the end, to answer one question. . . . I don't claim to know who you are," he began again after a pause. "But there are several of us who, since 1939, have known about your existence. The fact that you had appeared suddenly and independently of the traditions we knew induced us to believe, on the one hand, that you had a special mission, and on the other hand, that you had access to means of knowledge much superior to those at our disposal. There is no need for you to confirm what I'm saying. I have come to see you today because the discovery of the Essene manuscripts from the Dead Sea is the first sign of a well-known syndrome. There will follow, rather quickly, other discoveries, and with the same significance. . . ."

"Which is — ?" he interrupted, smiling.

The stranger scrutinized him before replying. "I see you are putting me to the test. Perhaps you're right. But the significance of the discoveries is clear: the manuscripts from Qumran reveal the doctrines of the Essenes, a secret community about which almost nothing precise is known. Likewise, the Gnostic manuscripts discovered recently in Egypt and still unstudied will reveal certain esoteric doctrines, ignored for almost 1,800 years. Soon there will follow other similar discoveries disclosing other traditions that have remained secret until our day. The syndrome to which I refer is this: the revelation in series of secret doctrines. The cycle is closed. This I knew long ago, but after Hiroshima I knew also the way it would end."

"Very true," he whispered absently.

"The question I wanted to ask you is this: employing all the knowledge that has been transmitted to you, do you know precisely the way the 'Ark' will be arranged?"

"The ark?" he asked, surprised. "Are you thinking of a replica of Noah's ship?"

106

The other looked at him again, puzzled and irritated at the same time.

"It's only a metaphor. A metaphor that's become a cliché," he added. "You find it in all the so-called occultist pulp literature. . . . I refer to the transmission of the tradition. The essential is never lost, I know, but I'm thinking of the many other things that, although they do not represent the essential, seem to me nevertheless indispensable to a truly human existence: for instance, the Occidental artistic treasury, above all music and poetry, but also a part of classic philosophy and certain sciences."

"I believe you can imagine what those few survivors of the cataclysm will think about science," he interrupted, smiling. "Probably post-historic man, as I have heard him called, will be allergic to science for at least a century or two!"

"It is very probable," the stranger agreed. "But I was thinking of mathematics. . . . Anyhow, that's what I wanted to ask about."

He sat thinking for a long time, hesitating to reply. "To the extent I understand your question, I can say only that . . ."

"Thank you, I understand!" the other exclaimed, unable to conceal his joy. He bowed low, shook his hand with genuine sincerity, and strode toward the door. It seemed to him, watching the man leave in such haste, that someone must have been waiting for him just outside in the street.

"I signaled to you several times," said the proprietor in a confidential tone, "but you didn't see me. He used to be a regular customer of ours; everyone knows him: Monsieur Olivier, but some say he is a doctor, Dr. Olivier Brisson. For some time he was a school teacher, but one day he left the school and the city without informing anyone in advance. I don't believe he's all there. He strikes up conversations with people and introduces himself as Comte de Saint-Germain."

He remembered that meeting when he observed that, in a

curious way, the scenario was beginning to be repeated. That year he became friends with a young Californian, Linda Gray, who among other things had, for him, the great merit of not knowing jealousy.

One evening, unexpectedly, when he had not yet poured their second cups of coffee, she said to him, "I found out that you were a good friend of a famous French doctor. . . ."

"He died," he interrupted her. "He was killed in an airplane accident in the winter of 1943."

The young woman lit a cigarette and after inhaling the first smoke she continued, without looking at him, "Some believe it wasn't an accident. They say the plane crashed because . . . Actually, I don't understand it very well, but you'll find out all about it when he gets here. I told him to come at 9:00," she added, looking at her watch.

"Who's coming at 9:00?"

"Dr. Monroe. He's the director, or something else important, at the Gerontology Laboratory in New York."

He recognized him immediately. He had seen the man several times at the library and then, just a few days ago, at the cafe. The man had begged leave to sit at his table, and he had no more than sat down when he asked him if he knew Dr. Bernard. "I knew him very well," he had replied. "But I promised never to discuss the history and significance of our friendship."

"Forgive me if I needed to resort to this stratagem," he began, extending his hand. "I'm Dr. Yves Monroe, and I have investigated the materials of Dr. Bernard in New York. As a biologist and gerontologist, I'm interested in one thing in particular: to stop the proliferation of new, dangerous myths — for example, the belief that youth and life can be prolonged in any way other than by the means we use today, that is, purely biochemical ones. Do you know what I'm referring to?"

"No."

"I refer, in the first place, to the method proposed by Dr. Rudolf: electrocution by means of a million or more volts. That's insane!"

"Fortunately, I believe his method was never tried."

The doctor picked up his whiskey glass and began to turn it around absently between his fingers.

"No, it was not," the doctor continued, giving him an icy stare. "But the legend was circulated that Dr. Bernard knew a somewhat analogous case of a rejuvenation induced by the electrical charge from a bolt of lightning. The materials on deposit at the Rockefeller Laboratory are so general and confused, however, that it is impossible to draw any conclusions. Moreover, I was told that part of the recordings were lost; more precisely, they were destroyed by mistake in an attempt to transfer them to perfect phonodiscs. At any rate, to the extent they are usable, the documents recorded by Professor Bernard refer exclusively to the phases of psycho-mental recuperation and reintegration of the patient struck by lightning."

He broke off his monologue and, without having put his glass to his lips, set it carefully back on the table.

"I have permitted myself to force this meeting," he resumed, "in the hope that you could furnish some explanations with regard to a rather obscure question. You have admitted knowing Dr. Bernard well. Recently the rumor has been going around that he had with him the most important documents, in two valises, and that the airplane in which he was to have crossed the Atlantic crashed because of those two valises. It is not known exactly what they contained, but one of the rival services wanted to assure itself, to avoid — how to say? — any risk. Now, do you know anything precise about the contents of those valises?"

He shrugged in confusion. "I believe that only Dr. Bernard's assistants in Paris would be able to explain."

The doctor smiled with some effort, without trying to hide his disappointment.

"The one who remembers declares he knows nothing. While the others claim they have forgotten. . . . I've also read articles by Professor Roman Stănciulescu in *La Presse médicale.* Unfortunately, Stănciulescu died in the fall of 1939. One of the colleagues on a mission in Bucharest wrote me recently that

109

all his efforts to find out more from Professor Stănciulescu's assistants have been fruitless."

He picked up his glass of whiskey again, and after turning it around several times between his fingers, he put it to his lips with great care and began to sip very slowly.

"Through the intervention of Dr. Bernard you had, for some three to four years, a Rockefeller stipend. What was the area of your research?"

"Materials for a history of medical psychology," he replied. "I sent them in 1945 to Dr. Bernard's collaborators in Paris."

"Interesting," he said, suddenly lifting his eyes from the glass and scrutinizing him at length.

That night he returned home wistful, preoccupied. He was not sure that Monroe had guessed his identity. On the other hand, he did not understand who Monroe believed him to be: a personal friend of Bernard? A patient? If, however, Monroe had listened to the recordings made at Geneva in 1938–39, he ought to have recognized his voice.

Linda's question the next day calmed him. "What did the doctor mean when he took me aside last evening and said, 'If he ever tells you he's past seventy, don't believe him!'?"

Several weeks later, in front of a cafe that had recently opened, he heard someone calling to him in Romanian, "Domnul Matei! Domnul Dominic Matei!" He turned his head in fright. A tall youth, blond and bare-headed, was hurrying toward him, trying at the same time to open a briefcase.

"I've learned a little Romanian," he said in an awkward French, "but I don't dare speak it. I knew you were here at Geneva, and with all the photographs I had, it wasn't hard to recognize you."

He rummaged nervously in the briefcase and brought out several photographs, frontal views and profiles, from various angles. They had been taken in the fall of 1938 by the surgeon who had succeeded in modifying his facial features so radically.

"And, for any eventuality," he added, smiling, "I'm

also carrying with me in the briefcase your family photo albums. Let's go inside this cafe a moment. You can't imagine how excited I was when I saw you a little while ago! I was afraid that when you heard me call 'Domnul Matei!' you wouldn't turn your head."

"I almost didn't," he replied, smiling. "But, I admit, I was curious."

They sat down at a table and after they had ordered a hot lemonade and a bottle of beer, the stranger began to stare at him in fascination and disbelief.

"A few weeks ago, on January 8, you were eighty years old!" he whispered. "You don't look more than thirty or thirty-two. And you look that old only because you're trying to hide your age. . . ."

"I still don't know with whom I have the pleasure to be speaking."

"Excuse me," he said, after sipping a little from his beer. "I'm still very excited. As bettors at a race track say, I put everything on one horse—and I won! . . . I'm Ted Jones, Jr., correspondent for *Time* magazine. It all began some ten years ago when I read your interview, "Struck by Lightning." I was extremely impressed, even after I found out it was apocryphal. But then came the War, and very few people still remember that interview."

He emptied the glass of beer and asked if he could continue in English and if pipe smoke annoyed him.

"Two years ago, when the famous secret archive of Dr. Rudolf was discovered, people began talking again about your case—of course, to the extent it was known from the materials collected by Dr. Gilbert Bernard. But nothing else was known, not even whether or not you were still alive. Unfortunately, since Dr. Rudolf was a notorious Nazi—and besides, he had committed suicide during the last week of the War—everything having to do with his experiments is suspect."

"What kind of experiments?"

"The electrocution of animals, of mammals in particular. Beginning with 1,200,000 volts, up to two million."

"And with what results?"

He tried to laugh, then refilled his glass with beer. "It's a long story," he began.

It was indeed a long, obscure, and inconclusive tale. The first investigations of Rudolf's archive seemed to indicate that in certain cases the victims had not been killed by the electric shock, but since the experiments were stopped a few months later, the consequences of the electrocution could not be followed. In other cases, a modification of the genetic system appeared to have been indicated. Several investigators apparently interpreted such modifications as the prodrome of a mutation. But under somewhat obscure circumstances, a good number of items from the archive—among them the most valuable—had disappeared. At any rate, in the absence of any data relative to experimentation with human beings, the Rudolf dossier was not conclusive. On the other hand, the great majority of American scholars rejected *a priori* the hypothesis of regeneration through electricity.

"You were the only argument, and you still are!" he exclaimed. "It was therefore to be expected that the few materials saved from Professor Bernard would be systematically depreciated and, in some cases, destroyed."

"Do you believe that was the way it happened?" Matei interrupted.

The other hesitated a few moments before replying. "I have strong motives for so believing. Fortunately, I was sent as correspondent to Romania."

Even before going to Romania, he had learned Romanian well enough to be able to read it and go about by himself on the street and in stores. He had the luck to meet and become friends rather quickly with Dr. Gavrilă, in whose possession he found the family album and all the documentation assembled by the Professor.

"What an extraordinary article could be published! 'Man Rejuvenated by Lightning!' With photos, documents, the declarations of Professor Roman Stănciulescu, Dr. Gavrilă, and others who took care of you, with the interview I'm having now, and lots of other pictures taken here in Geneva, in February 1948!"

Jones stopped himself and tried to relight his pipe, then gave it up and looked deeply into his eyes.

"Although your English is perfect, I see that you aren't saying anything."

"I'm waiting for what comes next."

"Good thinking! What I'm about to say is as spectacular and mysterious as your experience. For ethical and political reasons, the article *cannot* be published. Anything that might give rise to confusions, anything that might seem in one way or another to confirm the theory of Dr. Rudolf, must be kept from publication. Especially now when the voting of massive funding for institutes of gerontological research is at stake. . . . You have nothing to say?"

He shrugged. "I believe everything has happened as it had to happen. I'm sorry about your work and the time you've lost, but the consequences of the article would be disastrous. If men — more precisely, certain men — were sure that electrocution could solve the problem of regeneration and rejuvenation, we could expect anything. I believe it's preferable to let biochemists and gerontologists continue their investigations. One day, sooner or later, they'll arrive at the same results."

Jones smoked, watching him drink from his glass of hot lemonade. "In any event," he said presently, "you also must be considered. When we planned the article, we didn't think about what could become of your life after its publication."

"In a way, something's already begun to happen," Matei interrupted good humoredly. "How did it happen that you discovered me so easily? I supposed that Dr. Gavrilă and all the others in Romania believed me dead long ago, killed in an auto accident."

"So they do believe, the majority of them. Dr. Gavrilă believed it too, until I informed him, in great secrecy, that you were alive and living in Geneva. . . . Don't think I found this out from anyone," he added, smiling enigmatically. "I discovered it by myself, when I was told that Dr. Monroe had come to Geneva to discuss certain details with a friend of Professor Bernard. I guessed immediately that that friend could only be you! Of course, obviously, neither Monroe nor any of the others at the Laboratory of Gerontology believe — *nor can they believe* — such a thing."

"That's good news!"

"The truth *will* come out," Jones continued, not trying to hide his satisfaction. "The story's too wonderful to be buried under a pall of silence. I am going to write a novel," he added, beginning to clean his pipe. "In fact, I've already started. For you it presents no danger. The action takes place in Mexico, before and during the war years, and the majority of the characters are Mexicans. Of course, I'll send you a copy of it if, when it appears, you're still on the same terms of friendship with Linda. I knew her brother well; he was a pilot, killed on Okinawa."

He stopped abruptly and, as though he had just remembered something important, he opened the briefcase. "I was about to forget the family photo album," he said. "I promised Dr. Gavrilă that if I was successful in finding you, I'd give it to you. They are precious documents: memories from — how shall I put it? — memories from your first youth!"

Back at his place, he wrapped the album in a sheet of white paper, placed it inside a large envelope, and sealed it. In the upper left-hand corner he wrote: "Received February 20, 1948 from Ted Jones, Jr., correspondent for *Time* magazine in Bucharest. Brought on behalf of Dr. Gavrilă."

Things have become simplified and complicated at the same time, he said to himself, opening his writing pad. He began writing in French, telling about the meeting and summarizing the conversation with Jones. Then he added:

> He confirms Dr. Monroe's information: the systematic
> destruction of the documents from 1938–39. The only

reports concerning the process of physiological reconstruction and anamnesis. The only scientific proofs
of regeneration and rejuvenation by means of a massive
electrical discharge. This means that the *origin* of the
phenomenon of mutation no longer matters. *Why?*

He interrupted his writing and remained pensive for some
moments.

> Obviously, from the autobiographical sketch and
> from other notes grouped in Portfolios A, B, and C,
> the reader eventually will be able to learn the essentials.
> But without the materials collected and annotated by
> Professors Stănciulescu and Bernard, my testimony
> has lost its documentary value. Moreover, almost all
> of my notes refer to the consequences of the anamnesis,
> in a word, to the experiences of a mutant that anticipate
> the existence of post-historic man. The Stănciulescu-
> Bernard documents did *not* contain information rela-
> tive to those experiences, but, to a certain extent,
> they ensured their credibility. I can draw but one
> conclusion: my testimony is addressed to a reader in
> the near future, let us say in the year 2000. But to
> whom?
> A provisional answer could be this: in the aftermath
> of nuclear wars that will have taken place, many civili-
> zations, beginning with the Occidental one, will be
> destroyed. Undoubtedly, the catastrophe will unleash
> a wave of pessimism heretofore unknown in the history
> of mankind, a general despondency. Even if all the
> survivors do not fall prey to the temptation of suicide,
> very few will still have enough vitality to be able to
> hope in man and the possibility of a human species
> superior to *homo sapiens*. Discovered and deciphered
> then, this testimony could counterbalance the despair
> and universal wish for extinction. By virtue of the
> simple fact that they exemplify the mental potential of

a humanity that will come to birth in a far-off future, such documents demonstrate, because they anticipate, the reality of post-historic man.

This hypothesis presupposes the preservation of all the material deposited today in the safe-deposit box. I am ignorant as to how this safeguarding will be assured. But, on the other hand, I do not doubt that the material will be preserved. Otherwise, my experience would have no meaning.

He put the pages he had written into another envelope, sealed it, and set off for the bank. As he was locking the door, the telephone began to ring. He could hear it ringing all the way down the stairs.

4

The summer of 1955 was an unusually rainy one, and in Ticino thunderstorms occurred daily. Nevertheless, no one remembered having ever seen the sky as black as it was on the afternoon of August 10. When the first flashes of lightning crossed the sky above the city, the power station shut off the current. For almost half an hour lightning bolts fell in rapid succession, as if there were one endless explosion. From the window he watched where the lightning struck, toward the west, on the rocky hills that sprouted up abruptly in the direction of the mountains. The torrential rain gradually abated, and by three the sky had begun to lose its jet-black hue. Soon the street lights were turned on, and, from the window, he could see the street now, all the way to the cathedral. He waited for the rain to stop; then he went downstairs and headed for the police station.

"A little before noon," he began in a neutral, purely informative tone, "two women started out, intending to drive up to Trento. They asked me if I knew a road that was not too winding. I gave them directions, but I advised them to postpone their excursion, because they were in danger of being overtaken by a storm before reaching shelter at Helival. They replied that they were used to mountain storms and that in any event they could not postpone the trip. Their vacation would be over in a few days and they would have to return home."

The policeman listened to him politely, but without showing much interest.

"I don't know them," he continued. "I did hear the older lady addressing the younger: she called her Veronica. I believe I can guess what's happened. When the storm broke out, they were probably on the road that runs under the walls of the mountain, at Vallino, right where most of the lightning struck. I was at the window and I saw them," he added, realizing that the other was looking at him curiously, almost incredulously. "I imagine many rocks were dislodged. I'm afraid they were struck or even buried by the rockslide."

He knew it would not be easy to convince him.

"I can go by myself in a taxi and look for them," he resumed. "But if it happened as I suspect, we could not—the two of us, the driver and I—get them out from under the rocks by ourselves. We would need picks and shovels."

In the end, however, he had to accept that solution. If he needed help, he would telephone from the first service station and the police would send ambulances and everything needed. When he was approaching Vallino, the sky became clear, but here and there rocks were scattered on the highway, and the driver reduced his speed.

"I don't believe they had time to reach the shelter. Probably after the storm broke, they took refuge in one of the crevices in the walls."

"Some of them are as large as the mouth of a cave," observed the driver.

They both saw her at the same moment. Probably she had died of fright when lightning struck a few steps away. She was a woman well along in years, with gray hair cut short. She did not appear to have been killed by falling rocks, although a boulder had come to rest right beside her and had caught a corner of her skirt. Then he thought he heard a moan, and he began to search among the rocks.

"Veronica!" he called out several times.

They both heard a groan, then several short cries, followed by words in an unknown tongue pronounced rapidly, like an incantation. The falling rocks had piled up in front of the niche where Veronica had taken shelter, almost entirely blocking it. If he had not heard her groaning and crying out, he would never have suspected she was buried there. Just above, at a height of over two meters, a fissure opening into the cave could be seen. Scrambling up with difficulty, he saw her and called out her name, gesturing at the same time. The girl looked up, startled yet happy to see him. She tried to stand upright, but although she was not injured the place was too cramped and she could only half rise.

"The police will soon be here," he told her in French.

Then, because the girl looked as if she didn't understand, he repeated himself in German and Italian. Veronica wiped her hand across her cheek several times and started to speak. At first he realized she was speaking in a dialect of Central India, and then he distinguished whole sentences pronounced in Sanskrit. Bending closer to her, he whispered, *"Shanti! Shanti!"* and recited several canonical benedictions. The girl responded with a smile, then held up one hand to him, as though she wanted to show him something.

He stayed there pressed against the cliff, listening to her, trying to calm her and encourage her with familiar Sanskrit expressions until the ambulance and the police wagon arrived. They managed to move the rocks by digging underneath the edge of the slide that was nearest the road. After an hour the girl succeeded in getting out with the help of a rope ladder. At the sight of the police and the van she began to scream in fright. She took Dominic's hand, drawing very close to him.

"She's had a shock," he explained awkwardly, "and I think she's suffering from amnesia."

"But what language is she speaking?" someone in the group asked.

118

"I suspect it's an Indian dialect," he replied cautiously.

From her identification papers it was learned that she was Veronica Bühler, age twenty-five, a school teacher who lived in Liestal, in the Canton Bâle-Campagne. Her companion was Gertrude Frank, a German national, resident for some years in Freiburg, an administrative functionary in a publishing house. The autopsy confirmed the first assumption: death had been caused by a cardiac arrest.

Since he was the only one who could understand Veronica, and the only one in whose presence she was calm, he spent a considerable time at the clinic. He brought a tape recorder that he took care to camouflage. He recorded her voice several hours per day, especially when she was speaking about herself. She asserted that her name was Rupini, daughter of Nagabhata of the Kshatrya class, descended from one of the first families of Magadha to have been converted to Buddhism. Before her twelfth birthday she had decided, with her parents' consent, to consecrate her life to the study of the Abhidharma and had been accepted into a community of *bhikuni* (female ascetics). She had studied Sanskrit grammar, logic, and Mahayana metaphysics. The fact that she had memorized over 50,000 sutras had created for her a prestige not only among the instructors and students at the famous Nalanda University but also among many masters, ascetics, and contemplatives. At the age of forty she had become a disciple of the famous philosopher Chandrakirti. She spent several months in a cave, meditating and copying the works of her master. That was where she was when a storm had broken out and she had heard the lightning strike above her on the mountain. Many large rocks were dislodged and, pouring down like a river of stones, they had blocked the mouth of her cave. She had tried in vain to get out. Then suddenly she had seen him overhead, waving and speaking to her in an unknown language.

He was not sure he had understood everything, and even what he knew he understood he kept for the most part to himself. To the doctors he said that the young woman believed she was living in Central India twelve centuries ago and insisted she was a Buddhist anchorite. Thanks to sedatives she slept most of the time. Several medical doctors and psychologists from Zurich, Basel, and Geneva came to see her. As was to be expected, the newspapers published articles every day, and the number of foreign correspondents who roamed the clinic and interviewed the doctors grew unceasingly.

Fortunately, the solution that he had had in mind from the beginning was the course finally accepted. On the second day, after listening to a tape recording of her autobiographical confessions, he had sent a long telegram to the Oriental Institute in Rome. Then, on the third day, at the hour specified in the telegram, he had transmitted by telephone certain of the girl's statements. At the same time he informed one of C. G. Jung's closest collaborators. Two days later Professor Tucci came from Rome, accompanied by an assistant from the Institute. For the first time Rupini could discuss at length, in Sanskrit, Madhyamika philosophy and could talk about her master, Chandrakirti. All the conversations were recorded and the assistant translated some passages into English for the benefit of the doctors and reporters. The discussion became delicate whenever Rupini asked exactly what had happened to her, where she was, and why no one understood her although she had tried speaking in several Indian dialects in addition to Sanskrit.

"What do you say to her?" he asked Professor Tucci one evening.

"Of course, I begin always by reminding her of *Maya*, the great sorceress, cosmic illusion. It is not, properly speaking, a dream, I tell her, but it participates in the illusory nature of dreaming because it is a matter of the future, therefore of time; now, time is par excellence unreal. . . . I don't believe I've persuaded her. But fortunately, she's enthusiastic about logic and dialectics, and that's mainly what we discuss."

As soon as he suggested a journey to India, more precisely to the province of Uttar Pradesh, where the cave in which Rupini had meditated was located, Professor Tucci agreed that the Oriental Institute should sponsor the expedition. Thanks to the intervention of Jung, the basic expenses were covered by an American foundation. When they learned of this project, several daily papers offered to pay all incidental costs of the expedition in exchange for exclusive rights to the story. It was almost impossible to avoid publicity, especially since the consent of the director of the clinic had to be obtained, as well as that of the Indian government and the family of Veronica Bühler. But inquiries about her family made at Liestal yielded no results. Veronica had been a resident of the city for just five years. Her friends and colleagues knew nothing about her family. It was learned, however, that she had been born in Egypt, that her parents had been divorced when she was five; that her father, who had remained in Egypt, had remarried and no longer had any contact with her, while her mother, with whom she had never gotten along very well, had established herself in the United States, but the address was not known.

Eventually, the clinic permitted the journey to India, on the condition that the patient be accompanied by one of the doctors who had treated her. It was, naturally, understood that she would be put to sleep before leaving the clinic and would continue to sleep until they reached the vicinity of Gorakhpur.

From Bombay a military airplane transported them to Gorakhpur. Here six carloads of reporters and technicians were waiting, together with an Indian television crew in a large van. They journeyed from there toward the frontier of Nepal, to the region where, according to Rupini's account, the cave in which she was accustomed to meditate would be found. Fortunately, in addition to Matei, a pandit from Uttar Pradesh familiar with the Madhyamika philosophy was at Rupini's side when she awoke. At the insistence of the doctor, all the others had camouflaged themselves among the trees ten meters away. As if she recognized him, she addressed the pandit in a threatening way, asking him several questions but not waiting for a reply. Rather, she set off quickly up one of the paths, looking straight

121

ahead, repeating her favorite benedictions, which she had recited so many times at the clinic. After some twenty minutes
of climbing, she began to run, panting. With her arm out-
stretched, she pointed to the crest of a large rock resting against
the face of the mountain.

"That's it!" she exclaimed.

Then, using both hands, she began to scramble up the
cliff with surprising agility. When she reached the spot, she
pulled up a stunted shrub, cleaned the area of moss and dead
branches, uncovered an opening, and, trembling, put her face
to the rock and looked inside. Then she remained motionless.

"She's fainted!" someone exclaimed from below, even
before Matei had reached her.

"It's true!" he called back, lifting her head gently.

With difficulty, he brought her down and handed her
over to the team of technicians. They carried her on a stretcher
to the automobile. She was still unconscious and the car was
some ten miles distant when the first charge of dynamite
exploded. In less than half an hour they had succeeded in
reaching the bottom of the cave by means of a rope ladder.
With the help of searchlights they saw the skeleton: it was
sitting upright, as if death had overtaken it in a posture of
yogic meditation. Alongside, on the gravel, were a clay pot,
two wooden platters, and several manuscripts. Only when they
touched the manuscripts did they realize that they had turned
to dust long ago.

The nurse stopped him outside the door. "She's awake," she
said, "but she hasn't opened her eyes. She's afraid. . . ."

He went to her bed and laid his hand gently on her
forehead.

"Veronica!" he whispered.

She opened her eyes suddenly and, recognizing him,
her face brightened in a way he had never before seen it. Taking
his hand, she tried to sit up.

"Who are you?" she asked. "I remember you. We asked

directions of you earlier today. . . . But where's Gertrude? Where is she? . . ."

He had known from the first, as had all the others in the group, that it would be impossible to avoid publicity. The Indian television had recorded the most dramatic scenes, and tens of millions of spectators who had listened to her speaking in Sanskrit and a Himalayan dialect saw her in the end declaring in a timid English that her name was Veronica Bühler and that she knew well only two languages, German and French, declaring likewise that she had never tried to learn any Oriental language and, with the exception of a few popular books, she had never read anything about India or Indian culture. As was to be expected, precisely this fact excited the Indian public and, twenty-four hours later, worldwide opinion. For the vast majority of Indian intellectuals a clearer demonstration of the doctrine of the transmigration of the soul could not be found: in an earlier existence, Veronica Bühler had been Rupini.

"But I don't believe in metempsychosis," she whispered, frightened, one evening, taking his hand. "I never existed before! Maybe I was possessed by another spirit," she added, seeking his eyes.

And because he didn't know what to say and hesitated, caressing her hand, Veronica hung her head wearily.

"I'm afraid I'll go mad," she said.

The members of the expedition who remained were staying in one of the most deluxe hotels in India, guests of the Indian government. In order to avoid photographers, reporters, and the boldness of the curious, the whole group took their meals in a dining room reserved exclusively for them, kept well guarded. Every day they visited museums or institutes and met great personalities. For their transportation, limousines were provided, and they were always accompanied by a squad of motorcycle police. Otherwise, they did not dare leave the floor on which they were staying. They dared not even go walking in the corridors. Along with the doctor and the nurse, Dominic and Veronica had tried once, after midnight, to go out, hoping to catch a taxi and take a walk in the streets somewhere far away from the hotel. But a great throng was waiting at the exit. They were forced to return, fleeing under the protection of the police.

"I'm afraid I'll go mad," she repeated as they were leaving the elevator.

The next day he succeeded in having a conversation with an American reporter who had tried in vain to accompany them to Gorakhpur. He promised the reporter a long, exclusive interview and other hitherto unpublished material if he would arrange for them to be transported, incognito, to a Mediterranean island, where he and Veronica could live in seclusion for several months.

"Until the cyclone of television cameras and rotary presses has passed," he added. "In less than a year, things will be forgotten and each of us will be able to return to his own business."

Two weeks later they were installed in a villa built after the war on a hill a few kilometers from La Vallette. But the preparations and the recording of the interview had taken longer than expected, and Veronica had begun to show signs of impatience.

"We've talked so much and about so many things, yet I don't understand the essential thing: the transmigration of the soul."

"I'll explain it when we're finally alone."

She looked at him with unexpected warmth. "Will we ever be alone?" she whispered.

At Delhi she had said to him one evening, "When I opened my eyes and saw you, and when you told me about Gertrude, I realized I was thinking about two things simultaneously. I said to myself that although, very probably, both my parents were still alive, without Gertrude I was an orphan. And yet, at the same time, I was thinking: if I were five or six years older, and if he were to ask me to marry him, I'd accept!"

"I'm eighty-seven," he said in jest, smiling.

Then he had seen her laugh for the first time. "I'd be older than that if I were to add the years Rupini lived! But as I told you, I don't believe in that. I *can't* believe it."

"In a sense, you're right. But, I repeat, only *in a sense*. We'll discuss the problem later."

He avoided discussing it in the interview, contenting himself with citing classical Indian conceptions, from the *Upanishads* to Gautama Buddha, referring also to several contemporary interpretations, especially to the commentaries of Tucci. He succeeded in preserving his own anonymity; he was a young Orientalist who had recently become friends with Veronica. He succeeded above all in preserving the same face he had begun to construct in August, with the hair combed over the forehead and a thick, blond moustache covering his upper lip.

One evening when they were alone on the terrace, Veronica stepped over to his chaise-longue.

"Now explain it to me. But, above all, explain *how you knew*."

"I have to begin very far back," he said.

It was not until one evening at the beginning of October that he understood. They were seated beside each other on the sofa, watching the lights of the port above the railing of the terrace. Veronica seemed to be looking at him strangely.

"You want to say something, but you don't dare. What is it?" he asked.

"I've been thinking: seeing us together all the time, and living in the same house, people will think we're in love."

He sought her hand and squeezed it gently.

"But, it's so, Veronica. We are in love, we sleep in the same room, in the same bed."

"Is it true?" she asked in a whisper.

Then she sighed, laid her head on his shoulder, and closed her eyes. A few moments later she raised her head suddenly and, looking at him as though she did not recognize him, she began speaking in a foreign language, one he had never heard before. So, that's what it was! he said to himself. That's why we had to meet. That's why all those things happened. Slowly, without haste, in order not to startle her, he went to the study and got the tape recorder. She continued to speak more and more rapidly, looking at her hands. Then she put her wristwatch to her ear and listened, surprised and happy at the same time. Her face lighted up, as if she were about to laugh. But all of a sudden she came to her senses. Startled, she blinked several times and began rubbing her eyes. She staggered sleepily, dizzily toward the couch, and when he saw her swaying, he caught her in his arms. He carried her into the next room and laid her on the bed, covering her with a shawl.

She awoke after midnight.

"I'm scared!" she whispered. "I had an awful dream!"

"What did you dream?"

"I don't want to remember it! I'm afraid it will scare me again. I was somewhere beside a great river, and someone, a stranger, with a head like a dog mask, was coming toward me. In his hand . . . I don't want to remember!" she repeated, reaching out to embrace him.

From that night on, he never left her alone; he was afraid the paramediumistic attack would recur without warning. Fortunately, the gardener and the two young Maltese women who took care of the house disappeared every night, right after dinner.

"Tell me more," she would urge him each evening, as soon as they were alone. "Explain it to me! Sometimes I'm sorry I don't remember any of all that Rupini knows."

One evening, returning from the garden, she asked him all of a sudden, "Doesn't it seem odd that they should be waiting for us beside the fence! It's as though they're spying on us."

"I hadn't noticed anyone," he replied. "Where were they?"

She hesitated a few moments, avoiding his eyes. "They

126

were there, by the gate, as though they were spying on us. Two men, dressed oddly. But maybe I was mistaken," she added, bringing her hand to her forehead. "Maybe there wasn't anyone at our gate."

He took her arm and drew her slowly along with him. "I'm afraid you've spent too much time in the sun," he said, helping her lie down on the couch.

A week has past, he said to himself, so this must be the rhythm, hebdomadal. Which means that the whole thing could last a month. But what will happen to us then?

When he was sure she was deeply asleep, he tiptoed to the study and returned with the tape recorder. For some time he heard nothing but the blackbirds outside and her slightly agitated breathing. Then her whole face was illuminated by a broad smile. Very softly she pronounced a few words; then there followed a concentrated, anxious silence as though she were waiting for a response that was delayed or that she did not succeed in hearing. Then she began to speak, softly as if she were talking to herself, repeating certain words several times, with different intonations, but all pervaded by a great sadness. When he saw the first timid teardrops on her cheeks, he shut off the recorder and pushed it under the couch. Then, with great care, he stroked her hand and began to wipe her tears. Later, he carried her in his arms to the bedroom. He remained beside her until she awoke. Setting eyes on him, she grasped his hand and squeezed it tightly.

"I was dreaming," she said. "It was a very beautiful dream, but very sad. There were two young people like us, who loved each other and yet couldn't remain together. I don't understand why, but they weren't allowed to stay together."

He was not mistaken: the rhythm was indeed hebdomadal, although the paramediumistic ecstasies (as he had decided to call them) occurred at various hours. Materials for the documentary history of language, he said to himself, classifying the four cassettes. After Egyptian and Ugaritic, there had followed, probably, a sample of Protoelamite and one of Sumerian. We are descending deeper and deeper into the past.

Documents for the Ark, he added, smiling. What wouldn't linguists give if they could study them now! But how far back will we go? To the inarticulate protolanguage? And then . . .?

In the middle of December the strangest experience occurred. Fortunately it happened a little before midnight and he had not yet fallen asleep. Veronica burst into a series of guttural, pre-human cries that at the same time exasperated and embarrassed him. It seemed to him that such a regression into animality ought to be attempted only with volunteers, not with an unconscious subject. But, after several moments, there followed groups of clear phonemes with vowels, of an infinite variety, interspersed with short, labial explosions such as he would not have believed possible for a European to reproduce. After half an hour Veronica fell asleep, sighing. Farther than this I don't believe they will go, he said to himself, switching off the recorder. Then he waited. He wanted to be wide awake beside her when she roused from her slumber. Toward morning, however, he fell asleep.

When he awoke, a little before eight, Veronica was still sleeping and he didn't have the heart to wake her. She slept until almost eleven. Discovering how late it was, she sprang frightened from the bed.

"What's wrong with me?" she cried.

"Nothing. Probably you were very tired. And perhaps you had a bad dream."

"No. I dreamed nothing. At any rate, I don't remember dreaming anything."

They decided to spend Christmas Eve and New Year's Eve at a famous restaurant in La Vallette. Veronica reserved a table under the names of Monsieur and Madame Gerald Verneuil. She invented the names and also selected the costumes for New Year's Eve.

"I don't believe we're in danger of being recognized," she said. "Even if our pictures appeared last fall on the front pages of all the popular magazines."

"You can be sure they *did* appear," he interrupted her, "and perhaps they're still appearing."

She started to laugh somewhat timidly and yet happily. "I'd like to see them," she said. "The photos in the magazines, I mean. I'd like to have a few as souvenirs. But maybe it's too risky to search for them."

"I'll look around," he volunteered.

But although he searched through many kiosks and bookstores, he found only one magazine, an Italian one, with three pictures of Veronica, all taken in India.

"I seemed younger and better looking then, three months ago," she observed.

A few weeks later he realized she was right. For some time she had not looked so youthful. The documents for the Ark are to blame, he said to himself. The paramediumistic ecstasies have exhausted her.

"I feel tired all the time," she admitted one morning, "and I don't understand why. I do absolutely nothing, and yet I feel tired."

At the beginning of February he succeeded in persuading her to consult a doctor in La Vallette. They waited, then, uneasily for the results of the numerous tests.

"Madame is not suffering from anything, anything at all," the doctor assured him when they were alone. "I have, however, prescribed a series of shots with vitamins and minerals. . . . Perhaps it's the nervous condition that precedes the climacteric in certain women."

"What age do you take her to be?"

The doctor blushed, and rubbed his hands together awkwardly. "Around forty," he said at length, avoiding his eyes.

"And yet, I assure you that she didn't lie to you when she told you she was not yet twenty-six."

The effect of the injections fell short of expectations. Each day she felt more tired; often, after she had been looking in the mirror, he would catch her crying. Once, when he was walking to the park, he heard footsteps coming up quickly behind him, and he turned his head.

"*Professore,*" whispered the cook in fright, "*la signora ha il malocchio!*"

I ought to have understood this from the beginning, he told himself. We both have done our duty, and now we must separate. And since a more convincing argument could not be found — aside from a fatal accident or a suicide — this way was chosen: a process of galloping senescence.

He did not dare to tell her, however, until the morning when she showed him her hair: it had turned gray overnight. She wept, leaning against the wall, her face buried in her hands. He knelt beside her.

"Veronica," he began, "I'm to blame for this. Listen to me and don't interrupt. If I continue to live with you, by fall you will have perished! . . . I can't tell you more, I don't have the right. But I assure you that, in reality, you *haven't aged!* Once I disappear from your life, your youth and beauty will return."

Veronica sought his hand in fear, clasped it between hers, and began to kiss it. "Don't leave me!" she whispered.

"Listen to me, I implore you! Listen to me for two or three more minutes. I have been fated to lose all that I love. But I prefer to lose you young and beautiful, the way you were — and will be again, without me — than to see you perishing in my arms. . . . Listen! I'm going to leave, and if in three or four months you don't find yourself as you were last autumn, I shall return. The minute I receive your telegram, I'll come back. I ask just this much: wait three or four months, somewhere far away from me!"

The next day, in a long letter, he explained why he would no longer have a right to live with her once she had regained her youth. And because Veronica seemed to have begun to be persuaded to try the experiment, they decided to leave the villa. She would spend the first few weeks in a rest house run by nuns, and he would take a plane for Geneva.

Three months later he received a telegram: "You were right.

I will love you all my life. Veronica." He replied, "You will be happy. Good-bye."

That same week he left for Ireland.

5

Without his blond moustache and the bangs that had made him resemble certain poets from the twilight of Romanticism, he was not afraid of being recognized by anyone. Besides, after returning from Malta he frequented other *milieux*, primarily circles of linguists and literary critics. Sometimes, in the course of discussions, the case of Veronica-Rupini came up; judging by the questions he asked, it was quickly understood how little, and how badly, he was informed. In the summer of 1956 he agreed to contribute to a James Joyce documentary album. He accepted because the project allowed him to visit Dublin, one of the few cities he wanted to know. He returned there each year, a little before Christmas or at the beginning of summer.

Not until the fifth trip, in June 1960, did he meet Colomban. He met him by chance one evening when entering a pub off O'Connell Street. When he saw him, Colomban headed straight for him, took his hand between his own hands, and pressed it warmly. Then he invited him to sit at his table.

"How long I've been waiting for you!" he exclaimed pathetically, almost theatrically. "This is the fifth time I've come here, expressly to meet you."

He was a man of indefinite age, freckled, half-bald, with copper-colored sideburns contrasting with the pale blond of his hair.

"If I were to say that I know you, that I know *very well* who you are, you wouldn't believe me. So I shall say nothing. But since I too am probably condemned to live to be a hundred, I want to ask you just this: *What do we do with Time?* I'll explain immediately."

He was gazing at him in silence, smiling, when Colomban suddenly rose from the table.

"Or better, let's ask Stephens," he added, heading toward the bar.

He returned with a young man, thin and carelessly dressed. The youth shook his hand timidly, then sat down opposite him at the table.

"You must forgive his little manias," he said, pronouncing the words slowly. "He asks me all the time to declaim — he believes, perhaps, that I have better diction — to declaim: 'What do we do with Time?' His great discovery would be this, that the question, 'What do we do with Time?' expresses the supreme ambiguity of the human condition. Because, on the one hand, men — *all men!* — want to live long, to exceed, if possible, a hundred years; but in the vast majority of cases, once they reach the age of sixty or sixty-five and retire, *i.e.*, become *free to do what they want*, they become bored. They discover they have nothing to do with their free time. And on the other hand, the older a man becomes the more the rhythm of interior time accelerates, so that those persons — those very few — who *would* know what to do with free time, do not succeed in doing much of importance. . . . Finally, add to it the fact that. . ."

Colomban interrupted him, laying a hand on his arm. "Enough for today. Another day you will say it better, more convincingly."

Then, turning to the other, he added, "We shall return to the problem of Time. Meanwhile, I will ask if this article has come to your attention?"

He handed him a page from an American magazine:

. . . He spoke sometimes of a new quality of life, insisting that it could be, and *must* be, discovered by everyone. The moment he awoke he discovered a great joy that he did not know how to describe; it was undoubtedly, the joy of feeling himself alive, whole, and healthy, but it was something more: the joy that other people exist, that there are different seasons and that no day is just like any other, the joy that he could see animals and flowers, that he could touch trees. On the street, even without returning the glances of others, he sensed that he was participating in an immense community, that he was a part of the world. Even ugly things — a vacant lot littered with garbage and refuse — were in some mysterious way seemingly illumined by an inner incandescence.

"Very interesting," he said, reaching the end of the column. "But there must be more."

"Certainly there is. It's a whole article, rather long, entitled: 'The Young Man of Seventy.' The author is Linda Gray."

He did not try to hide his surprise. "I didn't know she'd taken up writing," he said, smiling.

"She's been writing a long time, and she writes very well," continued Colomban. "But I wanted to be sure that we are in agreement: longevity becomes bearable, and even interesting, *only* if a technique for simple bliss has been discovered beforehand."

"I don't believe it *is* a matter of a technique," he interrupted amiably.

"With all due respect, I beg to differ with you. Do you know any examples of centenarians or quasi-centenarians who live the bliss described by Linda Gray, other than Taoist solitaries, Zen masters, or certain yogis and certain Christian monks? That is, in a word, practitioners of various spiritual disciplines?"

"Plenty of examples are known. Naturally, the majority are peasants, shepherds, fishermen — 'simple folk,' as they are called. They employ no technique, properly speaking. But, obviously, they practice a certain spiritual discipline: prayer, meditation. . . ."

He abruptly ceased speaking, seeing that someone had stopped at their table, a man well along in years, completely bald, smoking from a long cigarette holder made of amber.

"Your discussion's futile," the man said, addressing Colomban. "In both cases, the problem is the same: without that new quality of life of which Linda Gray speaks, longevity is a burden, and perhaps even a curse, and in that case, *what do we do?*"

"This is Dr. Griffith," Colomban said, introducing him. "He was there with us also when it happened."

He interrupted himself and sought his guest's eyes. "Perhaps it would be better if we explain to him what this is all about," he said to the others.

The doctor sat down and continued smoking intently, with his eyes riveted on one of the yellowing chromolithographs on the wall.

"Tell him," he said after a pause. "But begin with the essential. The essential being," he specified, "not Bran's biography, but the significance of the centenary."

Colomban raised both his arms, as if he wanted to interrupt him and cheer him at the same time.

"If you say one more word, Doctor, you'll have to begin with the end."

Then he turned to look at Matei in what seemed to the latter a somewhat provocative way.

"Although you have the reputation of being omniscient, I'm sure you don't know anything about Sean Bran. Even here in Dublin, few still remember him. He was a poet and at the same time a magician and a revolutionary — or rather, an irredentist. He died in 1825, and, thirty years later, in June 1855, his admirers — he still had, at that time, a good number of admirers — set up, in a square, a monument in his honor: a rather mediocre bust, having for its base a rock from the sea. On the same day they planted an oak tree, some three meters behind the statue."

"It was on June 23," Dr. Griffith specified.

"Correct. And five years ago we, the last admirers of the *poet* and *magician* Sean Bran, organized a ceremony in the square that bears his name. We hoped that as a result of this event there would be renewed interest in Bran's work. We were dreaming, because the few of us who prize his poetry today are not at all in sympathy with his magical ideas and practices, whereas the political activists, those who admire his irredentism. . . ."

"You've forgotten the essential," the doctor interrupted. "You forgot about James Joyce."

"That's very important," said Stephens.

"True," Colomban acknowledged. "If the hopes that we linked to *Finnegans Wake* had been fulfilled, Sean Bran would be a famous name today. Because, as you know," he added, seeking his eyes again, "everything that touches the life or work of the Great Man is destined for fame. An oral tradition, whose origin we have not succeeded in identifying, claims that Joyce in *Finnegans Wake* made many allusions to the aesthetics and above all to the *magical concepts* of Bran. This tradition asserts that Joyce refused to specify more or to indicate the context or even the pages where those allusions are located. For years several of us have labored to discover them: so far, without success. If the tradition is authentic, the allusions lie hidden in those 189 pages of *Finnegans Wake* that still await decipherment."

"Only after it had become necessary for us to admit this failure," Dr. Griffith interrupted, "did we decide to celebrate the centenary. Perhaps we made a mistake in choosing not a commemoration of a biographical nature, but the *centenary of a statue.*"

"At any rate," continued Colomban, "when we gathered in the square, we almost expected an irremediable fiasco. The morning had been torrid. . . ."

"It was the twenty-third of June," specified Dr. Griffith.

"Torrid," repeated Colomban, "and now, at the beginning of the afternoon, the sky was like lead. Even those few reporters who had promised us their support did not dare to remain. The smattering of spectators began to leave as soon as they heard the first thunder and felt the first drops of rain. When the storm broke no one was left but we six, the ones who had taken the initiative in holding the commemoration."

The doctor stood up suddenly. "I believe it's time we started for the square," he said. "It's not far."

135

"Still, if a taxi comes our way, we'll take it," Colomban added.

They found one before they reached the end of the block.

"So, there were only the six of us left," Colomban continued. "And because it was raining bucketsful, we took refuge under the oak."

"And of course, at a certain moment," he interrupted him, smiling, "at a certain moment . . ."

"Yes. At a certain moment—when, moreover, we weren't expecting it, because we thought the storm had almost passed, and we were wondering whether we should read the speeches we had in our pockets or whether we should wait for it to clear up in the hope that at least some of the guests would return."

"Yes," Dr. Griffith interrupted, "at a certain moment lightning struck the tree, setting it on fire from top to bottom."

"And yet, it wasn't burned up entirely," Colomban resumed. "Because, as you see," he added after paying the driver and getting out of the cab, "a part of the trunk still remains."

They took several steps forward and stopped at the iron railing surrounding the monument. It was not illuminated, but in the light of the street lamps on the square it could be seen rather well. The rock was impressive the way it stuck up obliquely from the ground, and the bust had acquired a noble, almost melancholic patina. Behind was profiled the thick, mutilated trunk of the oak. One could distinguish the greater portion, burned black, as well as a few timid green branches.

"But why have they left it this way?" he asked. "Why haven't they dug it out and planted another?"

Colomban broke into a short, ironic laugh and began to rub his sideburns nervously. "For the time being, the City considers it—the oak, I mean—an historic monument. Sean Bran has not become popular, but the story of the oak, the oak struck exactly on the centenary of the day it was planted, has been heard all over."

136

They walked slowly around the fence.

"Now you understand," Colomban resumed, "why the problem of Time interests us. It is said, and I'm convinced it's true — my father knew several cases — it is said that those who take shelter under a tree and escape safe and sound when the tree is struck by lightning are destined to live a hundred years."

"I didn't know before that such a belief existed," he said, "but it seems logical."

It was such an impressive spectacle — the marine rock viewed from behind, with that trunk three meters in diameter, peeled, charred, and yet preserving a few living branches — that he asked permission to go back and look at it again.

"Even more curious," the doctor began a little later when they had returned to the front of the statue again, "curious and yet also sad, is the fact that the next day the police discovered a charge of dynamite hidden under the rock's pedestal. If it hadn't rained, it would have exploded during the speeches and destroyed the statue, or at least mutilated it."

On hearing this, Matei stopped walking and sought the speaker's eyes.

"But why?" he asked, lowering his voice. "Who would have been interested in destroying a historic monument?"

Dr. Griffith and Colomban exchanged knowing glances.

"Many," replied Stephens. "First of all, the irredentists, indignant that the revolutionary Bran was being claimed and honored by a few poets, philosophers, and occultists."

"In the second place," continued Colomban, "the church, more precisely the Ultramontanists and obscurantists who see in Bran the prototype of the satanic magician — which is absurd, because Bran follows the Renaissance magical tradition, the conception of Pico or of G. B. Porta. . . ."

"It's unnecessary to go into detail," Griffith broke in. "What is certain is that the ecclesiastical hierarchy is not disposed to accept him."

All four of them were now walking in the middle of the deserted, dimly lit street.

"But," Colomban resumed, "to return to the essential, that is, to our problem: condemned to live a hundred years, what do we do with Time?"

"I'd prefer to discuss this another time," Matei interrupted. "Tomorrow, if you wish, or the day after. Suppose we meet toward evening in a public garden or a park."

He had agreed to meet them again because above all he wanted to find out who Colomban thought he was. At a certain moment he had addressed him as if he considered him a specialist on *Finnegans Wake*. On the other hand, he had saved that page from "A Young Man of Seventy" and he knew who Linda Gray was (he knew the prestige she had acquired as an author).

Stephens escorted him all the way to his hotel. As they were about to separate, after looking all around several times, Stephens said, " 'Colomban' is a pseudonym. And it's better that you know—he practices black magic, he and Dr. Griffith. Ask them what happened to the other three who were with them under the oak tree when the lightning struck! And ask them about the title of the book they're writing in collaboration. . . . No, I'll tell you: *The Theology and Demonology of Electricity*."

He liked the title. He set it down in his private notebook after he had summarized the first meeting and tried to specify the significance of the incident of June 23, 1955. He was intrigued by the fact that the explosion which, for political motives, was to have blown up the statue, had been prevented by the rain and replaced by a bolt of lightning that set fire to the centennial oak. The presence of the dynamite constituted an element characteristic of our contemporary era. From that point of view, the incident looked like a parody, almost a caricature, of the epiphany of lightning. And yet the substitution of the object—the tree instead of the statue—remained enigmatic. But nothing he learned in the three meetings that followed contributed to clarifying the problem.

He was reminded of the title four years later, in the summer of 1964, when, at a colloquium on Jung's *Mysterium*

Conjuctionis, a young man interjected into the discussion the expression, the "eschatology of electricity." He began by recalling the union of opposites in a single totality, the psychological process which, he said, must be interpreted in the light of Indian and Chinese philosophy. For Vedanta as well as for Taoism, opposites are annulled if they are viewed from a certain perspective, good and evil lose their meaning, and, in the Absolute, being coincides with non-being. "But, what no one dares to say," continued the young man, "is that, in the horizon of these philosophies, atomic wars must be, if not justified, at least accepted."

"I, however," he added, "go even further: I justify nuclear conflagrations in the name of the eschatology of electricity!"

The tumult that erupted in the hall obliged the chairman to withdraw the privilege of the floor from him. A few minutes later, the young man left the room. Matei followed him and caught up with him on the street.

"I regret you were kept from expressing your views fully. Personally, I'm very interested in the idea of the 'eschatology of electricity.' What were you referring to exactly?"

The young man looked him over in disbelief, then shrugged. "I'm not in much of a mood for discussion now," he said. "The cowardice of contemporary thought exasperates me. I'd rather have a beer."

"With your permission, I'll join you."

They sat down on the terrace of a cafe. The younger man did not attempt to hide his irritation.

"Probably, I'm the last optimist in Europe," he began. "Like everyone else, I know what's in store for us: hydrogen, cobalt, and so on. But unlike the others, I try to find a meaning in this imminent catastrophe, and thereby reconcile myself with it, as the old man Hegel taught us. The true meaning of the nuclear catastrophe can only be this: the mutation of the human species, the appearance of the superman. I know, atomic wars will destroy populations and civilizations and will reduce a part of the planet to a desert. But this is the price that must be paid if we are to radically liquidate the past and form a new species, infinitely superior to the man of today. Only an enormous quantity of electricity, discharged over a period of several minutes or hours, could modify the psychomental structure of the unfortunate *homo sapiens* that up to now has dominated history. Taking account of the unlimited potential of post-historic man, the reconstruction of a planetary civilization could be achieved in record time. Of course, only a few million individuals will survive. But they will constitute so many million supermen. Therefore, I use the expression the eschatology of electricity; both the *end* and the *salvation of man* will be obtained by means of electricity."

He stopped speaking and, without looking up, drained his glass of beer.

"But why are you so sure that the electricity discharged by nuclear explosions will force a mutation of a superior order? It might just as well provoke a regression of the species."

The young man jerked his head around and gave him a severe, almost furious look.

"I'm not *sure*, but I *want* to believe it will be that way! Otherwise, neither the life nor the history of man would have any meaning. I'd be forced then to accept the idea of cosmic and historical cycles, the myth of eternal repetition. . . . On the other hand, my hypothesis is not only the result of despair; it's based on fact. Have you by chance heard of the experiments of a German savant, Dr. Rudolf?"

"By chance, I have heard. But his experiments, the electrocution of animals, are not conclusive."

"So they say," the young man interrupted him. "But since the Rudolf archive disappeared almost in its entirety, it's hard to judge. At any rate, during the time that that secret archive could be consulted, no indication was found of biological regression. On the other hand, you have read, surely, the novel by Ted Jones, *Rejuvenation by Lightning*."

"No. I didn't know it existed."

"If the problem interests you, you ought to read it. In an afterword, the author leaves the impression that the novel was based on facts; only the nationality and names of the characters were changed."

"And just what is this novel about?" he asked, smiling.

"Jones describes the regeneration and rejuvenation of an old man who was struck by lightning. A significant detail: the lightning struck in the center of the cranial cap. At eighty years of age the character — who, I repeat, is real — does not look more than thirty. Therefore, we are sure at least of one thing: that in certain cases, electricity in massive doses provokes a total regeneration of the human body, hence a rejuvenation. Unfortunately, concerning the modification of the psycho-mental experience the novel gives no precise indications; it only makes allusions to hypermnesia. But you can imagine what radical transformations will be brought by the electricity discharged by several dozens or hundreds of hydrogen bombs."

When Matei rose from the table and thanked him, the young man looked at him for the first time with interest, almost with sympathy. On reaching home, he wrote in his pocket notebook: "July 18, 1964. The eschatology of electricity. I believe that I can add: *The End*. I doubt I shall have occasion to record other events or meetings of equal interest."

And yet, in spite of this, two years later, on the tenth of October 1966, he wrote: "Evacuation of the materials. I receive a new passport." Normally, he would have related these two episodes in detail. Especially the admirable (and mysterious) transfer of the materials. He had received through the bank a letter from an air transport firm advising him that the expenses for the transportation of the boxes of manuscripts and tape recordings had already been paid at a branch in Honduras. In accordance with a previous understanding, one of the employees of the bank in Geneva would come to Matei's residence to supervise the packing of the materials. He was, certainly, a specialist and had been informed of the nature of the objects to be packed. After two large boxes, almost full, had been delivered from the bank, both of them worked until almost sunset. With the exception of the private notebooks and a few personal items, everything was packed in bags and boxes,

sealed, and numbered. For some time he feared that the evacuation of the materials might indicate an imminent catastrophe,
but a consecutive series of dreams reassured him.

Then, although they were succinct and enigmatic, the
notes increased in number and frequency. December 1966:
"I shall have to write him and thank him. The book is more
intelligent than I expected." This referred to the novel that
Jones had sent him. He started to add, "Even more extraordinary, how has he guessed my name and found my address?"
but he decided against it. February 1967: "Inquiry in connection with the destruction of the Dr. Rudolf archive." In April:
"Met R. A. by accident. He tells me in great secrecy that the
preliminary investigations have been concluded. He is certain
now that Dr. Bernard was carrying in the two valises the
most valuable documents (I suspect: The recordings and photostats of the reports of the Professor, and the notebooks of
1938–39)."

On June 3, 1967 he noted: "In India the polemics regarding Rupini-Veronica have begun again. An increasingly large
number of savants doubt the authenticity of the recordings
made at the clinic. The decisive argument: Veronica and her
companion disappeared without trace a little while after the
return of the expedition to Delhi. 'Now that almost twelve
years have passed,' writes a great materialist philosopher, 'any
confrontation with the witnesses has become impossible.' " On
October 12: "Linda received the Pulitzer Prize for her book, *A
Biography*. Whose?"

Then, on June 12, 1968: "Veronica. Fortunately, she did
not see me." After a few moments he added: "In the railway
station at Montreux, with two beautiful children by her side,
explaining to them a tourist advertising poster. She looked her
age, perhaps even somewhat younger. The only thing that
matters: she is happy."

On January 8, 1968 he celebrated his one-hundredth
birthday in a sumptuous restaurant in Nice, in the company
of a young Swedish woman, Selma Eklund, whom he admired
for her intelligent and original interpretation of Medieval drama.
That same month Selma would be twenty-eight, and he avowed,

half in jest, that he was almost forty. But the evening was a failure; probably she was not accustomed to champagne, and before dessert he had to take her back to her hotel. He spent the rest of the evening until after midnight walking on little frequented streets.

He wanted, nevertheless, to mark his "first centennial" (as he liked to call it) by taking a spectacular trip. Many years before, he had been to Mexico, and later to Scandinavia. He wanted now to visit China or Java. But he did not rush to make his decision. I have the whole year at my disposal, he repeated to himself.

One autumn evening he returned home earlier than usual. A hard, chilling rain had forced him to give up his long stroll through the park. He wanted to telephone a girlfriend, but changed his mind, and went to the record cabinet. For a cold night like this, only music . . . Only music, he repeated absently, surprised to find, lost among the records, the family photo album. He pulled it out, frowning. All at once, he felt a chill come over him, as though someone had just opened the window. For a few moments he hesitated, holding the album. *And the third rose?* he heard himself thinking. *Where do you want me to put it? Lay the album down, and show me where you want the rose put. The third rose.*

Baffled, he began to laugh bitterly. I am after all a free man, he said to himself, sitting down in the easy chair. Very carefully and with much excitement he opened the album. A freshly picked rose, maybe such as he had seen but once before, was there in the middle of the page. Happy, he picked it up. He would never have believed a single rose could perfume a whole room. For a long while he hesitated, then he placed it beside him, on the arm of the chair. His eyes came to rest on the first photograph. It was pale, faded, blurred, but he recognized without difficulty his parents' house in Piatra Neamț.

6

It had begun snowing several hours earlier; then, just past

Bacău a blizzard was unleashed; but as the train was entering the station the snow ceased to fall, and in a clear blue sky there rose, twinkling, the first stars. He recognized the square, immaculate beneath the fresh snow, although on all sides stood recently constructed apartment houses. And yet it seemed strange that a few days before Christmas there were so few windows lighted. He stood a long while holding his valise, looking with deep emotion at the boulevard that stretched before him. He came to his senses at the moment when the family with whom he had shared the compartment engaged the last taxi. But the hotel where he had reserved a room was rather close. Turning up the collar of his coat, he crossed the square without haste and set off down the boulevard. Only after reaching his destination did he realize his left arm had become stiff. The valise was heavier than he had supposed. He presented his passport and the receipt of the Office of Tourism.

"You speak Romanian very well," remarked the woman at the reception desk after she had examined his passport. She had gray hair, and was wearing eyeglasses without rims. Her distinguished face and the quality of her voice impressed him.

"I'm a linguist," he explained. "I have specialized in the study of Romance languages. And I've been to Romania before. I've even been to Piatra Neamț. I was a student. . . . By the way, does the Cafe Select still exist?"

"How could it not exist! It's an historic monument. Calistrat Hogaş frequented it — probably you've heard of him."

"Of course!"

"He frequented it from 1869 to 1886, the whole time he was professor here at Piatra Neamț. They say he liked it . . . . You have Room 19, on the third floor. Take the elevator."

"I believe I'll go first to the Select. It isn't far. I'll be back in an hour, an hour and a half."

It seemed to him that the woman was looking at him in wonderment over her spectacles.

"Don't catch cold," she warned. "The streets are still clogged with snow and more snow is forecast."

144

Ten minutes later he was convinced the woman was right: certain streets were indeed clogged and he made his way with difficulty. But in the vicinity of the cafe the sidewalk had been cleared of snow and he walked faster. Outside the door he stopped to catch his breath and calm the beating of his heart. On entering he recognized the smell of beer, of freshly ground coffee, and of cheap cigarette smoke. He headed for the back room, where he and his friends used to gather. The room was almost empty; there were just three men at a table, finishing tankards of beer. That explains why they have only one bulb, the weakest one, lighted on the ceiling — to save electricity. He sat down on the couch next to the wall and stared vacantly. As he waited for the waiter, he did not know whether he would ask for a mug of beer or a bottle of mineral water and a cup of coffee. Soon the three rose noisily from their chairs, preparing to leave.

"We haven't arrived at any conclusion again this time," exclaimed one of them, wrapping a woolen shawl around his neck.

"It doesn't matter!" said the second.

"It doesn't matter!" echoed the third, laughing and looking at the other two knowingly. "You know what I mean," he added.

Alone, he wondered if it was worthwhile waiting for the waiter any longer, when it seemed that someone was approaching him timidly, hesitantly, looking at him curiously. Only when he stopped in front of him did he recognize who it was: Vaian.

"It is you, Cucoane Dominic?" exclaimed Vaian, taking his hand with both of his own hands and shaking it over and over. "Praise God, you've returned! You've returned!"

Then he turned his head and called out, "Doctor! Come quickly. He's back! Cuconul Dominic!"

He was still squeezing his hand, pumping it. A few moments later the whole group invaded the room, with Dr. Neculache in front and Nicodim holding a bottle of Cotnar in his left hand and a half-full glass in his right. They all looked at him closely, repeating his name, exclaiming. He was so moved that he was afraid he would soon feel tears on his cheeks, but with an effort he managed to laugh.

"In other words," he said, "the story begins all over again, from the beginning. I'm dreaming, and when I wake up, it will seem I've just started to dream indeed! Like that story of Chuang-tze and the butterfly."

"Chuang-tze?" Vaian repeated in a whisper. "The story about Chuang-tze and the butterfly?"

"I've told it to you many times," he interrupted, suddenly very well disposed.

Then he heard a voice in the back say, "Send someone to tell Veta!"

"Leave Veta in peace!" he exclaimed. "I'll believe you without Veta. I realize very well I'm dreaming, and that in a minute or two I'll wake up."

"Don't tire yourself, Cucoane Dominic," the doctor spoke up, approaching and laying a hand on his arm. "You've been through a great deal. Don't tire yourself."

He started laughing again. "I know," he began, seemingly trying not to become angry. "I know that all this, our meeting here and all that will follow — all this could have happened really in December 1938."

"But that is when it *is* happening, Cucoane Dominic," Vaian interrupted. "This is December 20, 1938."

"I don't dare tell you what year we are living in, we who are outside this dream. If I were to make the effort I'd wake up."

"You *are* awake, Cucoane Dominic," the doctor said gently. "But you're tired. In fact, you look very tired."

"All right!" he exclaimed suddenly, losing his temper. "Between December 20, 1938 and this evening, many things have happened. The Second World War, for example. Have you heard of Hiroshima? Of Buchenwald?"

"The Second World War?" asked someone in the back. "It's coming, all right; coming fast!"

"Many things have happened since you disappeared

146

and gave us no sign of life," Nicodim began. "Your house has been opened more than once. Books were taken from your library."

"I know, I know!" he interrupted, raising his arm. "I told them what books to look for and bring to me. But that was long ago, long ago."

He was beginning to be irritated by the fact that he could not wake up, even though he knew he was dreaming and he wanted to awaken.

"We've looked all over for you," he heard a familiar voice saying. "The doctor looked for you in several hospitals."

"We heard you'd gone to Bucharest," said Neculache, "and that you were mistaken for someone else there."

"That's what happened," he interrupted. "I was taken for someone else because I was rejuvenated."

He hesitated a moment, then continued triumphantly yet enigmatically.

"Now I can tell you the truth. After the lightning struck me — struck me right on the top of my head — I was rejuvenated. I looked twenty-five to thirty, and after that I didn't change. For thirty years, I've looked the same age."

He noticed how the others were staring at him, and, exasperated, he raised his arms, trying to laugh.

"I know you can't believe it. But if I were to tell you how many other things happened, all on account of the lightning, how many Oriental languages I have learned — that is, I didn't even have to learn them, because it occurred to me all of a sudden that I knew them. What I'm telling you now, it's because I'm dreaming, and no one will know."

"You're not dreaming, Cucoane Dominic," Nicodim insisted gently. "You're here with us, your friends; you're at the cafe. This is what we imagined would happen. When Cuconul Dominic comes to his senses, when he recovers from his amnesia, and returns, you'll see — he'll go straight to the Cafe Select!"

He began laughing again and looked at them all with a sudden intensity, as if he were afraid he would wake up at

147

that very moment and lose all trace of them.

"But if I'm not dreaming, then you would know about Hiroshima and the hydrogen bomb and Neil Armstrong, the astronaut who landed and walked on the moon last summer, in July."

They were all silent, not daring to look at one another.

"So, that's what it was," the doctor spoke up at length. "You were mistaken for someone else."

He started to respond, but he was beginning to feel tired. He wiped his hand across his cheek several times.

"It's like the story of . . . of that Chinese philosopher. . . . You know who; I've told you several times."

"Which Chinese philosopher, Cucoane Dominic?" asked Vaian.

"I told you a little while ago," he replied irritably. "The name escapes me now. That story with the butterfly . . . Anyway, it's too long to repeat again."

He felt a strange fatigue throughout his body, and for a moment he was afraid he was going to faint. But maybe it would be better if I did, he said to himself. If I should faint, I'd wake up immediately.

"I've called for a sleigh to take you home, Domnu Matei," said someone. "Veta has a fire lit in the stove."

"I don't need any sleigh," he managed to say, rising from the table. "I'm going on foot. The next time the problem is raised, I'll know how to answer!"

"What problem, Domnu Matei?" Nicodim asked.

He started to reply, "The problem which worries all of us!"—but suddenly he felt all his teeth rattling, and embarrassed, furious, he clamped his jaws together tightly. Then he took several steps toward the exit. To his surprise, the others moved aside and allowed him to leave. He wanted to go back again and salute them all, raising his arm, but every movement exhausted him. Hesitantly, breathing heavily through his nostrils because he was holding his mouth tightly shut, he went out onto the street. The cold air revived him. I'm beginning to wake up, he told himself. When he thought no one would see him, he cupped his hand to his mouth and spat out his teeth, two or three at a time. He remembered vaguely, like some half-forgotten dream, that this same thing had happened to him once before: for some time he had been unable to speak because all of his teeth were loose. So, it's the same problem! he said to himself calmly, reconciled.

That night the doorman waited in vain for the return of the guest in Room 19. Then, when it began to snow, he telephoned the Cafe Select. He was told that a stranger, a gentleman, had come that evening and had gone directly to the back room. But after a little while, perhaps because the room was empty and poorly lighted, he had left without saying good evening, holding his right hand to his mouth.

In the morning, on strada Episcopiei, in front of house number 18, there was found, frozen, a stranger, very old, in an elegant suit and an expensive fur-lined overcoat. Both the overcoat and the other clothing were much too large for him, leaving no room for doubt that they were not his. Moreover, in the pocket of the jacket a billfold was found containing foreign currency and a Swiss passport bearing the name of Martin Audricourt, born in Honduras, November 18, 1939.

Paris, November–December 1976

Nineteen Roses

Nineteen Roses

1

For several minutes he sat gazing silently out the window. I closed my notebook and stuck it in my pocket.

"If you wish," I ventured finally, "I'll come tomorrow an hour earlier, or even two. And I'll bring the typewritten text."

"For tomorrow," he replied, slowly turning his head, "I've made other plans. . . . Nevertheless," he resumed after a pause, "nevertheless, I believe that's the best solution."

Just then we heard a knocking on the door. Startled, I rose quickly from the easy chair, but the next moment the door opened and in came a tall, blond young man, looking, it seemed to me, abnormally pale. He advanced toward us rather timidly, yet with a firm, resolute step.

"I beg your pardon," he said, heading toward the desk. "Are you domnul Anghel D. Pandele? The Maestru?"*

"But what do you want?" I interrupted.

As if he didn't hear me, he approached the desk and repeated his question. "Maestre Dumitru Anghel Pandele? The writer?"

*Maestru in Romanian is a form of address equivalent to "maestro," but is not limited chiefly to musicians. Maestru (vocative Maestre) is used in reference to any artist (writer, painter, or musician) enjoying wide recognition.

153

"I am," replied Pandele, smiling in his usual enigmatic and somewhat ironic way.

The young man stopped in front of the chair beside the typewriter and passed his left hand across his forehead several times.

"I beg your pardon," he murmured, "but in that case . . ."

He breathed deeply, then continued, gradually raising his voice and pronouncing his words slowly, with solemnity.

"Please don't be angry, but in that case . . . in that case you are — please excuse me for telling you this . . . but you are my parent, my father. . . ."

At that, Pandele sat down on the chair and turned his head toward me desperately, as though imploring me to come to his rescue. I don't know why, but that look of his, like that of a condemned man, annoyed me.

"How did you get into the house?" I asked, taking a step toward the young man.

"Through the kitchen. I found the door open, and so . . ."

"And why have you come?" I interrupted. "Is it an attempt at blackmail? Are you suffering from schizophrenia, or what?"

"Please, don't get upset," he said, rising slowly, with dignity. "I knew it would be hard, even painful. But I had to do it. I promised. . . ."

"Promised whom?" asked Pandele.

Pandele appeared calm, somewhat indifferent, but I knew him well. I knew that, as he liked to say, he was a prey to that maligned but noble vice of curiosity.

"My fiancée, Niculina. I promised her I'd come to ask your consent. Your consent to our marriage," he specified, flushing slightly. "Of course, it's just a formality. We aren't asking for anything else. And we won't tell anyone. If you don't like us, we won't come back again."

As I listened, I realized I could find him very congenial. In another outfit and minus a tie, he would have been an

154

interesting young man; he had the profile of an Alexandrian medallion.

"Your name?" asked Pandele.

"Serdaru. Laurian Serdaru. I'm twenty-eight, and both Niculina and I are graduates of the Conservatory in Bucharest. But I'm a swimming instructor at Uricani Factory, while Niculina gives private lessons in French and Latin."

Pandele continued to look him straight in the eye, deeply, concentrating. He was no longer smiling.

"But, actually, what makes you believe you could be my son? Did your mother tell you that?"

Again the young man passed his hand across his brow several times.

"No. Mother never told me anything about it. I suspect, however, that she intended to tell me after I had finished lycée. But Mother died when I was nine."

"Then how," I interrupted him, "do you know that she would have told you this later, after you had finished lycée?"

Serdaru turned his head toward me; he was as pale now as he had been when he first entered the study. "I don't believe I have the right to reveal that," he said after a moment.

"Actually," Pandele intervened, "if you don't know it from your mother, where did you get the idea? Who told you?"

The youth looked back and forth at each of us, and his face shone, as if he had just remembered a wonderful secret.

"I know it from Niculina. She discovered it this past winter, before we were engaged. She discovered it at Predeal, during the time of the rehearsals. We were rehearsing *Steaua sus răsare* (The Star Is Rising); both of us had parts as extras."

Pandele shrugged, and I surmised that the whole episode was beginning to amuse him. "I don't understand," he said with his inimitable false gravity.

"You're quite right not to understand, because things are more complicated than they seem at first glance. What I mean is, you couldn't understand before knowing that at first we were rehearsing *Orpheus in the Underworld*. We'd been rehearsing it for some three weeks; and in that play, in the last act, we had

155

parts—modest ones, of course, but anyhow we weren't just extras. Then, all of a sudden, the administration—probably they'd received orders from the Center—the administration decided to break off the rehearsals. And because the Christmas holidays were approaching, they replaced *Orpheus* with *The Star Is Rising*. You know," he added, lowering his voice, "*The Star Is Rising* is considered, and rightly so, the most successful antireligious comedy—or 'antiobscurantist' as they say."

He ceased speaking and stared at Pandele as though expecting something—a response, a gesture.

"I still don't understand."

"Doesn't this switching of programs remind you of anything?"

"No."

"It's true, almost thirty years have passed since then. . . . But, pardon me for asking: didn't you thirty years ago write *Orpheus and Eurydice*, a tragedy in two acts and five scenes?"

Pandele relaxed in his easy chair and, leaning his head back slightly, he began to laugh. He seemed in very good spirits, and I wondered why.

"But how on earth did you find out about *Orpheus and Eurydice*? That's the only play I ever wrote in my life; it was never played and I never published it, except for some excerpts in reviews of that day."

"It was a play in blank verse," Serdaru resumed, "a play more religious than philosophical, although it bore the subtitle, 'Introduction to the Most Ancient Metaphysics.' "

"Most of all, it was a bad play, precious and artificial."

"But once, once only, in December 1938, rehearsals for it were held. At the National Theater in Sibiu."

"You've found out about that too?" exclaimed Pandele, even more amused. "It is true: rehearsals were started, but after about three weeks the director of the theater, Mithu, resigned—he was forced to resign, in fact—and the new director took my play off the program."

Serdaru listened fascinated, unable to stop looking

156

straight into Pandele's eyes.

"That week you were at Sibiu. You attended rehearsals. And you stayed on after the rehearsals were stopped, hoping to persuade the new director. . . ."

"I was naive, very naive."

"You were young. . . ."

"Not so young, really," Pandele interrupted, smiling melancholically. "I had recently turned thirty-three."

They both fell silent, no longer looking at each other directly. I felt I must intervene, and do so as quickly as possible.

"But I still don't understand. I don't understand what connection the one has with the other. . . . Just that in both instances there was an interruption of the rehearsals."

Serdaru gave me a look of gratitude, as if I had extricated him from a great predicament. "I didn't understand either, until Niculina pointed it out to me. She noticed that, in both cases, rehearsals of plays representing Orpheus' descent into Hades were halted a little before Christmas. And in both cases there followed a play evoking the mystery of the Nativity, the birth of Jesus in Bethlehem."

"But," interrupted Pandele, "you know that *The Star Is Rising* was written much later; it was written some seven or eight years ago."

The young man looked at us both again, smiling mysteriously. "I'm not referring to the antiobscurantist comedy, Aurel Veriga's play, but to the song of the star, 'Steaua sus răsare, ca o taină mare . . .' (The star is rising like a great mystery). Because, I repeat, you were at Sibiu, and Christmas was approaching."

"True. It had begun snowing, and I was afraid the trains would be snowed in. . . . As it happened, in fact," he added dreamily.

"You spent the first days of Christmas at Sibiu," Serdaru continued, "and then you suggested to several actors and actresses who had been rehearsing *Orpheus and Eurydice* that they organize a Christmas performance: carols, the song of the star. . . ."

Pandele listened to him pensively, slightly frowning, squinting now and then.

"I don't believe it was *I* who had that idea," he said at length, in a low voice. "Otherwise, I'd remember. All I remember is that I was very depressed because I had failed to persuade the new director to perform my play and also, especially, because I couldn't be in Bucharest for Christmas. I wanted at all costs to spend the holidays in Bucharest."

"And yet," Serdaru persisted, "don't you remember that on Christmas Eve you went with a whole group that included several students from the Conservatory at Cluj—you went with them to the residence of a friend of yours, who was waiting for you with a table prepared, and there, after listening to 'Steaua sus răsare, ca o taină mare,' you told the actors—but you were speaking especially to the actress who had rehearsed the role of Eurydice—you told them that only then had you understood *what a deep and significant resemblance there is between Orpheus and Jesus. . . .*"

Pandele shook his head several times and interrupted him. "No, no you're mistaken! The resemblance between Orpheus and Jesus was something I discovered much later. I even tried to write a novella on that theme, but the subject seemed inappropriate at the time, and I abandoned it. And I don't remember having had any friend at Sibiu who was waiting for me on Christmas Eve with a table spread. The only person I'd begun to be friends with was Mithu, the former director of the theater."

Then I heard for the first time the voice. "Laurian, admit you've failed!"

I turned my head, startled. The large door leading to the drawing room was wide open, and in the doorway, with a valise in her hand, stood a young woman. She was curiously, I should even say provocatively, attired: a very long dress, the color of unripe grapes, which had been, probably, ten or fifteen years earlier, an elegant gown, but since then it had been worn continually and had been adjusted and readjusted numerous times.

158

"But, as you know," she continued, "rarely does anamnesis succeed at the first attempt."

Never had I heard such a voice. It in no way resembled the voice of any other woman, actress, or prima donna that I had ever heard. I rose, embarrassed, and, as I expected he would, Pandele too stood up at his desk a few moments later. He seemed as surprised as I.

"I am the fiancée, Niculina Nicolaie, and I beg your pardon for listening at the door. But it was a matter of great importance to us — especially to me." She set the valise very carefully on the edge of the rug.

Only then, watching her approach us, smiling, and walking with a slow, liturgical gait, alternating long steps with short pauses, as in a processional — only then did I realize how beautiful she was. She approached Pandele and held out her hand, at the same time bowing her head as if presenting herself to royalty.

"I'm happy that finally we can meet, even in such delicate circumstances. Ever since I first read your novels long ago in lycée, I've regretted that you never wanted to write for the theater."

As he admitted to me later, not only was Pandele surprised, but, without understanding why, he was frankly moved. He turned toward me and introduced me.

"Domnul Eusebiu Damian. My tireless secretary and diligent collaborator. If some day you read a volume of memoirs signed with my name, know that in the main it was written by him, by Eusebiu. Because I dictate them to him, and I don't know how to dictate."

Niculina inclined her head slightly but did not offer me her hand.

"I've brought several costumes in the valise," she resumed, "but I don't believe this is the most suitable moment for a 'performance.' We've prepared several skits," she added with a sad smile.

She could not avert her eyes from Pandele's.

"We were thinking of at least four, if not five, dramatic

159

pieces," Serdaru specified. "Depending on how the interview developed."

Pandele gave me a curious look, as if he wished to be convinced he was hearing correctly.

"I'm sorry," he said. "I would have liked to hear you interpreting a great role, right here in my study."

"We were thinking of something else," Niculina interrupted. "Not so much of characters from universal dramatic literature as of traditional plays, with or without masks, but utilizing scenarios of mime and choreography, accompanied by certain ancient melodies, almost forgotten in our day. Laurian, for instance, knows . . ."

"Perhaps you'd better not insist," Serdaru broke in. "The only thing that matters . . ."

"That's true," continued Niculina, "the only thing that matters is that you give us your consent. The wedding will take place tomorrow. In the strictest intimacy, as they say. In fact, there will be just the two of us — and the persons required by law."

"Interesting! Very interesting!" I whispered.

"Indeed, very interesting," Pandele echoed.

He sought my eyes again. Never had I seen him so helpless. If I hadn't known better, I'd have thought him paralyzed by an absurd, inexplicable fright.

"Really, why don't we all sit down?" I exclaimed, pointing with both hands to chairs about the room.

"Indeed, why don't you have a seat?" Pandele repeated, addressing Niculina and preparing to adjust the position of the armchair. Of course, I was beside him in a moment; I knew he had to avoid any physical exertion.

"We thank you," said Niculina, after Pandele had circled the room and reoccupied his seat at the desk. "We thank you from the bottom of our hearts. We've been dreaming of this meeting for 243 days."

"Exactly 243 days," repeated Serdaru. "I counted them again just before we came."

2

I had barely shut the door behind them when Pandele said, "This evening you're eating here with me. I'll ask Ecaterina to throw something together."

I wanted to interrupt, but he didn't give me time. He spoke rapidly, excitedly.

"She knows how to manage. Maybe an omelet with ham and a salad. And we have whiskey, and *ţuică,** and wine. I say, let's begin with a whiskey. But perhaps you'd prefer a *ţuică.*"

"No, I'll drink a whiskey too. But I must inform you," I added quickly, "that Ecaterina left at three or three-thirty."

Pandele was walking toward his chair at the desk, but he wheeled around suddenly and looked at me in surprise. "But what came over her? Why did she leave like that, without telling us?"

I held out to him the page torn from the calendar. In five short propositions, written in capital letters—the only letters she could write with any accuracy—Ecaterina excused herself. Hearing him "dictating inspired," she had not dared to enter the study to inform him she was leaving again for twenty-four hours. Her reason: this time she was sure she had seen *him* (Ioanid, the seducer) in a car, and she knew where to find him.

"Very well," he said, crumpling the page from the calendar, "it doesn't matter. We'll manage without Ecaterina." He paused; then smiling he resumed: "But where was the message posted this time?"

"It was fastened to the Japanese lantern."

I was ready to tell him how I'd found it there. A little while after Niculina had begun speaking to us about the rehearsals at Predeal, I suddenly thought about Ecaterina, and I wondered how she had allowed a stranger to enter, especially one dressed so oddly and carrying a valise. I got up quietly

*Ţuică (pronounced tzuí-ka) is a dry plum brandy, the Romanian version of slivovitz.

and almost tiptoed into the parlor. There I discovered quickly the calendar page on the shade of the Japanese lamp, attached, as usual, with a ten bani stamp.

"Actually," Pandele interrupted me, "it doesn't matter. Sit down and tell me: what do you think of all that's happened? Weren't you shocked?"

"Yes, indeed! I was shocked from the start. . . ."

"It is indeed extraordinary," he interrupted me again, seemingly more excited. "It's extraordinary that that young stranger who believes he's my son came to talk to me about *Orpheus and Eurydice* less than an hour after I'd recalled to you that anniversary with Mihail Sebastian, Camil Petrescu, and many other writers and artists when we spent almost the whole night talking about theater — when we discussed the possibility of reinterpreting classical myths and I spoke about the myth of Orpheus."

I stared at him, perplexed; I didn't know quite what to say. "You never actually spoke to me about all this. You just said, 'I suddenly realized I was thirty-three . . . ,' and you fell into a kind of reverie. You gazed out the window and for a long while I didn't dare interrupt your meditation."

"And yet," Pandele resumed, "I spoke to you about the symbolism of the age thirty-three — the age of Jesus — and I began to recall the discussions we had that night when I almost quarreled with Camil, because he challenged *en bloc* all attempts to update classical myths, while I maintained, at least in the case of Orpheus and Eurydice, that a contemporary dramatization was possible. . . ."

I pulled the notebook out of my pocket and opened it to the last page. "If you will, allow me to read your last sentences as I took them down in shorthand. You said: 'As I did every year, on that evening of September 21 I invited all my friends to my house. But that year *something*, I don't quite know what, but something seemed different. Suddenly I realized I had reached the age of thirty-three.' And after that you were silent and turned your face toward the window."

I was afraid I had upset him, and I didn't dare lift my

eyes from the notebook.

"Curious," he said at length. "I was sure I'd dictated more. Perhaps I was dictating to myself mentally. . . . But, at any rate, wasn't it a striking coincidence?"

"Yes indeed. But other things struck me, too. For instance, I don't understand how Niculina knew that one of the keys to the front door is always hidden under the mat. . . ."

"Never mind that!" he interrupted me, without trying to control his impatience. "Women of her type have a devilish sort of intuition, almost a kind of divination. But what do you say about her audacity when she took off that awful dress of an old cocotte, the second time, and started to dance in black tights, clapping her hands? Did you notice how elegantly she raised her arms over her head and how she snapped her fingers as though she had castanets?"

For some time I'd been wanting to say that I was thirsty, that I'd gladly drink a glass of whiskey and soda, but that I'd even be satisfied with a big glass of water. But I didn't dare interrupt him.

"What did that dance remind you of? I mean, the second dance, which for me was the most successful, the most fascinating?"

"To tell you the truth," I confessed, "I didn't get to see very much of it. I had gone into the bedroom to answer the other telephone, and when I returned, Niculina had almost finished the dance. She just made a few movements, knelt, then put on the dress and returned to her seat in the armchair."

Pandele stared at me, frowning, as he does when he hasn't understood me very well.

"I believe you're confused," he said. "The telephone rang later, after the third 'performance,' as they called it, had started, the one in which the boy had the principal role. . . . But, anyway, it doesn't matter," he continued without giving me a chance to reply. "I liked the second dance best. It reminded me of the dance of Salome in the play by Oscar Wilde, which I saw in my youth, in Berlin. But it reminded me also of Indian dances, of the performances of Udhai Shankar."

"I've seen them too, three years ago, here in Bucharest. But," I ventured, standing up suddenly, "I'd very much like a glass of soda to drink. I know where it is," I continued, starting for the kitchen. "I'll bring a bottle of whiskey, too."

When I returned, I found him pacing the floor, preoccupied, with his hands behind his back.

"You know, this adventure is beginning to interest me," he said, after I had offered him the glass and the bottle of whiskey. "Of course, the whole story about his mother who would have told him the truth after he finished lycée, and that inscription which, according to Niculina's interpretation, reveals the boy's paternity — the whole story seems an obvious fabrication. The children came here with another end in view. But *what?* What do you think? What do you believe they're after?"

I didn't care to speak the whole truth, to confess what I believed, namely that the inscription in *The Mill Wheel,* Pandele's most popular novel: "Sibiu, Christmas, 1938, Orpheus, *Steaua sus răsare"* — the inscription to which Serdaru's mother had added later, in 1945: "For Laurian, when he is grown, so that he will understand and forgive us" — that the inscription was, as Niculina had observed, as troubling as it was mysterious.

"According to the impression they made on me," I began after a brief pause, "I believe they're both very enthusiastic about theater, about what they call 'spectacle.' And she, the girl, is certainly a great artist — perhaps that's why she hasn't found a place in any theater and earns her living by giving lessons in French and Latin. In any event, both of them look upon play-acting as a sacred 'spectacle.' "

"So then?" Pandele interrupted me, obviously disappointed with my interpretation. "Why then did they come to me? They knew very well I'm not a playwright, and even if I wanted to, I couldn't do anything for them."

"My impression is that, taking 'spectacle' seriously, considering it as a ritual, they came to ask your consent to the ritual of their marriage."

Pandele was silent for some time. Then he picked up

his glass and began to sip slowly, pensively.

"It could be that, too," he said. "That's why I played along with their game and gave them my consent. Actually, why shouldn't I have given it? What does it cost me?" he added, trying (but without success) to imitate the vulgarity of Paraschiv Simionescu, his great rival. "It was just a formality."

"But you saw that for them, especially for the girl, your consent was more than a mere formality. It was a true ritual. You saw how moved she was when they were leaving and she fell suddenly to her knees, grasped your hand, kissed it, and said, '*Bénissez-nous, mon père!*' "

I realized instantly that I had made a blunder, but I didn't understand why. Pandele stared at me quizzically.

"Yes, it was an awkward moment," he said at length. "I didn't expect her to fall to her knees right in front of me and kiss my hand. I didn't know what to do."

"In your place," I ventured, "I'd have stood up and kissed her on both cheeks."

Pandele gave me a look of surprise, almost of fury.

"But that's what I did!" he exclaimed. "Except that I didn't kiss both her cheeks. I kissed her on the forehead and afterward on one cheek."

I felt myself blushing, and that symptom of weakness humiliated me.

"I beg your pardon. Perhaps I didn't see well. I was standing by the door, glad that they had finally decided to leave, and certain gestures must have escaped me."

Pandele stared at me, frowning harder and harder.

"Eusebiu," he began finally, very gravely, "if I hadn't known you all these years, I'd think that you wanted to make fun of me, or else that you were in the last degree of exhaustion from overwork."

"Why, Maestre?" I asked, intimidated.

"Because the scene with the falling to the knees and the kissing of my hand didn't take place at the door when they were leaving. It happened much earlier, after the third performance, when both of them approached me. I had just risen from my chair at the desk to congratulate them, and they approached me, the boy took her hand, as if he were going to present her to me, and she bowed deeply, and then . . ."

"You're right!" I exclaimed, and, not knowing what else to do, I put my hand to my forehead. "That's how it was, just as you say. Now I remember very well."

But I said all this out of desperation, because I didn't want to make him angry. The fact of the matter was, *the scene had happened the way I had said: when they were leaving, at the door.* Niculina had put on her dress for the last time and had even picked up her valise. But the moment I opened the door for them, she dropped the bag and fell on her knees.

"You're tired," Pandele said, continuing to stare at me suspiciously. "You ought to slow down with your nocturnal adventures. You aren't twenty any longer!"

3

The next morning I was awakened by the telephone.

"I hope you've had enough rest," he began in a hearty voice. "And I hope you aren't angry if I allowed myself, last evening, to be so frank with you."

I mumbled a few words in reply, but I don't believe he heard them.

"Forget that, please," he continued. "I inquired around and found out that the ceremony will be held at the Court House of Sector IV, at 11:00 today. Go buy nineteen roses, please, and at the end of the ceremony, give the bouquet to Niculina on my behalf, with these words. . . ."

I felt my heart beating faster and faster, and I interrupted him, very much excited. "Just a moment, please, till I find a pencil."

When I put the receiver to my ear again, I heard him coughing. "I choked," he began with some hesitation. "Imagine: last night, after you left, I was taken with a terrible urge to smoke. I went then to the Select and purchased a pack of

American cigarettes."

At first I thought he was kidding me. I remembered Ioniţǎ's indignation. "It's impossible!" he had said, "and it's proof of bad upbringing, to invite people to your house and then, at the door, show them a sign with carved letters: 'Smoking is strictly prohibited.' You can do this if you're ill, or if you're allergic to tobacco smoke, but he, A. D. P., is neither one nor the other!"

". . . and by midnight," he added in a tone that sounded provocative, almost aggressive, "I had smoked the whole pack! As in the good old days . . ."

"I didn't know you had ever smoked."

"I smoked a great deal in my youth," he continued in the same tone. "I smoked a very great deal. That's why I had to give it up."

Probably he tried to laugh, but he choked again, coughing. When I thought he could hear me, I asked him, "What words shall I write on the card?"

He hesitated for some time. "Perhaps it would be better if you presented the bouquet without any card. Just say, 'On behalf of domnul Anghel D. Pandele.' "

"Shall I say you wish them happiness, or luck, or something else like that?"

Again, a long pause. I surmised that he had not succeeded in deciding what to say, and as usual in such situations he was about to lose his temper.

"No!" he exclaimed brusquely. "I don't think it's necessary to add anything else. A bouquet of nineteen roses, presented by yourself, my friend and coworker, is enough, I believe. And if it's not asking too much of you," he added, "come to see me immediately after the ceremony."

As I had expected, when I entered the flower shop I found the roses had already been selected by him, by telephone. And of course he had selected the ones with the longest stems. I felt a little ridiculous carrying that enormous bouquet in my arms, especially since I had made the mistake of wearing my best suit, the only one A. D. P. liked. Fortunately, I found a cab rather quickly. I arrived at the courthouse at ten minutes before eleven, and excitedly climbed the stairs. The waiting room was crowded. Making my way through the throng, I tried to catch sight of Niculina. All at once I realized that my nervousness was accentuated by the thought that Niculina might be wearing that hideous dress. I didn't dare imagine myself bowing in front of her and offering her, with some solemnity, the bouquet of roses.

But after searching the hall from one end to the other without setting eyes on the couple, I was seized by panic. Maybe the ceremony had already taken place, or maybe it was being held at that very moment in another room. I asked the first man I met if there were other waiting rooms. He didn't know, but he directed me to the information office. Several persons were already there, waiting. At last I reached the window, but I didn't know very well what to ask. At first I was intimidated by the tired, severe voice of the young woman clerk, as I helplessly struggled to protect the roses, but luckily she began to laugh. The first thing she asked me were the names of the young people. After I had repeated them three times, she lifted her eyes from the register and informed me, somewhat disappointedly, "They aren't here. Perhaps you have the wrong courthouse. Perhaps they're at Sector 5 on strada Colonel Locusteanu."

"They're both actors," I insisted. "Perhaps those are their stage names, pseudonyms."

The clerk looked at me wonderingly for a long moment, then smiled. "But then, how could I identify them?"

"Indeed, it seems almost impossible."

Embarrassed, I thanked her and made my way to the exit. As soon as I reached the street I looked at my watch: eleven-thirty. I hesitated, wondering if I ought to call A. D. P., when, some ten or fifteen meters away, in a pickup truck which at that moment was just starting to leave, I thought I saw Niculina's silhouette. (Actually, I recognized her dress.) I began running, shouting her name, but very likely she didn't hear me, and in a few moments the truck had disappeared around the corner.

I waited on the sidewalk for half an hour for a taxi to pass, but in vain. Eventually, I took the trolleybus to the C. A. Rosetti Statue; then I headed for Pandele's residence. I walked slowly, because I felt tired, but especially because I didn't know what to say to him. I wondered if I ought to tell him I had seen — or, at least, *thought* I had — the silhouette of Niculina.

To my surprise, Ecaterina was waiting for me at the front door. "He's gone!" she exclaimed. "He packed a suitcase and left!"

In order not to betray my surprise and disappointment, I held out the bouquet of roses to her.

"I believe we ought to put them in the big vase, the big white one in the parlor. And with plenty of water." I started off calmly in the direction of the study. Ecaterina followed me meekly, carrying the flowers in both arms, like a baby.

"First there was a very long phone call, at 9:30," she began mysteriously. "After that, he asked me to bring him his new suitcase, the one with the tag. I started to help him, but he said he'd do it himself. Then he made a phone call. . . ."

"Didn't he leave any message for me?"

"Yes indeed. He left you an envelope on the desk — a *sealed envelope*." She stressed the last words.

Evidently, he had sealed it to be sure Ecaterina wouldn't open it. Seeing that she kept standing next to me, curious, hoping to guess the content of the letter from my facial expression, I pointed gently to the roses.

"If you don't trim the stems and put them in water immediately, they'll wilt."

As I had feared, the message was laconic and enigmatic. "Decisive events seem about to happen in the immediate future. Decisive and important for both of us. I don't know how long I will be gone. Please be, as before, my deputy in this study. And whatever may happen, the *Memoirs* are to appear at the date set by the publishing house." I put the letter in my pocket and went to the kitchen.

"What does he say?" Ecaterina asked. "What's the matter?"

169

"He doesn't say what the matter is. Probably a theme for a novel. You know, things like this happen whenever he gets obsessed by an idea for a new novel."

"Or perhaps," Ecaterina interrupted, smiling slyly, "perhaps he's met a new heroine. Like three years ago."

"That could be, too. We'll find out later."

It was that way the time before: we had found out the truth last of all, just a few days before he returned. We both learned of it through an indiscretion: Ecaterina from the chauffeur, I from the secretariat of the publisher. A. D. P. had not disappeared in order to begin a new novel. He had secluded himself at Sighişoara with a coed from the School of Journalism.

"We'll find out later," I reported. "In the meantime, we'll attend to things. I'll come every afternoon and work till evening. You, if the telephone rings, will answer always in the same way: that domnul Pandele has gone away, and if the caller wants to know more, he should call me here, between two and six. *Only in the event that the Maestru himself should call, morning or evening*—only in that case, call me immediately at home."

Ecaterina listened to me with an absent look, carefully separating the roses one from another.

"You know, there was someone here last evening," she began in a mysterious voice. "Or maybe there were several. They smoked nineteen cigarettes; I counted them, because since they didn't have an ashtray, they crushed them out on a plate."

"I know," I interrupted her. "The Maestru telephoned me this morning. . . . But how is it you've come back so soon? I was expecting you at three, three-thirty."

Whenever he brought up the matter of Ioanid's disappearance, Ecaterina lost her unbearable air of mistress of the house and softened, becoming almost humble.

"I was mistaken," she said in a hushed voice, blushing. "It wasn't him." Then, lest I should see she was crying, she concentrated on the roses.

"At any rate," I added, "so long as the Maestru is away, it would be better if you stayed home as much as possible."

At the door I turned and asked, "How did he leave? By taxi, or did a car come for him? Or the limousine of the Society?"

Without looking up, because she had pricked herself several times already cutting the stems of the roses, Ecaterina answered in a bored, almost forced tone.

"Not by car, or taxi, or limousine of the Society. It was a sort of pickup truck, old and rusty. I was ashamed for the neighbors to see us, so I came back in the house quick."

4

Depressed, I sat down at the desk. If he thought he was in love with Niculina, and was hoping for a new adventure, it meant that A. D. P. hadn't understood anything, or that he didn't want to understand. I regretted now I hadn't told him the truth, firmly: that in all probability, Laurian was his son. Although enigmatic, the inscription on the flyleaf of the novel, *The Mill Wheel* — "Sibiu, Christmas, 1938, Orpheus, *Steaua sus răsare*," — revealed its meaning through the words added in pencil seven years later: "For Laurian, when he is grown, so that he will understand and forgive us." Niculina had guessed rightly: Serdaru's mother was the actress who was to have played the role of Eurydice in Pandele's play. A little while before her death at the hospital, she had entrusted the volume to a friend, with the request that he deliver it to the boy after he had taken his baccalaureate. At that time, in Sibiu, in December 1938, when she was rehearsing the role of Eurydice, she was married to Doctor Serdaru, but a few years later they separated. She did not remarry, and the doctor died in the last year of the war. Laurian was raised by an aunt. He had seen the doctor only a few times, because the latter lived in Cluj; and the only objects left behind by his mother were a little silver cross and the one copy of *The Mill Wheel* with that mysterious inscription. . . . All these things I reconstructed from Serdaru's narration, interrupted by dances and pantomimes.

Feeling ill at ease, I got up from the desk and headed toward the chair where Niculina had sat at first. Obviously, I ought to have asked him how they had counted those 243 days: had they counted them one by one, tearing pages off a calendar? But I was still dumbfounded, and a little while after that Niculina had told us how she had recalled the inscription as soon as she had seen the announcement for *Steaua sus răsare*. With a few surprisingly big steps, she was beside the valise; she took out the book and the next moment she was at the desk showing him the lines written there in ink and in pencil. But Pandele did not seem impressed.

"It's a copy of the first edition," he said.

Niculina looked deeply into his eyes, moved, with a great sadness in her gaze; then she returned to the still-open valise and replaced the book between what appeared to be two layers of veils.

"We ought to try anyway," she whispered to Serdaru.

The young man rose solemnly from his chair and, looking very pale, he addressed Pandele, pronouncing his words slowly.

"The first 'spectacle'! Pantomime based on an Indian legend. Matsyendranath, suffering from amnesia as a prisoner of the women in the land of Kadali."

We were so surprised and in a way fascinated listening to those exotic names that we didn't notice when Niculina slipped off her dress and was left in a silver-gray jersey. I saw her bending slowly, letting her hands touch the carpet, beginning to caress it, sleepily, and I thought I heard her murmuring unintelligible words. But I soon realized it was not she who was murmuring them, but Serdaru, who was still standing close to the wall. A little while later I heard him singing a strange, sad melody, and only then did I notice he had turned up the collar of his coat, hiding his tie and shirt. He looked now like a different man, older, with a lock of gray hair falling over his forehead and his eyes half closed. But when did he take out a stubby little whistle from which came forth improbable sounds — resembling the grunting of a wild animal, blending gradually into a long sigh, an unnatural lamentation, in which it seemed to me I heard the approach of a tempest, with the noise of great, heavy branches breaking? To be sure, I had been following Niculina's pantomime, as had A. D. P., and I had not observed Serdaru's movements. The cry of a wounded wild boar brought me suddenly to my senses, almost frightening me—and only then did I see the whistle.

I was recalling that detail, sprawled in Niculina's armchair, staring at the ceiling, when the telephone rang. It was Ghiţă Horia, the director of the publishing house.

"Well, what are the instructions?" he asked sarcastically.

"The Maestru has left for the country, and meanwhile. . . ."

"I know, I know," he interrupted. "He phoned me this morning and told me he was going away for some time, 'to attend to duties' — that's just what he said, 'to attend to duties' —but he added that he would leave you precise instructions."

I didn't want him to realize my predicament. "If it has to do with the first volume of his *Memoirs* . . . ," I began.

"It's not about the *Memoirs*," he interrupted me again, irritated. "He spoke to me about a sensational project: a volume of drama, and he told me he'd leave you precise instructions."

"I know nothing about it."

"Then he was just kidding me!" he exclaimed, slamming down the receiver.

I began to pace the floor, nervous and perplexed. I didn't know what to think. Not twenty-four hours before, A. D. P. had declared that in his whole life he had written but a single play, *Orpheus and Eurydice,* and that, he had said, was pretentious and artificial. In his archive of manuscripts—at least in the files that were available to me—I had never come across any notes relative to the theater. I had never even found the manuscript or a typed copy of the five scenes of *Orpheus and Eurydice.*

At last I sat down in the chair at the desk, took the letter out of my pocket, and reread it carefully. "Decisive and important events"; but why "important for *us both*"? Perhaps, speaking to him on the telephone this morning, one of them — Serdaru or Niculina — had revealed other particulars about the rehearsals at Sibiu in the winter of 1938. Probably there are other witnesses still alive. Otherwise, how would Serdaru have known that Pandele had suggested the actors go caroling with the star at his friend's house? How would Serdaru know what Pandele had said to them, that only then had he understood *how profound and significant the resemblance between Orpheus and Jesus is*?

All of a sudden I found myself wondering: how did Niculina manage to remove her dress so quickly, and in so many ways? I couldn't be sure now at which "spectacle" she had removed it by pulling it over her head, and at which she had let it drop to her feet, stepping out of it as out of a laundry basket. And there were many other things that intrigued me. I didn't understand how Niculina had changed her jerseys — first silver, then black, then the color of ripe prunes, then black again — or how the veils and scarves seemed to appear and disappear, until after the last "spectacle" she collected them carefully and put them into the valise. And how had Serdaru changed his appearance and age, his hair seeming to be sometimes almost gray and at other times red, gleaming like copper in the sunlight? He removed things several times from the valise: once a mask (which he actually never used), another time several handkerchiefs, which he distributed meticulously among his various pockets. I had not remembered to take notice of the appearance of other objects, although he used several instruments — musical instruments, I'd call them, although quite small, minuscule, but which altogether took up considerable space, as I saw when he gathered them up in the valise before leaving.

I could find only one explanation: the two had studied not only dramatic arts, dance, and music but also certain sleight-of-hand tricks. Perhaps that is why they impressed us so profoundly that sometimes, when one of the performances ended, neither Pandele nor I could utter a word but just looked at each other, blinking our eyes as though waking from sleep.

I came to my senses at the sound of Ecaterina's footsteps.

"I'll bet you haven't eaten anything since morning, and it's almost two-thirty. Can I fix you something? A fried egg or an omelet? We have also cheese and fruit," she added, staring at me, I thought, with some wonder.

Of course, I chose the omelet. Ecaterina was unsurpassed; she had learned the recipe from the famous Felix.

"But before you fix the omelet, I'll have something to drink: a *ţuică* — or better yet, a whiskey. I feel rather tired."

In the dining room, I sat down at the table with the glass in my hand. I remembered that A. D. P. had held his glass in the same way when he was talking with Serdaru and Niculina about their conception of dramatic performance. He held it in his hand, turning it around slightly, as though he could not bear to bring it to his lips. Probably he was troubled; perhaps he realized he could no longer remember the sequence of the dances and pantomimes. . . . On the way home that night I had asked myself if it were not perhaps something more serious, the beginning of the loss of memory, provoked by poor circulation. I even thought about telephoning the Professor, but finally I had decided to wait a day or two.

Seeing Ecaterina coming with the omelet, I swallowed half the glass of whiskey quickly, without stopping. At the same time I remembered how elegantly Pandele had put the glass to his lips, and I felt myself beginning to blush.

"The roses weren't all fresh," she said, "or maybe you didn't know how to hold the bouquet right. I had to throw six of them out."

I thought she spoke these last words with a touch of sadness in her voice, and I tried to console her.

"There are still thirteen roses left — thirteen, a lucky number!" I exclaimed, smiling.

"Don't make God angry!" Ecaterina whispered, crossing herself quickly.

175

5

The next morning dawned hot, presaging a torrid day, and I left home early, immediately after breakfast.

"The phone's ringing right now," Ecaterina announced, greeting me. "It's rung three times." But as soon as I put my hand on the receiver, the ringing stopped.

"It's hot," I said, "and Bucharestians lose patience quickly."

In the parlor I paused in front of the blue vase. There were eleven roses left, and this time I noticed their fragrance. On the desk a pile of letters was waiting, together with several packages: books of poetry with long dedications and, from the publishing house, the proofs of the most recent edition of *The Mill Wheel*. As usual, the majority of the letters were from fans or young professors and journalists in the provinces, announcing various projects — articles, studies, "original interpretations" — and requesting biographical or bibliographical inforation. To such letters I replied directly via the typewriter according to models established three or four years earlier. A. D. P. merely signed them, and sometimes, when he was rushed or out of sorts, he would ask me to sign for him.

Because over the past year *The Mill Wheel* had been republished repeatedly, I had read and reread it so many times that I couldn't bear to go over it again. Fortunately, I could count on the proofreaders of the publishing house. "But when will there be another masterpiece?" friends and acquaintances kept asking me. I invented all sorts of excuses; most recently I had spoken about the *Memoirs*. It could become A. D. P.'s most important book, I told them, because it is the most candid, the most personal. But I knew I was exaggerating; as a matter of fact, it wasn't a *real* book, a written work, because he was dictating it to me; and, as he often said, he didn't know how to dictate, while I didn't dare interfere very much with the fabric of the prose. The truth was that for several years A. D. P. hadn't written anything other than a few excellent letters — which he did not always address to friends or fellow writers, but to persons chosen at random, to the first name that struck his eye in the morning when the urge to write was upon him: an unknown reader, a lycée pupil still learning to spell, an old pensioner he had met by chance on a bench in Cişmigiu Park, a distant relative who had wished him a happy New Year. In vain had I tried to persuade him to reply to some of the more important letters he had received. The mood struck him but rarely, and, he said, only in the morning; and although I kept those few important letters in a large manila envelope above the dictionaries in the bookcase, he pretended not to be able to find them.

I worked without enthusiasm but productively, copying the model responses. As I was just beginning the fifth letter, I suddenly remembered this detail: when Niculina had begun to dance in an increasingly frenzied way, whirling round and round and flinging her arms now to the right, now to the left, it seemed to me that for a few moments she had bared her breasts so that she resembled an Asian maenad, her hair twisting around her back, shoulders, and chest like writhing serpents. I believe I clenched my teeth, because I was afraid she'd begin to shriek at any moment. But that wild frenzy lasted less than a minute, and suddenly the rhythm of the dance changed, becoming slow, almost lazy. Then, half-consciously, I saw her gathering her hair in a crest on top her head, enclosing it in a kind of turban of cherry-colored cloth, and indeed — but I can't explain how she did it — I saw she had a turban of silk. A little while later she waved it several times, then she stood stock-still, hieratically, resembling a statue, and only then did she utter a cry, a few short guttural words in an unknown tongue. Then her usual smile and serene look returned. Niculina turned to Pandele and almost whispered, "A Syrian spell for calming the sea."

I rose abruptly from the desk and headed toward the chair where I had sat. Perhaps only from that angle was it possible to see how she had uncovered her breasts while dancing. I sat down on the chair and looked attentively, suspiciously in all directions. It was curious that A. D. P. had not called my

177

attention to that highly dramatic moment. At that instant I understood, marveling that it had taken me two days to grasp such an obvious thing: the veils, the scarves, the turban, and perhaps even the varicolored jerseys, were hidden in the folds of the dress, or more precisely they *constituted part of the dress.* Niculina had put them on and taken them off as she had removed or replaced her dress. To be sure, everything had happened in a few seconds, at the very moment when Serdaru was beginning a new song or surprising us with a new instrument. But I wondered why I hadn't noticed from the first, from the time Niculina had crossed the study in long, processional-like steps, that that extraordinary dress was, in fact, a walking wardrobe that she must have worn whenever she planned to present a "spectacle." I was sorry I couldn't share my discovery with A. D. P. immediately. Yet, I didn't rule out the possibility that he had discovered the same thing himself on the trip he had taken yesterday in the truck. Niculina was wearing that same wardrobe-gown; she was going somewhere, certainly, where at least a few "spectacles" were to take place.

I seated myself at the desk again, and in order to quiet the excitement that had come over me, I concentrated on the correspondence. Later, just as I was about to ask Ecaterina to make me some coffee, she appeared in the doorway.

"A young motorcyclist's here. He's come with a letter from the Maestru, but he says he's got orders to give it to you personally."

He was sitting on a chair in the kitchen, the envelope in his left hand. In his right hand was a large, colored handkerchief, with which he was meticulously wiping his face. He stood up quickly, gave me the envelope, and spoke shyly.

"Please sign the receipt and indicate the time. It's 3:45," he specified after glancing at his watch. "Keep the letter," he continued, holding out a penknife, "and give me back the envelope."

There were several sheets of paper, pages torn from

a notebook. "My dear friend," he had written me, "I am experiencing one of the most revelatory moments of my life. Impossible to say everything in a letter composed in great haste, because the courier leaves in ten minutes and I learned of his existence only a little while ago, when I heard—and they surprised me, irritated me—the first sounds of the motorcycle. Here is the essence of it: these simply extraordinary young people are both orphans. That's why they understand each other so well, why they fell in love with each other— *at the same time.* Niculina has been searching for her father for five years, ever since she learned he didn't die in a prison camp as she had believed, but was repatriated with a group of prisoners some fifteen or sixteen years ago. The details of this 'Quest' are moving and revealing. And, as Serdaru told us, it was she who deciphered the enigma of the inscription which you know, which is beginning to obsess me —not because it seems inauthentic, but because I find it *impossible* to remember how I spent those days of the Christmas season at Sibiu in 1938. In the meantime, Laurian has become quite as dear to me as Niculina, and the possible confirmation of my paternity could not, I believe, deepen that sincere affection I feel for him. But there are so many other things to add! I'll tell you about them, in part, when we see each other again; but more than that, you will discover them for yourself, once you too enter into this universe of legend, art, and dreams where I have been for nearly fifty hours. I hope you will guess more than these lines say. So be prepared spiritually (ah! I haven't used that expression since youth, and yet I do not blush to write it). Soon! As always, A. D. P."

I reread those notebook pages three times, not trying to contain my happiness. Never had he written me so much, or about such intimate things. Never had he said, "My dear friend." Never had he signed himself, "As always, A. D. P."

And there was something else. I was sure now that it wasn't just another "adventure," that obviously he was not enamored of Niculina.

6

The next day I arrived late on strada Fântânelor. I heard the clock in the dining room striking three, and I had scarcely entered the study when the phone began to ring.

"If you haven't heard the latest news," Ghiţă Horia began, "I'll tell you. I've received a letter, sent via a motorcyclist. A simply sensational letter; I repeat, *sensational!* A. D. P. declares that he is just now beginning to write his masterpiece — and this masterpiece will not be a novel, or an autobiography, but — hear this! — I'm quoting his very words, it will be 'an original group of plays for the theater.' Modern themes, even very *modern* — and he underscored the word 'modern' — but with *'extensions into mythology'* — and these last three words also were underscored. And in order for you to understand what he means, I read you this passage: 'The error all contemporary dramatists have made, the error I myself have made (because, I must confess, I once wrote a play, in my youth) is that we have tried to reinterpret ancient drama, that is, mythology, in the perspective of modern history. Now, we must, on the contrary, extend and complete ancient mythology through all that man has learned in the last hundred years. That's why my plays must be published first, that is, made accessible for study by each reader individually, and only after that performed (and not necessarily on the stages of great theaters). Especially since these plays presuppose and imply one another, just as the whole of Greek mythology is implicated in every one of the great Greek tragedies. For that reason, I'm asking you to make a place for my first volume of *Drama* in your winter schedule, postponing the *Memoirs* until spring.' Now, what do you say? How do you explain it?" Horia asked me sarcastically.

But he didn't give me a chance to answer. As if he had suddenly foreseen the innumerable complications that would result from modifying the winter schedule, he could not resist a sigh of despair; then he hung up the receiver.

I was quite as surprised as he. If A. D. P. was speaking seriously, he had undergone in less than three days a true conversion. Probably the "spectacles" he had witnessed had so excited him that he had decided to try his luck again at writing for the theater. But I didn't understand what made him think that the plays he would write would constitute his true masterpiece. And how would he be able to write them so fast, in a few months — or perhaps even more quickly than that, since he had asked Horia to announce the first volume of *Drama* in the winter schedule?

Ecaterina entered silently, bringing a tiny tray with sweets, coffee, and a glass of water. From the way she looked up I guessed she had been in the bedroom listening in on the telephone conversation.

"I wanted to call Aneta," she said blushing, "and when I picked up the receiver I heard the Director." She smiled mysteriously. "So, he's writing plays. But why hasn't he told us too?"

"Maybe he wanted to surprise us," I said, trying to make a joke of it.

She stood silent for some time, staring at me inquiringly.

"I know him better than you, and I'd say there's something more to it. You'll be convinced later."

What satisfaction it would have given Ecaterina to have listened in that evening when A. D. P. was giving me instructions, as mysterious as they were precise! But Pandele called me at home, a few hours later. I didn't get to ask him how he was or what he was doing, because he asked me immediately if I had ever seen a dance of the Călușari.

"I've never seen it, but I know the dance. That is, I've seen photographs, I've read about the Călușari, and I've even seen a few of their dances at the cinema."

"You know, then," he interrupted me, "that in every troupe there is a character who is not allowed to speak."

"I know. He's called 'the Mute' ".

"Exactly, the Mute. And now, listen closely. Pack a small valise with what you think you'll need for a few days. Nothing fancy, because I'm not inviting you to a formal reception. Tomorrow afternoon, at 3:30 to 4:00 probably, someone will come to your house to pick you up — of course, don't say anything to Ecaterina about it; just tell her you're going to a friend's place for a few days. A young man, very dark-skinned, will come with a car for you. He will ring the doorbell and ask for you. And these will be the only words you will hear from him (unless, of course, there should be — knock on wood! — an accident on the road and he should need to give you information). The young man will not speak at all during the trip, because, for various reasons (too complicated to explain over the phone) — for certain reasons, *he is practicing a ritual of silence*. . . . There's nothing mysterious about it," he added, with some timidity. "It's just a matter of — how to say it? — of the ritual function of spectacle."

"I was very excited by your letter of yesterday," I said, taking advantage of a brief pause.

"Bravo! I felt certain you would be. . . . Tomorrow, then. And be careful. Don't give yourself away to Ecaterina. Be as natural as possible. . . . The trip will take about three hours," he added.

7

In reality, it lasted less than that, but I never knew just how long. I was certainly extremely tired, because — as happens very seldom — I had hardly closed my eyes the whole night. An insomnia provoked, probably, by the conversation with A. D. P. It was past four A.M. when I set the alarm to ring at ten, but I don't believe I fell asleep before six. The sun had long since risen and the street had begun to stir. I arrived on strada Fântânelor a little before noon. I opened the mail listlessly and, as I was leaving, I told Ecaterina I would be spending a few days at Sinaia, as a guest of a friend. As A. D. P. had advised, I tried to seem as natural as I could, but from Ecaterina's suspicious expression I could tell I hadn't convinced her.

"At what address in Sinaia?" she began to interrogate

me. "Because there were three phone calls today already, and I told them to call back after two, to talk to you. Now what am I going to tell them?"

I shrugged. "Tell them I've gone to visit a friend, to rest, and ask them to call again in three days."

"And what if the Maestru calls?"

"He won't call!" I assured her, smiling, without realizing I'd given myself away.

Ecaterina looked me straight in the eyes, severely, almost harshly. "In other words, he has called."

I tried to get out of my predicament by pretending to laugh. "Since no matter what answer I give you, you won't believe me, I prefer not to answer at all."

Then I shook her hand warmly (I knew how responsive she was to that friendly gesture) and left. But the closer to home I got, the more humiliated and exasperated I became over the blunder I'd made. After packing my bag, I set the clock to waken me at three, and I lay down on the bed. I'd have been able to rest at least an hour if I had managed to fall asleep immediately. But then, probably, I wouldn't have heard the timid knock at the door. I recognized the signal and I sprang excitedly out of bed. In the doorway Valeria stood smiling, and, since she was quite tanned, her teeth seemed to be sparkling.

"I came this morning and I'm staying for two days," she said. "I wanted to surprise you. I looked for you first on strada Fântânelor, but Ecaterina told me that you weren't there, that you'd left already for Sinaia."

"I'm leaving in half an hour. A car's coming to take me."

"Don't you want to take me, too?"

"Impossible!" I exclaimed. "I'll explain why later."

She seemed so disappointed that I had to tell her the truth, or at least part of it. I said that A. D. P. had gone away unexpectedly four days ago; that he was staying at a location he insisted on keeping secret, but he was doing this, probably, because it was a matter of a new experiment; that he was doing something I couldn't have imagined until a few days ago: *he had undertaken to write drama!* I stressed the last few words, but Valeria did not seem very intrigued about this sudden conversion of A. D. P.'s.

"Actually, then, I've interrupted my vacation to see you for a half an hour."

"But, to use the same word — 'actually,' why *did* you come this way, so unexpectedly?"

"I missed you and I wanted to surprise you. . . ."

I realized she was about to burst into tears, and I put my arms around her. Fortunately, a little later there came a knock at the door.

"He's come to get me," I whispered. "You mustn't be surprised if I don't introduce you. I don't know who he is or what his name is. And A. D. P. told me the boy does not have permission to speak."

Then I opened the door. I gave a start when I set eyes on him: he was indeed very dark, almost black. If we had met on the street, I should not have thought him to be Romanian. He bowed slightly, smiling at me, and asked: "Domnul Eusebiu Damian?"

"I am. And this young lady is my fiancée, Valeria Nistor."

He bowed again, more deeply. Valeria stared at him, fascinated, as if he were an oriental prince.

"And now my dear," I said to her after embracing her again, "we must leave. Please don't forget to put the key where it belongs," I added in a whisper.

The car was waiting for us at the corner. An elegant vehicle, almost new; probably a foreign make.

"I know the stipulations," I said when the young man opened the door, indicating by his eyes the place where I was to sit: beside him on the front seat. The car was full of an assortment of packages, blankets, and large pillow cases filled and tied with string, like sacks. After leaving the city I tried to guess the direction we had taken. But my eyelids closed from drowsiness; probably a little while afterward I fell asleep, because I felt my companion's hand slapping me gently on the knee.

"I beg your pardon," I said softly. "I'm very tired. I had a terrible case of insomnia all night."

The youth nodded his head sympathetically, then pointed to a little box on the seat between us, signaling for me to open it. Inside were two thermoses, two glasses, two cups, and several sandwiches wrapped in cellophane. I opened one of the thermoses; it was full to the brim with piping hot coffee.

"This really hits the spot!" I exclaimed, filling my cup. "And you?"

He shook his head, smiling; then frowning, he fixed his eyes ahead, on the highway. The car was approaching a convoy of trucks; he had to reduce his speed, and this seemed to annoy him. Still, after he saw that I had finished my coffee, he turned toward me again with a smile and pointed to the other thermos. I filled a glass with water.

"Aren't you thirsty?" I asked, offering him the glass. He was not, and I emptied it, sipping slowly. After that, I don't know exactly what happened. I remember that after putting the second thermos bottle, the cup, and the glass back in place, I closed the box and rested my head against the back of the seat. Very likely I fell asleep again and he let me sleep as the car was moving slowly behind the trucks. But when I felt his hand clapping me on the knee again, and I awoke with a start, the trucks had disappeared and the highway opened clearly ahead of us. I apologized again and looked around wonderingly at the landscape; I didn't recognize it. We were not, at any rate, headed for Sinaia, as I had imagined. The road wound through low hills covered with vineyards and plum orchards. To keep from going to sleep again, I dug my fingernails into my legs suddenly. And yet, after a while, I realized I was moving my fingers, one by one, trying to count in my mind to one hundred. I was still counting when the young man opened the door and made a sign for me to get out. Beside him I recognized immediately Serdaru. He was dressed in a pair of dungarees, old and faded.

"Aren't you feeling well?" Serdaru asked, seeing me alight from the car with difficulty and stumble at my first steps.

"I'm dead tired! Falling asleep on my feet!" I repeated, making no effort to smile.

"And I wonder why. . . . True, I suffered from a terrible attack of insomnia last night, but anyway, I did get a few hours' sleep. And I've drunk I don't know how many cups of coffee."

"That's what happens when, as you Bucharestians say," he specified, winking his left eye mysteriously, without my understanding why, "—when you 'change the atmosphere.' Here, as you'll see," and again he gave me the sign with his eyes, "here the 'air' is different."

I glanced around and it did not seem to me we were in a mountain region. As far as I could tell in my state of torpor, the little hills looked more like mounds of clay and sand. I saw, at some distance, several stores and farther off, the smoke-stack of a factory.

"From now on, you're in my care," said Serdaru, pointing with his arm to the pickup truck some twenty meters away, half-hidden among trees. "The road is bad, because it's not yet finished. It was supposed to have been ready this spring, but something happened—I don't know just what—and the work was interrupted. And after so much rain, you can imagine. . . ."

Only when we had almost reached the truck did I realize that the vehicle in which I had come was gone.

"And I haven't even had a chance to thank him!" I said aloud.

"It doesn't matter," Serdaru assured me. "You can thank him tonight at midnight, after the last performance."

8

As far as I can calculate, seeing how awfully tired I was, A. D. P. had let me sleep until 10:30 that evening. He woke me with a hard shake.

"Now, sleepy or not, tired or rested, you must get up! The first part, the part for the 'general public,' that is, for the whole camp, is ended. Excerpts from several historical dramas and short, one-act comedies. All excellently performed. But now we're ready for Part Two. Don't say anything; just wait and see!"

I had been sleeping fully clothed on an army cot in a rather large room. It was not, certainly, a dormitory, because except for two other beds I saw only boxes, big and little, barrels, and sacks. Probably it was a storeroom, because I could distinguish various smells — of cooking oil, of boxes of preserves, of clean blankets and linens. Over the door hung a single bulb of rather low wattage. When we went out, A. D. P. felt for the switch, flicked off the light, and turned on a flashlight. Taking my arm he said in a whisper, "Now we must walk very carefully. In this part of the camp, the lights are turned out at 10:45, allowing just enough time for every spectator to get to his dormitory."

I let him guide me, not daring to lift my eyes from the beam of the flashlight on the ground ahead of us.

"Here, on the right," continued Pandele, "as you will see tomorrow, is the gymnasium. Here, twice a week, performances for the public are held. But the true 'spectacles' are improvised *extra muros*, outside the camp, in a ruined building abandoned many years ago. It was, I've been told, a sort of storage garage for trucks and tankers; the boys have identified next to it the site of a former repair shop and gasoline pumps. . . . From here on we won't need the flashlight. Keep your eyes closed a few moments to accustom them to the dark, and then you'll be able to see."

I looked around, thrilled. It had been a long time since I had seen such a clear, August night, far from any city, illumined only by stars. Very soon I began to distinguish far off, profiled against the sky, the undulating line of the hills; and closer, some telegraph poles, a few poplars growing here and there in the field; while just ahead, a few hundred meters away, the contours of a bizarre building — apparently consisting of several big blocks, one rather tall, the others truncated at various heights.

"When the fire broke out," Pandele explained, "they

187

hoped they'd be able to control it, and they concentrated on those parts where they knew trucks were parked. Thus they were able to save the walls and part of the roof. The rest burned more or less completely, according to how the wind blew. But fortunately for Ieronim, the steel skeleton remained standing."

We walked faster, and the farther we progressed, the louder and more strident became the chirping of the crickets. Soon we found ourselves in front of the ruins.

"They're waiting for us," whispered Pandele. "Probably all the others are in their seats. . . . Eusebiu," he added, "don't ask me anything; I'll tell you about it later. It's simply extraordinary! But pay very close attention during the performance, because I doubt you'll understand it at first."

"It's a shame I'm so tired! I'm fighting to stay a-wake. . . ."

"Keep fighting and conquer sleep!" Pandele interrupted. "It's too important — for you and for me, both!"

I didn't realize how mammoth the ruins were until we went inside. It might have been said we had entered a cave whose walls we could discern — now close to us, on the right and left, now far away — and whose vault rose higher and higher the farther we went. I realized we were walking down an aisle between rows of benches, the majority of them empty, but I sensed that behind us the benches were filling, almost noiselessly, with spectators who up till then had been standing against the walls in the darkness.

All at once someone approached us and whispered, "Here, Maestre. We have reserved two seats."

I smiled and sat down. They were lawn chairs, equipped with pillows. Although our seats were in the second row, we were still a good distance from the stage. Perhaps ten or twelve meters separated us from a weakly lighted podium that I took to be a stage — or at least part of a stage, because in the back, between two improvised curtains, I could make out the first steps of an amphitheater. Sometimes I thought I saw stars twinkling overhead. At other times I felt a gentle breeze, and it seemed that the walls began to quiver from top to bottom, like the folds of a curtain. When my eyes had become accustomed to the spaces of darkness and semidarkness, I discovered at the right of the stage a compact group of shadows. If I hadn't been so tired, I would have tried to decipher the other mysterious forms that I seemed to see stirring in one corner of the stage after another.

Then suddenly I recognized the voice of Niculina, and I snapped to attention, much excited.

"As before, we shall begin with an exercise of anamnesis. We shall recollect, as we have learned to do, the role of certain animals in universal history: the she-wolf in the founding of Rome, the ass on which Jesus entered Jerusalem, St. Nilus' camel, Napoleon's horse. . . ."

"Attention, attention!" I heard several voices saying together, but so perfectly that the words seemed like a single polyphonic voice. "Attention! You have guessed the allusion: it is a famous saying of Hegel's: 'In Napoleon, the Universal Spirit entered History, riding on horseback.' "

"But this time," continued Niculina, "our story begins with a mule and it will not end with Hegel."

"With Georg Wilhelm Friedrich Hegel," the chorus recited solemnly. "It will not end with him, with the great Hegel."

"Our story begins with a mule," Niculina resumed. "More precisely, our history, that of us Romanians, begins with a mule. Because two great Byzantine historians wrote about that mule in the sixth century."

"Theophanes and Theophylactus Simocatta," intoned the chorus.

"Hear what I say," Niculina began, changing slightly the timbre of her voice. "It was the year 580. Hordes of Avars were plundering and devastating the Eastern Empire."

There began to flicker, far off, beyond the amphitheater hidden by the curtains, a reddish flame, and a muffled murmuring was heard, in which there seemed to be mixed the voices and cries of thousands of people, with lamentations and screams quickly stifled.

"But the New Rome is keeping watch!" the chorus

189

exclaimed. "The Roman Empire of the East is keeping watch! Once again Byzantium vanquishes sleep!"

"Two Roman generals . . ."

"Comentiol and Martin . . ."

"The two generals have hidden their legions in the forests of the Balkan mountains. . . ."

For the next several moments it seemed to me that I saw on either side of us, stealing along next to the walls, an endless line of shadows. Pandele leaned over to me and whispered, "They're Laurian's best pupils. They're all excellent swimmers. You'll see now!"

"And one day," continued Niculina, "or perhaps it was toward evening, before nightfall, the legions swept down upon the Avars. And, say the two Byzantine historians, victory would have been certain if . . ."

"Remember!" shouted the chorus with a metallic, trumpet-like timbre, "Remember Napoleon's horse!"

"Victory would have been certain if it had not been for the mule."

"Like all mules," the chorus added in a whisper, "he was heavily laden. He had carried for hours, he had carried for days and nights, the burden of his master. . . ."

"The load came loose," Niculina resumed, "and it slipped, without the master's noticing. Then one of the soldiers walking behind shouted to him, at the top of his voice — he shouted to him to turn around and adjust it. He shouted, *'Turn, turn, brother!'*"*

"He shouted with all his might," echoed the chorus, *"'Turn, turn, turn around, brother!'"*

"And the other soldiers," Niculina went on, "took up the call, *'Turn, turn, brother!'* — and then those at the head of the column heard the shout. . . ."

"'Turn, turn, turn around, brother!'" repeated the chorus, more and more rapidly.

"And they believed that the order to retreat had been

---

*These words are *torna, torna, fratre!* and they are the first recorded words of the Romanian language.

given," Niculina continued in a trembling voice, seemingly choked with emotion, "and they turned around, taking up the cry, 'Turn, turn, brother!' and they were thrown into disorder."

For a while I thought I was dreaming, because that mass of shadows which had gathered on the stage began to stir, murmuring, "Turn, turn, return brother!" and started toward us like a single, monstrous creature. In a few moments it overtook and swallowed up the chorus and Niculina, and it kept advancing with the muffled, menacing sound of feet tramping, tramping upon the earth. It seemed to me that any moment I would be caught by that gigantic octopus with truncated arms which was approaching faster and faster. I sprang to my feet and began to shout, "Turn, turn, brother!" and, turning my back to the stage, I tried to run to the exit. It seemed as though the whole great room was emptying and the spectators were running, some pushing from behind, some beside me. But I don't know how far I ran. I don't believe I had managed to escape from that huge barn when I stumbled and fell.

9

"Probably I fainted," I whispered upon seeing Serdaru.

"You were sleeping so soundly that the Maestru didn't try to wake you. But what's the matter?" he asked.

The morning light blinded me and I rubbed my eyes automatically. "When I saw that crowd bearing down on us and saw how everyone else was running away, I tried to save myself, and I ran, too."

Serdaru looked at me, smiling. "That was all part of the spectacle. But they weren't running toward the exit. They were just spreading out around the walls, to be able to slip back quietly toward the stage. They were preparing for the second scene. Only with Scene Two did the true spectacle begin. A pity, a great pity! . . . I leave you now. The bath is down the hallway. I'll be back in fifteen minutes."

I found I was in a dormitory with six beds, but all the

other occupants had awakened and gone long before, because the beds were made. Embarrassed by my naiveté and fatigue, I washed and dressed as quickly as I could. Then I walked the length of the hall to the exit, and went outside into the yard.

"Bravo!" Serdaru greeted me with what seemed to be genuine pleasure. "Three minutes early is a good sign! They told me you could take tea in the kitchen."

"What's the Maestru doing?" I asked him rather timidly. "Probably my foolishness and harebrained behavior surprised him."

"He's sorry about it, too. But he'll see you later, a half hour before lunch. He's working now," Serdaru added, lowering his voice. "It's unbelievable how much he's been able to write here in the past three days."

In the kitchen we sat down at a table by the window. I was still dazed by the intensity of the light. Soon Niculina came in with a full tray.

"I beg your pardon," I said, bowing my head. "I don't know what came over me last night. Exhaustion, probably."

Niculina set the tray down in front of me and shook my hand. "We're sorry, too. It was one of the most successful spectacles we've had this summer. And the big surprise for all of us was the dialogue between Hegel and the representative of contemporary historiography. I say surprise, because the scene was introduced into the spectacle at the last moment. It was practiced in great secrecy in Ieronim's chambers."

The tea wasn't very hot, but the homemade bread, butter, and honey tasted as good as they had when I was a child.

"Of course," Serdaru interjected, "because you watched only the first scene, you couldn't understand that the spectacle, in its entirety, illustrated the mode of being of historical events and at the same time the structure of historiography."

"Maybe you'll smile at this," I ventured, taking courage suddenly, "but I still don't understand the point of the 'performance.' Why did you start with '*Turn, turn, brother?*'"

Just as I had expected, they looked at each other, smiling. "You explain it to him," Serdaru said to Niculina. "You're

192

more of an expert."

"But where to begin? . . . I'll begin at the beginning. You remember from lycée how important for us Romanians the testimony of the Byzantine Chronicles is. It's the first document in the archaic Romanian language: *Stră-română*. And the fact that the cry *'Turn, return, brother,'* spoken in that archaic Romanian, was understood by the whole army, confirms the presence of a massive population of 'Stră-Romanians' in the sixth century in the Balkan peninsula."

Just then I realized that her blouse was so transparent that her breasts could be distinguished quite clearly. Probably she was not wearing a bra. I blushed and looked down at my plate; fortunately there was still a slice of bread left, and a little butter. But it is very likely that I missed the point of several sentences having to do with interpretations of those two words, *torna* (or *retorna*), and *fratre*, given by historians and philologists.

"Now, the most important thing is the plurality of meanings this event bears. On the one hand, an account of a tragedy — the defeat of a Romanian army — becomes one of the most prized, most exalted documents of Romanian historiography. On the other hand, the document illustrates admirably the precariousness and fortuitous nature of historiography: if that mule had not lost his pack, there would be no proof, so early — the sixth century — of the Stră-Romanians and the Stră-Romanian language. But especially illuminating is the light it throws on the structure of a historical event in general: any accident, however insignificant or ridiculous it may be, can have considerable consequences for the history of a people or, in certain cases — for instance, Cleopatra's nose — for a continent or a civilization."

"But," I ventured to interrupt, although I didn't see the latter part, "I don't understand how these interpretations of the historical event and historiography could constitute the theme of a dramatic spectacle."

Niculina gave Laurian a meaningful look. "The best thing would be for you to tell him all that followed. I have to go; the boys are waiting for me."

I didn't understand very well what Serdaru told me, although it certainly wasn't all his fault. My mind wandered — sometimes to the thought of Pandele and his sudden literary inspiration, at other times to visualizing again that transparent blouse of Niculina's and her breasts. Later, in Bucharest, I asked A. D. P. about it, but he had seen the spectacle differently, and he had not always understood the connection between the scenes. In brief, the next scene had presented other famous episodes illustrating the role of animals in world history: the doe that had shown the Huns the way out of the Maeotic marshes; the aurochs chased by Prince Dragoş, which led to the founding of the principality of Moldavia. Then in the third scene, a series of dances, pantomimes, and songs showed what admirable folkloric masterpieces such myths and legends had produced. The fourth scene had illustrated, *"as dramatically as possible,"* Serdaru stressed, the confrontation between the artistic and philosophical valorization, on the one hand, and the historiographic interpretation on the other hand, of these exemplary events.

"All right, all right," I interrupted him finally, "all these things are very interesting, and, as you say, they can even inspire dramatic spectacles. But why did you pick *this* theme, the theme of historiography and exemplary events? To me it seems to be a didactic one: basically a minor, peripheral problem."

"On the contrary," replied Serdaru in a voice that was firm and, I thought, almost pathetic. "It's the cardinal problem of our time. Because *if Hegel is right, we are lost!*"

I didn't fully understand him, but I let him continue. The next scene, according to Serdaru, had illustrated this very confrontation with Hegel. But it was beyond me to imagine it performed — that is, *staged.*

"I have to confess," Serdaru acknowledged, "that I haven't read Hegel. I know only excerpts that Ieronim has translated for us and commented on. But I believe I understand his *system of thought,* because I have experienced it so many times, in everyday life, and even more so because I've

relived it in rehearsing for certain performances under Ieronim's direction. The best thing would be for you to have him,
Ieronim Thanase, explain the Hegelian interpretation of History
to you."

It seemed odd that Pandele told me the same thing
later on, in the course of the same day. But before escorting
me to the room where A. D. P. was working, Serdaru showed
me the gymnasium and swimming pool of the camp. I understood that he belonged to a team of athletic coaches at the
Uricani Factory, while Niculina and the "boys" worked in the
summertime with the dramatic ensemble at the camp. At the
swimming pool I had a surprise. The excellent form and vigor
of several of his pupils impressed me: they didn't seem tired
even after swimming several times a course of a hundred meters.
But still I didn't know what to make of the secret of these
performances, a secret Serdaru revealed to me, with the request
that I keep it to myself. (And rightly so, because not only
would no one have believed me, but also he risked losing his
job.) When he discovered any pupil with real talent, Serdaru
would lead him to the fish pond at the entrance to the camp
and enjoin him to spend a long time watching the fish swimming; then he was to imagine — more precisely, to let his imagination carry him, to dream — that in the swimming pool he
would propel his body with the same ease and spontaneity as a fish.

"It's an exercise of self-suggestion," I said, "and thus
a kind of magical act."

"It's that, but the secret is deeper: it is an exercise of
anamnesis."

10

"Like all of us," A. D. P. remarked that morning, "the boys
indulge in clichés. But many times they're right: the great secret
of all techniques, physiological and spiritual, is anamnesis."

Now, in the light of a noonday summer's sun, he
seemed younger and more rested than ever. There was a stack

195

of written pages on the desk in front of him, and alongside a rather voluminous portfolio. I had prepared several questions: what had they said to him on the telephone, and why had they come to get him in the pickup truck? What's Niculina's story? Why had he spoken about a Quest? What makes him think his future masterpieces will be dramas? — and other such queries. But A. D. P. gave me no chance to ask them. He talked almost constantly; I contented myself with answering his questions. I did attempt, nevertheless, to apologize for the scene I made the night before.

"It surprised me, too, but Ieronim gave it a different interpretation: you were so impressed by the spectacle that you really relived the disastrous retreat of the Romanian cohorts. But it was not an anamnesis; rather, it was an experience comparable to a possession. That's why you didn't awaken until late this morning and missed the remainder of the performance. So I'll say your initiation into that kind of theater was a failure."

"You can't imagine how sorry I am," I murmured.

"It doesn't matter; there will be other occasions. But I am sorry, because, since you missed last night's spectacle, all I tell you and all you read here (he pointed to the portfolio and the written pages) about the possibilities of the theater will seem like mere theoretical considerations to you. But, anyway, we have other urgent things to discuss."

He lit a cigarette (this was the first time I had seen him smoke) and looked at me, smiling.

"How are things going at home? What's Ecaterina doing?"

I blushed, but I confessed the truth. He was content to pass it off with a shrug; it did not seem to upset him. I took advantage of that brief pause to summarize the telephone conversations with Ghiţă Horia.

"Yes, I wanted to pique his curiosity, to make him reverse himself and publish my first volume of *Drama*."

"But when have you had time . . . ?"

"To write the first volume?" he interrupted me, in high spirits. "I haven't written it yet, but if I can stay here as I would

196

like for two or three weeks, I can finish it. In any event, I already have plenty of material ready to publish. Look here," and he pointed to the portfolio, "there are some two hundred pages here — written by hand, it's true, with not too many lines to the page. That text constitutes a long Introduction to a dramatic art and technique suitable to our time."

"But when . . . ?" I tried to ask again.

"Eusebiu!" he interrupted me in a mysterious, excited voice. "I wrote you already that this is a decisive experience for me *and you*. All I've told you so far is to remain strictly between us. You'll see directly that it's a matter of extreme importance. This Introduction is not written by me. But it explains the plays I'm writing now, and in any event it must be published under my name so it can appear quickly — and be read and taken seriously. If it were to appear under the name of the author — something I doubt would be possible at the present moment — this Introduction would pass unnoticed. Of course later, perhaps even in the second edition, I shall reveal the author's name. The fact that I'm telling you all this, and that I will beg you to preserve the original manuscript with the greatest care and send it back to me by courier as soon as you've made a typed copy — this very fact shows, I like to believe, that it is not a question of plagiarism."

He paused suddenly and crushed his cigarette absently.

"But the plays I'm writing now," he resumed, "are inspired by this theory of the dramatic spectacle, a theory you will understand after reading the Introduction. I say 'plays,' plural, because, although they can be cited and produced separately, they disclose their true meaning only when they are played in a group. For the time being, in the first volume, there will be four or five plays, but the series will be continued in subsequent volumes. If I were younger, I could write sixty to seventy plays, and all of them together would constitute *a single work*."

I was ready to interrupt, to assure him that he had many productive years ahead, and if he succeeded in writing four or five plays in a few weeks, he could write sixty or seventy in the next five years. But I didn't get to utter a single word.

"The idea for this sort of dramatic literature," he continued, "came to me the same night I arrived here, after watching the first 'spectacle.' In brief, I can tell you that I understood then, as in a lightning flash, the meaning of many events in my life. Then, that night, while talking with Ieronim Thanase, the author of the manuscript" — and he pointed to the portfolio again — "I became convinced that my experience did not constitute an exceptional case. *Anyone, any spectator, any reader can have a similar revelation.* I realized then the importance of that type of 'spectacle' for all our contemporaries, in all lands and on all continents."

He stopped a moment, gazed deeply into my eyes, and then declared with gravity: "My dear friend, in our day the spectacle is the only chance we have to know *absolute freedom*, and this will be even truer in the near future. I specify *absolute freedom*, because it has nothing to do with freedom of a social, economic, or political type."

"That's simply extraordinary!" I whispered, suddenly moved.

"You'll be convinced for yourself, and perhaps sooner than you expect. But we'll talk about these things later. In the meantime, here is what I'm asking. If you have no objection, a car — a different one, not the car you came in — will take you tomorrow afternoon to Bucharest. I'm entrusting you with the manuscript of the Introduction, and I ask you to type a copy of it as quickly as possible, without letting anyone set eyes on the original. If Ghiţă phones, answer that you're preparing the Introduction for publication and indicate, approximately, the number of pages it will be. Assure him that very soon, perhaps within a week, you'll receive the manuscript of the first play. If he asks for details about the Introduction, tell him I have entitled it 'Introduction to a Possible Dramaturgy.' "

"An interesting title," I observed. "But no less enigmatic."

He looked at me again with warmth, smiling. But the smile was a sad one, almost melancholic.

"It is indeed enigmatic, because I don't dare, as yet, say more. I spoke a little while ago about anamnesis. There have been so many important events in my life, events that I remember rather well; although, as I told you, only a few days ago, after watching the first spectacle, did I understand their meaning — and yet not completely. But I realized recently that there is one extremely important event in my life of which I remember almost nothing. I have only very vague recollections of that Christmas of 1938 spent at Sibiu. Until a few days ago I couldn't have suspected that *something* happened then, *something* that changed my life radically."

He became silent and took a pack of cigarettes from his pocket.

"In other words," I began, not knowing why I felt so excited, "you are convinced that Laurian Serdaru . . ."

"It's not only that," he continued. "There's also the fact that from that time, after the experience at Sibiu, I abandoned playwriting completely. Since then, I've written nothing but novels and short stories. Why?" he asked, looking me straight in the eyes. "What other writer ever renounced his vocation after one failure? And actually it wasn't even a failure, because the play was taken off the program before the premiere. If it had been performed, it might have been successful — or perhaps it would not have been. That doesn't matter. I'd have written another play, I'd have continued. *Why did my interest in drama cease so abruptly and definitively after my return from Sibiu?*"

He paused to light a cigarette. I thought he was very wrought up, and his hand was trembling slightly.

"Ever since then I've believed that *Orpheus and Eurydice* was a bad play, a dud, and I never had the curiosity to reread it. I don't know what came over me, but after Niculina phoned me I hunted up the manuscript and put it in the suitcase. Well! I reread it twice, and the play doesn't seem bad at all. It is, of course, a youthful effort with defects characteristic of beginners. But if I had continued, I'd have written better and better. I'd have been today, I don't hesitate to say, a *great* dramatic author. But something intervened, something I can't succeed in remembering, which had a traumatic effect. Since then . . ."

He suddenly broke off and turned toward the window. I wondered what I should say, how I could change the subject without making him sadder.

"There's no doubt about it," he resumed in a flat, neutral tone, "that traumatic incident was produced as a consequence of my meeting with Eurydice — I mean, with the actress who played the role of Eurydice, Laurian's mother. How is it possible to have *forgotten everything*? Such an amnesia certainly must have a deep cause. If I were to use mythological terminology, I'd say that my amnesia expresses in the most concrete way possible the death of Eurydice. For me, Eurydice has *died forever,* in a way she never died for Orpheus, not even after she remained forever in Hades. But if that interpretation is correct, it means that in the winter of 1938 I did not see in that young actress the incarnation of Eurydice, but I saw *someone else*! But, I keep asking myself, *who?*"

"Indeed, *who?*" I repeated in a whisper, much moved.

We were brought to our senses suddenly by the sound of the bell calling us to dinner.

11

Only on the way back to Bucharest in the car the next day did I try to recapitulate all the events and discoveries of the past twenty-four hours. To the extent that I could remember them, I realized that many of the puzzles I had hoped to have explained remained unsolved. Every time I had been ready to ask if he had guessed the secret of Niculina's "wardrobe-dress," A. D. P. had cut me short: he seemed obsessed with the problems of the spectacle and anamnesis. Just once had he said to me in passing: "For her, costumes symbolize, but at the same time *realize,* the different modalities and situations of man. Whenever an actor removes a costume, he is freed from a certain mode of being. They learned this technique from Ieronim."

Since I had seen only one scene, I didn't know what other costume Niculina might wear. That night, as sleepy as I was, I didn't notice if she was wearing her wardrobe-dress or not. The next day, in the camp, she had on the transparent blouse and a long skirt, and that evening a kind of shalwars of blue silk. It seemed odd to me, in the car, that I couldn't recollect precisely the color of her hair or how she had worn it. As if he had been reading my thoughts, the young man beside me said abruptly, "Niculina changes her hair style every day."

"Even the color of it?" I questioned him.

"When she wants to, she changes the color too. But not every day."

Like all the other pupils of Serdaru, this young man seemed to be enamored of Niculina. I discerned in his expression a total adoration, as for a goddess.

"What would the true color of her hair be?" I inquired, trying to smile.

"Serdaru says that when he first met her, she was a blonde. But now, usually, the color is auburn, and sometimes a brighter red."

"Curious!" I murmured.

In order to put an end to the conversation, I opened the notebook again and began paging through it as though I were looking for a certain item. "If Hegel is right," I read by chance, "then we are lost." I had set down that note immediately after dinner. When, a little later, I had repeated it to Ieronim Thanase, he said: "True. That's why we have to correct Hegel and carry his thought further."

I had not imagined how he would look: still youthful, very handsome — with a stern, romantic face — tall, robust, and yet paralyzed in an armchair, with two canes beside him. But when A. D. P. and I entered the room, he was waiting for us on his feet. Only after shaking my hand firmly did he sit down, assisted by two young men. Fortunately, at the last moment, just before we had arrived at his door, A. D. P. had informed me, lowering his voice, that Ieronim was half-paralyzed.

"It's my fault," Ieronim said at a certain moment. "Somewhere I made a mistake; somewhere, I don't know where, in a role I played badly, in an erroneous staging of something, I don't know. . . . But when I discover the cause — because the doctors have wracked their brains for a year and they can't make sense of it — when I discover it, the healing will come of itself. The dramatic art becomes, domnule Damian, what it was in the beginning, a magical art!" He burst into a surprisingly youthful laugh. "So beware, because many things can happen to you!"

Then, in a different voice, equally seductive, he asked me to describe in as much detail as possible my experience of the night before. After some time, taking advantage of the fact that Niculina and Serdaru had entered bringing coffee, I mentioned Hegel. Suddenly his whole expression changed, as if illumined by an inner fire.

"What an extraordinary destiny!" he exclaimed. "To remain misunderstood for almost a hundred years, and then to be discovered, praised to the skies, revered as the greatest thinker since Aristotle — while those who think they have understood him best prevent us, by their exegesis, from deciphering his message and, therefore, from completing him and going beyond him. Because, while everyone agrees that Hegel was truly convinced that the Universal Spirit is manifested in any historical event, all the exegetes interpret this idea in a simplistic way: namely, that we must accept the historical events, the manifestations of the Universal Spirit, even in their most monstrous expressions, for instance in the crematoriums of Auschwitz — must accept them and justify them. If they happened, if they occurred in History, it means they are rational, and therefore, justified and justifiable."

He broke off abruptly and, turning to Laurian and Niculina, asked, "Who made the coffee today? I want to know what herbs you put in it: belladonna or basil?"

"I made it," confessed Niculina, smiling. "But why do you ask? Do you taste the mandrake?"

"Ah, Circe! the peerless sorceress!" Ieronim exclaimed

in jest, parodying, probably, some first-year Conservatory student.

Niculina waited a few moments, watching him drink the coffee; then she began to recite, almost in a whisper:

"'*Quel grand miracle! quoi! sans être ensorcelé, tu m'as bu cette drogue! Jamais, à grand jamais, je n'avais vu mortel résister à ce charme. . . . Il faut qu'habite en toi un esprit invincible. C'est donc toi qui serais l'Ulysse aux mille tours?*' The *Odyssey*, Canto 10, Victor Bérard's translation."

"Too bad we don't know Greek, so we could listen to you recite it to us in the original," said Ieronim, somewhat melancholically, I thought. Then he added, turning in my direction, "But don't think I've forgotten what I started to say. I started to say that Hegel's idea can be understood differently. I, at any rate, *dare to understand it differently*, and to correct it. Agreed, every historical event constitutes a new manifestation of the Universal Spirit, but that doesn't mean we have to accept it and justify it. We must go further, and decipher its *symbolic meaning*. Because every historical event, as well as every everyday happening, carries a symbolic significance, illustrates a primordial, transhistorical, universal symbolism. . . . I believe you've heard this a hundred times!" he exclaimed, addressing Niculina and Laurian, and he broke into his adolescent laugh. "And you, Maestre, you have met these ideas, or you will meet them, on almost every page of the Introduction."

"It's my fault," I apologized, "because I asked the question."

"It is not your fault, Domnule. The repetition and continual reformulation of these thoughts constitutes for me something more, even, than an intellectual delight. It compares with the aesthetic thrill of rereading a poem. I like to compare it to the effect produced in the soul of a believer by the ritual recitation of great prayers, especially that of the first prayer, "The Lord's Prayer." Therefore, to return to the *true* interpretation of historical events, and to conclude: I like to repeat whenever I have the opportunity — to repeat in a somewhat *ritualistic* way — that the decipherment of the secret, symbolic meanings of historical events can constitute a *revelation*, in the religious sense of the term. Moreover, this is the purpose of all the arts."

Seeing me staring absently at the highway stretching out ahead of us, the young man tried to continue the conversation.

"But that Serdaru is quite a fellow himself," he said, smiling. "Have you seen how he swims?"

"No, him I didn't see. Yesterday, at the pool, I saw only you, his pupils."

"Serdaru Laurian," he declared solemnly, "swims like a fish!"

"Even as fast as a fish?" I asked jokingly.

"Not in the pool, of course. No matter how large it might be — and the pool at the camp isn't very big — the water stands in a swimming pool as it does in a jar: it has no currents, no waves. But you should see Serdaru swimming in the Olt or the Danube: he cuts the water like a loach! To say nothing of how he swims in the Black Sea," he added, smiling mysteriously. "He doesn't like me to talk about it. But in your case, it's different. . . . I am, as Serdaru says himself, his right-hand man. Until last year, when he became engaged, he took me with him everywhere he was hired as an instructor."

He told me that three years ago they had been together at Eforie. Once, after midnight, Serdaru had awakened him and, signaling him to walk on tiptoe, they had left the dormitory of the colony and had gone down to the beach.

"I'll show you right here what I learned that night. But I'll show only you."

Then Serdaru had entered the water, and because the breakers were so high, coming in rapid succession, he had dived under them; a few moments later he emerged some ten or twelve meters' distance away, and waved. Knowing his skill, the boy had not been overly impressed, and he even wondered why Serdaru had wakened him. But he quickly realized his instructor had dived again, and he waited to see how long he could stay under. After a quarter of an hour he became alarmed and began walking up and down the beach, wondering if he ought to notify the maritime police. At last, convinced that there had been an accident — because by this time almost an hour had elapsed since he had seen Serdaru wave — he informed the police. A motor launch, with lights, began searching a hundred meters away offshore. Soon the lights were turned off, because daylight had come. At a certain moment they saw him far out, swimming valiantly and so fast they couldn't believe their eyes.

"I'm sorry," he had apologized after climbing aboard the boat. "I didn't realize I'd gone so far."

"Moreover," the young man continued, lowering his voice, "Serdaru says that some of his ancestors were fish. But I can't believe that."

And so, I said to myself, the same thing again: anamnesis through actions, incantations, drama. As Ieronim said, this is the purpose of all the arts: to reveal the universal dimension, that is the spiritual meaning, of any object, or gesture, or event, however banal or ordinary it may be.

"But through the dramatic spectacle," he added, "the decipherment of the symbolic, therefore religious, meanings of events of any kind can become an instrument of illumination — more precisely, of salvation — of the masses."

"That's why I told you this morning," Pandele intervened, turning toward me, "that that way of practicing dramatic art is, today, the only means of obtaining absolute freedom."

I was enthusiastic and at the same time puzzled. Without realizing that I might be thought less intelligent than I consider myself to be, I confessed very frankly: "But I still don't see what connection Hegel has with this kind of dramatic art!"

I breathed more easily hearing Ieronim laughing harder than ever. He lifted one of his canes in the air, and shook it as though he wished to announce he was about to say something very important.

"Bravo! You're perfectly right, and I thank you for calling it to my attention. Because precisely that point, of

205

capital importance for our discussion, was left aside. Obviously, I reproach Hegel for foundering on the equation: historical event equals a new manifestation of the Universal Spirit, instead of carrying his analysis further and revealing the symbolic meanings of events and happenings. But that revelation, or decipherment, of symbolism which breaks the shell of the apparently banal events of every day and *opens them to the universal* — that spiritual exercise is only rarely accessible to the man of our time. The revelation of the symbolic meaning of our gestures, actions, passions, and even beliefs is obtained by participating in a dramatic spectacle *as we understand it* — that is, one comprising dialogues, dance, mime, music, and action, or, if you will, 'plot.' Only after the experience of several spectacles of that sort will the spectators succeed in discovering the symbolic, transhistorical meanings of every commonplace event or incident."

"In other words," Pandele interjected, "the dramatic spectacle could become, very soon, a new eschatology or soteriology, a technique of salvation."

"Obviously," said Ieronim, "such terms must never be pronounced because, in our day, they are disqualified. 'Eschatology' and 'soteriology' belong to the vocabulary of the so-called obscurantist ideologies."

"And we could be accused not only of superstition and obscurantism," Niculina spoke, grinning, "but even of black magic."

Ieronim looked at her in feigned surprise, and burst into laughter again. "Look who's talking!" he exclaimed.

12

I found the ideas of Ieronim again, that same night, while reading the manuscript of the Introduction. But the further I read, the more I realized that the argument was more complex and nuanced than I had thought. Thanase recalled the magical origins of the arts, described in detail several gymnastic and psycho-physiological techniques, and showed their role in the history of the dramatic spectacle. I wondered what the reaction would be from the drama critics and the historians of literature. But actually only one thing really interested me: what would A. D. P. *create* under the inspiration of these theories, and what would become of him, the man, obsessed as he seemed to be by the mystery of those three days of Christmas spent at Sibiu in 1938?

Fortunately, Ecaterina showed more understanding than I had expected. She asked only how A. D. P. felt and if anyone was taking care of him.

"He phoned me yesterday morning," she added, without hiding her satisfaction. "He told me which linens and which clothes to get ready for him. And this evening, late, a motorcyclist came — not that young fellow who was here before, but a different one — and I gave him the suitcase."

In the office I quickly went over the mail, and in accordance with A. D. P.'s instructions, I classified all the letters in two files: the urgent ones, to which I would reply right away, and all the others. Then I began to type the Introduction. I worked until evening, and when I heard Ecaterina coming with a tray of sweets and coffee, and later, with a platter of fruit, I covered Thanase's manuscript with a page of typing from the Memoirs. On leaving, I crammed all the material into my briefcase and took it home with me.

The next day I arrived on strada Fântânelor well before noon, sure that Ecaterina would prepare me her inimitable omelet. I was determined to finish the typing of the Introduction as soon as possible: the precautions I had to take to keep the secret had become annoying. By evening I had reached page 168 of the manuscript. This left some forty pages to type. I was happy thinking of how pleased A. D. P. would be on hearing of my accomplishment. But he didn't telephone, either that day or the third, after I had typed the last page and begun a review of the whole typescript of 99 pages. I'd have called him if I had known the telephone number of the camp. For a moment I was tempted by the thought of notifying Ghiţă Horia, but I changed my mind immediately; he would be even more surprised when he called me. I decided, in any event, to give myself a day's vacation. I informed Ecaterina that I wouldn't be coming the next day. If the Maestru should call, she was to tell him I had finished what he had asked and was awaiting instructions.

I stayed in bed later than usual. Then after a gourmet luncheon at the House of Men of Science, I returned home, walking slowly along the boulevard. I had promised myself to begin Volume 2 of Saint-Simon. I was ready to take off my jacket and shoes and put on lounging pajamas when the doorbell rang. After a brief hesitation, I went to the door and opened it. A middle-aged man with thin, faded-blond hair combed flat across his head held out his hand and smiled.

"Emanoil Albini," he said. "I permitted myself to come at this hour because I knew I'd find you alone. Domnişoara Valeria will not return until tomorrow evening."

I blushed, confused, and indicated a comfortable chair. Then I sat down at the desk and looked at him questioningly.

"I don't understand exactly what it's about. Something to do with Valeria?"

I thought he tried to laugh but didn't succeed. "No, no!" he exclaimed. "Domnişoara Valeria Nistor is taking advantage of her last day at the beach. And I admit, I envy her."

He thrust his hand automatically into his shirt pocket and pulled out a silver cigarette case.

"May I smoke a cigarette?" he added, with exaggerated politeness. "I understand you yourself don't smoke. But one never knows what tomorrow will bring. You have seen Maestru Pandele. . . ."

Involuntarily I gave a start. "But how did you find out?"

"Everybody knows! . . . *A propos*, how's the Maestru doing?"

"He's working. He writes day and night. It's simply extraordinary!"

He stared at me steadily, searchingly, but without severity. I had the impression that he was appraising me; he still didn't know in what category of "men without a past or future" to classify me.

"A new novel? The sequel to *The Mill Wheel* for which we've been waiting for thirty years?"

This time I stared at him in surprise. "But A. D. P. never said he would write a sequel to *The Mill Wheel*. Besides I don't see how it could have a sequel, since both the leading characters died — or, more precisely, Manole disappeared after Otilia's death, but the way he disappeared amounts to a death."

Albini smiled, but with some effort, it seemed to me. "Perhaps I'm mistaken," he began. "But, in any event, it's a detail of no importance. The important thing is that Comrade Horia is correct in announcing a volume of *Drama,* to appear very soon."

"It's no secret. On the contrary, A. D. P. is delighted by the publicity arranged by Ghiță Horia. He realized what a sensation the news will make that soon a volume of *Drama* will appear."

"It is as though it had been announced in Paris, in 1922–1927, that Marcel Proust was writing a play. . . ."

I looked at him astonished and with some alarm, but I had no time to reply.

". . . And according to all appearances," continued Albini, "he is enjoying himself at Camp Bolovani, in the company of 'the boys' and Ieronim Thanase."

"It is an environment he finds stimulating. Because he hasn't written for the theater since youth."

"Since *Orpheus and Eurydice,*" Albini interrupted. "He was thirty-two or three then."

"Correct," I repeated, blushing slightly, "since *Orpheus and Eurydice*. But this time it's a different matter. A new way of writing drama. And the presence of Ieronim's group, or should I say troupe, stimulates him. Perhaps you know that these young people have been trying all sorts of theatrical experiments over the past several years. Their conception of performance is extremely bold and original. . . ."

"I hope you're right," Albini interrupted. "But that's

not the point. It's a matter of Thanase's group. Among them there are several curious persons — I might even say suspect."

"In what sense 'suspect?' " I asked him, intimidated.

"In the proper sense of the word. Unstable elements, hot-headed youths, lacking in maturity, easy victims of any obsolete and dangerous ideology. But, actually, that may not be so serious. What seems to me, if not serious, at least risky, is the interest the Maestru shows in the rather mysterious pair, Serdaru and Niculina."

"They're both orphans!" I exclaimed with fervor. "They're searching for a father. Moreover, it was due to this fact — the search for a father — that A. D. Pandele met them. He was profoundly impressed with their desire to identify him as their father. For example, Niculina . . ."

"Since you have brought up the matter," began Albini, meticulously crushing out his cigarette, "I must tell you what the Maestru will discover one day sooner or later. Niculina has been, if indeed she is not still, a whore. For years she's slept with whomever she needed to and whomever she liked. That's why she could never get a permanent position, at any theater."

"She's looking for her father!" I repeated irritably, aware I was blushing. "She's been searching for five years! . . ."

Albini looked at me again with exaggerated surprise; then his face brightened, as though he were about to laugh.

"Do you suffer from insomnia?" he asked me.

"Very seldom. Once in several years . . . And just a few days ago."

"My congratulations! I've suffered from insomnia since youth. Now I've learned not to try to cure myself of it, and not to take sleeping pills. I have come to believe that insomnia has its solution, but specialists have not yet succeeded in finding it. In my case, however, I believe I understand: insomnia allows me to read books I otherwise should never open. So it has happened that, for several years, I've spent part of the night reading Gnostic texts and books about Gnosticism."

Probably he caught the bewilderment in my expression, because he explained: "You know, those Eastern sects, some pre-Christian, others Christian but heretical."

"I remember very vaguely," I said apologetically. "Actually, I don't know anything precise about them."

"That was my case too until, three or four years ago, Hans Leisegang's book on Gnosticism fell into my hands, and it fascinated me. What especially intrigued me was the system of a great Gnostic thinker, Valentinus. And listening to you just now talking about Niculina *seeking her father*, I recalled Valentinus' explanation about the creation of the universe and the presence of evil in the world. The tragedy began, says Valentinus, when Sophia . . . But perhaps I'm boring you?"

"On the contrary, on the contrary!" I exclaimed with an exaggerated fervor.

"The tragedy began when Sophia, that is, Wisdom, was blinded by the desire to know her father. But the Father, in Valentinus' view, is transcendent, invisible, and unknowable. This aberrant wish of Sophia's to know directly, in a concrete way, that which by definition cannot be known, was the cause of all the falls, all the evils and sins that characterize the world in which we human beings live. I won't further summarize the system, which is grandiose and grotesque at the same time. But listening to you a little while ago I was struck by the symmetry between Valentinus' Sophia — the Girl who, wishing to know the Father, introduces disorder, suffering, and sin into the world — and Niculina, who, for the same reason, behaves like a common prostitute and provokes scandal, endless crises, and all sorts of predicaments."

I listened, simultaneously frightened and fascinated, not daring to take my eyes off his face, not daring to interrupt him.

"I don't quite see the connection," I almost whispered at length. I thought I discerned a subtle, enigmatic satisfaction in Albini's look.

"This comparison with the Gnostic myth of Valentinus I made as something of a joke, to see how you'd react: if, for instance, you'd smile, or shrug, or become pensive. Since you've done neither, I'll abandon Sophia and limit myself to Niculina. I must tell you first that her name is not Niculina Nicolaie, but Elena Niculescu. Her mother, Irina Bogdan, although she was born to nobility and lived among landowners and wealthy people, had from youth socialistic convictions. That explains, perhaps, why she married a young typographer, Nicolaie Niculescu. All who knew him say only good things about him. He was, in any event, a handsome youth, intelligent and very industrious, because he became, rather quickly, the director of the largest printing establishment before the war, the Official Monitor. His political views are not very well known, although they were not, certainly, those of his wife, because when war was declared, he insisted on leaving for the front, although he could have remained at home, assigned to the Official Monitor. He became a prisoner and after some time his wife was informed through the Red Cross of his death. Elena, or Niculina as she calls herself now, was born soon after her father left for the front. Therefore, she never knew him except from photographs."

He stopped to light another cigarette.

"And yet, despite all this, Niculina is sure her father *didn't* die in a prison camp."

"That is true," Albini resumed. "He was repatriated in 1950, but Niculina, who was then nine, did not learn about this until much later. Besides, very soon the family began to believe that the repatriation of Nicolaie Niculescu had been just a rumor, because they never received word from him, either from the camp or after he arrived in Romania."

"And yet, it seems it was not a rumor."

"That is correct also. There exists definite proof that he crossed the Prut with a group of repatriated prisoners, and that he stayed for several days in a train station in Moldavia, waiting for a train to be formed for Bucharest. But this is all; after that, there is no trace of him. There is no evidence that he died, or that he changed his name and stayed in some village of Moldavia, or that he crossed back over into Russia. He simply *disappeared*. This means, very probably, that he *died*.

So Niculina believed, until five years ago. Her mother died a year before that, in 1960. She passed away as discreetly as she had lived. I say this because she lived exclusively for her daughter, more precisely, for her daughter's education. Indeed, the girl, very intelligent, acquired a culture I should call quite exceptional."

"She gives lessons in French and Latin. . . ."

Albini looked at me curiously, and, I thought, with some disappointment.

"That wouldn't be anything. Her friends and colleagues consider her a second Iulia Haşdeu. She knows many other things besides Latin and French. She has studied music and drama and took many courses at the Faculty of Letters."

"That's true!" I exclaimed suddenly. "She's studied literature. She knows the *Odyssey* by heart!"

"Unfortunately," Albini continued as if he hadn't heard me, "five years ago she met one of the repatriated officers who had become friends with her father; he had not met him in the camp in Russia, but in Moldavia, when they were waiting for the train to be formed for Bucharest. This was enough to drive her out of her mind. She became convinced — no one understands why because that officer couldn't tell her more than we knew already — she became convinced that her father was still alive. And so she decided to search for him."

"But how?" I asked.

Albini shrugged. "We don't have time to go into details. Of course, she needed to seek out all who had known her father, especially those who had talked with him those few days when they were waiting for the train to form. But she had to track them down, to find out if they were still living and where. All these investigations entailed time and expense, but more importantly numerous visas and special permits; hence, acquaintances and connections with the right persons. In order to obtain them, Niculina did not shrink from anything. Since she was young and very good-looking, it was not hard for her to get into the good graces of various heads and directors of the different services whose help she needed. Soon the news got around — and not just in the Capital — that she might well be the most eccentric cocotte since the war. If she had not been the protégée of a very important personage, probably she would have disappeared from circulation, especially since she had been banished from the National Theater and had not been able to find a place in any troupe in the Capital."

"I can hardly believe it," I whispered. "It hasn't been a week since I saw her playing and since I heard her talking about Hegel. . . ."

"It's true that now, recently, she has changed," continued Albini. "Perhaps, the influence of Thanase, or the engagement to Serdaru. But the troubles provoked by Veronica Bogdan, as she called herself then, still aren't ended. I repeat, I can't go into the details. It suffices for me to say that, *at the highest level*, many marriages were ruined and many careers were compromised. But, I must admit," he added, smiling bitterly, "Veronica-Niculina's a lucky one! To be precise, no matter what predicament she gets into, she always finds a protector strong enough to save her. Although, one never knows what the future will bring. . . ."

There followed several moments of silence.

"And the father," I asked. "Is she still searching for her father?"

"Probably she still is, but with other, more discreet methods. At any rate, her searches haven't given rise to any new public scandals."

I had the impression that while Albini was slowly crushing out his cigarette, he was wondering if he ought to add other details.

"I apologize for this overly long introduction. But I wanted to inform you as precisely as possible so you'd understand why it would be well for you to alert the Maestru. It would be a shame for a great writer like A. D. P. — an academician and artist emeritus of the people, one of the glories of the nation — to let himself be drawn into an intimacy with those young people that could become risky."

"Of course, I shall tell him all you told me. Although,

I don't understand. . . ."

"Because there would be much to say about Laurian Serdaru also," Albini continued. "For many years he could have been an international swimming champion, but every time he appears in a race — more precisely, is forced by his superiors to appear — he fails lamentably. Some say he does it on purpose. He claims to be an actor, and he did indeed attend the Conservatory; and he is a great master of various musical instruments no longer in use. And yet, instead of making capital of these talents, he prefers to do walk-on parts in provincial troupes."

"But now he's working with Ieronim Thanese's troupe!" I exclaimed.

Albini looked at me again, almost severely. "That's another story," he added, getting up to leave.

13

That same evening A. D. P. called. He had concluded already, from what Ecaterina had said, that I had finished typing the Introduction, and he congratulated me warmly several times.

Taking advantage of his first pause, I said quietly, "This afternoon I had an unexpected visitor. Emanoil Albini."

I got the impression the news didn't particularly surprise him. "Go on," he urged me. "I'm listening."

I summarized the conversation, without dwelling on the "Veronica Bogdan" episode, but stressing Albini's insistence that "intimacy with those young people could become risky."

"Nonsense!" he interrupted me, obviously irritated. "There's no risk. These children are both exceptional."

"But Albini says . . ."

"He's wrong," Pandele interrupted again. "At any rate," he added in a calmer tone, "if difficulties should arise, whatever they may be, Ieronim has the ability to clear things up."

I was ready to repeat what Albini had said, that Niculina is the one who enjoys protection from high places, but A. D. P. continued.

"But never mind that. You will receive tomorrow the manuscript of two plays. There is no great rush, but the sooner you start typing the better, so we can see how many pages we will have."

"The Introduction has 99 pages."

"So much the better!" he exclaimed. "An enigmatic number. Probably these two plays will not run over 150 pages. I have two others in progress. So, if Ghiţă calls, you can say that a manuscript of around four hundred pages of typing will be ready before the end of September."

I remembered just then that Valeria was returning the next day, September 1, and that I would no longer be able to spend the whole day on strada Fântânelor. As if he had read my thoughts, A. D. P. asked:

"What's the matter? Does the number of pages frighten you?"

"No, no!" I tried to protest.

"But soon you will receive your reward. Then you'll see it was worth all that effort. Courage! I'll phone you in a few days to find out the news."

I knew the only news that interested him were possible conversations with Ghiţă Horia and the number of pages of the two plays. I don't believe he cared much about my opinions on his literary production.

Ten minutes later he called me again.

"I forgot the most important thing. Please package the portfolio with the manuscript of the Introduction, seal it, and give it tomorrow to the motorcyclist. Have him sign a receipt."

The next day Valeria phoned just as I was beginning to decipher the first play.

"Meet me in half an hour!" she whispered.

"Impossible!" I exclaimed. "A. D. P. has just sent me an important manuscript. I'll explain this evening. Allow me just this afternoon. I'll come to get you at seven. . . . Hello! Hello!"

I hadn't noticed when she hung up. I dialed the number

of her house several times, but she didn't answer. I was angry, irritated with myself for my lack of tact; I could just as well have postponed till tomorrow the reading of the play. But, I realized, I was simply intrigued by those few pages I had managed to read. I didn't understand why, after he had specified that the action takes place in our day, in a park in autumn, and from the wings the conversation of young couples begins to be heard — why A. D. P. had written: "Conversation can be found in every French novel from Stendhal on, up to and including Proust. But it must not last more than three or four minutes. The final sentence will be spoken by a man (not necessarily one whose voice has been heard previously). Then there appears on stage a young man dressed rather simply, with an open book in his hand, leafing through it at random, trying to find an adequate rejoinder."

I had reached that point when the telephone rang. I reread the passage, but I couldn't concentrate. My thoughts kept running to Valeria. A little presence of mind, I said to myself, and everything would have developed as usual. I could have made a joke of it: Why exactly half an hour? How about twenty-five or forty-five minutes? — or something of that sort.

I realized that I had read some five pages without remembering what I had read. Again I tried to call her, but there was a busy signal. When I attempted to reach her again, Valeria did not answer. In order to calm myself, I began typing the manuscript. I pounded at the machine in a mechanical way, without following the sense of the dialogue. But from time to time I stopped to decipher a reply or a notation added in red pencil on the margin of the page. Since I didn't understand what it was all about, I wasn't sure I deciphered correctly.

There were some pages where I recognized the influence of the "spectacle" as conceived by Ieronim and the others. For instance, at a certain place A. D. P. had written: "Here, the reader is advised to listen to a recording of Albinoni's *Adagio*. When the play is performed, a stereophonic record must be used."

But there were also enigmatic notations, for example:

"At this point, the reader is advised to close the book and take a walk on the street (preferably a quiet street with many trees), for not more than half an hour. But during this time he must maintain the *atmosphere* of the last scene and try to recapitulate the dialogues *in reverse order*, that is, starting from the last reply he read and ending with the first sentence spoken by the young women after coming on stage." Or another example: "After the second astrologer finishes his monologue, the reader is advised to open the first book that comes to hand at page 29 and read out loud the first fifteen to twenty lines, making himself find, that is *invent*, a connection between the two texts. If in the book he opens page 29 is blank, it means the exercise has not succeeded. In that case, he must go back and reread from the beginning the scene with the two astrologers. Of course, when the play is produced, the stage manager will take care to check all the books in the little library located in front of the stage, eliminating any in which the twenty-ninth page is blank."

Deciphering and typing the monologue of the second astrologer, I wondered how and when they had appeared on stage. I reread then the last ten pages and understood that they were the same two men who appear at the beginning and who, for no apparent reason, start at a certain point to declare themselves "astrologers" and address each other with that title. I couldn't concentrate enough to tell if their behavior and vocabulary changed at that point. The plot, if it could be called a plot, did not involve any occult or magical element. The titles — because the play had three titles: two for reading and one for the production — did not contribute very much to the decipherment of the "message" (the second female character comes on stage carrying a small object; A. D. P. indicated: "Modest enough not to attract attention: a colored egg, a ball of yarn, an old-fashioned watch, with or without a chain, etc." — and showing it to the audience, she cries: "Attention! Our spectacle, even if it should trouble you or anger you, carries a message. Do your best to guess what it is, as time allows!") The titles for the readers were: "Readings from Others" and "Invitation to Your Home"; and the title for the production: "In the Beginning Was the End. . . ."

I had reached the middle of page 42 — the fifth character had just appeared, a foreign sailor, speaking a language not understood by the readers, the spectators, or the other two male actors (astrologers?), but which the two female characters understood and immediately translated — when the phone rang.

"I've forgiven you," whispered Valeria. "But come to get me at six."

I couldn't have imagined until then that so few words could make a man so happy. I glanced at my watch: five after five. I shoved the manuscript into the briefcase and set off toward her house, very excited.

14

Toward morning I realized I couldn't sleep anymore. I put on my dressing gown and, walking on tiptoe, so as not to waken Valeria, I went to the study. It was not yet daylight. I turned on the lamp and took out the play, "In the Beginning Was the End." But in vain did I try to understand the pages I read. I began to wonder if A. D. P. had not deceived himself in thinking he had a gift for writing drama. I could hear already his colleagues and enemies making fun of the three titles and the many provocatively extravagant dialogues. He seemed to me most vulnerable in that which he, probably, considered his great contribution to the dramatic art: the innovations, somewhat artificial, epigonic, reminiscent of the experiments of the first surrealists. I had begun to suffer already; it wasn't right that a great writer like A. D. P., in the twilight of his life, should be compromised in such a ridiculous way. The only hope was that Ghiță Horia would refuse the manuscript.

"In the Beginning Was the End" concluded with a brief scene in which all five characters recited, or intoned, a curious text that seemed to me, however, very well written. It changed gradually into a beautiful tale, a sort of cosmogonic myth, evoking the appearance of light over the primordial ocean, and then, in the very last sentence, proclaiming the victory of the Demiurge and exalting the majesty of the Creation. Thrilled, I turned over this last page, and was surprised — because I had not imagined that anything else could follow — by the Epilogue. A. D. P. addressed the reader directly: "If you have had the curiosity to read this play in its entirety, the most charitable observation you will have made, dear reader, is that you haven't understood it. And you are right. This was my intention in writing 'In the Beginning Was the End.' In the beginning there was what there will be at the end, and then again at the beginning — in the beginning there was chaos. But from out of that chaos there will come into being a new world, because, in contrast to the other chaoses and nothingnesses that we know, alas! all too well — *this will be a cosmogonic chaos.* From it there will be created the imaginary Universe, which we shall dare to present in several volumes to come, a dramatic Universe, that is, created expressly to be performed — and which only accidentally is signed with my name. The authors are numerous. You have read, therefore — and I hope one day you will be able to contemplate it in a theater — the dramatic description of a type of decomposition and chaos that soon will give birth to a new world, with all its potentialities intact. The last scene concludes this cosmogony. Of course, we must not imagine that any chaos or any cosmogony resembles the traditional models we know, if not from the *Rig Veda* and the *Ennuma elish,* then at least from the Bible and Hesiod. . . ."

Valeria found me at the desk, sleeping with my head on the manuscript.

"A. D. P. is a great dramatic author," I said. "But I'm afraid he won't be understood."

Fortunately, although I was still tired and sleepy, I did not repeat the same formula when, a few hours later, Ghiță Horia phoned.

"It is a highly original dramaturgy, in the tradition of the so-called theater of the absurd. It continues Eugène Ionesco and Beckett, but it profits by the experiments of Ieronim Thanase."

"So, what do you mean?" Horia demanded.

I tried to explain, without going into detail, that A. D. P. anticipated a "theater of the future," and for that reason his plays must be read and pondered in expectation of great stage directors yet to come. "In any event," I assured him, "the manuscript will contain about four hundred pages and will be ready by the end of the month."

I had hoped, in vain, that the numerous cups of coffee Ecaterina brought me would eventually have an effect. Nevertheless, I stubbornly persisted in remaining at the typewriter all afternoon, deciphering and typing like a somnambulist. But whenever I finished a new page, I felt a strange, incomprehensible satisfaction. It was as though I were running in a race that I must, at all costs, win. Toward evening only the last scene and the Epilogue remained to be typed. I returned home exhausted, and yet proud, almost triumphant.

Only the next day, after I had finished the Epilogue, did I dare open the other manuscript. It seemed to be written even more carelessly, partly with ink, partly with red pencil. It bore only two titles: "Heroic Marches" (for the reading), and "The Trojan War" (for the performance). But, as I rather expected, up to page 14, where I had arrived when the telephone rang, I had not come upon any allusion to Troy.

"Well! What's the news?" A. D. P. greeted me.

He could scarcely believe it when I told him the first play was typed and that it came to 103 pages. "It's fascinating, but on the first reading the text seems difficult. Why not publish the Epilogue as a Prologue?" I suggested.

He began to laugh, in very good spirits.

"The idea tempted me too, but we must play the game as honestly as possible. If we announce to the reader at the beginning that he won't understand any of it, and that this was the author's intention, the reading will not produce the necessary shock. As you have seen very well, the reader *must* be shocked, startled, made indignant. Only after that can *metanoia,* as Niculina calls it, take place — the 'overturning,' the awakening, the reintegration. I believe you've understood that in this chaos rich in potentialities, certain individuals can achieve self-realization even now, immediately, in the midst of the general decomposition; they are not obliged, like all the others, to wait for a new Creation in order to regain the plentitude. . . ."

I was having difficulty following him, and it is probable that A. D. P. guessed my predicament, because he interrupted his monologue abruptly.

"But, that wasn't what I called you about," he resumed after a pause. "I had a long conversation just now with Ghiţă. He repeated to me what you said to him yesterday, that the plays I'm writing are an extension of the theater of the absurd, and he acknowledged that this could cause certain objections. . . ."

"I'm sorry . . ." I began.

"It's not your fault," he interrupted. "In any event, when he reads the text, he will be shocked, too. And all the others, in the hierarchy, who will read after him, will even be alarmed, as you understand. Therefore, we have reached an agreement to have available for publication the first volume of the *Memoirs.* I believe the best thing is to end the volume at the place we stopped the last time. Please check over the text one more time, because if Ghiţă hesitates to publish the *Drama.* . . . Although, I confess, I'd be very sorry," he added.

"What should I do with 'The Trojan War?' " I asked him. "Shall I stop work on it and put the final touches on the *Memoirs?*"

"No, no! By no means. The plays have priority. Work on the *Memoirs* in your spare time. In future weeks you will receive the other two plays—the best ones, in my opinion. Courage, Eusebiu!"

I shall never forget that month, September 1966. Insomnia kept its grip on me, and after a week I had to take sleeping pills to be able to get to sleep for even three or four hours toward morning. But in the daytime I was dazed and with great effort was barely able to decipher A. D. P.'s manuscript.

On the afternoon of September 9, when I had just finished typing "The Trojan War," the door to the parlor opened suddenly. I was flabbergasted to see him. In flannel trousers, a colored shirt, tanned, with hair combed over his forehead in bangs, A. D. P. seemed ten years younger. He gave me a hug (something he had never done before) and, laughing, exclaimed: "Eusebiu, I have grown children now; I've got to look younger, too!"

But after he sat down in the chair at the desk and had scrutinized me thoroughly, he became quite serious. "What's the matter with you? You're very pale and look tired."

"For some time now I've been suffering from insomnia. I'm following in Albini's footsteps. Maybe I ought to start reading the Gnostics, too!"

I told him all Albini had said to me about Valentinus, and about Sophia who had sought the Father, and so on. I ventured to speak in passing about the symmetry Albini had remarked between Sophia and Niculina, about the crises which their efforts to 'know the Father' had provoked. He listened to me quite attentively.

"Very interesting!" he exclaimed. "That Albini's a man who'd be worth meeting. He has curious, even unique, reading habits, I'd say."

He was silent for a while, smiling absently.

"But you mustn't be overly impressed by what he told you," Pandele resumed, lowering his voice. "Do you remember that very dark young man who brought you to the camp? I found out that he is the son of Number Two, and although he has ahead of him a great political future, as you can imagine, he's working with Ieronim. Moreover, he practices all the exercises Ieronim indicates: and he practices them with the knowledge and consent of his parents. This is just between you and me. Also just between us is this detail: the boy was a stutterer, it is said, from infancy, and until five years ago he couldn't pronounce certain consonants and diphthongs. He finished lycée and was admitted to the University owing entirely to his father's position. Many of his professors and classmates considered him almost mentally retarded. But the young man has proved to be, on the contrary, rather gifted. You understand now why the whole family is grateful to Ieronim."

Then he changed the subject. He said that he had come back for twenty-four hours, that the son of Number Two had brought him in his car, and that they would dine together in the city. The publication of *Drama* was something too important — to him and to us all — for him not to do everything in his power to ensure its happening, and as soon as possible. Even if it were published in a limited edition.

He unwrapped a package that, when he came, he had laid on the desk, and took from it a folder that seemed to me rather voluminous.

"Here you have the manuscripts of two more plays, both somewhat longer than the first. Unfortunately, I wrote them in pencil, and only you are capable of deciphering — and sometimes guessing — my infernal scribbling. How far along are you with 'The Trojan War'?"

"I finished it the moment you opened the door."

"Bravo! You're a marvel! And when do you believe you could deliver the *Memoirs* manuscript to Horia?"

I shrugged. "If I could get one or two good nights' sleep, I could wind it up by the end of next week."

"You're extraordinary! But for now, you are to concentrate on the third and fourth plays. But, in order to be able to concentrate you need to rest — and try to sleep. Without sleeping pills, if possible. Take the manuscripts to your house, please, and stay in bed all day tomorrow. I myself probably will remain until tomorrow evening or the morning of the next day. In any event, I'll call you at home the day after tomorrow, in the morning, to see how you feel."

I started to ask him several things having to do with Albini, Niculina, and Serdaru, but I had the impression he wanted to be rid of me as soon as possible, so I left. At home,

when I opened the folder, and began deciphering the manuscripts, I was horrified. They were almost illegible; with so
many words abbreviated, reduced sometimes to two or three
letters, one would have said A. D. P. wrote them in a trance.
I would have to decipher them line by line. If we had been
together and he were dictating them to me, the typing would
go much faster. But after deciphering a few random pages,
they seemed less eccentric. I even came upon some very moving
passages, resembling Oriental mystic-erotic poems. But I didn't
understand their point in a drama entitled "The United Prin-
cipalities."

When he telephoned me the morning of his departure,
I was more stupefied than ever. I had tried to sleep without
pills, but I hadn't fallen asleep until nearly daybreak.

"The situation appears more favorable than Ghiţă had
imagined it," he assured me. "Very probably both volumes can
appear at the same time, at the beginning of January. . . . I
hope that from here on you'll be able to sleep better and better."

On strada Fântânelor, Ecaterina was waiting for me in
the parlor.

"We had all sorts of guests," she told me, smiling
mysteriously. "They came in several cars, each one more stylish
than the one before. And they drank champagne. And one of
the guests . . ."

It is odd now I've forgotten the rest of what she told
me, although I listened to her, doing my best to smile, pretending to be interested in all those details. The day passed before
I knew it, with my deciphering and typing, word by word,
like a beginner. By evening, I had reached only page 12. But
I retained in my mind nothing of that text, outside of the fact
that the two protagonists were telling each other their dreams,
and A. D. P. invited the reader to repeat the exercise with a
friend of either sex, but not, he specified, with a member of
one's family.

Valeria didn't think I'd succeed in finishing the work
by the twenty-fifth or twenty-sixth of September, as I had
promised. And yet somehow, by some miracle, I *did* succeed.

On the morning of September 25 I phoned Ghiţă Horia, inform-ing him that the whole volume of *Drama* — the Introduction and four plays, 398 pages — was now at his disposal. He asked how A. D. P. felt. Very frankly I replied that I didn't know. The last time I heard from him, the twentieth of September, he had called from Sibiu. At that time, tired as I was, I didn't understand what he was referring to when he said that the further his anamnesis progressed, the more certain would become the journey that would have a great importance in my life. "It could take place any time after October 15. So be prepared for any eventuality."

To our surprise, mine and Valeria's, that night I fell asleep as soon as my head touched the pillow, and I didn't awake until lunchtime the next day.

"But who's Eurydice?" Valeria asked, frowning. "You talked with her all night in your sleep."

15

A. D. P. was right. That journey — the reward he had promised me — played a decisive role in my life.

On the afternoon of October 15 he was waiting for me in front of the library. In an ordinary tone of voice he told me: "You are being sent on a cultural mission. Two months, with a per diem in hard currency. Which do you prefer: India or the United States?"

"India!" I whispered without hesitation.

"You have chosen very well! But you should know you have to be ready to leave in a few days."

I had the impression that, in addition to the satisfaction it gave him to have succeeded in arranging this exceptional trip, for reasons I couldn't imagine, A. D. P. was delighted that I would be gone from the Capital for two months. I was sur-prised especially at how easily he accepted my absence at the very time he would have great need of me. Indeed, the galley proofs of the two volumes had to be corrected by the first of

November, and Pandele had a horror of proofreading. Undoubt-edly, he had assured himself of the assistance of someone else, in addition to the publisher.

For the first time I crossed the frontier of Europe. And for the first time also I wrote something besides texts and letters in the name of A. D. P. To my surprise and delight, the pages I sent regularly, every week, to the *Literary Gazette* had great suc-cess. "You have reinvented literary reportage and rehabilitated exotic literature," A. D. P. wrote me at Delhi. (My "reportages" were, in fact, my real letters to Valeria.) And after he read my impressions from Hardwar and Rishikesh, he congratulated me, specifying: "I am convinced now that your reading of those four plays had the result I was banking on. You will understand, on your return, things which very few others understand."

On returning home, even before I set eyes on Valeria (she was still at work), I found stuck under my door a letter from Ecaterina. She had written it that same morning. She informed me that the Maestru had gone away again, without saying where he had gone or when he would return. She *absolutely must* talk with me (she had underlined the words), but not at my house nor on strada Fântânelor. She proposed we meet as if *accidentally* (underscored) on one of the streets around the Statue. She would go walking there every morning between ten and eleven, and again between four and five.

I telephoned the house on strada Fântânelor anyway. An unknown, surly young masculine voice answered. As soon as I identified myself, the young man became affable. He was Nicolaie Voinea, my replacement; he was occupied with proof-reading and correspondence. The Maestru, he said, was in Transylvania, in a village near Sibiu, attending rehearsals of a "spectacle" Ieronim was preparing. He concluded by saying that he would be phoning A. D. P. that evening, and that very probably the Maestru would call me the next morning.

I had not begun to unpack my suitcase when Valeria returned. The first thing she said to me was the date she had set for our wedding: the twenty-ninth of December, that is, in eight days.

"It's my birthday," she added, smiling sheepishly.

I looked at her in surprise, trying to guess what she meant, "You've always told me your birthday was January 29. It's even recorded that way on your identification papers."

"I wanted to make myself a year younger," she explained, blushing slightly. "It seemed ridiculous that for two or three days . . . you understand what I mean."

Just then the telephone rang, and I lifted the receiver excitedly. I was almost certain A. D. P. was calling.

"I'm glad you've returned home on time!" he exclaimed. "I was afraid you might stay several days at Pondichery. And that would have been a pity. We are approaching . . ."

The connection was then cut off, and I slammed the receiver down angrily. Some ten minutes passed before the phone rang again. This time his voice was far off, muffled, and I understood the words with difficulty.

"Very important things . . . But I don't know what's wrong with the connection. Do you hear me? *Very important*! Can you hear? . . . Then it's no use. . . . I'll call back tomorrow, at the same time."

"What did he say?" asked Valeria, seeing my disappointment.

I shrugged. "I didn't understand the point. The connection was very bad. Probably he was speaking from that village near Sibiu."

"Then it's on account of the snow," Valeria interrupted. "It's been snowing all over northern Transylvania for two days and nights. But what do you think he wanted to tell you?"

"He repeated several times that it was a matter of something *very important*. Probably having to do with the 'spectacle' Ieronim is preparing. I found out about it a little while ago from my 'replacement,' a certain Nicolaie Voinea. It seems that A. D. P. is attending all the rehearsals. Somewhere in a village near Sibiu."

Valeria suddenly became pensive. "But I hope he'll come to the wedding," she said presently. "I understand he doesn't want to hold the marriage crown over our heads, nor

even be a witness, but I do hope he'll come to the ceremony.*
All my family, and especially Mother, have been waiting for
this more than anything: to meet, *personally*, the greatest living
Romanian writer."

I realized then that since she had entered the door,
Valeria had not asked me a single question about my trip to
the East, and I hadn't asked her anything about what she had
been doing during the two months of our separation; we had
spoken of nothing except the date of the wedding and A. D. P.
Laughing, I took her in my arms.

"But Pandele has never claimed to be the greatest living
Romanian writer," I said.

"Anyway, I hope he'll come to the wedding," she continued in the same tone. "If not, it would be a great blow for
all of us, but for Mama especially."

16

From a distance, Ecaterina looked the same. Once she recognized me, her face brightened and she hurried toward me.
But no sooner had she taken my hand and shaken it, than
she turned her head and began looking suspiciously up and
down the street, searching the balconies with cautious eyes,
prying into the paved courtyards. Never had I seen her so
frightened.

"There's no one around," I assured her, smiling.

I continued to hold her hand, but she jerked it away
suddenly, almost fiercely, and thrust it into the pocket of her
coat as though she wanted to hide it. Then she burst out in a
loud voice, almost shouting:

"How are you, domnule Eusebiu! When did you get
back? Did you arrive yesterday? What a pleasant surprise!"

It seemed to me she was signaling me with her eyes

*In Eastern Orthodox weddings, the best man holds a crown,
usually consisting of a wreath of flowers, over the heads of the bride and
the groom, to symbolize their day of divine majesty.

to say something else.

"How's the Maestru?" I asked.

"Louder, please, louder; I don't hear very well."

"How is the Maestru?" I repeated, as loudly as I could. "How are things going at the house?" But raising my voice made me choke, and I began to cough.

"Now we can go," Ecaterina whispered. "And if I make a sign with my glove, like so" (and she showed me), "you pretend you have to cough again. . . . So, as I was saying," she resumed in the same loud voice, "everything's going very well."

We walked on slowly, side by side, and although I guessed from the start that she was afraid of something, I did not understand the meaning of these exaggerated precautions.

"So, as I was saying," she repeated again. Then, with her eyes fixed straight ahead, twirling one of her gloves unconsciously, she began her story.

From the day of my departure, much had happened on strada Fântânelor. Niculina and Serdaru had taken up residence there: they slept sometimes in the study, sometimes in the drawing room. That wouldn't have been so bad, if there had not been such a succession of strange people coming and going through the house, day and night. Once, sometime after two-thirty in the morning, a car stopped in front of the house and began honking its horn. She jumped out of bed and ran to the window to see what the matter was. As she was drawing the curtains apart, with great caution, she began to hear an uproar in the drawing room and laughter, and someone shouted: "We're coming! We're coming!" The car was large and elegant, and just as she looked, that very dark youth, the one who had come several times in the summer (obviously, the son of Number Two), was getting out of it. He looked in the direction of the drawing room window and then, speaking very loudly, he addressed someone in the back seat of the automobile.

"Give me your cane, and I'll beat on the door!"

"Maybe they've gotten the dates mixed up!" the other

replied in an equally loud voice, handing him the cane. (Very probably, it was Ieronim Thanase.)

But while the young man was walking toward the front door, those who had been sleeping in the drawing room or the study appeared at the top of the steps.

"Were they Niculina, Serdaru, and someone else?" I asked.

"I don't know who they were. There were three persons. I didn't recognize any of them. I know that the 'young married couple' — because that's what the Maestru calls them — slept at our place, but I didn't recognize them. . . . And yet it was they," she added, lowering her voice even more, "because the next morning, when I went to the drawing room to tell them coffee was ready, there was no one there, and their beds — in a manner of speaking, because they weren't really beds; they slept sometimes on the sofa, sometimes on pallets — their beds were made. . . . But, as I was saying," she added, abruptly raising her voice and signaling with her glove.

I started coughing, at the same time reaching for my handkerchief. A few meters ahead, coming toward us, was an elderly man with a scarf wrapped snugly around his neck. As soon as he passed, Ecaterina signaled me to turn my head, to see if he was walking on.

"Because you have no idea how many there are or who they are," she said, breathing hard.

"But the Maestru — what did he say?"

That night A. D. P. had not been home. He returned — "from the provinces," Ecaterina emphasized with irony — some three days later. And when Ecaterina had tried to tell him about it, he had smiled and interrupted her.

"It was just a mistake," he said. "It wasn't their fault. Niculina and Laurian were sure that the rehearsals would take place the following Wednesday, at one A.M. They had been so informed by Tudorel — the young chap who slept in the kitchen or the hallway" (I understood that he was Serdaru's favorite pupil, the one who had brought me back from the camp that summer). "Tudorel had written down the wrong day in his date book."

"So," I ventured to interrupt her, "the three were Niculina, Serdaru, and Tudorel."

"I'm sure they were, but who'd recognize them? Who knows what 'spectacle' they were practicing for that night before going to bed — because that's what they called them: 'spectacles.' And they practiced almost every night — *with all the doors shut,*" she emphasized, watching my expression closely. "Usually, only those three plus the Maestru, if he was at home. But sometimes ten or fifteen would gather . . . some of them tall as the door. I don't know what they were practicing, but I'd hear them laughing, singing — and they'd all sing, very beautifully, in chorus, or separately, and they had all kinds of musical instruments. . . ."

"What do the neighbors say?"

She turned toward me and smiled — a smile that seemed mysterious, yet ironic.

"After they found out who was meeting there and where the Maestru is being invited, they didn't dare say anything. Although . . ."

She hesitated a few moments, then she gave me a suspicious look again, as though trying to guess what I was thinking.

"I oughtn't to tell you, but you, who have been the Maestru's right-hand man . . ."

"And I hope to continue to be from here on," I tried to joke, smiling.

"May God grant it!" she sighed, "but so many things have changed since you left. I oughtn't to tell you, but . . ."

She lowered her voice still more.

"From time to time, toward midnight, a car parks in front of the doctor's house — you know where I mean, the third house from the corner — and stays there all night, with the lights out. But the car isn't empty. Once one night — the music wasn't bothering me, I'd gotten used to the rehearsals, but I seemed to have a premonition — I got out of bed and tiptoed to the window. At just that moment the very dark young man came out of the house with Serdaru. I saw them go to the car. I don't know what they talked about with the driver, or who else was inside, but soon afterward the car started away, moving slowly with the lights still off. . . . And there's something else, but it's a great secret, and I oughtn't to tell you. . . ."

"You know you can trust me completely," I encouraged her. "We didn't meet just yesterday or the day before. And we're both devoted to the Maestru. Really, what would the Maestru have done without you and me?"

She looked at me with warmth, gratefully, but she could not suppress a sigh.

"I know," she whispered. "That's why I've got to tell you. The next day after the episode with the car, when I was coming back from the cooperative, I was stopped by a gentleman — not young, not old — dressed very stylishly. When he lifted his hat to salute me, I saw he was almost bald. Very politely he told me his name, but I can't remember it now." (Evidently, it was Albini.) "He asked me if I had news from you, because, he said, all kinds of rumors were going around town — that you weren't coming back, that the Maestru had persuaded you to stay there, in India, if not permanently, then at least several years, until he should come himself. . . ."

I listened, fascinated, not daring to interrupt.

"I told him the truth, that is, what I knew from the publishing house: that you were coming back on the twentieth or twenty-first of December, but he quickly changed the subject. He told me he had admired the Maestru's books since his youth, and for that reason he was worried about all that's been going on in the past few months, that the neighbors have complained, that he knows . . . Why, he knows everything — he knows what the young married couple are doing, the 'spectacle' they're working on. And then, he took out a calling card and said, 'It so happens that the function I have opens many doors for me. If you ever have any difficulty, or any other sort of problem, call me at this number.' I kept the card, but I've never telephoned him," she added.

I breathed a sigh of relief and began to laugh.

"In other words that's why you were so afraid and almost didn't dare speak, even on the street. You were afraid you were being followed by the Security."

Ecaterina stopped walking and turned toward me with a look of amazement. "What would the Security have to do with me?!" she exclaimed. "I mind my own business. I don't meddle in politics or anything else. . . ."

"Then if you *know* you aren't being followed, why so many precautions?"

"If you'd let me finish," she whispered, "you'd understand why I'm so scared. . . . And when you've heard it all, you'll be scared too."

It had all begun some two weeks after my departure. One evening, on entering the drawing room to light the Japanese lantern, she discovered an elderly woman asleep on the sofa. Ecaterina screamed, and when the woman awoke, she asked her who she was and when she had come. The woman looked at her curiously, as though she didn't understand Romanian well. And indeed, when she got up from the couch, Ecaterina realized she was a foreigner. She was dressed oddly, though stylishly, in a long dress of red silk and was wearing shoes such as Ecaterina had never seen: they seemed coated with gold. The woman kept staring at her and smiling, and to all Ecaterina's questions, she shrugged her shoulders. She might have been fifty or fifty-five, but when she smiled, she seemed younger. Only when Ecaterina started for the telephone, the woman stretched out her arms toward her and said very softly, "Ecaterina, don't do that! Don't play with fire!"

"And didn't you recognize the voice?" I broke in. "Didn't you realize it was Niculina, sleeping there on the couch in the costume she wore at rehearsals?"

Ecaterina looked straight at me again and frowned. "I couldn't recognize the voice, because it was *not* Niculina. She didn't sound like Niculina. Her voice was weak, like an old woman's. She was taller than Niculina. Her hair was gray."

"Then, who was she?" I asked, troubled.

"I don't know. And that's why I'm scared. Because after she said, 'Don't play with fire!' she added, 'Now, I can tell you because we're well acquainted. I am the wife of Laurian Serdaru; therefore, if you have learned the secret, I'm the Maestru's daughter-in-law. Everyone calls me Niculina, and I like that name very much. But it isn't my name. Niculina you will meet in an hour or an hour and a half, because this evening we are guests of the Maestru.' And she made a deep bow, as at the theater, took her golden slippers in her hand, and headed toward the bathroom."

"And so, after all, it was she!"

Ecaterina shrugged her shoulders in exasperation and sighed. "I told you once, and I tell you again, it wasn't her. And I have proof that it *couldn't have been* Niculina."

Indeed, A. D. P. was not in Bucharest and on that evening there were no guests. When, about an hour later, she met Niculina, she had said, "You really gave me a scare a little while ago!" Niculina replied, "A scare? What do you mean?" and after Ecaterina had told her the story of the incident, Niculina shook her head. "It wasn't I. At that hour I was at rehearsal." "Then who could it have been?" Ecaterina had exclaimed in alarm. "Who could have gotten into the drawing room without my knowing it?" "Anyone of us can enter that room because we each have a key, the eleven of us in Ieronim's troupe. We had to have keys made so we wouldn't be bothering you all the time. Because, as you have seen, people come and go here day and night."

"So, it was someone from the troupe," I murmured, still troubled. "Didn't she tell you who?"

Ecaterina looked at me again, and I did not understand why she should be smiling in amusement.

"Do you know what she said when I asked her? She said, 'The way you describe her, fifty to fifty-five, with gray hair and a pair of golden slippers in her hand, it could have been anyone of the five girls, because that's how many there are of us in Ieronim's troupe: five girls and six boys.' "

"And the Maestru? What did the Maestru say when

you told him all this?"

According to what I understood, because Ecaterina was walking faster and faster and there were words that escaped me, A. D. P. had tried to calm her, assuring her that it *was*, in fact, Niculina. As to what was she up to, he had added that they are young and like to have fun; they're always playing jokes on one another.

"If that was only all it was," continued Ecaterina, "just jokes and games of young actors . . ."

But Ecaterina was convinced that there was *something else* at the bottom of it; she didn't know *what*, but it was enough to frighten her. Not a week after that episode Grigore at the Cooperative called her toward evening to say he was sending her four rabbits. In order not to attract the neighbors' attention, he asked her to stand at the window between five-fifteen and five-thirty, and as soon as the car stopped, to open the kitchen door so the driver would not have to wait. She followed the instructions, but the driver could not — or would not — get out, and he called to her to come. It was raining, and Ecaterina signaled to him to wait a little, while she put on her coat and found something to cover her head. But when she was ready to go out, a young man crossed the street on the run, went to the car, took the bag with the rabbits, and called to her to stay where she was, in the kitchen doorway. The car left immediately, a truck approached from the other direction, and seeing that the youth was waiting there, for a few seconds she thought she had been hoodwinked. But after a little while the boy entered the kitchen laughing with the sack of rabbits bouncing on his back. Ecaterina wanted to give him something and she started searching her pockets.

"Don't trouble yourself, Ecaterina," the boy said. "I'm from this house."

And since Ecaterina stared at him in surprise, trying to recognize him, he added, "After all these weeks, don't you know me? I'm Laurian, Niculina's husband."

"He must have just come from a rehearsal," I said.

So she also believed. But she couldn't get enough of

looking at him, marveling, repeating over and over: "Gracious me! What luck! You're ten years younger — you, of all people, who didn't need it. . . ."

A few moments later Niculina entered the kitchen with an empty carafe, headed for the faucet.

"What do you say about this domnul Laurian?" Ecaterina asked. "Sheer magic!"

The young man looked perplexed and began to wipe his hand nervously across his face.

"Laurian's in the drawing room, with all the others," was Niculina's response. "And they're all thirsty."

"You see, she doesn't wish to recognize me," the young man whispered through his teeth, and opening the door suddenly, almost angrily, he disappeared into the rain.

And to the present day Ecaterina had not known what to believe. When she was alone, she had taken off her coat, unfastened the sack, and looked in the drawer for some heavy cord and hooks with which to hang the rabbits in the pantry, but a little while later she found herself shivering, and she put her coat on again. However, she soon realized that she was shivering from fear, not the cold. She started crossing herself, but her eyes fell on the rabbits, which she still had not removed from the sack, and she was ashamed. She jerked off the coat roughly and forced herself not to think. But curiosity kept gnawing at her, and after she had hung up the four rabbits in the pantry, she made a decision. She knew that only at night were the drawing room doors locked, but A. D. P. had strictly charged her several times that *under no circumstances* was she to enter that room during rehearsals. After she had found a reason (Niculina had said they were thirsty), she took from the refrigerator a bottle of mineral water, selected several glasses, and with a full tray in her right hand she knocked briefly on the drawing room door and went in. There were six or seven young people there, curiously costumed: each seemed to have a long cape, every one a different color, hanging over his shoulders. They turned their heads toward her, startled. She stood speechless, with an arm upraised, her mouth half open.

237

Beside her, in a mantle of bright red, was Laurian Serdaru. He too looked at her with surprise. But Ecaterina was sure, and perhaps would even swear, that at a certain moment Serdaru had smiled at her meaningfully and winked.

17

Walking home, I realized that those events from early November had provoked in Ecaterina a trauma that might possibly lead to a persecution complex. Since that evening when she had interrupted a "rehearsal," she had thought she was being followed by all manner of strange personages, each of whom, ultimately, proved to be one of the habitués of the house, usually Niculina or Serdaru, but sometimes others — Tudorel, for instance, or one of the actresses, the one called Vera. She would stop now and then at a shop window, and suddenly someone would appear behind her, and by the way he or she looked at her, or by the way he or she smiled, Ecaterina would discover that the person belonged to Ieronim's troupe. But the difficulty had just begun, because it was not easy to identify the person exactly. Sometimes it took two or three days and nights.

"I've been waiting for you as for a god!" she exclaimed as we parted, clasping both my hands. "As for a god!" she repeated several times.

Only after I had taken off my overcoat and sat down at the desk did I remember that I would have to go to the publishing house. I wanted to see how A. D. P.'s two books looked, but even more, I wanted to find out what Ghiță Horia thought about my project of collecting my articles about India in a volume. The idea of the volume had been suggested to me by A. D. P. in his last letter: "I knew you were a good writer, because you wrote the *Memoirs* in a way I never could have been able to write them. But I didn't suspect you were a good writer in a *style very different than mine.* We have worked together almost eight years, and I never suspected this *specific quality* of your literary talent."

I hesitated: should I telephone Horia — it was almost 12:00 — or just go to see him unannounced at the beginning of the afternoon? A few moments later the telephone rang.

"Where've you been all morning?" A. D. P. demanded, sounding, I thought, somewhat annoyed.

"I happened to run into Ecaterina, and we had a long talk. Poor woman, she's afraid that . . ."

"Never mind Ecaterina!" he interrupted. "We have more important things to discuss. And we can't discuss them over the phone. You will have to come to Sibiu. I've reserved a seat for you on the plane tomorrow morning. Call the agency, or better still, go there yourself before four and pick up your ticket. I'll be waiting at the airport. And right after lunch . . ."

With an effort I ventured to interrupt. "But, Maestre, you see, it's almost Christmas Eve, and I've just returned. I want to spend the holidays with Valeria. Especially since we're getting married on the twenty-ninth of the month."

I had the impression this piece of news surprised him, because, after a brief silence, he continued in a different tone of voice.

"Very well, but today is December 23. We still have a week. We'll return on the twenty-sixth, or at the latest the twenty-seventh. Since I'm holding the crown for you, the wedding can't take place without me."

I flushed suddenly with excitement, and I felt my mouth become dry. "But you've told me so many times," I murmured weakly, "you've said you didn't wish to hold the crown for us. . . ."

"What I said another time," A. D. P. interrupted, in very good spirits, "doesn't matter! I want very much to crown you. And we'll celebrate the event on strada Fântânelor with Niculina, Laurian, and several other friends."

"Obviously," I resumed in a firmer voice, "obviously Valeria will be happy and grateful. As well as myself, needless to say. But I think if I leave her alone at Christmas . . . "

"Eusebiu!" he exclaimed, almost pathetically. "It's very

important! I can't tell you why now, but you *must* come tomorrow. I'll wait for you at the airport. And thank Valeria for me, for accepting this sacrifice!"

After hanging up the phone, I sat for a long while staring into space. As I came to my senses, I realized I was thinking of something else entirely. I was striving to remember a scene from Pandele's third or fourth play, a scene which, it seemed to me, might explain why he had insisted so pathetically on having me with him from Christmas Eve until two or three days afterward. Someone (impossible for me to remember who), finding himself in a desperate situation (but why, *why?*), makes a pathetic appeal to a younger friend; he asks him for something, apparently ridiculously commonplace (a glass of water, a handkerchief?), at the same time announcing a reward: *there will be a fairytale wedding,* and he, *He* himself, will crown them, and will invite to the dinner not only friends, but also . . . Impossible to remember who the others are who will be invited to the "banquet" (in the text the word was *agapa*).

Excited, I dialed Horia's number. I did not expect to find him, since it was past one, but I knew his secretary would answer.

"I was just going to lunch," Horia answered. "So please be as brief as possible."

But he left me no time to say anything, continuing in a dry, almost severe tone. "If it's about your *India*, we'll have to discuss that seriously."

"But it's not about my book, " I interrupted. "I wanted to say . . ."

"I don't say your texts aren't interesting," he continued as though he hadn't heard me. "But you've got to vary them. You dwell too much on 'Indian spirituality,' on hermits and monasteries. . . ."

"But I'm telling you, it's not a matter of my book. . . ."

"You have to evoke other aspects of Indian history and society: poverty, social injustices, caste, the untouchables. . . . You don't say anything about the untouchables. . . ."

240

With an effort I succeeded in keeping my temper. "Comrade Horia," I began pronouncing clearly and plainly each separate word. "I repeat, it is not a matter of my book. I only want to know if A. D. P.'s book, *Drama*, has appeared yet, and if I can come by after lunch and pick up a copy."

It seemed he hesitated too long before replying. "To be perfectly frank, the volume is printed, but I haven't seen it yet. It could appear in about two weeks, if, in the meantime, what I was afraid from the start . . ."

"Very well," I interrupted him politely, "I don't wish to detain you. I'll phone you again after the holidays."

As soon as I had replaced the receiver I realized I had made a blunder. Suspicious as he was, who knew what Horia would imagine? I should have gone directly to my "replacement"; he certainly would have a set of page proofs. But to my surprise, Voinea told me that all the material — the manuscripts, galleys, and page proofs — had been sent, at his request, to A. D. P., by courier, at the beginning of the month. What had seemed strangest to him, he added, lowering his voice slightly, was that a few days later he had received a phone call from the publishing house saying that they needed the manuscripts and proofs for a final review. But Voinea knew very well that the final editorial review had been made the previous week; he himself had given the copy to the printer. He had had the impression — and saying this he lowered his voice still more — that when Horia's secretary learned what had happened, namely, that all the material was in the hands of A. D. P., he had not known what to say, and so had asked him to wait a moment and speak to the Director. After listening to Voinea, Ghiţă Horia had said, "Very well!" and had hung up the phone.

Again, it seemed to me I had made a blunder: who knows how Voinea would interpret my desire to reread a text I myself had typed three months earlier? And what if, in an hour or two, Horia should phone him and ask, "Has Damian perhaps called you about . . . ?" Maybe I ought to warn him, to tell him, for instance, that if anyone should inquire about me, to tell him that . . . Just then I remembered Ecaterina, and I rose from the chair, unable to sit still.

Valeria had prepared a lunch of cold cuts and grapes for me. I ate absently, without much appetite. But soon I saw the first flakes of snow, and my spirits brightened as if by magic. I stood a long while at the window, watching the snow fall. When I set off for the travel agency an hour later, the snow in places was several centimeters deep. As I expected, the ticket had been prepaid by Pandele.

"But if it snows all night," the clerk said, "I don't believe you will be able to leave tomorrow morning. At any rate, be at the airport at least a half hour early."

I wanted to wander about the city for a while, to go down to Cişmigiu, but I said to myself if the snow doesn't let up, very probably Pandele will telephone to change the schedule.

While waiting for the call, I fell asleep in the easy chair. Valeria awakened me, shaking the snow off her galoshes vigorously in front of the door. When I told her A. D. P. would hold the crown for us, she stopped stock-still in the middle of the floor; then she threw her arms around me and began to dance, pulling me along, humming — but more and more softly, because she could not hold back her tears. She wanted to call home immediately, to announce the great news, but I held her back.

"Of course, all joys have their prices. Pandele insists I come tomorrow to Sibiu. He absolutely must have me there."

And because she looked so surprised, as if she hadn't understood, I added quickly, "It's just a matter of twenty-four hours, or thirty-six at the most. We'll be back, both of us, the second day after Christmas at the latest."

"But that's impossible!" Valeria interrupted, brightening. "No airplanes are leaving for Transylvania. I heard it on the radio."

"So I was told also at the agency. But if A. D. P. doesn't call, then tomorrow morning I shall have to . . ."

242

18

As a matter of fact, I didn't know if our plane would be able to land at Sibiu until the last moment, when, after waiting almost two hours, I was ready to give up. Fortunately, as we neared Sibiu, the landscape became like a fairyland. I had never seen that part of the country buried under snow. The sky cleared suddenly, and we were blinded by the glare of a harsh, polar light. Soon the airplane checked its engines and descending we were able to distinguish more and more clearly the railroad tracks and country houses. Then, we saw the city, we passed over a newly constructed quarter, and a few minutes later we landed.

A. D. P. was waiting for me, beaming, accompanied by Serdaru and Tudorel. He embraced me, I thought, with unusual feeling. Then he shook my hand a long time.

"Thank you for coming," he said softly. "I know you made a sacrifice."

I didn't know what to think. He looked even younger than he had the past autumn, yet despite this he had trouble hiding his nervousness. He seemed restless, preoccupied.

"The Maestru is tired," said Serdaru, as if he had read my thoughts. "He slept only a few hours last night. He stayed up till 2:30 to see the end, although all of us, and Ieronim especially, kept trying to . . ."

"Never mind that," A. D. P. interrupted, managing nevertheless to smile. "We have so many other things to talk about."

Then, turning to me and taking my hand, he continued. "I'm not asking you anything about India. We shall discuss that later. Let me give you the schedule from here on: lunch at the Majestic — I've reserved a table; then by military vehicle — in fact, a sort of jeep — to Călina. It's less than ten kilometers, but the highway's snowed under in spots, and with a regular automobile it would be too risky. We're staying in a former hunting lodge, transformed into a rest house; rather comfortable, and, although it has been remodeled twice, still rather picturesque. And from there on," he continued, smiling at me enigmatically, "we can't count on anything but sleighs."

"But you can't imagine what kind of sleighs," Serdaru added. "Like those from olden times. No longer seen, except in period films."

"But they're more beautiful than those in *Anna Karenina*, a film of last year," said Tudorel.

"Perhaps we'll make a film, too," added A. D. P. "We'll see."

"You shouldn't have told him," whispered Serdaru, somewhat disappointed. "I wanted it to be a surprise."

Pandele looked at him and shrugged. "It will suffice for him to see the sleighs, the horses, and the equipment in the dining room, and he'll understand what it's all about."

I don't know if I would have guessed so quickly. I had no way of knowing that the jeep which brought us to the rest house, as well as the horses of peerless beauty which were led out of the stable the moment we arrived, belonged to the Corps of the Army in Sibiu. Likewise I had no way of knowing that the sleighs I saw in the courtyard had been built that fall on the model of the sleighs of the Hungarian nobles of 1840, preserved in the Museum of Ethnography. Nor did I wonder at the picturesque costumes of the young men in the entryway and corridor; I assumed they were coming from or going to a rehearsal. But I believe I would have begun to suspect certain scenes were to be filmed when I set eyes on the floodlights in the dining room and the high platform on wheels in the hallway.

Once we were alone in the room he had chosen for me, next door to his own, A. D. P. seated himself on the edge of the bed and motioned for me to draw my chair closer.

"I have so many things to tell you," he began, in a voice that was almost hushed, "that I don't know where to start. I'll begin, however, with what seems to me least important."

As I listened, I wondered why it seemed "least important" to him. To me it sounded rather serious. It was a matter of a secret struggle for power between Number Three and Number Two. The tension had been building for some time, but in the past few weeks it was threatening to explode. "Obviously," A. D. P. added, "this complicates Ieronim's situation. Number Three's men have their eyes on him, ready to take advantage of the first slip he makes. Very probably, many of the technicians and operators are informers for Number Three. Some of them — of course, without realizing it — betrayed themselves that morning when they saw Ieronim handing over his canes to a minor actor and climbing onto the platform to adjust the spotlights.

"Yes," continued A. D. P., giving me no time to interrupt, "about ten days ago Ieronim sensed that he didn't need his canes anymore. 'I finally identified the error I committed on the evening of August 11, 1964,' Ieronim explained to me, 'and, just as I expected, at the same moment I was healed.' "

"Extraordinary!" I exclaimed. "Simply extraordinary!"

"Yes," resumed A. D. P., "so said we all. But you see, that mysterious healing took place at a very inconvenient moment for all of us, and for Ieronim especially. As I told you, several mechanics and operators betrayed themselves instantly; they rushed to telephone the news to Bucharest. Neither Ieronim nor Number Two finds it convenient to speak about this miracle just now. . . . But, anyway, as I said, this is not the most important thing."

More serious, it seemed to him, was the intrigue plotted against him, which could lead to the prohibiting of his volume of *Drama*. This intrigue had no direct connection with the tension between Number Two and Number Three, but, undoubtedly, some of his colleagues, jealous and envious, were ready to take advantage of the combination of circumstances. (I understood that he was thinking especially of Paraschiv Simionescu, who could not rest easy so long as A. D. P. was on intimate terms with the family of Number Two.) For that reason A. D. P. had taken the necessary precautions: he had made ten photocopies of the *Drama* volume and had put them in secure places, in different locations — *even in several different countries*, he emphasized. I wanted to interrupt him just then, to say that perhaps the situation wasn't as critical as he imagined it, when he stood up suddenly, strode to the door, and opened it quickly. Seeing no one in the corridor, he sighed with relief and smiled.

"As you can see," he resumed in a different tone of voice, "one might say I'm following in Ecaterina's footsteps. But *here,* and *at this moment,* we must keep our eyes wide open. Except for ourselves — those we know — anyone could be an agent."

"I'm sorry," I began somewhat tentatively, seeing that the silence was lengthening. "I, on the contrary, believe that . . . "

"Eusebiu!" he exclaimed, cutting me short, "all I've been saying to you confirms what I've suspected for some time, for at least two weeks. The truth is, *I'm afraid*! I don't dare confess to you what I ought to confess, and then, in order to postpone that painful confession, I keep talking about this and that. All I've told you about Number Three, about Paraschiv's intrigue, is true. I haven't invented anything. But, I repeat, all of this isn't of much significance. The only important thing is the discovery I made recently, which I dare not reveal to you!"

I listened to him with mounting agitation. Pandele took several steps around the room, then sat down again on the edge of the bed.

"You have realized, surely," he began abruptly, "that the 'spectacle' organized by Ieronim has as its aim, first of all, the completion of the process of anamnesis begun last summer. But the thing only I know is that *I completed this anamnesis some time ago.* I've remembered all that happened the night of Christmas, 1938 — I've succeeded in remembering every detail. (It was not for nothing that I participated so enthusiastically in all Ieronim's rehearsals!) There's no need for me to go over them, because not all the particulars are interesting. It's enough to tell you that, at first, to be very frank and perhaps even vulgar, at first I believed that on that night I had drunk too much — I who was not used to strong alcohol — and I had gone to bed with the actress who played the role of Eurydice. And I said to myself that, very probably, the next day I had been ashamed of myself — not for going to bed with her, but because I had been drunk and probably had behaved like a brute — and being ashamed, I had avoided meeting her for the next two or three days. I said to myself that my conduct surely had been so odious that unconsciously I had wanted to forget — and *had succeeded* in forgetting — everything from the beginning until the time I left to return to Bucharest. I was aware that psychologically the process did not seem too plausible, but finally, I pretended to be convinced that it *had happened that way.*"

He stood up and began pacing the floor; he seemed not to know what to do with his hands.

"The truth is something else entirely. I was not drunk that night, and my behavior was as courteous as possible. In short, it was a very sincere, even romantic night of love that I should have preserved always as a fond, melancholy memory. I should have, and certainly I would have, if something else hadn't happened, a highly unusual episode. And that 'something else' provoked the amnesia."

He stopped in front of me and stared curiously, as if he were seeing me for the first time.

"But how," he began again after a pause, "can I speak about the cause of my amnesia without running the risk that you, or anyone else who hears me, will believe I've lost my mind? Apparently, everything seems normal. At a certain moment, Eurydice proposed we take a sleigh and go to visit a girlfriend of hers who lived in a forester's house some five or six kilometers from Sibiu. Of course, I agreed immediately and Eurydice began to laugh. She said she had been so sure I would accept the idea that she had told the friend to expect us for dinner. I needn't describe the trip to the forest, the two of us snuggled together in the sled. I felt myself already in love. We were both surprised when we arrived to find all the lights lit and the table set for dinner, but no sign of the friend. We were relieved, somewhat, reading the note she had left us. Just these enigmatic lines: 'If you are waiting for someone, I assure you you are not waiting for me.' A few minutes after I read the note, I forgot everything. But now I remember. The two of us were alone, the champagne was chilled and the dinner seemed excellent. I told you what happened next. . . . But how can I relate the rest?"

He stopped in front of me again and sought my eyes.

"And yet, *I must tell you*," he almost whispered. "Later, toward morning, I woke up, suddenly very thirsty. I don't believe I had ever experienced such a terrible thirst: it was as though I had swallowed hot coals. I got out of bed and went to the kitchen. I found a water faucet, put my mouth directly to it, and began to drink like an animal. For several moments I felt nothing, as though I were swallowing air, and sleepy as I was, a horrible thought struck me: *what if I can never quench this thirst?* I continued to drink, more and more alarmed, and then I saw a face at the window, almost pressed against the glass to be able to see me better — the face of a young woman with long, blond hair hanging to her shoulders. When she realized I had seen her, she gave me a sign to say nothing, putting her finger to her lips. The next moment she vanished."

He began pacing the floor again, from one end of the room to the other.

"It is odd that I wasn't frightened. But returning to the bedroom, I saw Eurydice. She had awakened and had turned on the flashlight that I had left on the stand by the bed. I felt as though I had taken a chill, but strangely, instead of getting back into bed quickly, I put on my overcoat (why I had left it there on the chair, I don't know).

" 'What does your friend look like?' I asked her. Eurydice smiled, but I thought there was much sorrow in her look.

" 'Why do you ask?'

" 'Because just now, when I was in the kitchen I saw a face at the window, the face of a young woman, and I wondered if some misfortune might have happened. If perhaps . . .'

"Eurydice began to laugh. 'To tell you the truth, there is no friend. *I* arranged this surprise in great secrecy. I came here this afternoon, prepared the meal, wrote the note, and lit the lamps. . . . But why are you looking at me that way?' she asked, in a troubled voice.

"I didn't know what to reply. I thought I was dreaming, but I couldn't imagine when the dream had begun.

" 'Did you think she looked like me?' Eurydice continued, speaking very softly. 'Did she have long, blond hair, like mine? And did she put her finger to her lips, to signal you to keep the secret?'

"From that point on, I remember nothing. I don't know how I got back to the hotel."

Just then we heard Niculina's voice. "Forgive me, but without meaning to I overheard what you were saying, from outside the door. But I made sure no one else was listening."

Then she went quickly to Pandele and took his hand.

"Forgive me, *mon père*, if I dare to contradict you. From a certain moment, perhaps when you began to drink from the tap and did not taste the water — from that moment on it can't be an anamnesis, but rather a figment of your imagination."

"Why do you say that?" asked A. D. P., embarrassed.

"Because, in no event could such a total amnesia be provoked by a shock of that nature. If it had been as you said, you could not have forgotten that scene, no matter how hard you tried. Events of that sort — hallucinations, or parapsychological phenomena, or whatever they are — are rather common. Perhaps long ago, you read a story like that, and you became convinced it had happened to you."

"And yet, I repeat to both of you, *that's how it happened!* And for that reason, I'm afraid. I'm not ashamed to say it: *I'm afraid!*"

"You have every right to be afraid," continued Niculina, smiling. "This is part of the process of anamnesis itself. Only, that fear of which you speak is *not* due to the scene you evoked just now: the face you saw at the kitchen window and which, several minutes later, you recognized as being that of Eurydice. This scenario is a last attempt you are making—or rather, not you, but something else, deep down in your unconscious — a last attempt *to prevent the truth from being revealed.* If you forgot everything, if in particular you renounced drama from that time on, it's because at the moment when you were tortured by thirst, and began to drink from the tap *without feeling you were quenching your thirst,* at that moment . . . Laurian!" she shouted suddenly, without averting her eyes from Pandele's, "Stay by the door to be sure no one listens to us. . . . At that moment, therefore, you had a shocking revelation, which so frightened you that, without any effort on your part, *you forgot it."*

"What kind of revelation?" asked A. D. P.

"We shall find out soon enough. But I know now it has to do with something else, something extremely important for us all. That's why Ieronim is so excited. What was revealed to you — that is: what simple and yet terrible truth did you learn, when you sensed that *you could never quench your thirst* — what was it, that it resists all our efforts at anamnesis?"

"Perhaps it was purely and simply," said A. D. P., pronouncing the words slowly, "that if I were to continue seeing Eurydice, and thus dedicate my life to the theater, I would soon die. . . ."

Niculina smiled, and her face seemed illuminated by a secret joy.

"Undoubtedly, it is partly a matter of death. But what kind of death? Not a death of the everyday sort, which we accept blindly without realizing what we do. It has to be something more simple and more profound; something which, if you had accepted it, would have changed your life *radically."*

"In any event," said Pandele, "how frightened I was in 1938, and, I repeat, I'm afraid again now!"

"I'm afraid too," whispered Niculina, seeking his eyes. "Who's not afraid on the threshold of his salvation? Even Jesus was afraid. . . ."

19

I believe that at the same moment I awoke and looked in astonishment at my bandaged fingers, I also recognized Albini's voice.

"Don't be frightened!" he said. "Neither your fingers or your feet are frozen."

Probably the fear he read in my eyes made him hasten to calm me and explain things at the same time.

"After eight or nine hours of being half-buried in the snow, much can happen! Luckily, it wasn't too cold. But, in any case, the doctors say that an hour or two more and the frostbite could have been so bad they would have had to amputate both feet."

I suddenly remembered about Valeria. "What day is this?"

Albini looked at me, it seemed, in a kindly way, almost with pity. "December 27, but it would be more accurate to say practically the twenty-eighth, since it's just twenty minutes before midnight."

"I've got to call Bucharest immediately, to tell Valeria!"

"We've taken care of that," said Albini, smiling. "We have informed domnişoara Valeria Nistor personally of all that has happened."

"But what *has* happened?" I asked him, frightened.

"That's what I want to ask you. . . . But not now. Maybe tomorrow morning."

I started to interrupt him, but he didn't give me the time.

"Domnişoara Nistor wanted by all means to come to Sibiu, but we assured her there was no need of that. In two or three days — so say the doctors — you'll be able to go home."

"On December 29, the Maestru is going to hold the marriage crown at our wedding." Then, suddenly remembering how we had been separated, I fairly shouted, "But what about the Maestru? What happened to the Maestru?"

Albini looked at me slightly frowning, and deliberately,

it seemed, postponing his response.

"We were perhaps deluding ourselves," he began at length. "We thought that you would tell us what happened to Maestru Pandele."

I looked, in utter astonishment, first at Albini, then at the nurse who had just entered. As she came toward me, smiling, holding a glass of water in her hand, I seemed to recognize her face, and I closed my eyes. But I had to open them again to take a few swallows. I realized immediately that it wasn't pure water; it had a salty taste. But despite this, I drank those few sips with an inexplicable joy.

"You were found, on the morning of December 25, some ten kilometers from the rest house," Albini continued. "You were found sitting on a stump in the snow, with a light jacket on, but bareheaded. A few meters away an overcoat, a fur hat, and a pair of wool-lined boots were found. No one understands, nor do I even now, why you weren't wearing your coat, why you didn't have the cap pulled down over your ears — as you did when you got into the sleigh. It was thought at first . . . you know, it was the holiday season, and it was thought you had drunk too much the night before. But the blood test showed no trace of alcohol. Some believed you'd been drugged, but the analyses were negative on that score, too."

I felt suddenly drained of strength. "But the Maestru?" I asked again with a great effort. "And Niculina? And Serdaru? . . . I hope nothing's happened to them."

"We hope so, too. But for the time being, we know nothing. We hope you will explain things to us."

Then he turned to the nurse and asked her something in a whisper. The young woman shook her head and smiled. Perhaps she said something, also in a whisper, but at that moment I closed my eyes. I believe I fell asleep immediately.

Because I had begun telling about the episode that was to have been filmed that night, Albini interrupted me, in a kindly but rather firm way.

"Let's come back to that episode later. For the time being, we have sufficient testimony on record about what happened on December 24, from morning until 11:30 that night. We are interested to know what happened after 11:30, when the sleigh you were riding, together with Maestru Pandele, Niculina, and Serdaru — when that sleigh, which was at the head of the column, disappeared."

I couldn't tell him that the *same thing* interested me, and that I was trying to gain time and to guess from his questions *what* and *how much* he knew.

"I don't remember when we got ahead of the others," I said, resuming the story. "At a certain moment as we were approaching the forest, the horses became frightened and began to gallop madly. Serdaru tried with all his might to bridle them, straining on the reins and leaning back as far as he could. Soon, however, he gave up. Suddenly we were blinded by the snow, falling thick and heavy, and the horses began to slow their gallop. After a few minutes, when it seemed the blizzard had diminished, we realized we had entered the forest."

Albini listened attentively, frowning slightly; undoubtedly our voices were being recorded, because he spoke very little and, I realized, weighed his words carefully.

"We were proceeding along a broad and well-tended path," I continued, "and here, in the woods, the snow seemed less deep."

"Please, be as precise as possible," Albini interrupted. "What forest are you referring to?"

"I don't know, I don't know its name. It was a rather extensive forest, well cared for, with tall, old trees."

Albini stared at me a few moments, as though he were going to ask me another question, but he decided against it and motioned for me to go on. "Continue, please!"

I told him all I could remember, with as many details as possible. I didn't want to tell him what I was thinking when we approached the forester's house, but I let myself be drawn along and I confessed everything. "It's not much farther," Pandele had said. "I recognize the road!" We were startled, hearing him speak; his voice was choked. "A hundred, two hundred meters to the cabin!"

" 'So, this was it!' I said to myself excitedly when we saw at a distance the lighted windows. 'The forester's house where Eurydice had brought him. But now, what will we say if the forester, or whoever lives here, asks us questions? That we're lost in the woods?' "

"Be more explicit, please," Albini interrupted. "Who said this?"

"No one said it. I thought it. I wondered, *this time*, when we meet the people who live in this cabin now, what will we say? How will we justify our visit — strangers, in the middle of the night, without having announced our coming? I was still asking myself this question when, after knocking on the door several times, louder and louder, we opened it and walked in. And, of course, we were utterly surprised: the table was set, the lights were burning, and on a chair was a large silver container full of ice and two bottles of champagne. But there was no one there. We went from one room to another — there was a small living room, a dining room, a sleeping room, a kitchen, and a bath — we clapped our hands. No one! And then Pandele spoke. 'Now I know what happened,' he almost whispered. 'There was no face of a girl. It had to do with the water I drank. While I was drinking the water, I looked at the window, and *I saw. Now I know what I saw!* ' "

Albini lifted his arm, interrupting me again.

"Please, be as precise as possible. All these things Pandele said. But what did he see? Didn't he tell you what he saw?"

"No. He didn't say. He turned toward Niculina and Serdaru, and motioned to them. 'Come with me. It isn't far!' "

But even though Albini was staring deep into my eyes as if trying to hypnotize me, I didn't tell him what I heard Niculina whisper to Serdaru: "So it's just as we suspected!"

" 'Eusebiu,' the Maestru added, turning to me, 'wait for us here. We won't be gone more than five or ten minutes.'

I saw them climb into the sleigh and I heard Serdaru whistling and calling to the horses, but strangely, after a few moments, I could no longer hear the sleighbells. I was too warm, and I took off my coat and boots. I didn't look at my watch, but I don't think more than five or ten minutes had passed, yet I felt myself becoming impatient. All at once I felt very thirsty. I went to the kitchen and found the water faucet, that faucet of which the Maestru spoke; I found a glass and I drank. Then I returned to the living room and sat down in an easy chair. I was sorry now I hadn't insisted they take me with them in the sleigh. . . . I don't know how long I sat there in the chair, waiting. Probably, very soon, I fell asleep."

Seeing Albini was silent, almost inattentive, I added in a timid, pleading voice, "Now, perhaps you can tell me what happened to Maestru Pandele."

Albini shrugged wearily. "I've told you several times, both last night and today, that very frankly we don't know anything definite."

"Well, then, what do you *think* might have happened? An accident?"

Albini looked me straight in the eyes again, then tried to smile. "What I think happened has no importance. We'll speak of that later. Meanwhile, let's return to your deposition — obviously, it is not a deposition properly speaking; that will come later — but, anyway, to your story."

He took out his cigarette case, toyed with it a little while, and put it back in his pocket.

"I don't know what to think," he resumed in a different tone of voice, almost harsh. "I can't believe you invented this story *ad hoc* to hide the truth — *whatever it may be.*" He spoke the last words slowly, so I would understand he was emphasizing them.

I felt my face flush, and I was ready to protest, but he stopped me, lifting his arm forcefully.

"I said, *I can't believe* you'd try to deceive us. In any event, you would have invented a less naive tale. You would have invented a series of events that, at least in part, would have seemed plausible. But the story you concocted . . ."

"I don't understand what you mean," I murmured in a choked voice.

"Let us begin with the more important things. I know the area very well, because I did my studies here, at Sibiu, after the evacuation of the University of Cluj in the fall of 1940. I've roamed this region from one end to the other, several times. I assure you that nowhere in the vicinity of the rest house, neither within five or ten, nor within twenty or thirty kilometers, does there exist any forest in any way comparable to the one you described just now. There are nothing but meadows, and the only trees of any considerable age are those that line the roadways."

I listened to him, fearful and incredulous. I had the impression he was trying to lead me into a trap.

"I don't know the environs of Sibiu," I said. "But the best thing would be for me to take a sleigh, like the four of us were in, and to take you with me. I believe I can recognize rather easily the spot where the horses were frightened and we started into the woods."

Albini scrutinized me more closely, almost severely. It seemed he was beginning to admire me, and yet the certainty with which I spoke annoyed him. Finally, his face lightened in a curious, ironic smile.

"It's not necessary for us to go right now. You're still tired. Don't forget you lay unconscious with a high fever almost three days. . . . But if it's a matter of an old, beautiful forest, such as you describe, and a roomy, comfortable house of a forester, I will show you photographs this afternoon. Probably they are reproduced in some old album about Sibiu."

"So, they exist!" I exclaimed. "Both the forest and the house. If you show me photographs, it means I didn't invent anything, that I told you the truth."

Albini seemed amused, but he could scarcely hide his exasperation. "It's true," he said. "You haven't invented anything. You have repeated just what you were *told to say*. Because the photographs will show the forest *as it existed prior to 1941*.

256

In the fall of 1941, under the Antonescu regime, the Alunarul Forest — which belonged to the State — was cut down, by order of the General Staff. I was here at Sibiu when it was cut. And although we students were indignant, we couldn't say anything, because, as we found out, the forest had been cut for the needs of the army. I never knew what those needs were. A sinister joke circulated then: it was said the General Staff needed coffins to bring back the bodies of the troops who had died in Russia."

I looked at him in amazement and felt my cheeks burning again. "You mean to say then, . . ."

"In view of your age," Albini continued, as if he had not heard me, "I don't believe you ever saw Alunarul Forest. Probably you know about it from Maestru Pandele. But what interests us is to find out *why* Pandele asked you to tell such an unlikely story when he could have invented something else, something more plausible."

"But, actually, what has happened to the Maestru?" I asked again, sincerely troubled.

Trying to hide his exasperation, Albini took out his cigarette case again and began to turn it around between his fingers.

"If you'd tell us the truth, you'd facilitate the inquiry greatly. We will know in what direction to concentrate the investigation. And perhaps we shall find him alive and be able to save him."

I listened as in a dream, as though I couldn't comprehend the sense of certain words. "But why do you say that you may still find him alive? What's happened?"

"We don't know what has happened, and your story doesn't help us in any way to find out what might have happened. The fact is that Maestru Pandele, Niculina, and Serdaru have disappeared."

He paused abruptly and was silent for some time, looking me straight in the eyes.

"That is —?" I whispered finally.

"Since that night, no one has seen anything of them. We don't know what has become of them."

20

Obviously, he had left so abruptly, vaguely waving good-bye, in order to put me to the test. He knew I would not be able to rest until I had learned more. That is why he did not come that afternoon, as he had promised, to show me the album. And probably it was on Albini's orders that I was given no sedatives or sleeping tablets. In fact, the nurse had come only to bring my lunch and an evening meal. That morning, the doctor had removed the bandages to examine my fingers, and he looked satisfied. He told me, however, that he would rebandage them that evening, to prevent me from scratching, because in the evening, and especially at night, the itching would become unbearable. But that evening he didn't come, and I spent a painful night, holding my hands under the pillow as much as possible, to keep from scratching. And, just as I feared, I was unable to go to sleep until late, toward morning.

On entering, Albini noticed the change (I had scratched my fingers bloody), but he asked nothing. (He knew, certainly, that neither the doctor or the nurse had come to see me.) He approached the bed and held out the album.

"This is how your forest looked in 1933–34. Do you recognize it?"

I didn't know what to answer. It was indeed a forest with old, tall trees, but it had been photographed in the summertime, and I couldn't tell if it was the same. Seeing I didn't say anything, Albini turned the page and showed me the forester's house. I felt my heart begin to race, although at first sight I couldn't say I recognized it as the same. But, looking more closely, I noticed the lamp beside the gate and I seemed to recognize one of the windows.

"I can't swear to it," I began, "because we came by sleigh, and the photograph was taken in the summer or autumn. I do believe, however, that I recognize the light fixture and one of the windows," and I pointed to them.

Albini closed the album absentmindedly and laid it on the stand beside the bed. The title caught my eye: *Picturesque*

Bukovina — and I blushed. "But that isn't . . . ," I began.

"The only interesting and enigmatic detail," Albini continued, "is the fact that the place where you were found, sitting on a stump, on the morning of December 25, was, until late 1941, a part of the Alunarul Forest."

Again I felt as though I were trying to awaken from a dream I had dreamed once before, recently. Albini took from his pocket an envelope of pictures, selected a few, and showed them to me.

"See," he continued, "you were found here, on that stump!"

I could scarcely distinguish anything in the picture, my eyes seeming to be covered with cobwebs, but in that field of white I succeeded at last in identifying a stump, half-buried in the snow.

"And here," said Albini, pointing to marks made in red ink, "were found your boots, hat, and overcoat. But owing to the fact that a highway has been constructed here" (which he showed me), "and some half kilometer to the left a group of workers' houses was built a few years ago — it was thanks to a worker from the power plant that you were found in time — we cannot be sure if the spot where you were found corresponds precisely to the space formerly occupied by the forester's house."

"Maybe I was dreaming," I whispered, not knowing what else I could say. "Maybe everything I told you yesterday I experienced in a dream."

Albini sat down on a chair and again took out his cigarette case, pensively. "Because the doctors have assured me that you are out of danger — the itching is inevitable, and will continue; try not to scratch too much — and because tomorrow you will return to Bucharest, to celebrate the New Year with your family, I've reserved a plane ticket for you already. Domnişoara Nistor will be waiting for you at the airport. Allow me to light a cigarette." He lit it without haste, taking great care, as though performing a ritual.

"Perhaps I dreamed . . . ," I repeated.

259

"It's possible. But that doesn't explain the rest. And the *rest* is what interests us. That is: what happened to Maestru Pandele and the other two. We might construct several hypotheses. One would be: they all died in an accident. But so far we have found no trace of them. It is true that throughout the whole area, all the way to the border, the snow is over a half meter deep. But still, it is a matter of *three* bodies."

"And of a sleigh, four horses, and the carbine that was in the sleigh," I added.

Albini smiled again, this time with considerable effort. "The sleigh, horses, and rifle were found the next day, in the evening."

"Where were they found?" I asked him in a whisper, eagerly.

"Strangely, they were found in the stable at the rest house: the horses in their stalls, and the sleigh, with the carbine inside, covered with a tarpaulin, under the shed. But no one could tell us how they had gotten there, or who had brought them."

Again I felt my heart pounding faster and faster. I thought I was suffocating, and I wanted to take a deep breath, but I didn't dare.

"And so," I whispered, "the three are alive. They returned with the sleigh, then left for other parts."

"That would be the simplest explanation, and the most rational one. And yet, I can't believe the Maestru abandoned you by the roadside, in the snow, in your jacket and bareheaded."

"If all I told you was true," I began, "and it was *not* a dream, he didn't leave me on the side of the road."

Albini shrugged and continued in the same dry, detached tone. "Thus, if we assume that they were not dead by the next day when they brought back the sleigh — although even this is not certain, because anyone from the rest house could have returned it — we don't know what happened to them after that. Let us suppose that in one way or another they found out that you had been taken to the hospital and were out of danger. What might they have done after that? Again several hypotheses suggest themselves. One would be that all three of them went to a little provincial town, *incognito*, in order to spend there a quiet vacation. Or, also *incognito*, they crossed the border to give occasion to all sorts of legends; because, you admit, it is tempting to have it said of someone that he has disappeared or vanished without a trace. If Niculina and Serdaru are, as people say, great prestidigitators, we must not rule out the possibility that Maestru Pandele has let himself be drawn into their game."

For some time I had had to make a great effort to follow him. My mind was running in several directions at once. I felt certain that A. D. P. had spoken to me at some time of such an adventure: hiding *incognito* in a village, or city, or foreign country, but why? *Why?* I suddenly realized that Albini was staring at me questioningly, suspiciously.

"I'm afraid I've tired you," he said.

"On the contrary, on the contrary!" I exclaimed. But I knew I was blushing, and I felt Albini's eyes on me, bearing down harder and harder.

"If only you'd told me the truth from the start. . . ."

I tried to protest, but Albini raised his arm forbiddingly.

"If only we knew *why* Maestru Pandele had asked you to repeat that story, down to the last detail, about the Alunarul Forest. . . ."

"Maybe I dreamed it," I interjected.

"And," continued Albini smiling ironically, "he suggested that finally you should say you might have dreamed it. . . . If we knew *why* he chose this defense posture, we'd know where to look for him."

I listened with difficulty, barely able to stand the itching, and I hid my hands under the pillow.

"In any event," he said, rising to leave, "if any of the hypotheses I've expounded is correct, in a day or two, or a week or two, the Maestru will give you some sign of life. . . . But we must not rule out other hypotheses, for instance, an accident in which all three were killed. Or, *something else . . .*"

261

Only after he had shut the door behind him did I remember. It wasn't A. D. P. who had spoken to me about that adventure. I had read it in one of the plays, the third or (more probably) the fourth. One of the characters evoked the example of Brâncuşi: how different he had become after he left his work in Bucharest behind; and then how he had believed in a different aesthetics while working in Munich, and how he had set off on foot for Paris. But, to the end of his life, not even Brâncuşi realized the great discovery he had made. Otherwise, at a certain moment, he would have had to leave Paris also, and *leave behind him* his supreme achievement. Leave his master-pieces behind, separate himself from them forever, and begin anew, from the *very beginning*.

And then another character asks him, "In other words, you would have asked him not to be what he was, the great Brâncuşi?"

"No, I couldn't have asked that of him," the other replies. "The great Brâncuşi he would still have remained, and perhaps he would have been even greater because his genius would have created something else. But I should have asked him, from then on, to live and create *incognito*."

21

Several days after returning to Bucharest, I realized how serious the consequences were. On the evening of my arrival, weeping in my arms, Valeria had said that, for the time being, our marriage was postponed *sine die*. Her family had announced everywhere that we would be crowned by A. D. P. And now, so long as nothing was known about him, we could not get married. And if it were to be learned that Pandele was dead, it would be more serious still; they say there is no more ill-fated sign than this: for the *naş*, the best man, to die a little before the wedding. So we had no other choice but to wait ("as we have been waiting up till now," Valeria added).

The next day, on my way to the publishing house, I

noticed I was being followed. I tried to bolster my courage, saying that since I had nothing to hide, I had no reason to be afraid. At the publishing house, my appearance produced a sensation. The employees and the several writers who happened to be there ogled me with great interest, but also with fear. Not one of the young writers I knew offered to shake hands, and soon, one by one, they left the office. One of the employees asked me "what it was like" in India, but I didn't have time to answer him because he was called to the telephone. After I had waited ten minutes or so, Ghiţă Horia's secretary informed me that the director had had to leave, having been summoned urgently to the Ministry, but he encouraged me to return the next week. However, he added with some embarrassment, it would be better if I called beforehand, so a definite appointment could be made.

"I just wanted to find out what he's decided about my volume about India."

The young man shrugged. "Telephone next week and talk with Comrade Director."

As I expected, whenever I called, the director was absent or in conference. I visited several bookstores to see if the volume of *Memoirs* had been put on sale. Fortunately, no one knew me there and I could listen to conversations unhindered. Several times, I thought people were talking about the disappearance of A. D. P., but I didn't dare get too close to learn the particulars. At any rate, Valeria, who followed the provincial press also, confirmed this: that nowhere — neither in newspapers nor in literary reviews — was the name of A. D. P. ever mentioned now.

A week later, with the same agent still trailing me, I went to strada Fântânelor. When Ecaterina opened the door, she was impassive. She pointed with her arm in the direction of the study, and then made herself invisible.

"I've been waiting for you a long while," Albini greeted me.

263

He was seated at the desk with a stack of files in front of him. I recognized them instantly: they were the letters from the last few years, with the replies I had typed.

"How are you feeling?" he asked, extending his hand to me across the desk, but without rising. "Take a seat, please, and tell me how you feel. And what's the news?"

"I feel rather well. As for the news, I was just going to ask you."

For some time he said nothing, looking at me absently; then he opened his silver case and selected a cigarette.

"Everyone suspects that they have not been found. Of course, a great many lakes are still frozen, and snow covers the mountains and valleys. If we could find Maestru Pandele's body, things would be simplified immediately. A state funeral, eulogizing articles in the press, several printings of the *Memoirs* exhausted in less than a week, and many other such things. . . . For instance," he resumed after a pause, looking me in the eye and gesturing broadly, "this house consecrated as 'Casa Memorială A. D. P.' and you named conservator of the collections. . . . Because," he added in a different, more intimate tone, "a copy of his will has been found, and you are named the sole heir."

I knew I had paled. Taking out my handkerchief, I passed it once across my face and then began to wipe my hands.

"Nevertheless, I hope the Maestru is still alive," I whispered.

"But *where is he?*" Albini interrupted. "If he's alive, he can only be somewhere abroad. And that's what I believe. I keep hoping to hear him on Radio Free Europe or to see he has given an interview to a reporter from the *New York Times*. But more than two weeks have gone by, and still no news."

"Nevertheless . . . ," I began meekly. But I stopped, embarrassed, not knowing what to say.

Albini crushed his cigarette slowly in the ashtray. "It is true," he continued in a flat voice, "you believe in 'miracles' and you are still impressed by Ieronim Thanase's phantasmagorias. Be informed, then, that you won't be hearing about

Ieronim's 'rehearsals' again for a long time. Measures have been taken with regard to them. No longer will the State's money be wasted, as was done until yesterday or the day before, to support a troupe of amateurs in the hope that they will someday make a brilliant film, so brilliant that it will win all the prizes at all the international competitions."

I listened to him, anxious, continuing to rub my fingers with the handkerchief.

"I admit, Ieronim is not lacking in good qualities, and he has made many victims — you aren't the only one he has charmed. . . . He is also very able. He succeeded in fooling a great many people with his so-called 'paralysis,' and then, when it was convenient, he threw away his canes — and everyone around him cried, 'Miracle!' "

"Nevertheless," I dared to interject, "when I saw him last summer, he couldn't walk without canes. He couldn't even stand without someone's supporting him."

"So I said myself," continued Albini. "He's as clever as can be. But, in fact, he was not suffering from bilateral sclerosis, as those around him said. I have inquired of several specialists. If it had been that, the illness would have been incurable and would have ended fatally, in a progressive paralysis. Therefore, Thanase was just 'acting' for two years, but he played the part so well that no one suspected anything."

He fell silent, smiled at me, took out his silver case, and lighted another cigarette.

"Do you perhaps remember what I said to you this summer about Valentinus and the Gnostics?"

I gave a start. "I remember very well."

"Then you'll like what I have to say now. In the time of the Apostles, there lived a great sorcerer, Simon Magus. He remained famous by virtue of the many pranks and follies he committed, but the most famous is his last mystification: one fine day he announced throughout Imperial Rome that he would rise to heaven in the sight of all. And indeed he began to rise up, but the Apostle Peter, who was present, prayed to the God he served, and Simon Magus fell down and broke into pieces. . . . This legend, Comrade Damian — because, obviously, it is nothing but a legend — illustrates perfectly the situation we are in today. The Apostle Peter represents the Church, that is, an institution admirably organized and with a well-established hierarchy. Such is also our socialist society today — or it is on the point of becoming such. Whereas Simon Magus represents the gnoses and heresies that threaten to raze the Church to its foundations. In our day, we find the same irrational and obscurantist heresies in individuals like Ieronim Thanase and Niculina."

I listened, fascinated, sensing fear beginning to arise within me.

"But I don't want to bore you," Albini resumed in a different, almost pretentious tone. "Tell me, please, what I may do for you."

I didn't know how to reply, and I smiled sheepishly, wrapping my handkerchief around first one hand, then the other.

"I've admired your devotion to Maestru Pandele and your work as an ideal secretary," continued Albini, pointing to the portfolio of letters. "Such a capacity ought not to be squandered. For the time being, I'll arrange for you to get a significant cash advance from the Writers' Association."

I ought to have thanked him, but I could manage only to nod my head, smiling.

"It is curious that no manuscript and no notes concerning the four plays have been found," Albini resumed. "I know from Comrade Horia that the Maestru had the manuscripts and proofs, but they weren't found in his baggage left at the rest house. It seems that the manuscripts were almost indecipherable, that only you. . . ."

Because he suddenly stopped speaking and was looking at me questioningly, I told him how difficult it had been to decipher and type the four plays. He listened, it seemed to me, with mounting interest.

"I too have read his volume of *Drama*," he said, smiling. "I am not adept in that kind of literature, although, in my youth, I was interested in so-called avant-garde poetry. Personally, I never got the point of any of those four plays, and when I was talking with Thanase the last time, I asked him to explain them to me. I must admit, Ieronim Thanase was very frank with me; he declared that the Maestru's *Drama* 'says all' — I repeat just what he said to me — it *says all*, if you know how to decipher it. But who could decipher it without having the code?"

"*All* about *what?*" I asked, surprised.

Albini began to laugh, and I asked myself if I had ever heard him laugh before.

"That's just the question!" he exclaimed, quite amused. "Thanase claims it is a matter of *absolute freedom*, the only freedom permitted to the man of contemporary societies. But we know it's a matter of *something else*, something quite important. When we discover the code — because no code can withstand our specialists and computers — when we discover it, we shall *understand* the four plays, we shall know what plans Pandele had made for the night of December 24–25, and we shall know what happened; more precisely, we shall learn which things transpired *differently* from what he had planned."

He became suddenly silent, frowning. Then he rose from the desk again, approached me, and held out a calling card.

"If you ever need me, you can reach me at one of these numbers."

22

"Actually, you went to India for nothing," Valeria said to me one evening, unable to conceal her sadness. "You haven't been interviewed once — not by the newspapers or on television. No one talks about you. . . ."

With an effort, I managed to joke. "I'd go even further. I'd say almost no one talks *with* me!"

I thought Valeria looked at me then with despair. "What are we going to do?" she asked, almost in a whisper.

"One day, sooner or later, we'll learn the truth. And I'm afraid that when we learn it, we'll be sorry. I'm afraid," I added, lowering my voice, "very much afraid that the Maestru and the other two have lost their lives in an accident. Otherwise, surely, I'd have heard from them by now."

"Maybe A. D. P. is living somewhere, a victim of amnesia," said Valeria.

It seemed odd that she spoke of amnesia, and I asked her, "Have you read something about this — about amnesia?"

She hadn't read anything, but this was the theory of her coworkers at the office. In fact, I recalled then overhearing this explanation proposed recently in a bookstore. But I found it hard to believe that all three had become amnesiacs.

Nevertheless, a few days later this version suddenly became official. I read it first in the morning newspaper, and I found it again, developed and nuanced, in the reviews of that week. A. D. P. began to be talked about for the first time. As the result of an accident, Pandele was suffering from amnesia and was a patient in a sanatorium (whether in Romania or elsewhere was not specified). On February 24, without advance notice, his *Memoirs* appeared in bookstores and, naturally, the printing was exhausted the same day. All the reviews I read lamented the accident. Only several weeks later did I understand why that version had been chosen. The Writers' Association had been informed confidentially that this year A. D. P. had a very good chance to receive the Nobel Prize (he had been proposed two years before and, it seemed, had received a considerable number of votes). It was necessary then, at all costs, that Pandele be found alive, although, being a victim of amnesia, he could not be visited by journalists. It was necessary, likewise, that he publish a new volume, to show that up till very recently he had been fully active.

Soon afterward Ghiţă Horia's secretary phoned me. The director would expect me at three o'clock to sign the contract for *India: Seen and Unseen*. As I expected, Horia brought up the matter of A. D. P.'s disappearance. I repeated what I had told all the others — actually, not very many — who had asked me the same question: at a certain moment the horses had become frightened and had taken off on the run, I lost consciousness, the sled disappeared into the darkness, and I was found the next day, almost frozen, buried in the snow. (To Valeria I had confessed all I had told Albini at the hospital, but not even to her had I dared to say more: nothing about A. D. P.'s confidential statements at the rest house, with Niculina and Serdaru keeping watch at the door of my room.) Ghiţă Horia did not hide his disappointment; he was expecting to learn more sensational details. He believed, as did Albini and probably many others, that the whole thing had been staged to camouflage A. D. P.'s flight abroad (although no one understood why he had done it, because Pandele could cross the border anytime he wished).

"But it's the beginning of March now," concluded Horia, "and there's been no word. Let us hope he isn't dead. Let's hope he's suffering from amnesia in a sanatorium somewhere. But, actually, if we don't know what sanatorium he's in, *how do we know he's lost his memory?*"

I had to admit he was right.

The next day, March 6, I felt a little homesick for the house on strada Fântânelor. In the kitchen was a policeman. The drawing room, study, parlor, and sleeping room — all had been sealed. The policeman had orders to record the name and Identity Card number of all who rang the bell at the front door or the kitchen. After I had put away my Identity Card, I asked him about Ecaterina. She had moved to her sister's place in Şoseaua Iancului, but she came once a week to "do the cleaning," the policeman said with a knowing smile, that is, to sweep the kitchen and pantry and to take care of the last two rubber trees left from the Maestru's famous collection ("A. D. P.'s jungle," as Paraschiv Simionescu sarcastically called it).

"But only till May," the policeman added, "because in May she's getting married and moving to the provinces."

"Has anyone told you whom she's marrying?" I inquired.

"His name wasn't mentioned. I just heard that they've been talking about it ten years. For a long time, he was a chauffeur, but now he's gone back to the factory where he worked when he was younger."

I smiled, not knowing why, with melancholy. So, finally . . . Ioanid had returned to Ecaterina. (He had known her not for ten, but for more like twelve years.) Probably he, the seducer, will cure her of her phantoms and persecution complex.

I was returning home, walking slowly, not thinking, when, in front of the Rosetti Statue I saw him. He was hurrying toward me. I felt as though I were suddenly awakening from a dream, that it was that night of December 24 again, when I saw him climbing into the pickup truck and sitting down beside the spotlights.

"I thought we'd never meet again," I said softly, shaking his hand.

Ieronim broke into the childlike laugh that made him seem ten years younger (although he never looked his age of forty, as he liked to repeat).

"I went to your place a little while ago and left you a note. I said I'd be back in an hour or two. I must see you, at all costs, *today.*"

I didn't ask him anything until we reached home. I did all the talking, and I spoke only of trifles: the success of the book of *Memoirs*, the contract I had signed, Ecaterina's marriage. After he had seated himself in the armchair I asked him, "Now, tell me: what's happened?"

"First, tell me what you know."

I repeated all I had told Albini at the hospital, adding also those few details I had kept to myself.

"She said that?" he interrupted me at a certain moment. "You're sure Niculina said, 'So, it's as we suspected'? And Serdaru didn't say anything? . . . All right, continue," he urged me.

He was especially interested in Albini's questioning of me, and he asked me to repeat — word for word, if possible —

all the questions he had asked. After I had reproduced the last conversation with Albini on strada Fântânelor, he began laughing again.

"Albini seems obsessed with the problem of Gnostics and heretics, but actually *he's afraid*: afraid that perhaps not only does *God* exist — to God, we Eastern Europeans can adjust ourselves — but also the Devil, and therefore demons, sorcery, and black magic. And so, Albini takes refuge in institution and hierarchy: if we are many, and obedient and well disciplined, he tells himself, the risks become minimal. . . . The comparison with Simon Magus doesn't suit us, no matter what you think of our ideas of drama. If you want to find something similar in the past, a more suitable comparison would be the conflict between the Inquisition and Giordano Bruno or Campanella. Both wished to *save* the Church, that is to renew it, purifying it of its dogmatic provincialism; basically, they wanted to prepare the Church and European Christianity in general for the crises that were sure to be released by the great scientific discoveries of the Renaissance."

He paused a little while, then resumed in a deep, severe voice.

"Albini is going to break his neck someday. . . . He's not so naive as to believe the legend Number Three had told him, in great secrecy. I mean, that the scenes we were going to film on Christmas Eve night were just a camouflage."

Because my face registered surprise, he explained what he was referring to. The "legend" fabricated by Number Three alleged that on that night, under the camouflage of a convoy of sleighs that we were filming, the son of Number Two was supposed to defect clandestinely to Czechoslovakia, carrying with him a set of documents compromising to Number One. Those documents (obviously fabricated), having reached their destination, would have brought about the dismissal of Number One and his replacement by Number Three. Fortunately, Number Two's son was in Bucharest from December 22 on; therefore he could not be implicated. But on that night of December 24 the sleigh carrying A. D. P., Niculina, and Serdaru

271

disappeared. And the next day I was found, almost frozen, by the side of the road. Number Three took advantage immediately of this combination of events, launched the rumor in the right places that the compromising documents had been taken by A. D. P. into Czechoslovakia. Ieronim and his whole company were isolated for questioning in a special building. During the three days I was lying unconscious in the hospital with a fever that seemed to indicate double pneumonia, Albini conducted the inquiry. But he was baffled by the way I kept insisting on returning to the Alunarul Forest; he didn't understand why A. D. P. had instructed me to tell such an improbable story. But inasmuch as there was no information from Czechoslovakia indicating the presence of a Romanian foreign agent, they suspected that A. D. P. had gone to Western Europe. That act would have been, in any event, compromising for Number Two. But neither was this hypothesis confirmed by the Special Services in the West.

Then on January 5, Ieronim and his whole group, which included, of course, several informers, were transported by plane to Bucharest and detained in one of the buildings belonging to Security. But from this point on, Albini was not the only one responsible for questioning. Among the examiners were some of Number Two's men who had managed to infiltrate the Security, and they kept Ieronim up to date on what was happening. The last hypothesis at which Albini had arrived was that of the fatal accident. During the month of January and for half of February Albini's men explored all the lakes, valleys, and woods where the three bodies might have been discovered. The compromising documents, Albini theorized, would have been hidden in the lining of A. D. P.'s overcoat.

Since I was almost convinced that Pandele was dead, I paled on hearing this last sentence, but Ieronim reassured me immediately.

"Have no fear. The danger has passed. Ten days ago, a very important individual, Number Three's right-hand man, abroad on an important mission, turned himself over to a West

European agency and disappeared. More precisely, the passage was made earlier, but it was confirmed only ten days ago. Naturally, repressions followed. Number Three was replaced, and Albini has been given another assignment. We were released, somebody arranged an official pardon for us, and all the workers and actors — all except me — received their wages for the weeks lost from work. And soon the filming will be resumed."

He paused a moment, smiling at me.

"You have observed, I believe, that since then you haven't been shadowed any longer."

"To tell you the truth, I hadn't noticed. I'd become so accustomed to my man that I didn't even see him. . . . But, now, tell me, please, what you know about the Maestru and the young married couple."

This time his laugh was less childlike. He stood up and took a few steps around the room, stopped in front of the window, and gazed briefly at the sky. Then he turned and spoke.

"Why are you asking me? Quite frankly, I doubt that I know any more than you."

I was disappointed, and Ieronim guessed it immediately.

"I'm asking you because I don't understand what happened on that Christmas Eve night, how I ended up on a stump beside the road and why the others disappeared. I realize now that all four of us had one of those incomprehensible experiences in which one seems to be in an alien space and a past time. I don't want to think about that experience, because I feel I might lose my mind. But I keep thinking all the time about the Maestru and the other two. *Why* did they disappear? *How* did they disappear? And *where*?"

Ieronim became suddenly grave. He sat down in the armchair again and looked me straight in the eyes.

"I told you I don't know any more about it than you do," he began, "because I imagined that you still have fresh in your mind the text of the four plays you typed last summer."

I could not help sighing.

"The truth is, even though I typed them, I remember almost nothing of their content. I deciphered them word for word, and I didn't understand what I was deciphering. I wanted to reread the book, but . . ."

"True," Ieronim interposed, "I remember the Maestru telling me you were tired, exhausted, suffering from insomnia."

"I'd like to ask you this: what do you think happened? Do you believe they're still alive? And will we be able to meet again someday, however long from now that may be?"

He was silent for a long while, pensive.

"I don't want to lie to you, to encourage any illusions of any sort. I want to be as candid with you as possible. And when you reread — or better said, *read* — those four plays, you'll understand why I told Albini that they illustrate and convey a method of absolute freedom, provided you know, when *reading* them or watching them *performed*, the corresponding code. Albini, obviously, thought it was a matter of a political and immediate freedom, therefore dangerous to socialism. But what we are accustomed to call 'absolute freedom' is something else entirely. Anyone who faces up to reality knows that soon we will be entering upon a phase of universal history in which none of the freedoms we have begun to know will be possible. This is the price at which nuclear catastrophe may be averted. We must, therefore, prepare now in order to be able to survive in the institutions of tomorrow's society. For some of our contemporaries with their eyes fixed nostalgically on the past, what lies ahead amounts to one of the hells evoked in the novel *1984* or other anticipations of the same sort. And it could be so, if we let ourselves be integrated into the socio-political organisms of tomorrow the way we are today: naive and unprepared."

Listening to him I could not hide my disappointment. I had heard such reflections before, perhaps from him or from A. D. P. He read the disappointment in my eyes, I'm sure, and he smiled.

"Please be patient a little, because I don't know how

else to answer your questions. . . . Thus, the gradual and fatal loss of all freedoms, of every sort, can be compensated for only by that which I have called absolute freedom. I want to believe, and I hope, that dramatic, gymnastic, and choreographic performances, dances, the recitation of poetry and songs will not be *completely* prohibited. In any event, meditations, silent prayers (repeated mentally, at night, or in any moment of solitude), certain physical exercises in a rhythm so slow that they become imperceptible to the uninformed eye — all these *cannot* be prohibited. And all these trifles — gestures, songs, poems, recited *differently* from the way they were learned; meditations, inner prayers, exercises of breathing and visualization — can become techniques of *escape*."

"Escape to where?" I interrupted almost involuntarily. "To what country, what continent?"

Ieronim looked at me in surprise, as though he could not believe his ears.

"You of all people ask me that? You who — at least, so you told me — who entered a forest destroyed twenty-five years ago, entered a house with all the lights lit and a table set and chilled champagne waiting, just as on Christmas Eve, 1938? And then you were found sitting on a stump on the edge of the road, almost buried in the snow?"

I blushed, perplexed. "I know. But that was all involuntary on my part, and it was, as I said, one of those incomprehensible experiences. . . ."

Ieronim looked straight at me again, but this time he grinned.

"You're right. It was involuntary, and it would have been better, perhaps, if the Maestru hadn't insisted on your accompanying him in the sleigh. But, anyway, that's what happened, and not something else. The *escape* of which I was speaking just now does not entail unknown cities, countries, or continents. You 'escape' only from the time and space in which you have been living — a time and space which, in a future unfortunately rather near at hand, will be equivalent to a perfectly programmed existence in an immense collective prison. Our descendants, if they do not know how to discover techniques of escape and how to utilize the *absolute freedom* that is *given* us in the very structure of our condition — as beings that are *free* although incarnate — our descendants will consider themselves truly captives, living in a prison without doors and windows . . . and eventually they will die. Because man cannot survive without belief in the possibility of freedom — however limited that freedom may be — and without the hope that some day he will be able to obtain, or reobtain, that freedom."

For some time I rubbed my forehead half-consciously. I understood, I believe, rather well, but I didn't see the connection with my question.

"So, then," I began in a hushed tone, "in that case . . ."

"I told you that I didn't intend to encourage any false hopes," continued Ieronim. "You asked me what happened to the Maestru and the other two. I answered you very frankly: I don't know exactly. I can't give you any news of them. I hope they're alive. And if they are alive, someday they'll give us a sign. If so far they haven't given us any sign of their being alive, it doesn't mean they aren't living. I don't know what kind of existence they have chosen or had to choose. I only know that absolute freedom *exists*, and that the one who finds it, or receives it as a gift, has at his disposal possibilities that none of us can imagine. I know this, because I was convinced long ago, down deep in my bones, that man as well as the Cosmos has more dimensions than those we've been taught about in school, here in the West, for three thousand years."

"So . . .?"

"I repeat, I know nothing precise. What we all know, unfortunately, is that every new freedom has been won with great sacrifices. Religious freedom and freedom of thought, social, economic, and sexual freedom — all have had their heroes and martyrs. We have no reason to believe that absolute freedom, *true spiritual freedom*, will be obtained without risks, persecution, and martyrdom."

"But if someone enjoys 'absolute freedom' . . ."

He regarded me with surprise again, but this time he smiled. "You've been to India; you know very well the dangers of such freedom."

I shrugged, embarrassed. "I didn't have enough time to become informed. . . ."

"At any rate, you know that the most dangerous temptations saints and yogins meet occur on the threshold of salvation, or at the moment they obtain absolute freedom. These same temptations are spoken of also in all the religious legends from pagan Antiquity and the Christian Middle Ages."

"This would mean . . ."

"This *may* mean," Ieronim corrected me, "that our friends might have perished at that moment when they awoke, wherever it was, and believed they could never return, and didn't understand that it was a matter of the final initiatory trial — didn't understand that they were *still here,* on earth, in *our* world."

He stood up abruptly and approached me.

"I wanted to see you today, because tomorrow morning I leave for Sibiu to continue the filming. I knew that for some time you wouldn't be going to Sibiu again."

He took my hand and shook it warmly.

"If you receive any sign, please, I beg of you, say nothing to anyone, not even your fiancée. And in any event, don't write me. I hope to finish the film at the beginning of May, and then I'll come to see you."

In the doorway, he turned toward me, smiling. "I hope from now on Albini will leave you in peace."

23

I thought it odd when, at the end of March, Albini came to call. More courteous than at the last interview, he did his best to smile all the time. He even offered me a cigarette from a full case: English cigarettes, he specified, the only ones that can't be counterfeited.

Then he told me he had read A. D. P.'s *Memoirs* "with youthful enthusiasm." But, unfortunately, there was no longer any doubt that the Maestru had suffered death in an accident. Probably the trio had tried to cross a frozen arm of the Târnavă, and the ice had given way. The same thing had happened to a group of four workmen at the end of January. And, of course, the bodies had not yet been found.

"This being the situation," he continued, seeking to catch my eyes, "why haven't we changed the slogan, 'A. D. P., an amnesiac in a sanatorium,' and begun saying instead, 'A. D. P. disappeared'? In that case the Memorial House could be established and you could be installed as curator of the collections."

I said that the amnesia hypothesis had been encouraged, I understood, by the rumor that A. D. P. might receive the Nobel Prize that fall.

"No chance!" he declared gravely. "We are informed that the Swedes know the situation perfectly. Several articles have appeared in the German press and now no one believes in the amnesia story anymore."

I agreed with him, but I confessed I didn't know what to do.

"As secretary, friend, and general legatee of Maestru Pandele, you could arrange an interview in which you state that unfortunately, now, three months after his disappearance, you no longer believe in the possibility of amnesia. Consult also with Comrade Horia; see what his opinions are."

Then, he stood up abruptly, shook hands with me politely, and left.

When I told Valeria about my talk with Albini (of course on that evening, March 6, I said nothing to her about my meeting with Ieronim), she became pensive.

"You know, then," she began after a while, "it would be better if we had our wedding ceremony while people still believe that Maestru Pandele is an amnesiac. To say that means that he is, at least, alive. When he is declared to have 'disappeared,' everyone will understand that, in fact, Pandele is dead. And, as I've told you. . ."

I agreed. From all points of view, it was better to speed up our wedding plans. Valeria wanted to have children now, while we were young. After I added that we could, in the near future, move into the house on strada Fântânelor, Valeria made the decision immediately. Excitedly, we consulted the calendar. We selected the date of April 11, for no particular reason. Then Valeria telephoned her family. "The Maestru's amnesia could last for years," she told them. "It would be a shame to waste our youth waiting." Everyone agreed. For the best man we had decided long since: the engineer Gheorghe Camilar, Valeria's uncle. But he had to be informed immediately, because he worked at Turda. We left it that we would call him the next day.

Since giving up hope of being crowned by A. D. P., we had decided to celebrate the marriage in a private ceremony at the Bogdan restaurant. Just the family — that is, Valeria's mother and her two sisters — and a few friends. I wanted there to be twelve persons, but in the end Valeria invited two girl friends, both married. There were sixteen of us — a lucky number, I said.

But unfortunately, the rain that began in the morning continued till late at night. For several hours no taxi could be found, and some guests arrived at the restaurant soaked to the skin.

I can't say that the reception was very successful, but because Valeria and her family seemed happy, I tried to appear to be enjoying it also. Nevertheless, we returned home early, before midnight.

Scarcely had we turned the key in the lock when the doorbell sounded. For an instant, we were both frightened. (I thought immediately of Albini.) We made no response. But after several light knocks on the door, we called out together, "Who is it?"

No reply. And yet I thought I heard footsteps rapidly descending the stairs, and I opened the door. On the threshold there lay, wrapped in cellophane, a huge, superb bouquet of roses.

"Probably from the publishing house," I muttered.

There were so many of them, and the stems were so long, and the fragrance so overpowering, that I felt my heart beginning to pound, and I counted them. There were nineteen — nineteen roses. Just then I saw the card, and I concealed it swiftly in my hand, lest Valeria see it.

Only when I went to the kitchen to fill the vase with water did I read the card: "As always, A. D. P. Remember, Niculina and Laurian."

24

I don't know how I kept from giving myself away. As I embraced her tightly, scarcely holding back the tears, Valeria began to kiss me.

"I knew, I knew long ago," she whispered, "I knew how much you love me."

Next morning I awoke earlier than usual and dressed quickly. As soon as Valeria had left for the office, I set off for the flower shop. They all knew me, and A. D. P. they had known for twenty years. I went up to Elvira and thanked her.

"That bouquet we received was the most beautiful I've ever seen."

She didn't know about our marriage, and she congratulated me. "But we didn't send the flowers," she added.

"Nineteen red roses, with extra-long stems; the kind the Maestru liked so well."

"Poor man!" whispered Elvira.

"I'd have sworn the bouquet was arranged here. Where else would one get such beautiful roses, with stems so long and wrapped so delicately in cellophane?"

Elvira shook her head. "At any rate not from us. For the past two days we haven't received any red roses. We've had only white, plus a dozen yellow ones."

I looked so upset and disappointed that Elvira looked at me in wonder. "Why don't you try at the Fan? They have lovely flowers there, too."

So I tried at that place, and I found the roses hadn't been sent from there. Then I went to the Florence and finally even the Athénée Palace. There were several customers ahead of me, and when my turn came and I asked her, the saleswoman could not help making a gesture of weariness and exasperation. "We don't deliver to residences!" she snapped.

Then she turned to the old man waiting in line behind me, and asked him with her eyes for his order.

"A bouquet of Parma violets," he said quietly.

I don't know why, but I felt sorry for him and gave him a smile.

Albini was right. Once the newspapers had announced that, although nothing certain was known, it was probable that A. D. P. had lost his life that winter in an accident, the number of articles and studies about him increased quite noticeably. That week I gave several interviews: to the *Morning Journal*, two literary reviews, and the television. I recalled, especially, my intimacy with Pandele, but avoided dwelling on the last days spent with him at Sibiu.

I knew that this sudden notoriety made Valeria happy. But every time I reread the interviews, I wondered what A. D. P. would say if he ever chanced to see them. I was waiting for another sign of life from him; I was waiting, above all, for some indication, however brief, as to how I should behave. And when, in June, my book, *India: Seen and Unseen*, appeared, I hoped I'd receive a few words from him. It was my first book and it was due to him, primarily, that it had been written. Several weeks later I said to myself that surely the Maestru must be living abroad somewhere, and did not yet know about my book's being published.

I began hoping again when I signed the contract for a volume of my reminiscences about A. D. P. and started going every day to strada Fântânelor for several hours to consult the archives. I didn't understand why Ieronim hadn't come to see me in May. For a while I thought it was because he hadn't finished the film. But shortly after *India* appeared, I read in a review of it that some pages of mine reminded the author of the review of certain scenes from *Nobody's Children*, Ieronim Thanase's film, which the reviewer had seen in an advance showing.

After that I awaited with increasing impatience the premiere. It was said it would be a masterpiece. When, at the beginning of October, the premiere took place, *Nobody's Children* was hailed as "the best Socialist film of the century." Valeria and I stood in line several times before we could get seats. We were both so overwhelmed that neither of us could utter a single word all the way home.

"After *Nobody's Children*," whispered Valeria, sitting on the edge of the bed, "I won't be able to watch another film for a long, long time!"

I ought to have said something, too, but I didn't know what to say. I had not believed it possible, by respecting precisely, to the letter, Socialist ethics and aesthetics, to create a masterpiece that in no way resembled anything done before.

"I'll never forget her expression, when she stops singing and begins listening to the bells on the sleighs coming nearer, and she understands. . . ."

Valeria became silent suddenly, then hung her head to keep me from seeing her tears. It was Niculina: she had found, hidden in an abandoned barn, the last children left from a whole school, who had fled from the village a week before when the bombing began; the children were dying, one after another, from hunger, cold, exhaustion. And because they did not have even so much as a crust of dry bread, Niculina began telling them stories, singing, dancing . . . and gradually an unnatural light transfigured the barn. And there began to appear, one after another as Niculina spoke of them, all sorts of dolls and animals, live or stuffed, and young girls who seemed first to be fairies, then servant girls, then acrobats, and Niculina danced in the midst of them. Now and then she would stop and begin laughing, and then all the children would start to laugh too, because Niculina would show them a white rabbit, holding it by the ears, or a miniature elephant made of cardboard, trying to hide its trunk. . . . And then, all at once, the sound of the sleighbells is heard, and one understands. . . .

The critics stressed that the fairytale atmosphere was perfectly compatible with the Socialist Realist vision. The four children who survive return later to their abandoned village, where the last inhabitants are dying amidst the ruins, and, improvising a workshop resembling a large doll house, they undertake to construct an immense barn, which soon proves to be something else: a dormitory, mess hall, school, infirmary, gymnasium, and library. Very skillfully Ieronim had introduced Socialist ideology and vocabulary; the spectator discovers that the four are Pioneers, that their workshop heralds the "construction of Socialism," that the legends they tell and the ballads they sing evoke the mythology of the Dacians and memorable scenes from the history of the Romanian peasants.

As was expected, *Nobody's Children* took first prize at the International Film Festival at Cannes. Several weeks later the film was being shown all over Europe and had been engaged for the United States and Latin America. I said to myself that Ieronim, very probably, had left the country. It was rumored that several film companies had offered to hire him and his entire company.

And then, without any reason being given, in November, the film was withdrawn. Later it was learned that many foreign critics who had written enthusiastically about *Nobody's Children* saw in that brilliant film the most virulent satire of the Socialist system.

25

1967, 1968, 1969. . . . What more is there to say? My *Remembrances* about A. D. P. appeared a year ago, and I signed the contract for a critical monograph to be accompanied by some posthumous texts. But in April 1968 we were so unwise as to go away for a week to Sinaia. When we returned, melancholy because it had rained almost the whole time, we found at the door a great bouquet of roses.

"Yesterday was our wedding anniversary!" I whispered to Valeria, rather sheepishly.

Trembling, I began to undo the cellophane wrapping, succeeding again in hiding the card.

"A pity!" said Valeria. "Some have wilted already."

When she took them to the kitchen to cut the stems, I quickly read the card: "As always, A. D. P. Remember, Niculina and Laurian."

Valeria filled the vase with water.

"Six of them have wilted," she said.

"There are thirteen left, then," I murmured dreamily. "A lucky number!"

In February 1969 our son was born: Adrian Gheorghe. And in March we moved to strada Fântânelor. The memorial house had been inaugurated two weeks before.

As the anniversary approached I said to myself, "This time, whatever happens . . ." On the night of April 10–11 I hardly slept. At daybreak, I dressed and went to the study. (I told Valeria I had something that needed finishing urgently.) When the doorbell rang, I looked at my watch: precisely a quarter to eight. I ran to the door on tiptoe and opened it. On the doorstep, the same sumptuous bouquet of roses. A youth of about sixteen or seventeen was crossing the street slowly. I ran after him and caught him by the arm.

"Did you bring the roses? Whom are they from?"

The youth looked at me candidly as though he didn't

understand.

"You just rang the bell at Number 43, and you left a bouquet of nineteen roses in front of the door."

The boy shrugged. "You've got me mixed up with somebody else, sir," he said politely but firmly. "I've got no use for roses. I have to take an exam today and I'm scared."

"An exam in what?" I asked him suspiciously.

"Modern French literature," he said with a bitter smile. "But I'm stuck on something."

He thrust his hand into his pocket and pulled out a folded page from a notebook.

"I have to translate and explain a text. Just a few sentences. But how do I explain them? *'Liberté absolue,'* that I understand: absolute freedom. But what's next? *'Nous sommes condamnés à la liberté!'* What does that mean?"

"It means exactly what it says, that we are condemned to absolute freedom."

He smiled as he listened, and at a certain moment I thought he gave me a signal with his eye.

"As they say, to quote an example from last year's exam, *A bon entendeur, salut!*"

He bowed low, somewhat as a joke, thrust both hands in his pockets, and walked away slowly, whistling.

Eygalières, August–September 1978
Chicago, February 1979

Notes on the Novellas in This Volume

"The Cape" ("Pelerina") was written in the summer of 1975 in ten days of unusual "inspiration," at a rate of ten to twenty handwritten pages a day (see entries for July 19, 21, 26, 28, and 31, 1975, in *Fragments d'un journal II*, Paris: Gallimard, 1981, pp. 243–44). It was first published in German, in the translation of Edith Silbermann, as *Die Pelerine* (Frankfurt/ Main: Suhrkamp, 1976). The original Romanian version was published six years later in the Paris-based émigré journal *Ethos*, 3 (1982): 5–36.

"Youth Without Youth" ("Tinerețe fără de tinerețe") was written at the end of 1976. Here are a few excerpts from Eliade's journal (from the entry for December 28, 1976): "A few days ago, more precisely on December 22, I finished the short novel I had started on November 6. . . . At the beginning I thought of calling it in Romanian *Youth Without Old Age* [after the title of the famous Romanian folktale, 'Tinerețe fără bătrî-nețe și viață fără de moarte,' meaning literally 'Youth Without Old Age and Life Without Death'], which might be rendered in French as *Le centenaire*. . . . I decided to start writing this novel after a night of insomnia, in which I had a vision of its beginning and of its drift. . . . Rereading the manuscript yesterday I thought it 'had weight.' But some episodes, I feel, are too summarily written" (*Fragments d'un journal II*, p. 307). "Youth Without Youth" was first published in Romanian in *Revista Scriitorilor Români* (Munich) 15 (1978): 49–82, and 16 (1979): 33–73. It appeared in French, in the translation of Alain Paruit, as *Le temps d'un centenaire* (Paris: Gallimard, 1981). The Romanian text was republished in Romania in 1981, in a censored version, in a volume collecting several stories by Eliade under the title *În curte la Dionis* (In the Court of Dionysus) (Bucharest: Cartea Româneasca, 1981).

An early version of what was to become "Nineteen Roses" ("Nouăsprezece trandafiri") is mentioned in the diary in December 1975. Eliade had just found, in a forgotten corner of his office at the University of Chicago, an old file folder containing several pages of an untitled novella written in great haste. "The piece starts with a young man entering: 'Excuse me, I hope I don't disturb you, but I found the door open . . .' He interrupts himself, looks attentively at his interlocutor, and then asks in a shy voice: 'You are Mr. X . . . , aren't you?' 'Yes.' 'All right, I am your son.' . . . I cannot recall the rest of the novella, nor the way it ended, and I regret it. I think I wrote these pages seven or eight years ago, at Santa Barbara, after one of my habitual walks on the beach" (*Fragments d'un journal II*, pp. 254–55). This means that the generative vision or idea of "Nineteen Roses" (a young man's search for his mythical father) goes back to February 1968, when Eliade was in Santa Barbara. The next identifiable reference to "Nineteen Roses" occurs on July 26, 1978, when Eliade confesses that he cannot think of anything except "the novella whose idea came to me a few weeks ago" (ibid., p. 378). On September 1, 1978, he writes that "Christinel [his wife] has finished typing the one hundred and ten pages of my novel. Her enthusiasm reassures me" (p. 383). The next day, September 2, he works on the manuscript: "I have written all day long. And what's more, I found a title for my novel: 'Nineteen Roses' " (ibid.). The Romanian original appeared as a separate volume, *Nouăsprezece trandafiri* (Paris: Ethos, 1980). The novella was translated into French by Alain Paruit as *Les dix-neuf roses* (Paris: Gallimard, 1982).